FAR-

SECRETS OF A
CAREER GIRL

BY
CAROL MARINELLI

MILLS &
BOON

Dear Reader

I really enjoyed writing Penny and Jasmine's stories which make up my SECRETS ON THE EMERGENCY WING duet. Even though they are sisters they are very different and that is what made them so real to me. I loved that, even though they had the same parents and shared the same pasts, because of their unique personalities they looked at things differently.

Penny and Jasmine don't look alike; they don't even get on. No-one could even guess that they are sisters—they really are two different sides of the same coin. Yet, for all their differences, there are similarities and I had a lot of fun with a little secret of Penny's that you shan't find out till near the end of the second book.

I really would love to know which sister ends up being your favourite? Except, as my mother tells me, you're not allowed to have favourites…

You may yet be surprised ☺

Happy reading!

Carol

x

SECRETS ON THE EMERGENCY WING

Life and love—behind the doors of an Australian ER

The **SECRETS ON THE EMERGENCY WING**
duet is also available in eBook format
from www.millsandboon.co.uk

DR DARK
AND
FAR-TOO DELICIOUS

BY
CAROL MARINELLI

First published in Great Britain 2013
by Mills & Boon, an imprint of Harlequin (UK) Limited.
Harlequin (UK) Limited, Eton House, 18-24 Paradise Road,
Richmond, Surrey TW9 1SR

© Carol Marinelli 2013

ISBN: 978 0 263 89901 6

Harlequin (UK) policy is to use papers that are natural, renewable and recyclable products and made from wood grown in sustainable forests. The logging and manufacturing process conform to the legal environmental regulations of the country of origin.

Printed and bound in Spain
by Blackprint CPI, Barcelona

Carol Marinelli recently filled in a form where she was asked for her job title and was thrilled, after all these years, to be able to put down her answer as 'writer'. Then it asked what Carol did for relaxation. After chewing her pen for a moment, Carol put down the truth—'writing'. The third question asked—'What are your hobbies?' Well, not wanting to look obsessed or, worse still, boring, she crossed the fingers on her free hand and answered 'swimming and tennis'. But, given that the chlorine in the pool does terrible things to her highlights, and the closest she's got to a tennis racket in the last couple of years is watching the Australian Open, I'm sure you can guess the real answer!

CHAPTER ONE

JUST CONCENTRATE ON WORK.

Jed said it over and over as he ran along the damp beach.

He ran daily, or tried to, depending on work commitments, but as much as he could Jed factored running into his day—it served as both his exercise and his relaxation, helped him to focus and to clear his head.

Just concentrate on work, he repeated, because after the last two hellish years he really did need to do just that.

Jed looked along the bay. The morning was a hazy one and he couldn't make out the Melbourne skyline in the distance. Not for the first time he questioned whether he had been right to take the position at the Peninsula Hospital or if he should have gone for a more prestigious city one.

Jed loved nothing more than a big city hospital—he had worked and trained at a large teaching hospital in Sydney and had assumed, when he had applied for jobs in Melbourne, that the city was where he would end up, yet the interview at Peninsula Hospital that he had thought would be a more a cursory one had seen him change his mind.

It wasn't a teaching hospital but it was certainly a busy one—it served as a major trauma centre and had an NICU and ICU and Jed had liked the atmosphere at Peninsula, as well as the proximity to the beach. Perhaps the deciding factor, though, had been that he had also been told, confidentially, that one of the consultants was retiring and a position would be opening up in the not-too-distant future. His career had been building up to an emergency consultant position and, his disaster of a personal life aside, it was where he was ready to be. When Jed had handed in his notice six months ago an offer had been made and he'd been asked to reconsider leaving, but Jed had known then that he had to get away, that he had to start again.

But with new rules in place this time.

Jed missed not just Sydney and the hospital he had trained and worked at but his family and friends—it had been the first birthday of Luke, his newest nephew, yesterday, another thing he hadn't been able to get to, another family gathering he had missed, when before, even if he hadn't been able to get there on the day, he'd have dropped by over the weekend.

A phone call to a one-year-old wasn't exactly the same.

But the decision to move well away had surely been the right one.

Still he questioned it, still he wondered if he had overreacted and should have just stayed in Sydney and hoped it would work out, assumed it was all sorted.

What a mess.

Jed stopped for a moment and dragged in a few breaths.

Over and over he wondered if he could have handled things differently, if there was something he could have said to have changed things, or something he had done that had been misconstrued—and yet still he could not come up with an answer.

It was incredibly warm for six a.m. but it wasn't a pleasant heat—it was muggy and close and needed a good storm to clear it but, according to the weather reports, the cool change wasn't coming through till tonight.

'Morning.' He looked up and nodded to an old guy walking his dog. They shared a brief conversation about the weather and then Jed took a long drink of water before turning around to head for home and get ready for work.

He should never have got involved with Samantha in the first place.

Still, he could hardly have seen that coming, couldn't have predicted the train wreck that had been about to take place, but then he corrected himself.

He should never have got involved with someone from work.

Jed picked up the pace again, his head finally clearing. He knew what he needed to focus on.

Just concentrate on work.

CHAPTER TWO

'JASMINE?' IT WASN'T the friendliest of greetings, and Jasmine jumped as the sound of Penny's voice stopped her in her tracks.

'What are you doing here?' her sister demanded.

'I'm here for an interview.' Jasmine stated what should be the obvious. 'I've just been for a security check.'

They were standing in the hospital admin corridor. Jasmine was holding a pile of forms and, despite her best efforts to appear smart and efficient for the interview, was looking just a little hot and bothered—and all the more so for seeing Penny.

Summer had decided to give Melbourne one last sticky, humid day before it gave way to autumn and Jasmine's long dark curls had, despite an awful lot of hair serum and an awful lot of effort, frizzed during the walk from the car park to the accident and emergency department. It had continued its curly journey through her initial interview with Lisa, the nurse unit manager.

Now, as Penny ran a brief but, oh, so critical eye over her, Jasmine was acutely aware that the grey suit she reserved for interviews was, despite hundreds of sit-ups and exercising to a DVD, just a touch too tight.

Penny, of course, looked immaculate.

Her naturally straight, naturally blonde hair was tied back in an elegant chignon—she was wearing smart dark trousers and heeled shoes that accentuated her lean body. Her white blouse, despite it being afternoon, despite the fact she was a registrar in a busy accident and emergency department, was still impossibly crisp and clean.

No one could have guessed that they were sisters.

'An interview for what, exactly?' Penny's eyes narrowed.

'A nursing position,' Jasmine answered carefully. 'A clinical nurse specialist. I've just been to fill out the forms for a security check.' Jasmine was well aware her answer was vague and that she was evading the issue but of course it didn't work—Penny was as direct as ever in her response.

'Where?' Penny asked. 'Where exactly have you applied to work?'

'Accident and Emergency,' Jasmine answered, doing her best to keep her voice even. 'Given that it's my speciality.'

'Oh, no.' Penny shook her head. 'No way.' Penny made no effort to keep her voice even, and she didn't mince her words either. 'I'm not having it, Jasmine, not for a single moment. You are *not* working in my department.'

'Where do you expect me to work, then, Penny?' She had known all along that this would be Penny's reaction—it was the very reason she had put off telling her sister about the application, the very reason she hadn't mentioned the interview when they had met up at Mum's last Sunday for a celebratory dinner to toast Penny's *latest* career victory. 'I'm an emergency nurse, that's what I do.'

'Well, go and do it somewhere else. Go and work at the hospital you trained in, because there is no way on earth that I am working alongside my sister.'

'I can't commute to the city,' Jasmine said. 'Do you really expect me to drag Simon for an hour each way just so that I don't embarrass my big sister?' It was ridiculous to suggest and what was even more ridiculous was that Jasmine had actually considered it, well aware how prickly Penny could be.

Jasmine had looked into it, but with a one-year-old to consider, unless she moved nearer to the city, it would prove impossible and also, in truth, she was just too embarrassed to go back to her old workplace.

'You know people there,' Penny insisted.

'Exactly.'

'Jasmine, if the reason you're not going back there is because of Lloyd…'

'Leave it, Penny.' Jasmine closed her eyes for a second. She didn't want to go back to where everyone knew her past, where her life had been the centre stage show for rather too long. 'It has nothing to do with Lloyd. I just want to be closer to home.'

She did—with her marriage completely over and her soon-to-be ex-husband having nothing to do with either her or her son and her maternity leave well and truly up, Jasmine had made the decision to move back to the beachside suburb to be close to the family home and the smart townhouse where her sister lived and to start over again, but with family nearby.

She wanted to be closer to her mum, to her sister and, yes, she wanted some support, but clearly she wasn't going to get any from Penny.

It was career first, last and always for Penny, but then again it was the same with their mum. A real estate agent, though now semi-retired, Louise Masters had made a name for herself in their bayside village for being tough and no-nonsense. It was the rather more dreamy Jasmine who did stupid things like take risks with her heart and actually switch off from work on her days off—not that she didn't love her work, it just wasn't all that she was.

'We'll talk about this later.' Penny's blue eyes flashed angrily—it was the only feature that they shared. 'And don't you dare go using my name to get the job.'

'As if I'd do that,' Jasmine said. 'Anyway, we don't even share the same surname, *Miss* Masters.'

Penny was now officially a Miss—the title given to females once they gained their fellowship. It caused some confusion at times, but Penny had worked extremely hard to be a Miss rather than a Doctor—and she wasn't about to have anyone drag on her coat-tails as she continued to ride high.

'I mean it,' Penny flared. 'You are not to even let on that you know me. I'm really not happy about this, Jasmine.'

'Hey, Penny.' Her sister turned, and so too did Jasmine, to the sound of a deep, low voice. Had Jasmine not been so numb right now, so immune and resistant to all things male, she might have more properly noticed just how good looking this man was. He was very tall and though his dark brown hair was cut fairly short it was just a bit rumpled, as was his suit.

Yes, a couple of years ago she might have taken note, but not now.

She just wanted him gone so that she could get back to the rather important conversation she had been having with Penny.

'It's getting busy down there apparently,' he said to Penny. 'They just called and asked me to come back from lunch.'

'I know,' came Penny's clipped response. 'I've just been paged. I was supposed to be speaking with Legal.'

Perhaps he picked up on the tension because he looked from Penny to Jasmine and she noticed then that his eyes were green and that his jaw needed shaving and, yes, despite being completely not interested, some long-dormant cells demanded that she at least deign to acknowledge just how attractive he was, especially when his deep voice spoke on. 'Sorry, am I disturbing something?'

'Not at all.' Penny's response was rapid. 'This nurse was just asking for directions to get back to Emergency—she's got an interview there.'

'You can hardly miss the place.' He gave a wry smile and nodded to a huge red arrow above them. 'Follow us.'

'Mrs Phillips?' Jasmine turned as she heard her name

and saw it was the receptionist from Security, where she had just come from. 'You left your driving licence.'

'Thank you.' Jasmine opened her mouth to say that she was soon to be a Ms, but it seemed churlish to correct it as technically she was still a Mrs—it was there on her driving licence after all. Still, in a few weeks' time she'd be a Ms and she'd tell everyone the same.

Jasmine couldn't wait for the glorious day.

For now, though, she followed Penny and her colleague towards Emergency.

'I didn't mean to literally follow,' Jed said, and he waited a second for her to catch up. Jasmine fell into reluctant step alongside them. 'I'm Jed...Jed Devlin—I'm a registrar in the madhouse, as is Penny.'

'Jasmine.' She duly answered. 'Jasmine Phillips.'

'So?' he asked as Penny clipped noisily alongside them. She could hear the anger in her sister's footsteps, could feel the tension that was ever present whenever the two of them were together. 'When do you start?'

'I haven't got the job yet,' Jasmine said.

'Sounds promising, though, if you've been sent up to Security.'

'They have to do a security check on everyone,' Penny said abruptly.

They all walked on in silence for a few moments.

'Here we are,' Jed said. 'See that big red sign that says "Accident and Emergency"?'

'How could I miss it?' She gave a brief smile at his teasing as they headed through the swing doors and stepped into Emergency. 'Thanks.'

'No problem.'

'Good luck,' Jed said.

Of course Penny didn't offer her best wishes. Instead, she marched off on her high heels and for a second Jasmine stood there and blew out a breath, wondering if she was mad to be doing this.

It clearly wasn't going to work.

And then she realised that Jed was still standing there.

'Do I know you?' He frowned.

'I don't think so,' Jasmine said, while reluctantly admitting to herself that they had definitely never met—his was a face she certainly wouldn't forget.

'Have you worked in Sydney?'

Jasmine shook her head.

'Where did you work before?'

She started to go red. She hated talking about her time there—she'd loved it so much and it had all ended so terribly, but she could hardly tell him that. 'Melbourne Central. I trained there and worked in Emergency there till I had my son.'

'Nice hospital,' Jed said. 'I had an interview there when I first moved to the area, but no.' He shook his head. 'That's not it. You just look familiar…'

He surely hadn't picked up that she and Penny were sisters? No one ever had. She and Penny were complete opposites, not just in looks but also in personality. Penny was completely focussed and determined, whereas Jasmine was rather more impulsive, at least she had been once. She was also, as her mother had frequently pointed out throughout her childhood whenever Jasmine had burst into tears, too sensitive.

'There you are!' Jasmine turned as Lisa came over and Jed made his excuses and wandered off.

'Sorry,' Jasmine said to Lisa. 'They took ages to find all the forms I needed.'

'That's Admin for you,' Lisa said. 'Right, I'll walk you through the department and give you a feel for the place. It just got busy.'

It certainly had.

It had been almost empty when Jasmine had first arrived for her interview and the walk to Lisa's office had shown a calm, even quiet department, compared to the busy city one Jasmine was more used to. Now, though, the cubicles were all full and she could see staff rushing and hear the emergency bell trilling from Resus. Not for the first time, Jasmine wondered if she was up to the demands of going back to work in a busy emergency department.

The last two years had left her so raw and confused that all she really wanted to do was to curl up and sleep before she tackled the process of healing and resuming work, but her ex didn't want to see their son, let alone pay child support, and there was no point going through appropriate channels—she couldn't wait the time it would take to squeeze blood from a stone, but more than that Jasmine wanted to support her son herself, which meant that she needed a job.

However much it inconvenienced Penny and however daunted she was at the prospect.

'We do our best with the roster. I always try to accommodate specific requests, but as far as regular shifts go I can't make allowances for anyone,' Lisa explained—she knew about Simon and had told Jasmine that there were a couple of other single mums working there who, she was sure, would be a huge support. 'And I've rung the crèche and said that you'll be coming over to have a look around, but you know that they close at six and that on a late shift you don't generally get out till well after nine?'

Jasmine nodded. 'My mum's said that she'll help out for a little while.' Jasmine stated this far more generously than her mother had. 'At least until I sort out a babysitter.'

'What about night shifts?' Lisa checked. 'Everyone has to do them—it's only fair.'

'I know.'

'That way,' Lisa explained, 'with everyone taking turns, generally it only comes around once every three months or so.'

'That sounds fine,' Jasmine said confidently while inwardly gauging her mother's reaction.

It was a good interview, though. Really, Jasmine was confident that she'd got the job and, as she left, Lisa practically confirmed it. 'You'll be hearing from us soon.' She gave a wry smile as Jasmine shook her hand. 'Very soon. I wish you didn't have to do orientation before you start—I've just had two of my team ring in sick for the rest of the week.'

Walking towards the exit, Jasmine saw how busy yet efficient everyone looked and despite her confident words about her experience to Lisa, inside she was a squirming mess! Even though she'd worked right up to the end of her pregnancy she hadn't nursed in more than a year and, again, she considered going back to her old department. At least she'd maybe know a few people.

At least she'd know where things were kept. Yet there would still be the nudges and whispers that she'd been so relieved to leave behind and, yes, she should just walk in with her head held high and face the ugly rumours and gossip, except going back to work after all she had been through was already hard enough.

'Jasmine?' She turned as someone called her name and forced back on her smile when she saw that it was Jed. He was at the viewfinder looking at an X-ray. 'How did you get on?'

'Good,' Jasmine answered. 'Well, at least I think I did.'

'Well done.'

'I'm just going to check out the crèche.'

'Good luck again, then,' Jed said, 'because from what I've heard you'll need it to get a place there.'

'Oh, and, Jasmine,' he called as she walked off, 'I do know you.'

'You don't.' Jasmine laughed.

'But I know that I do,' he said. 'I never forget a face. I'll work it out.'

She rather hoped that he wouldn't.

CHAPTER THREE

'HOW DID YOU GO?' her mum asked as she let her in.

'Well,' Jasmine said. 'Sorry that it took so long.'

'That's okay. Simon's asleep.' Jasmine followed her mum through to the kitchen and Louise went to put the kettle on. 'So when do you start?'

'I don't even know if I've got the job.'

'Please,' her mum said over her shoulder. 'Everywhere's screaming for nurses, you hear it on the news all the time.'

It was a backhanded compliment—her mother was very good at them. Jasmine felt the sting of tears behind her eyes—Louise had never really approved of Jasmine going into nursing. Her mother had told her that if she worked a bit harder at school she could get the grades and study medicine, just like Penny. And though she never came right out and said it, it was clear that in both her mother's and sister's eyes Penny had a career whereas Jasmine had a job—and one that could be done by anyone—as if all that Jasmine had to do was put on her uniform and show up.

'It's a clinical nurse specialist role that I've applied for, Mum,' Jasmine said. 'There were quite a few applicants.' But her mum made no comment and not for the first time Jasmine questioned her decision to move close to home. Her mum just wasn't mumsy—she was successful in everything she did. She was funny, smart and career-minded, and she simply expected her daughters to be the same—after all, she'd juggled her career and had independently raised Jasmine and Penny when their father had walked out.

Jasmine wanted nothing more than to be independent and do the same; she just wanted a pause, a bit of a helping hand as she got through this bit—which in her own way her mother had given. After four weeks of living at home Louise had had a very nice little rental house come onto her books—it was right on the beach and the rent was incredibly low and Jasmine had jumped at it. It was in other areas that Jasmine was struggling, and nursing with all its shift work wasn't an easy career to juggle without support.

'I'm going to have to do nights.' Jasmine watched her mother's shoulders stiffen as she filled two mugs. 'A fortnight every three months.'

'I didn't raise two children just so that I could raise yours,' Louise warned. 'I'll help you as much as I can for a couple of months, but I take a lot of clients through houses in the evenings.' She was as direct as ever. 'And I've got my cruise booked for May.'

'I know,' Jasmine said. 'I'm going to start looking for a regular babysitter as soon as I get the offer.'

'And you need to give me your off duty at least a month in an advance.'

'I will.'

Jasmine took the tea from her mum. If she wanted a hug she wasn't going to get one; if she wanted a little pick me up she was in the wrong house.

'Have you thought about looking for a job that's a bit more child friendly?' Louise suggested. 'You mentioned there was one in Magnetic...' She gave an impatient shrug when she couldn't remember the terminology.

'No. I said there was a position in MRI and that even though the hours were fantastic it wasn't what I wanted to do. I like Emergency, Mum. You wouldn't suggest Penny going for a role she had no interest in.'

'Penny doesn't have a one-year-old to think of,' Louise said, and then they sat quietly for a moment.

'You need to get your hair done,' her mum said. 'You need to smarten up a bit if you're going back to work.' And that was her mum's grudging way of accepting that, yes, this was what Jasmime was going to do. 'And you need to lose some weight.'

And because it was either that or start crying, Jasmine chose to laugh.

'What's so funny?'

'You are,' Jasmine said. 'I thought tea came with sympathy.'

'Not in this house.' Her mum smiled. 'Why don't you go home?'

'Simon's asleep.'

'I'll have him for you tonight.'

And sometimes, and always when Jasmine was least expecting it, her mum could be terribly nice. 'My evening appointment cancelled. I'm sure you could use a night to yourself.'

'I'd love that.' Jasmine hadn't had a night to herself since Simon had been born. In the weeks when she'd first come home and had stayed with her mum, the only advantage she had taken had been a long walk on the beach each morning before Simon woke up. 'Thanks, Mum.'

'No problem. I guess I'd better get familiar with his routines.'

'Can I go in and see him?'

'And wake him up probably.'

She didn't wake him up. Simon was lying on his front with his bottom in the air and his thumb in his mouth, and just the sight of him made everything worth it. He was in her old cot in her old bedroom and was absolutely the love of her life. She just didn't understand how Lloyd could want nothing to do with him.

'Do you think he's missing out?' Jasmine asked her mum. 'Not having a dad?'

'Better no dad than a useless one,' Louise said, then gave a shrug. 'I don't know the answer to that, Jasmine. I used to feel the same about you.' She gave her daughter a smile. 'Our taste in men must be hereditary. No wonder Penny's sworn off them.'

'Did she ever tell you what happened?' Jasmine asked, because one minute Penny had been engaged, the next the whole thing had been called off and she didn't want to talk about it.

'She just said they'd been having a few problems and decided that it was better to get out now than later.'

Before there were children to complicate things, Jasmine thought, but didn't say anything. It was her mum who spoke.

'I know it's tough at the moment but I'm sure it will get easier.'

'And if it doesn't?'

'Then you'd better get used to tough.' Louise shrugged. 'Have you told Penny you're applying for a job at Peninsula?'

'I saw her at my interview.'

'And?' Louise grimaced. They both knew only too well how Penny would react to the news.

'She doesn't want me there—especially not in Accident and Emergency,' Jasmine admitted. 'She wasn't best pleased.'

'Well, it's her domain,' Louise said. 'You know how territorial she is. She used to put thread up on her bedroom door so she'd know if anyone had been in there while she was out. She'll come round.'

And even though she smiled at the memory, Jasmine was worried that Penny wouldn't be coming round to the idea of her little sister working in her hospital any time soon.

Jasmine was proven right a few hours later when, back at her own small house, adding another coat of paint in an attempt to transform the lounge from dull olive green to cool crisp white, there was a loud rap at the door.

'Can you knock more quietly?' Jasmine asked as she opened it. 'If Simon was here—'

'We need to talk,' Penny said, and she brushed in and straight through to the lounge.

If Louise hadn't exactly been brimming with understanding, then Penny was a desert.

Her blouse was still crisp and white, her hair still perfect and her eyes were just as angry as they had been when she had first laid them on Jasmine in the hospital corridor earlier on that day. 'You said nothing about this when I saw you last week,' Penny said accusingly. 'Not a single word!'

'I didn't exactly get a chance.'

'Meaning?'

She heard the confrontation in her sister's voice, could almost see Pandora's box on the floor between them. She was tempted just to open it, to have this out once and for all, to say how annoyed she still felt that Penny hadn't been able to make it for Simon's first birthday a couple of months earlier. In fact, she hadn't even sent a card. Yet there had been no question that Jasmine herself would be there to join in celebrating her sister's success.

Or rather celebrating her sister's *latest* success.

But bitterness wasn't going to help things here.

'That dinner was to celebrate you getting your fellowship,' Jasmine said calmly. 'I knew you'd be upset if I told you that I had an interview coming up, and I didn't want to spoil your night.'

'You should have discussed it with me before you even applied!' Penny said. 'It's my department.'

'Hopefully it will be mine soon, too,' Jasmine attempted, but her words fell on deaf ears.

'Do you know how hard it is for me?' Penny said. 'All that nonsense about equal rights... I have to be twice as good as them, twice as tough as any of them—there's a consultancy position coming up and I have no intention of letting it slip by.'

'How could my working there possibly affect that?' Jasmine asked reasonably.

'Because I'm not supposed to have a personal life,' was Penny's swift retort. 'You just don't get it, Jasmine. I've worked hard to get where I am. The senior consultant, Mr Dean, he's old school—he made a joke the other week about how you train them up and the next thing you know they're pregnant and wanting part-time hours.' She looked at her sister. 'Yes, I could complain and make waves, but how is that going to help things? Jed is going after the same position. He's a great doctor but he's only been in the department six months and I am not going to lose it to him.' She shook her head in frustration.

'I'm not asking you to understand, you just have to believe that it is hard to get ahead sometimes, and the last thing I need right now is my personal life invading the department.'

'I'm your sister—'

'So are you going to be able to stay quiet when the nurses call me a hard witch?' Penny challenged. 'And when you are supposed to finish at four but can't get off, are you going to expect me to drop everything and run to the crèche and get Simon?'

'Of course not.'

'And when I hear the other nurses moaning that you hardly ever do a late shift and are complaining about having to do nights, am I supposed to leap to your defence and explain that you're a single mum?'

'I can keep my work and personal life separate.'

'Really!'

It was just one word, a single word, and the rise of Penny's perfect eyebrows had tears spring to Jasmine's eyes. 'That was below the belt.'

'The fact that you can't keep your work and personal life separate is the very reason you can't go back to Melbourne Central.'

'It's about the travel,' Jasmine insisted. 'And you're wrong, I can keep things separate.'

'Not if we're in the same department.'

'I can if they don't know that we're sisters,' Jasmine said, and she watched Penny's jaw tighten, realised then that this was where the conversation had been leading. Penny was always one step ahead in everything, and Penny had made very sure that it was Jasmine who suggested it.

'It might be better.' Penny made it sound as if she was conceding.

'Fine.'

'Can you keep to it?'

'Sure,' Jasmine said.

'I mean it.'

'I know you do, Penny.'

'I've got to get back to work. I'm on call tonight.' And her sister, now that she had what she came for, stood up to leave. Jasmine held in tears that threatened, even managed a smile as her sister stalked out of the door.

But it hurt.

It really hurt.

CHAPTER FOUR

IT WAS HER favourite place in the world.

But even a long stretch of sand, the sun going down over the water and a storm rolling in from the distance wasn't enough to take the harsh sting out of Penny's words.

Jasmine hated arguments, loathed them and did her very best to avoid them.

She could still remember all too well hearing the raised voices of her parents seeping up the stairs and through the bedroom floor as she had lain on her bed with her hands over her ears.

But there had been no avoiding this one—Jasmine had known when she'd applied for the role that there would be a confrontation. Still, she couldn't just bow to Penny's wishes just because it made things awkward for her.

She needed a job and, no matter what her mother and sister thought of her chosen career, nursing was what she was good at—and Emergency was her speciality.

Jasmine wasn't going to hide just because it suited Penny.

It had been cruel of Penny to bring up her relationship with Lloyd, cruel to suggest that she wasn't going back to Melbourne Central just because of what had happened.

It was also, Jasmine conceded, true.

Finding out that she was pregnant had been a big enough shock—but she'd had no idea what was to come.

That the dashing paramedic who'd been so delighted with the news of her pregnancy, who'd insisted they marry and then whisked her off on a three-month honeymoon around Australia, was in fact being investigated for patient theft.

She'd been lied to from the start and deceived till the end and nothing, it seemed, could take away her shame. And, yes, the whispers and sideways looks she had received from her colleagues at Melbourne Central as she'd worked those last weeks of her pregnancy with her marriage falling apart had been awful. The last thing she needed was Penny rubbing it in.

'I knew I recognised you from somewhere.' She looked over to the sound of a vaguely familiar voice.

'Oh!' Jasmine was startled as she realised who it was. 'Hi, Jed.' He was out of breath from running and— she definitely noticed this time—was very, very good looking.

He was wearing grey shorts and a grey T-shirt and he was toned, a fact she couldn't fail to notice when he lifted his T-shirt to wipe his face, revealing a very flat, tanned stomach. Jasmine felt herself blush as for the first time in the longest time she was shockingly drawn to rugged maleness.

But, then, how could you not be? Jasmine reasoned.

Any woman hauled out of a daydream would blink a few times when confronted with him. Any woman would be a bit miffed that they hadn't bothered sorting their hair and that they were wearing very old denim shorts and a T-shirt splashed with paint.

'You walk here?' Jed checked, because now he remembered her. Dark curls bobbing, she would walk—sometimes slowly, sometimes briskly and, he had noticed she never looked up, never acknowledged anyone—she always seemed completely lost in her own world. 'I see you some mornings,' Jed said, and then seemed to think about it. 'Though not for a while.'

'I live just over there.' Jasmine pointed to her small weatherboard house. 'I walk here every chance I get—though I haven't had too many chances of late.'

'We're almost neighbours.' Jed smiled. 'I'm in the one on the end.' He nodded towards the brand-new group of town houses a short distance away that had been built a couple of years ago. Her mother had been the agent in a couple of recent sales there and Jasmine wondered if one of them might have been to him.

And just to remind her that he hadn't specifically noticed her, he nodded to another jogger who went past, and as they walked along a little way, he said hi to an elderly couple walking their dog. He clearly knew the locals.

'Taking a break from painting?' He grinned.

'How did you guess?' Jasmine sighed. 'I don't know who's madder—whoever painted the wall green, or me for thinking a couple of layers of white would fix it.

I'm on my third coat.' She looked over at him and then stated the obvious. 'So you run?'

'Too much,' Jed groaned. 'It's addictive.'

'Not for me,' Jasmine admitted. 'I tried, but I don't really know where to start.'

'You just walk,' Jed said, 'and then you break into a run and then walk again—you build up your endurance. It doesn't take long.' He smiled. 'See? I'm addicted.'

'No, I get it.' Jasmine grinned back. 'I just don't do it.'

'So, how did you go with the crèche?' He walked along beside her and Jasmine realised he was probably just catching his breath, probably pacing himself rather than actually stopping for her. Still, it was nice to have a chat.

'They were really accommodating, though I think Lisa might have had something to do with that.'

'How old is your child?'

'Fourteen months,' Jasmine said. 'His name's Simon.'

'And is this your first job since he was born?' He actually did seem to want to talk her. Jasmine had expected that he'd soon jog off, but instead he walked along beside her, his breathing gradually slowing down. It was nice to have adult company, nice to walk along the beach and talk.

'It is,' Jasmine said. 'And I'm pretty nervous.'

'You worked at Melbourne Central, though,' he pointed out. 'That's one hell of a busy place. It was certainly buzzing when I went for my interview there.'

'Didn't you like it?'

'I did,' Jed said, 'but I was surprised how much I

liked Peninsula Hospital. I was sort of weighing up between the two and this…' he looked out to the bay, '…was a huge draw card. The beach is practically next to the hospital and you can even see it from the canteen.'

'I'm the same,' Jasmine said, because as much as she loved being in the city she was a beach girl through and through.

'You'll be fine,' Jed said. 'It will take you ten minutes to get back into the swing of things.'

'I think it might take rather more than that.' Jasmine laughed. 'Having a baby scrambles your brains a bit. Still, it will be nice to be working again. I've just got to work out all the shifts and things.'

'What does your husband do?' Jed took a swig from his water bottle. 'Can he help?'

'We're separated,' Jasmine replied.

'Oh. I'm sorry to hear that.'

'It's fine,' Jasmine said. She was getting used to saying it and now, just as she was, it would be changing again because she'd be divorced.

It was suddenly awkward; the conversation that had flowed so easily seemed to have come to a screeching halt. 'Storm's getting close.' Jed nodded out to the distance.

Given they were now reduced to talking about the weather, Jasmine gave a tight smile. 'I'd better go in and watch my paint dry.'

'Sure,' Jed said, and gave her a smile before he jogged off.

And as she turned and headed up to her flat she wanted to turn, wanted to call out to his rapidly departing back, *'It's okay, you don't have to run—just because I don't have a partner doesn't mean that I'm looking for another one.'*

God, talk about put the wind up him.

Still, she didn't dwell on it.

After all there were plenty of other things on her mind without having to worry about Jed Devlin.

CHAPTER FIVE

THERE WAS, JASMINE decided, one huge advantage to being related to two fabulously strong, independent women.

It sort of forced you to be fabulously strong and independent yourself, even when you didn't particularly feel it.

The hospital squeezed her in for that month's orientation day and after eight hours of fire drills, uniform fittings, occupational health and safety lectures and having her picture taken for her lanyard, she was officially on the accident and emergency roster. Lisa had, as promised, rung the crèche and told them Simon was a priority, due to the shortage of regular staff in Emergency.

So, just over a week later at seven o'clock on a Wednesday morning, two kilograms lighter thanks to a new diet, and with her hair freshly cut, Jasmine dropped her son off for his first day of crèche.

'Are you sure he's yours?' Shona, the childcare worker grinned as Jasmine handed him over. It was a reaction she got whenever anyone saw her son, even the midwives had teased her in the maternity ward. Simon was so blond and long and skinny that Jasmine felt as if she'd borrowed someone else's baby at times.

Until he started to cry, until he held out his arms to Jasmine the moment that he realised he was being left.

Yep, Jasmine thought, giving him a final cuddle, he might look exactly like Penny but, unlike his aunt, he was as soft as butter—just like his mum.

'Just go,' Shona said when she saw that Simon's mum looked as if she was about to start crying too. 'You're five minutes away and we'll call if you're needed, but he really will be fine.'

And so at seven-twenty, a bit red-nosed and glassy-eyed, Jasmine stood by the board and waited for handover to start.

She never even got to hear it.

'I've decided to pair you with Vanessa,' Lisa told her. 'For the next month you'll do the same shifts, and, as far as we can manage, you'll work alongside her. I've put the two of you in Resus this morning so don't worry about handover. It's empty for now so I'll get Vanessa to show you around properly while it's quiet—it won't stay that way for long.'

'Sure,' Jasmine said, in many ways happy to be thrown straight in at the deep end, rather than spending time worrying about it. And Lisa didn't have much choice. There wasn't much time for handholding—experienced staff were thin on the ground this morning, and even though she hadn't nursed in a year, her qualifications and experience were impressive and Lisa needed her other experienced nurses out in the cubicles to guide

the agency staff they had been sent to help with the patient ratio shortfalls this morning.

Vanessa was lovely.

She had been working at the hospital for three years,
she told Jasmine, and while it was empty, she gave her
a more thorough tour of the resuscitation area as they
checked the oxygen and suction and that everything
was stocked. She also gave her a little bit of gossip
along the way.

'There's Mr Dean.' Vanessa pulled a little face. 'He
likes things done his way and it takes a little while to
work that out, but once you do he's fine,' she explained
as they checked and double-checked the equipment.
'Rex and Helena are the other consultants.' Jasmine
found she was holding her breath more than a little
as Vanessa worked through the list of consultants and
registrars and a few nurses and gave titbits of gossip
here and there.

'Penny Masters, Senior Reg.' Vanessa rolled her
eyes. 'Eats lemons for breakfast, so don't take anything
personally. She snaps and snarls at everyone and jumps
in uninvited,' Vanessa said, 'but you have to hand it to
her, she does get the job done. And then there's Jed.'
Jasmine realised that she was still holding her breath,
waiting to hear about him.

'He's great to work with too, a bit brusque, keeps
himself to himself.' Funny, Jasmine thought, he hadn't
seemed anything other than friendly when she had met
him, but, still, she didn't dwell on it. They soon had their
first patients coming through and were alerted to expect a patient who had fallen from scaffolding. He had

arm fractures but, given the height from which he had fallen, there was the potential for some serious internal injuries, despite the patient being fully conscious. Resus was prepared and Jasmine felt her shoulders tense as Penny walked in, their eyes meeting for just a brief second as Penny tied on a large plastic apron and put on protective glasses and gloves.

'This is Jasmine,' Vanessa happily introduced her. 'The new clinical nurse specialist.'

'What do we know about the patient?' was Penny's tart response.

Which set the tone.

The patient was whizzed in. He was young, in pain and called Cory, and Penny shouted orders as he was moved carefully over onto the trolley on the spinal board. He was covered in plaster dust. It was in his hair, on his clothes and in his eyes, and it blew everywhere as they tried to cut his clothes off. Despite Cory's arms being splinted, he started to thrash about on the trolley

'Just stay nice and still, Cory.' Jasmine reassured the patient as Penny thoroughly examined him—listening to his chest and palpating his abdomen, demanding his observations even before he was fully attached to the equipment and then ordering some strong analgesia for him.

'My eyes...' Cory begged, even when the pain medication started to hit, and Penny checked them again.

'Can you lavage his eyes?' Penny said, and Jasmine warmed a litre of saline to a tepid temperature and gently washed them out as Penny spoke to the young man.

'Right,' Penny said to her young patient. 'We're going to get some X-rays and CTs, but so far it would seem you've been very lucky.'

'Lucky?' Cory checked.

'She means compared to how it might have been,' Jasmine said as she continued to lavage his eyes. 'You fell from quite a height and, judging by the fact you've got two broken wrists, well, it looks like as if you managed to turn and put out your hands to save yourself,' Jasmine explained. 'Which probably doesn't feel very lucky right now.'

'How does that eye feel?' She wiped his right eye with gauze and Cory blinked a few times.

'Better.'

'How's the pain now?'

'A bit better.'

'Need any help?' Jasmine looked up at the sound of Jed's voice. He smelt of morning, all fresh and brisk and ready to help, but Penny shook her head.

'I've got this.' She glanced over to another patient being wheeled in. 'He might need your help, though.'

She'd forgotten this about Emergency—you didn't get a ten-minute break to catch your breath and tidy up, and more often than not it was straight into the next one. As Vanessa, along with Penny, dealt with X-rays and getting Cory ready for CT, Jasmine found herself working alone with Jed on his patient, with Lisa popping in and out.

'It's her first day!' Lisa warned Jed as she opened some equipment while Jasmine connected the patient to the monitors as the paramedics gave the handover.

'No problem,' Jed said, introducing himself to the elderly man and listening to his chest as Jasmine attached him to monitors and ran off a twelve-lead ECG. The man was in acute LVF, meaning his heart was beating ineffectively, which meant that there was a build-up of fluid in his lungs that was literally drowning him. Jim's skin was dark blue and felt cold and clammy and he was blowing white frothy bubbles out through his lips with every laboured breath.

'You're going to feel much better soon, sir,' Jed said. The paramedics had already inserted an IV and as Jed ordered morphine and diuretics, Jasmine was already pulling up the drugs, but when she got a little lost on the trolley he pointed them out without the tutting and eye-rolls Penny had administered.

'Can you ring for a portable chest X-ray?' Jed asked. The radiographer would have just got back to her department as Jasmine went to summon her again.

'What's the number?' Jasmine asked, but then found it for herself on the phone pad.

Jed worked in a completely different manner from Penny. He was much calmer and far more polite with his requests and was patient when Jasmine couldn't find the catheter pack he asked for—he simply went and got one for himself. He apologised too when he asked the weary night radiographer to hold on for just a moment as he inserted a catheter. But, yes, Jasmine noticed, Vanessa was right—he was detached with the staff and nothing like the man she had mildly joked with at her interview or walked alongside on the beach.

But, like Penny, he got the job done.

Jasmine spoke reassuringly to Jim all the time and with oxygen on, a massive dose of diuretics and the calming effect of the morphine their patient's oxygen sats were slowly climbing and his skin was becoming pink. The terrified grip on Jasmine's hand loosened.

Lisa was as good as her word and popped in and out. Insisting she was done with her ovaries, she put on a lead gown and shooed them out for a moment and they stepped outside for the X-ray.

Strained was the silence and reluctantly almost, as if he was forcing himself to be polite, Jed turned his face towards her as they waited for the all-clear to go back inside. 'Enjoying your first day?'

'Actually, yes!' She was surprised at the enthusiasm in her answer as she'd been dreading starting work and leaving Simon, and worried that her scrambled brain wasn't up to a demanding job. Yet, less than an hour into her first shift, Jasmine was realising how much she'd missed it, how much she had actually loved her work.

'Told you it wouldn't take long.'

'Yes, well, I'm only two patients in.' She frowned as he looked up, not into her eyes but at her hair. 'The hairdresser cut too much off.'

'No, no.' He shook his head. 'It's white.'

'Oh.' She shook it and a little puff of plaster dust blew into the air. 'Plaster dust.' She shook it some more, moaning at how she always ended up messy, and he sort of changed his smile to a stern nod as the red light flashed and then the radiographer called that they could go back inside.

'You're looking better.' Jasmine smiled at her patient because now the emergency was over, she could make him a touch more comfortable. The morphine had kicked in and his catheter bag was full as the fluid that had been suffocating him was starting to move from his chest. 'How are you feeling?'

'Like I can breathe,' Jim said, and grabbed her hand, still worried. 'Can my wife come in? She must've been terrified.'

'I'm going to go and speak to her now,' Jed said, 'and then I'll ring the medics to come and take over your care. You're doing well.' He looked at Jasmine. 'Can you stay with him while I go and speak to his wife?'

'Sure.'

'I thought that was it,' Jim admitted as Jasmine placed some pillows behind him and put a blanket over the sheet that covered him. After checking his obs, she sat herself down on the hard flat resus bed beside him. 'Libby thought so too.'

'Your wife?' Jasmine checked, and he nodded.

'She couldn't remember the number for the ambulance.'

'It must have been very scary for her,' Jasmine said, because though it must be terrifying to not be able to breathe, to watch someone you love suffer must have been hell. 'She'll be so pleased to see that you're talking and looking so much better than when you came in.'

Libby was pleased, even though she promptly burst into tears when she saw him, and it was Jim who had to reassure her, rather than the other way around.

They were the most gorgeous couple—Libby chatted enough for both of them and told Jasmine that they were about to celebrate their golden wedding anniversary, which was certainly an achievement when she herself hadn't even managed to make it to one year.

'I was just telling Jasmine,' Libby said when Jed came in to check on Jim's progress, 'that it's our golden wedding anniversary in a fortnight.'

'Congratulations.' Jed smiled.

'The children are throwing us a surprise party,' Libby said. 'Well, they're hardly children...'

'And it's hardly a surprise.' Jed smiled again. 'Are you not supposed to know about it?'

'No,' Libby admitted. 'Do you think that Jim will be okay?'

'He should be,' Jed said. 'For now I'm going to ring the medics and have them take over his care, but if he continues improving I would expect him to be home by the end of the week—and ready to *gently* celebrate by the next.'

They were such a lovely couple and Jasmine adored seeing their closeness, but more than that she really was enjoying being back at work and having her world made bigger instead of fretting about her own problems. She just loved the whole buzz of the place, in fact.

It was a nice morning, a busy morning, but the staff were really friendly and helpful—well, most of them. Penny was Penny and especially caustic when Jasmine missed a vein when she tried to insert an IV.

'I'll do it!' She snapped, 'the patient doesn't have time for you to practise on him.'

'Why don't you two go to lunch?' Lisa suggested as Jasmine bit down on her lip.

'She has such a lovely nature!' Vanessa nudged Jasmine as they walked round to the staffroom. 'Honestly, pay no attention to Penny. She's got the patience of a two-year-old and, believe me, I speak from experience when I say that they have none. How old is your son?' She must have the seen that Jasmine was a bit taken aback by her question, as she hadn't had time to mention Simon to Vanessa yet. 'I saw you dropping him off at crèche this morning when I was bringing in Liam.'

'Your two-year-old?'

'My terrible two-year-old,' Vanessa corrected as they went to the fridge and took out their lunches and Vanessa told her all about the behavioural problems she was having with Liam.

'He's completely adorable,' Vanessa said as they walked through to the staffroom, 'but, God, he's hard work.'

Jed was in the staffroom and it annoyed Jasmine that she even noticed—after all, there were about ten people in there, but it was him that she noticed and he was also the reason she blushed as Vanessa's questions became a bit more personal.

'No.' Jasmine answered when Vanessa none-too-subtly asked about Simon's father—but that was nursing, especially in Emergency. Everyone knew everything about everyone's life and not for the first time Jasmine wondered how she was supposed to keep the fact she was Penny's sister a secret.

'We broke up before he was born.'

'You poor thing,' Vanessa said, but Jasmine shook her head.

'Best thing,' she corrected.

'And does he help?' Vanessa pushed, 'with the child-care? Now that you're working...'

She could feel Jed was listening and she felt embarrassed. Embarrassed at the disaster her life was, but she tried not to let it show in her voice, especially as Penny had now walked in and was sitting in a chair on the other side of the room.

'No, he lives on the other side of the city. I just moved back here a few weeks ago.'

'Your family is here?' Vanessa checked.

'Yes.' Jasmine gave a tight smile and concentrated on her cheese sandwich, deciding that in future she would have lunch in the canteen.

'Well, it's good that you've got them to support you,' Vanessa rattled on, and Jasmine didn't even need to look at Penny to see that she wasn't paying any attention. Her sister was busy catching up on notes during her break. Penny simply didn't stop working, wherever she was. Penny had always been driven, though there had been one brief period where she'd softened a touch. She'd dated for a couple of years and had been engaged, but that had ended abruptly and since then all it had been was work, work, work.

Which was why Penny had got as far as she had, Jasmine knew, but sometimes, more than sometimes, she wished her sister would just slow down.

Thankfully the conversation shifted back to Vanessa's son, Liam—and she told Jasmine that she was on her own, too. Jasmine would have quite enjoyed learning all about her colleagues under normal circumstances but for some reason she was finding it hard to relax today.

And she knew it was because of Jed.

God, she so did not want to notice him, didn't want to be aware of him in any way other than as a colleague. She had enough going on in her life right now, but when Jed stood and stretched and yawned, she knew what that stomach looked like beneath the less than well-ironed shirt, knew just how nice he could be, even if he was ignoring her now. He opened his eyes and caught her looking at him and he almost frowned at her. As he looked away Jasmine found that her cheeks were on fire, but thankfully Vanessa broke the uncomfortable moment.

'Did you get called in last night?' Vanessa asked him.

'Nope,' Jed answered. 'Didn't sleep.'

Jed headed back out to the department and carried on. As a doctor he was more than used to working while he was tired but it was still an effort and at three-thirty Jed made a cup of strong coffee and took it back to the department with him, wishing he could just go home and crash, annoyed with himself over his sleepless night.

He'd had a phone call at eleven-thirty the previous night and, assuming it was work, had answered it without thinking.

Only to be met by silence.

He'd hung up and checked the number and had seen that it was *private*.

And then the phone had rung again.

'Jed Devlin.' He had listened to the silence and then

hung up again and stared at the phone for a full ten minutes, waiting for it to ring again.

It had.

'Jed!' He heard the sound of laughter and partying and then the voice of Rick, an ex-colleague he had trained with. 'Jed, is that you?'

'Speaking.'

'Sorry, I've been trying to get through.'

'Where are you?'

'Singapore... What time is it there?'

'Coming up for midnight.'

'Sorry about that. I just found out that you moved to Melbourne.'

He had laughed and chatted and caught up with an old friend and it was nice to chat and find out what was going on in his friend's life and to congratulate him on the birth of his son, but twenty minutes later his heart was still thumping.

Two hours later he still wasn't asleep.

By four a.m. Jed realised that even if the past was over with, he himself wasn't.

And most disconcerting for Jed was the new nurse that had started today.

He had found it easy to stick to his self-imposed rule. He really wasn't interested in anyone at work and just distanced himself from all the fun and conversations that were so much a part of working in an emergency department.

Except he *had* noticed Jasmine.

From the second he'd seen her standing talking to Penny, all flustered and red-cheeked, her dark curls bobbing, and her blue eyes had turned to him, he'd noticed her in a way he'd tried very hard not to. When he'd heard she was applying for a job in Emergency, his guard had shot up, but he had felt immediate relief when he'd heard someone call her Mrs Phillips.

It had sounded pretty safe to him.

There had been no harm in being friendly, no chance of anything being misconstrued, because if she was a Mrs then he definitely wasn't interested, which meant there was nothing to worry about.

But it would seem now that there was.

'Thanks, Jed.' He turned to the sound of Jasmine's voice as she walked past him with Vanessa.

'For?'

'Your help today, especially with Jim. I had no idea where the catheter packs were. It's good to get through that first shift back.'

'Well, you survived it.' He gave a very brief nod and turned back to his work.

'More importantly, the patients did!' Jasmine called as she carried on walking with Vanessa.

They were both heading to the crèche, he guessed. He fought the urge to watch her walk away, not looking up until he heard the doors open and then finally snap closed.

Not that Jasmine noticed—she was more than used to moody doctors who changed like the wind. For now she was delighted that her first shift had ended and as she and Vanessa headed to the crèche, Jasmine realised she had made a friend.

'He's gorgeous!' Vanessa said as Jasmine scooped up Simon. 'He's so blond!'

He was—blond and gorgeous, Simon had won the staff over on *his* first day with his happy smile and his efforts to talk.

'This is Liam!' Vanessa said. He was cute too, with a mop of dark curls and a good dose of ADD in the making. Jasmine stood smiling, watching as Vanessa took about ten minutes just to get two shoes on her lively toddler.

'Thank goodness for work,' Vanessa groaned. 'It gives me a rest!'

'Don't look now,' Vanessa said as they walked out of the crèche, 'they're getting something big in.' Jed and Lisa were standing outside where police on motorbikes had gathered in the forecourt. Screens were being put up and for a moment Jasmine wondered if her first day was actually over or if they were going to be asked to put the little ones back into crèche.

'Go.' Lisa grinned as Vanessa checked what was happening. 'The screens are for the press—we have ourselves a celebrity arriving.'

'Who?' Vanessa asked.

'Watch the news.' Lisa winked. 'Go on, shoo…'

'Oh,' Jasmine grumbled, because she really wanted to know. She glanced at Jed, who looked totally bored with the proceedings, and there was really no chance of a sophisticated effort because Simon was bouncing up and down with excitement at the sight of police cars and Liam was making loud siren noises. 'I guess I'll have to tune in at six to find out.'

And that was the stupid thing about Emergency, Jasmine remembered.

You couldn't wait for the shift to finish—even today, as much as she'd enjoyed her shift, as soon as lunchtime had ended, she had been counting the minutes, desperate to get to the crèche and pick up Simon.

Except that the second she had finished her shift, she wanted to go back.

'I've missed it,' she told Vanessa as they walked to the car park. 'I was looking at a job in MRI, but I really do like working in Emergency.'

'I'm the same,' Vanessa admitted. 'I couldn't work anywhere else.'

'The late shifts are going to be the killer, though,' Jasmine groaned, 'and I don't even want to think about nights.'

'You'll work it out.' Vanessa said. 'I've got a lovely babysitter: Ruby. She's studying childcare, she goes to my church and she's always looking for work. And if she can deal with Liam she can more than handle Simon. She's got really strict parents so she loves spending evenings and sometimes nights at my place.' She gave Jasmine a nudge. 'Though I do believe her boyfriend might pop over at times. Just to study, of course...'

They both laughed.

It was nice to laugh, nice to be back at work and making friends.

Nice to sit down for dinner on the sofa, with a for-once-exhausted Simon. 'Come on,' Jasmine coaxed, but he wasn't interested in the chicken and potatoes she was feeding him and in the end Jasmine gave in and warmed up his favourite ready meal in the microwave. 'I'm not buying any more,' Jasmine warned as he happily tucked in, but Simon just grinned.

And it was nice to turn on the news and to actually feel like you had a little finger on the pulse of the world.

She listened to the solemn voice of the newsreader telling the viewers about a celebrity who was '*resting*' at the Peninsula after being found unconscious. She got a glimpse of Jed walking by the stretcher as it was wheeled in, holding a sheet over the unfortunate patient's face. Then Jasmine watched as Mr Dean spoke, saying the patient was being transferred to ICU and there would be no further comment from the hospital.

It wasn't exactly riveting, so why did she rewind the feature?

Why did she freeze the screen?

Not in the hope of a glimpse at the celebrity.

And certainly not so she could listen again to Mr Dean.

It was Jed's face she paused on and then changed her mind.

She was finished with anything remotely male, Jasmine reminded herself, and then turned as Simon, having finished his meal and bored with the news, started bobbing up and down in front of the television.

'Except you, little man.'

CHAPTER SIX

JED DID CONCENTRATE on work.

Absolutely.

He did his best to ignore Jasmine, or at least to speak to her as little as possible at work, and he even just nodded to her when they occasionally crossed paths at the local shop, or he would simply run past her and Simon the odd evening they were on the beach.

He was a funny little lad. He loved to toddle on the beach and build sandcastles, but Jed noticed that despite her best efforts, Jasmine could not get him into the water.

Even if he tried not to notice, Jed saw a lot as he ran along the stretch of sand—Jasmine would hold the little boy on her hip and walk slowly into the water, but Simon would climb like a cat higher up her hip until Jasmine would give in to his sobs and take him back to the dry sand.

'You get too tense.' He gave in after a couple of weeks of seeing this ritual repeated. He could see what Jasmine was doing wrong and even if he ignored her at work, it seemed rude just to run past and not stop and talk now and then.

'Sorry?' She'd given up trying to take Simon into the water a few moments ago and now they were patting a sandcastle into shape. She looked up when Jed stood over her and Jasmine frowned at his comment, but in a curious way rather than a cross one.

He concentrated on her frown, not because she was resting back on her heels to look up at him, not because she was wearing shorts and a bikini top, he just focused on her frown. 'When you try to get him to go into the water. I've seen you.' He grinned. 'You get tense even before you pick him up to take him in there.'

'Thanks for the tip.' Jasmine looked not at Jed but at Simon. 'I really want him to love the water. I was hoping by the end of summer he'd at least be paddling, but he starts screaming as soon as I even get close.'

'He'll soon get used to it just as soon as you relax.' And then realising he was sounding like an authority when he didn't have kids of his own, he clarified things a little. 'I used to be a lifeguard, so I've watched a lot of parents trying to get reluctant toddlers into the water.'

'A lifeguard!' Jasmine grinned. 'You're making me blush.'

She was funny. She wasn't pushy or flirty, just funny.

'That was a long time ago,' Jed said.

'A volunteer?'

'Nope, professional. I was paid—it put me through medical school.'

'So how should I be doing it?'

'I'll show you.' He offered her his hand and pulled her up and they walked towards the water's edge. 'Just sit here.'

'He won't come.'

'I bet he does if you ignore him.'

So they sat and chatted for ten minutes or so. Simon grew bored, playing with his sandcastle alone, while the grown-ups didn't care that they were sitting in the water in shorts, getting wet with each shallow wave that came in.

Jed told her about his job, the one he'd had before medical school. 'It was actually that which made me want to work in emergency medicine,' Jed explained. 'I know you shouldn't enjoy a drowning...'

She smiled because she knew what he meant. There was a high that came from emergencies, just knowing that you knew what to do in a fraught situation.

Of course not all the time; sometimes it was just miserable all around, but she could see how the thrill of a successful resuscitation could soon plant the seeds for a career in Emergency.

'So if I drown, will you rescue me?'

'Sure,' Jed said, and her blue eyes turned to his and they smiled for a very brief moment. Unthinking, absolutely not thinking, he said it. 'Why? Is that a fantasy of yours?'

And he could have kicked himself, should have kicked himself, except she was just smiling and so too was he. Thankfully, starved of attention, Simon toddled towards them and squealed with delight at the feeling of water rushing past his feet.

'Yay!' Jasmine was delighted, taking his hands and pulling him in for a hug. 'It worked.'

'Glad to have helped.' Jed stood, because *now* he was

kicking himself, now he was starting to wonder what might have happened had Simon not chosen that moment to take to the water.

Actually, he wasn't wondering.

Jed knew.

'Better get on.' He gave her a thin smile, ruffled Simon's hair and off down the beach he went, leaving Jasmine sitting there.

Jed confused her.

Cold one minute and not warm but hot the next.

And, no, being rescued by a sexy lifeguard wasn't one of her fantasies, but a sexy Jed?

Well...

She blew out a breath. There was something happening between them, something like she had never known before. Except all he did was confuse her—because the next time she saw him at work he went back to ignoring her.

As well as confusing, Jed was also wrong about her getting right back into the swing of things at work. The department was busy and even a couple weeks later she still felt like the new girl at times. Even worse, her mum was less than pleased when Lisa asked, at short notice, if Jasmine could do two weeks of nights. She had staff sick and had already moved Vanessa onto the roster to do nights. Jasmine understood the need for her to cover, but she wasn't sure her mum would be quite so understanding.

'I'm really sorry about this,' Jasmine said to her mum as she dropped Simon off.

'It's fine.' Louise had that rather pained, martyred

look that tripped all of Jasmine's guilt switches. 'I've juggled a few clients' appointments to early evening for this week so I'll need you to be back here at five.'

'Sure.'

'But, Jasmine,' Louise said, 'how are you going to keep on doing this? I'm going away soon and if they can change your roster at five minutes' notice and expect you to comply, how are you going to manage?'

'I've a meeting with a babysitter at the weekend,' Jasmine told her mum. 'She's coming over and I'll see how she gets on with Simon.'

'How much is a babysitter going to cost?' Louise asked, and Jasmine chose not to answer, but really something would have to give.

Paying the crèche was bad enough, but by the time she'd paid a babysitter to pick Simon up for her late shifts and stints on nights, well, it was more complicated than Jasmine had the time to allocate it right now.

'How are things with Penny at work?' Louise asked.

'It seems okay.' Jasmine shrugged. 'She's just been on nights herself so I haven't seen much of her, and when I do she's no more horrible to me than she is to everybody else.'

'And no one's worked out that you're sisters?'

'How could they?' Jasmine said. 'Penny hasn't said anything and no one is going to hear it from me.'

'Well, make sure that they don't,' Louise warned. 'Penny doesn't need any stress right now. She's worked up enough as it is with this promotion coming up. Maybe once that's over with she'll come around to the idea a bit more.'

'I'd better get going.' Jasmine gave Simon a cuddle and held him just an extra bit tight.

'Are you okay?' Louise checked.

'I'm fine,' Jasmine said, but as she got to the car she remembered why she was feeling more than a little out of sorts. And, no, she hadn't shared it with her mum and certainly she wouldn't be ringing up Penny for a chat to sort out her feelings.

There on the driver's seat was her newly opened post and even though she'd been waiting for it, even though she wanted it, it felt strange to find out in such a banal way that she was now officially divorced.

Yes, she'd been looking forward to the glorious day, only the reality of it gave her no reason to smile.

Her marriage had been the biggest mistake of her life.

The one good thing to come out of it was Simon.

The *only* good thing, Jasmine thought, stuffing the papers into her glove box, and, not for the first time she felt angry.

She'd been duped so badly.

Completely lied to from the start.

Yes, she loved Simon with all her heart, but this was never the way she'd intended to raise a child. With a catalogue of crèches and babysitters and scraping to make ends meet and a father who, despite so many promises, when the truth had been exposed, when his smooth veneer had been cracked and the real Lloyd had surfaced, rather than facing himself had resumed the lie his life was and had turned his back and simply didn't want to know his own son.

* * *

'Are you okay?' Vanessa checked later as they headed out of the locker rooms.

'I'm fine,' Jasmine said, but hearing the tension in her own voice and realising she'd been slamming about a bit in the locker room, she conceded, 'My divorce just came through.'

'Yay!' said Vanessa, and it was a new friend she turned to rather than her family. 'You should be out celebrating instead of working.'

'I will,' Jasmine said. 'Just not yet.'

'Are you upset?'

'Not upset,' Jasmine said. 'Just angry.'

'Excuse me.' They stepped aside as a rather grumpy Dr Devlin brushed passed.

'Someone got out of the wrong side of bed,' Vanessa said.

Jasmine didn't get Jed.

She did not understand why he had changed so rapidly.

But he had.

From the nice guy she had met he was very brusque. *Very* brusque.

Not just to her, but to everyone. Still, Jasmine could be brusque too when she had to be, and on a busy night in Emergency, sometimes that was exactly what you had to be.

'You've done this before!' Greg, the charge nurse, grinned as Jasmine shooed a group of inebriated teenagers down to the waiting room. They were worried about their friend who'd been stabbed but were starting to fight amongst themselves.

'I used to be a bouncer at a night club.' Jasmine winked at her patient, who was being examined by Jed.

Greg laughed and even the patient smiled.

Jed just carried right on ignoring her.

Which was understandable perhaps, given that they were incredibly busy.

But what wasn't understandable to Jasmine was that he refused a piece of the massive hazelnut chocolate bar she opened at about one a.m., when everyone else fell on it.

Who doesn't like chocolate? Jasmine thought as he drank water.

Maybe he was worried about his figure?

He stood outside the cubicle now, writing up the card. 'Check his pedal pulses every fifteen minutes.' He thrust her a card and she read his instructions.

'What about analgesia?' Jasmine checked.

'I've written him up for pethidine.'

'No.' Jasmine glanced down at the card. 'You haven't.'

Jed took the card from her and rubbed his hand over his unshaven chin, and Jasmine tried to tell herself that he had his razor set that way, that he cultivated the unshaven, up-all-night, just-got-out-of-bed look, that this man's looks were no accident.

Except he had been up all night.

Jed let out an irritated hiss as he read through the patient's treatment card, as if she were the one who had made the simple mistake, and then wrote up the prescription in his messy scrawl.

'Thank you!' Jasmine smiled sweetly—just to annoy him.

She didn't get a smile back.

Mind you, the place was too busy to worry about Jed's bad mood and brooding good looks, which seemed to get more brooding with every hour that passed.

At six a.m., just as things were starting to calm down, just as they were starting to catch up and tidy the place for the day staff, Jasmine found out just how hard this job could be at times.

Found, just as she was starting to maybe get into the swing of things, that perhaps this wasn't the place she really wanted to be after all.

They were alerted that a two-week-old paediatric arrest was on his way in but the ambulance had arrived before they had even put the emergency call out.

Jasmine took the hysterical parents into an interview room and tried to get any details as best she could as the overhead loudspeaker went off, urgently summoning the paediatric crash team to Emergency. It played loudly in the interview room also, each chime echoing the urgency, and there was the sound of footsteps running and doors slamming, adding to the parents' fear.

'The doctors are all with your baby,' Jasmine said. 'Let them do their work.' Cathy, the new mum, still looked pregnant. She kept saying she had only had him two weeks and that this couldn't be happening, that she'd taken him out of his crib and brought him back to bed, and when the alarm had gone off for her husband to go to work... And then the sobbing would start again.

She kept trying to push past Jasmine to get to her baby, but eventually she collapsed into a chair and sobbed with her husband that she just wanted to know what was going on.

'As soon as there's some news, someone will be in.' There was a knock at the door and she saw a policeman and -woman standing there. Jasmine excused herself, went outside and closed the door so she could speak to them.

'How are they?' the policewoman asked.

'Not great,' Jasmine said. 'A doctor hasn't spoken to them yet.'

'How are things looking for the baby?'

'Not great either,' Jasmine said. 'I really don't know much, though, I've just been in with the parents. I'm going to go and try to find out for them what's happening.' Though she was pretty sure she knew. One look at the tiny infant as he had arrived and her heart had sunk.

'Everything okay?' Lisa, early as always, was just coming on duty and she came straight over.

'We've got a two-week-old who's been brought in in full arrest,' Jasmine explained. 'I was just going to try and get an update for the parents.'

'Okay.' Lisa nodded. 'You do that and I'll stay with them.'

Jasmine wasn't sure what was worse, sitting in with the hysterical, terrified parents or walking into Resus and hearing the silence as they paused the resuscitation for a moment to see if there was any response.

There was none.

Jed put his two fingers back onto the baby's chest and started the massage again, but the paediatrician shook his head.

'I'm calling it.'

It was six twenty-five and the paediatrician's voice was assertive.

'We're not going to get him back.'

He was absolutely right—the parents had started the resuscitation and the paramedics had continued it for the last thirty-five futile minutes. Jasmine, who would normally have shed a tear at this point before bracing herself to face the family, just stood frozen.

Vanessa cried. Not loudly. She took some hand wipes from the dispenser and blew her nose and Jed took his fingers off the little infant and sort of held his nose between thumb and finger for a second.

It was a horrible place to be.

'Are you okay?' Greg looked over at Jasmine and she gave a short nod. She dared not cry, even a little, because if she started she thought she might not stop.

It was the first paediatric death she had dealt with since she'd had Simon and she was shocked at her own reaction. She just couldn't stop looking at the tiny scrap of a thing and comparing him to her own child, and how the parents must be feeling. She jumped when she heard the sharp trill of a pager.

'Sorry.' The paediatrician looked down at his pager. 'I'm needed urgently on NICU.'

'Jed, can you…?'

Jed nodded as he accepted the grim task. 'I'll tell the parents.'

'Thanks, and tell them that I'll come back down and talk to them at length as soon as I can.'

'Who's been dealing with the parents?' Jed asked when the paediatrician had gone.

'Me,' Jasmine said. 'Lisa's in there with them now. The police are here as well.'

'I'll speak first to the parents,' Jed said. 'Probably just keep it with Lisa. She'll be dealing with them all day.'

Jasmine nodded. 'They wanted a chaplain.' She could hear the police walkie-talkies outside and her heart ached for the parents, not just for the terrible news but having to go over and over it, not only with family but with doctors and the police, and for all that was to come.

'I'll go and ring the chaplain,' Greg said. 'And I'd better write up the drugs now.' He looked at the chaos. There were vials and wrappers everywhere, all the drawers on the trolley were open. They really had tried everything, but all to no avail.

'I'll sort out the baby,' Vanessa said, and Jasmine, who had never shied away from anything before, was relieved that she wouldn't have to deal with him.

'I'll restock,' Jasmine said.

Which was as essential as the other two things, Jasmine told herself as she started to tidy up, because you never knew what was coming through the door. The day staff were arriving and things needed to be left in order.

Except Jasmine *was* hiding and deep down she knew it, had been so relieved when Jed had suggested keeping things with Lisa. She screwed her eyes closed as screams carried through the department. Jed must have broken the news.

She just wanted to go home to her own baby, could not stand to think of their grief.

'Are you okay, Jasmine?' Vanessa asked as she stocked her trolley to take into Resus, preparing to wash and dress the baby so that his parents could hold him.

'I'll get there.' She just wanted the shift to be over, to ring her mum and check that Simon was okay, for the past hour not to have happened, because it wasn't fair, it simply was not fair. But of course patients kept coming in with headaches and chest pains and toothaches and there was still the crash trolley to restock and plenty of work to do.

And now here was Penny, all crisp and ready for work.

'Morning!' She smiled and no one really returned it. 'Bad night?' she asked Jed, who, having told the parents and spoken to the police, was admitting another patient.

'We just had a neonatal death,' Jed said. 'Two weeks old.'

'God.' Penny closed her eyes. 'How are the parents?'

'The paediatrician is in there with them now,' Jed said. Jasmine was restocking the trolley, trying not to listen, just trying to tick everything off her list. 'But they're beside themselves, of course,' Jed said. 'Beautiful baby,' he added.

'Any ideas as to why?' Penny asked.

'It looks, at this stage, like an accidental overlay.

Mum brought baby back to bed and fell asleep feeding him, Dad woke up to go to work and found him.'

She heard them discussing what had happened and heard Lisa come in and ask Vanessa if the baby was ready, because she wanted to take him into his parents. She didn't turn around, she didn't want to risk seeing him, so instead Jasmine just kept restocking the drugs they had used and the needles and wrappers and tiny little ET tubes and trying, and failing, to find a replacement flask of paediatric sodium bicarbonate that had been used in the resuscitation. Then she heard Penny's voice...

'The guidelines now say not to co-sleep.'

And it wasn't because it was Penny that the words riled Jasmine so much, or was it?

No.

It was just the wrong words at the wrong time.

'Guidelines?' Jasmine had heard enough, could not stand to hear Penny's cool analysis, and swung around. 'Where are the guidelines at three in the morning when you haven't slept all night and your new baby's screaming? Where are the guidelines when—?'

'You need to calm down, Nurse,' Penny warned.

That just infuriated Jasmine even more. 'It's been a long night. I don't feel particularly calm,' Jasmine retorted. 'Those parents have to live with this, have to live with not adhering to the *guidelines*, when they were simply doing what parents have done for centuries.'

Jasmine marched off to the IV room and swiped her ID card to get in, anger fizzing inside her, not just towards her sister but towards the world that was now minus that beautiful baby, and for all the pain and the grief the parents would face. Would she have said that if Penny hadn't been her sister?

The fact was, she *would* have said it, and probably a whole lot more.

Yes, Penny was right.

And the guidelines were right too.

But it was just so unfair.

She still couldn't find the paediatric sodium bicarbonate solution and rummaged through the racks because it had to be there, or maybe she should ring the children's ward and ask if they had some till pharmacy was delivered.

Then she heard the door swipe and Jed came in.

He was good like that, often setting up his drips and things himself. 'Are you okay?'

'Great!' she said through gritted teeth.

'I know that Penny comes across as unfeeling,' Jed said, 'but we all deal with this sort of thing in different ways.'

'I know we do.' Jasmine climbed up onto a stool, trying to find the IV flask. She so did not need the grief speech right now, did not need the debrief that was supposed to solve everything, that made things manageable, did not really want the world to be put into perspective just yet.

'She was just going through the thought process,' Jed continued.

'I get it.'

He could hear her angrily moving things, hear the upset in her voice, and maybe he should get Lisa to speak to her, except Lisa was busy with the parents right now and Greg was checking drugs and handing over to the day staff. Still, the staff looked out for each other in cases like this, and so that was what Jed did.

Or tried to.

'Jasmine, why don't you go and get a coffee and…?' He decided against suggesting that it might calm her down.

'I'm just finishing stocking up and then I'm going home.'

'Not yet. Look—' he was very patient and practical '—you're clearly upset.'

'Please.' Jasmine put up her hand. 'I really don't need to hear it.'

'I think you do,' Jed said.

'From whom?'

'Excuse me?' He clearly had no idea what she was alluding to, but there was a bubble of anger that was dangerously close to popping now, not just for this morning's terrible events but for the weeks of confusion, for the man who could be nice one minute and cool and distant the next, and she wanted to know which one she was dealing with.

'Am I being lectured to by Dr Devlin, or am I being spoken to by Jed?'

'I have no idea what you're talking about. You're distressed.' He knew exactly what she was talking about, knew exactly what she meant, yet of course he could not tell her that. Jed also knew he was handling this terribly, that fifteen minutes sitting in the staffroom being debriefed by him wasn't going to help either of them.

'I'm not distressed.'

'Perhaps not, but I think it would be very silly to leave like this. It would be extremely irresponsible to get into a car and drive home right now, so I'm suggesting that you go to the staffroom and sit down for fifteen minutes.' She stood there furious as she was being told what to do, not asked, she knew that.

'Fine.' She gave a terse smile. 'I will have a coffee and then I'll go home, but first I have to put this back on the crash trolley and order some more from pharmacy.'

'Do that, and then I'll be around shortly to talk to you.' Jed said, 'Look, I know it's hard, especially with one so young. It affects all of us in different ways. I know that I'm upset...'

She didn't say it, but the roll of her eyes as he spoke told him he couldn't possibly know, couldn't possibly understand how she felt.

'Oh, I get it,' Jed said. 'I can't be upset, I don't really get it, do I? Because I don't have a child, I couldn't possibly be as devastated as you.' His voice was rising, his own well-restrained anger at this morning's events starting to build. 'I'm just the machine that walks in and tells the parents that their baby's dead. What the hell would I know?'

'I didn't mean that.' She knew then that she was being selfish in her upset, but grief was a selfish place and one not easy to share.

'Oh, but I think you did,' Jed said. 'I think you meant exactly that.'

And he was right, she had, except that wasn't fair on either of them, because she had cried many times over a lost baby, it just felt different somehow when you had one at home. There was a mixture of guilt and pain tempered with shameful relief that it hadn't happened to her, because, yes, she'd taken Simon into bed with her, despite what the guidelines might say, and it wasn't fair on anyone.

It simply wasn't fair.

Jasmine had no idea how the next part happened. Later she would be tempted to ring Security and ask if she could review the security footage in treatment room two between seven twenty and seven twenty-five, because she'd finally located the sodium bicarbonate and stepped down from the stool and stood facing him, ready to row, both of them ready to argue their point, and the next moment she was being kissed to within an inch of her life.

Or was it the other way around?

She had no way of knowing who had initiated it, all she was certain of was that neither tried to stop it.

It was an angry, out-of-control kiss.

His chin was rough and dragged on her skin, and his tongue was fierce and probing. He tasted of a mixture of peppermint and coffee and she probably tasted of instant tomato soup or salty tears, but it was like no other kiss she had known.

It was violent.

She heard the clatter of a trolley that moved as they did.

It was a kiss that came with no warning and rapidly escalated.

It was a kiss that was completely out of bounds and out of hand.

She was pressed into the wall and Jed was pressing into her; his hands were everywhere and so too were hers; she could feel his erection pressing into her. More than that she too was pushing herself up against him, her hands just as urgent as his, pulling his face into hers, and never had she lost control so quickly, never had she been more unaware of her surroundings because only the crackle of the intercom above reminded them of their location—only that, or shamefully she knew it could have gone further. Somehow they stopped themselves, somehow they halted it, except they were still holding each other's heads.

'And you thought driving would be careless and irresponsible,' Jasmine said.

He sort of blew out his breath. 'Jasmine...' He was right on the edge here, Jed realised, shocked at himself. 'I apologise.'

'No need to apologise,' Jasmine said. 'Or should I?'

'Of course not.' His mouth was there, right there, they were holding each other, restraining the other, and both still dangerously close to resuming what they mustn't. She could hear their breathing, fast and ragged and fighting to slow, and slowly too they let go of each other.

Her blouse was undone, just one button, and she didn't really know how, but he looked away as she did it up and moved away from him to pick up the flask she had dropped. She left him setting up his IV and went to head back out, but she could still taste him, was still not thinking straight. And then Lisa came in.

'Shouldn't you be heading home?'

'I couldn't find the paediatric sodium bicarb,' Jasmine said. 'There's only one left after this.'

'Thanks,' Lisa said. 'I'll get Joan to add it to the pharmacy order. Thanks for everything, Jasmine. I know that can't have been an easy shift.'

'How are the parents?'

'They're spending some time with him. The hospital chaplain is in with them and the police have been lovely.' Lisa looked at Jasmine. 'Maybe go and get a coffee before you go home.'

'I think I just want my bed,' Jasmine admitted. 'I just need to finish the crash trolley off and order some more of this.'

'I'll do that.' Lisa took the flask from her and they stepped aside as Jed walked past with his IV trolley. Very deliberately, neither met the other's eye.

'You go to bed and get a well-earned rest,' Lisa said.

Fat chance of that.

Jasmine did have a cup of coffee before she drove home.

Except she certainly wasn't hanging around to see Jed. Instead, she chose to head to the kiosk and get a takeaway.

And, of course, on the way to her car, she rang her mum.

'How was Simon last night?' Jasmine asked the second her mum answered.

'Fantastic. I haven't heard a peep out of him.'

'He's not up yet?'

'No, but he didn't go down to sleep till quite late.'

'You've checked him, though?' Jasmine could hear the anxiety in her voice

'I checked him before I went to bed. Jasmine, it's eight a.m. Surely it's good if he's having a little lie-in when he often has to be up at six for crèche?'

'Mum…'

She heard her mother's weary sigh as she walked through the house and then silence for a moment. She was being ridiculous, but even so, she needed the reassurance.

'He's asleep,' her mum said, 'and, yes, he's breathing.'

'Thank you.'

'Bad night?'

'Bad morning.'

'I'm sorry.' And then Louise started to laugh. 'He's just woken up—can you hear him?'

Jasmine smiled at the lovely morning sounds Simon made, calling out to anyone who was there, but she was dangerously close to tears a second later as she realised again just how lucky she was.

'Go and have a nice sleep and I'll see you here for dinner.'

'Thanks, Mum.'

Her mum could be so nice, Jasmine mused as she drove home. When she had Simon she was wonderful with him. Jasmine completely understood that her mother didn't want to be a permanent babysitter and she decided that when she woke up she *was* going to ring

Ruby, Vanessa's babysitter, and maybe get together and see if they could work something out.

All the drive home she thought very practical thoughts, aware she was a little bit more than tired.

And upset.

And confused.

She parked in the carport and looked over at the beach, wondered if a walk might be soothing, but knowing her luck Jed would be running there soon and another encounter with him was the last thing either of them needed now.

So she showered and tried to block out the day with her blinds, set her alarm and did her level best not to think of those poor parents and what they were doing right now, but even trying not to think about them made her cry.

And it made her cry too, that she had been here twelve weeks now and Simon's father hadn't even rung once to see how he was, neither had he responded to the occasional photo of his son she sent him.

And then she got to the confusing part and she wasn't crying now as she went over the latter part of her shift.

Instead she was cringing as her mind wandered to a man who at every turn bemused her, and then to the kiss that they had shared.

She hadn't been kissed like that, ever.

Their response to each other's kiss had been so immediate, so consuming that, really, had the intercom not gone off, they'd have been unstoppable, and she burnt in embarrassment at the thought of what Lisa might have come in and found.

And she burnt, too, because in truth it was a side to him she had known was there—something she had felt the second he had jogged up to her on the beach. Jed was the first man to move her in a very long time, but she had never thought her feelings might be reciprocated, had never expected the ferocity of that kiss.

And she'd do very well to forget about it!

They had both been upset, Jasmine decided.

Angry.

Over-emotional.

It had been a one-off. She turned over and very deliberately closed her eyes. Yes, it would be a bit awkward facing him tonight but, hell, she'd faced worse.

She'd just pretend it had never happened.

And no doubt so would he.

She had her whole life to sort out without confusing things further.

And a man like Jed Devlin could only do that.

CHAPTER SEVEN

'MUM!' SIMON SAID it more clearly than he ever had before, and Jasmine scooped him up and cuddled him in tight the second she got to her mum's.

'You're early,' Louise commented. 'I said you didn't need to be here till five.'

'I didn't sleep very well,' Jasmine admitted. 'I'm going to go shopping at the weekend for some decent blinds.' Not that that was the entire reason! 'How has he been?'

'Okay. He's been asking after you a lot,' Louise said, when Jasmine rather wished that she wouldn't as she already felt guilty enough. 'Right, I'd better get ready.'

Louise appeared a little while later in a smart navy suit, with heels and make-up, looking every bit the professional real estate agent. 'How did you do it Mum?' Jasmine asked. 'I mean, you had evening appointments when we were little.'

'You were older than Simon when your dad left,' Louise pointed out. 'Penny's a good bit older than you and she was born sensible—I used to ask the neighbour to listen out for you. It was different times then,' she admitted.

Maybe, but nothing was going to fill the well of guilt Jasmine felt leaving Simon so much and it was only going to get more complicated for him when she added a babysitter to the mix.

Still, she did her best not to worry about next week or next month, just concentrated on giving him his dinner, and when he spat it out she headed to her mum's freezer and, yes, there were chicken nuggets. He could eat them till he was eighteen, Jasmine thought, and let go of worrying about the small stuff for five minutes, just enjoyed giving him his bath and settling him, and then got herself ready for work.

There really wasn't time to stress about facing Jed, especially when her mum didn't get back till after eight, and by the time she raced into work the clock was already nudging nine but, of course, he was one of the first people she saw.

It was a bit awkward but actually not as bad as she'd feared.

As she headed to the lockers Jasmine met him in the corridor and screwed up her face as she blushed and mouthed the word, 'Sorry.'

'Me too,' Jed said, and possibly he too was blushing just a little bit.

'Upset, you know,' Jasmine said.

'I get it.'

'So it's forgotten?' Jasmine checked.

'Forgotten,' he agreed.

Except it wasn't quite so easy to forget a kiss like that, Jasmine knew, because through a restless sleep she had tried.

So too had Jed.

He was a master at self-recrimination, had been furious with himself all day, and that evening, getting ready for work, he'd braced himself to face her, to be cool and aloof, yet her blush and her grin and her 'sorry' had sideswiped him—had actually made him laugh just a little bit on the inside.

'I got you a present.' Vanessa smiled as, still blushing, Jasmine walked into the locker room and peered into the bag being handed to her. It was a bottle with ribbons tied to the neck. 'I think it should be real champagne, but sparkling wine will have to do. You can open it when you're ready to celebrate.'

'Thank you!' Jasmine was touched. 'I'll have a drink at the weekend.'

'I mean properly celebrate.' Vanessa winked. 'You can't pop that cork till…'

'It will be vintage by then.' Jasmine grinned.

It was a very different night from the one before.

It was quiet and the staff took advantage. Greg, the charge nurse, put some music on at the work station and when at four a.m. there were only a few patients waiting for beds or obs, instead of telling them to restock or reorder, he opened a book as Jasmine and Vanessa checked each other's blood sugars. They were low enough to merit another trip to the vending machine, they decided. Then they came back and checked each other's BP.

'It's so low!' Vanessa pulled a face as she unwrapped the cuff and Jasmine grinned, proud of herself for keeping her pulse and blood pressure down, with Jed sitting at the station.

He noticed how easily she laughed.

She noticed him, full stop.

Noticed that this time when she cracked open her chocolate he took a piece.

'Do you want your blood pressure checked, Jed?' Vanessa asked.

'No, thanks.'

Vanessa pulled a face at his grumpy tone. 'Do you work on it, Jed?' It was ten past four, well into the witching hour for night nurses, a quiet night, lights blazing, the humour becoming more wicked. 'Do you work on being all silent and moody?'

'No,' he said. 'I just work.'

'And that beard you're growing,' Vanessa pushed as Greg looked up and grinned, 'is it designer stubble?'

'No,' Jed said patiently. 'I went for a run when I got in from work and I was too tired to shave afterwards, and then I overslept.'

'You're sure about that?' Vanessa said. 'You're sure you're not a male model on the side?'

Jed had forgotten those times of late. He hadn't partaken in chit-chat and fun for a very long time, he'd been too busy concentrating only on work. Maybe he needed a coffee, maybe *his* blood sugar was down, because he was kind of remembering the harmless fun he had once had at work before it had all become a nightmare.

He sat there recalling the laughs that had been part of the job and he was almost smiling as Vanessa chatted on. There was such a difference between playing and flirting. Jed had always known that, he'd just forgotten how to mix the two of late, had lost one for fear of the other, but the atmosphere tonight was kind of bringing it back.

'When you go to the hairdresser's, do you ask them to leave that bit of fringe?' Vanessa teased. 'Just so it can fall over your eye?'

As he turned, Jasmine waited for a frown, for a sharp word, for a brusque put-down, but her smirking grin turned to a delighted one as he flopped his fringe forward, pouted his lips and looked over their shoulders in a haughty model pose.

And then as they screamed in laughter and even Greg did too, Jed got back to his notes.

Enough fun for one night, Jed told himself.

Except he'd set them off and now they were walking like models.

Greg was joining in too as he filled in the board, standing with one hand on his hip and talking in deliberately effeminate tones. Jed tried not to smile, not notice as he usually managed to—he had just blocked out this side of Emergency, had chosen to ignore the black humour and frivolity that sometimes descended.

And yet somehow it was coming back.

Somehow he was starting to remember that it wasn't all just about work.

And Jed knew why.

It was just that he didn't want to know why.

'I'm going for a sleep.' He stood. 'Call me if anything comes in or at six if it stays quiet.'

He could hear them laughing as he tried to rest.

And whatever they were doing it must be funny because he even heard the po-faced nursing supervisor, who must be doing her rounds, start to laugh.

Jed turned on the white noise machine but still he couldn't sleep.

He could do without this!

'Morning, sunshine!' Greg rapped on the door at six, but Jed was awake. He rolled out of bed and brushed his teeth, headed out, took a few bloods and discharged a couple of patients, and wished the place would pick up.

He got one query appendicitis and one very grumpy old man called Ken Jones. He had a chronically infected leg ulcer, which was being dressed by a visiting nurse twice a week, but he had decided at five-thirty a.m. that it was time to do something about it and had called an ambulance. He was very grubby and unkempt and had his radio with him, which was tuned in to a chat show.

'What's his blood sugar?'

'Eight,' Jasmine said.

'You're taking all your diabetic medication, Ken?' Jed checked.

'I just do what I'm told.'

'Okay.' Jed had already carefully examined the man and his leg and he chatted to him for a little while. 'I'm going to get the medics to come down and have a look at you,' Jed said, 'but it might take a while. We're really quiet down here but I know they're very busy up on the ward, so you might have to stay with us for a while. And we could look at the dressings nurse to come and have a good look at your wound and maybe try something new.'

'Up to you.'

'It could be a few hours,' Jed said.

'I don't make a fuss.'

Jed grinned as he walked out. 'He'll be ringing up the radio station to complain about how long he has to wait soon.'

'Does he really need to see the medics?'

'Probably not,' Jed said. 'Penny will probably clear him out by eight, but...' he gave a shrug, '...the old boy's lonely, isn't he? Anyway, he could do with a good looking over, his chest is a bit rattly and he's a bit dry. I'll run some bloods.'

'I'll order him breakfast,' Jasmine yawned.

She ordered a breakfast from the canteen and then checked on the query appendicitis. His drip was about through so she headed over to the IV room. When she swiped her card and saw that Jed was in there, sorting out his trolley to take the bloods, she nearly turned and ran.

But that would be making a big deal of things so instead she stepped in.

'We need to talk,' Jed said without looking up from his task.

'No we don't,' Jasmine said. 'Really, it's fine.'

'Sure about that?' Jed said, and then looked over.

And, no, she wasn't sure about that because the ghost of their kiss was there in the room. She could see the exact spot where he'd pressed her to the wall, feel again every feeling she had yesterday—except the anger, except the upset.

'What about we meet for coffee after work?' he suggested.

'People will see,' Jasmine said. 'You know what this

place is like.' She certainly didn't want a hint of this getting back to Penny.

'I meant away from the hospital. Just to talk.'

She shook her head. She'd hardly slept yesterday and had to work tonight as well as stop by her mum's at five and give Simon his dinner.

'I just want to go to bed.' She opened her mouth to correct herself and thankfully they both actually laughed.

'I really,' Jasmine said slowly, 'and I mean *really* am in no position to start something. I know people say that, but I've got a whole lot of things to sort out before...' She shook her head. 'I'm not going there.'

'I get that,' Jed said. 'Believe me, I had no intention of getting involved with someone at work but yesterday, hell, these past weeks...' He wondered how something he had spent all yesterday regretting should be something he would happily do again right this minute.

'Is that why you've been so horrible?'

'I haven't,' he said, then conceded, 'Maybe a bit. We need to talk, maybe clear the air—because if we don't—'

'If we don't,' Jasmine interrupted, 'we're going to be caught making out in the IV cupboard.' She gave him a grin. 'And I have no intention of going there again.'

Except she was lying.

She was looking at his mouth as she said it.

And he was looking at hers.

Had Greg not come in, that was exactly what would have happened and they both knew it.

Yes, the air needed clearing.

CHAPTER EIGHT

'WHY IS HE waiting for the medics?'

Despite not having to start till eight, Penny was in at a quarter to seven, standing and staring at the admission board and determined to make the most of a rare opportunity to clear the board and start her working day with not a single patient.

'He's brewing something.' Jed shrugged.

'We're not a holding pen,' Penny said. 'I'll get the nurses to order him transport home.'

'Let him have his breakfast at least.'

'Of course he can have his breakfast—by the time transport gets here he'll probably have had lunch as well.' She glanced briefly at a weary Jed. 'You look awful.'

'It's easier when it's busy,' Jed yawned.

'Go home,' she said.

'I might just do that.' And then he looked at Penny, who was rather determinedly not turning round to face him, just staring fixedly at the board. 'Speaking of looking awful…' he waited till she reluctantly turned to face him and he saw her red swollen eye '…what happened?'

'I walked into a branch.'

'Ouch.' Jasmine walked over just as he was taking a look.

'Ooh.' She winced when she saw Penny's red eye. 'Penny, what happened?' And then she remembered she wasn't supposed to be her sister.

'My neighbour's tree overhangs,' she said darkly. 'Though it won't by the time I get home—I've left them a note, telling them what's happened and that they'd better cut it.'

Jasmine could just imagine she had, and what was in it. And she could picture the branch, too, and Penny's gorgeous old neighbours who would be so upset.

Trust Penny to handle things so sensitively!

Of course she said nothing.

'I'll have a look,' Jed said, and went to buzz Reception to get Penny an admission card.

'I don't need to be registered,' Penny snapped. 'It's just a scratch.'

'A nasty scratch on your cornea,' Jed confirmed a few minutes later. Penny was sitting at the nurses' station and Jed had put some fluorescein drops into her eye. It made her eye bright yellow but any scratches showed up green. 'You need antibiotic drops and to keep it covered. When was your last tetanus booster?'

'I can't remember,' Penny said. 'I'm sure I'm up to date.'

'Penny?' Jed checked, as Jasmine walked in.

'Ken Jones just spiked a temp—his temp's thirty-eight point nine.'

'I'll do cultures.' Jed grinned, and Penny rolled her

tongue in her cheek because now the old boy would have to be admitted.

'I'll do them,' she sighed.

'Not yet,' Jed yawned. 'I'll just give you your tetanus shot.'

'I'll go to my GP.'

'Don't be ridiculous,' Jed said, already opening a trolley and pulling out a syringe.

It was then that Jasmine *had* to say something.

'I'll do that.' Jasmine smiled. 'You can do the cultures.'

'I'll do the cultures,' Penny said. 'You go home, Jed, and think about shaving.'

Jasmine said nothing, not a single word as they headed into a cubicle and Penny unbuttoned her blouse. She just handed her a wad of tissues as Penny started crying.

Penny was, as Jasmine knew only too well, petrified of needles.

Not a little bit scared, completely petrified of them, though she didn't blink when sticking them in others.

'If you breathe a word of this...'

She was shaking on the seat as Jasmine swabbed her arm.

'No, wait!' Penny said.

'For what?' Jasmine said, sticking the needle in. 'Done.' She smiled at her. 'You big baby.'

'I know, I know.' Penny shuddered. 'Just give me a minute, would you? Go and set up for those blood cultures.' She had snapped straight back to being Penny, except this time Jasmine was smiling.

* * *

Jed didn't think about shaving.

He had a shower and tried not to think about Jasmine.

And then he pulled on some running clothes and ran the length of the beach and told himself to just concentrate on work.

Only this time it didn't work.

And he saw where she lived and her car pull up in her carport and he saw Jasmine minus an armful of Simon but holding a bottle of champagne, which confused him, and he tried to continue to run.

What on earth was he going to say to her if he knocked at her door?

At least nothing would happen, he consoled himself, as ten minutes later he found himself doing just that, because given he wasn't exactly fresh out of the shower, there would be no repeats of yesterday.

Except *she* was fresh out of the shower when she opened the door and he prided himself on the fact that he did not look down, that he somehow held her eyes, even though her dressing gown did little to hide her womanly shape.

'Bad timing?'

'A bit.'

'Well, I won't keep you from your champagne.' He didn't want to make her laugh, except he did so, only he wasn't here for that.

'It's in the fridge.'

'Good.'

'A present.'

'That's nice.'

'Well?' Jasmine demanded. 'Which Jed am I talking to this morning?' And she looked at him standing there, and she knew who it was—the beachside Jed, the man who made her smile, the Jed who had made his first appearance at work just a few hours ago.

'I like to keep my work and personal life separate,' he offered as way of an explanation, only it didn't wash with Jasmine. Penny did too but she was a cow both in and out of work. Yet with Jed sometimes she felt as if she was dealing with two completely different people.

But she liked this one.

Really liked this one, and, no, maybe they weren't going anywhere, maybe it was just all a bit much for him, she was a mother to one year old after all, but that he was here, that at this hour of the morning he stood at her door, when sensible shift workers should be firmly asleep, proved the undeniable attraction.

'I just wanted to say that I am really sorry and that it won't happen again. There'll be no more inappropriateness.'

'And it won't happen again at this end,' Jasmine said. 'Nothing inappropriate…'

Jed nodded and turned to go, except she didn't want him to. She was tired of running from the past, tired of saving for the future—she just wanted a little bit of living for now.

'At least, not at work.'

And for two years Jed had kept things separate. Despite some temptations, he had kept fiercely to his rule.

But Jed's rules had never been tested at this level.

Had they not kissed yesterday he might have been able to walk away.

Had he not tasted lips that were exactly suited to his, he might have headed back to the beach and then home.

But more than that, her blush and eye roll and 'sorry' last night, her total lack of pursuit or demands meant more to Jed than Jasmine could possibly know.

Bottom line?

They wanted each other.

Not a little bit of want, it was a morning after a sleepless nights want. It was twenty-five hours since yesterday's kiss and for twenty-five hours it had been on both of their minds.

He walked into the hallway and his mouth met hers.

And his chin was even rougher than yesterday.

And yesterday, though their kiss had been fierce it had been on both sides with bitter restraint.

But now they could have what they wanted.

Each other.

For now, at least, it could be as simple as that.

She didn't care that he was damp from running. He smelt fresh and male and she knew what was under that T-shirt, and as she pulled it up and over his head she didn't just get to glimpse, she got to feel, and, no, he wasn't annoyed at the intrusion this time.

He tugged at her dressing gown as his mouth was everywhere—on her lips, on her neck and on her breasts. Meanwhile, she pulled at his shorts, because he was pressed so hard into her, and they pulled apart just enough to get to the bedroom—they weren't in the treatment room now and they quickly celebrated the fact.

She wanted to see what she had felt and she manoeuvred his shorts and all things unnecessary and he kicked off his running shoes and stepped out of them and they were naked in seconds, and seconds from impact.

'Condoms.' She was on the floor, going through his shorts.

'I don't run with them.' Jed laughed.

She was at eye level with his crotch as she knelt up and pressed her lips to him, pleased with a brief taste. Too selfish to continue, she dashed to her tiny bathroom and pulled the cupboard under the sink apart for condoms that were somewhere in a box she hadn't sorted in ages.

She was uncaring as Jed watched her bottom sticking up as she searched in the cupboard and her breasts jiggling as she turned round and it was safer that he go back into the bedroom.

Oh, my.

It was all Jasmine could think as she walked back towards him, because he was better than anything she had fashioned in her mind. He was incredibly fit and toned. She should have been shy as she walked over, but shy was the furthest thing from her mind and anyway, he didn't wait for her to finish walking—both of them were happy to collide.

He was just so into her body, so wanting, and he didn't need to worry about speed or things moving too quickly for her because as his hands slid between her thighs and met her heat she was moaning and he was pushing her onto the bed, with Jasmine wondering where her inhibitions had gone.

She had hundreds of them, Jasmine reminded herself as he knelt over her and examined every inch of her, his eyes greedy with want.

A telephone book full of them.

Or she had, but they had just all disappeared today.

It was almost impossible to tear the packet for him.

And she found herself licking her lips as he slid it on.

She had never had sex like it.

She had never felt less mechanical in her life.

Thought had been replaced by pure sensation.

Him, she thought as he got back to kissing her.

Her, he thought as he reclaimed her mouth.

And then the power that remained sort of fused into one.

His fingers were there and she was wet and warm and wanted this just as much as he did.

'First time since…' She sort of braced herself and he held back and took a moment to not be selfish, even if she wanted him to be. Instead, he slid deeper into her with fingers that were skilled and frantic, and she left it to him, because he knew what he was doing. If they were quick it was mutual, if they were fast it was with begging consent.

Even with much preparation she was incredibly tense when the moment came and she willed him to ignore her. Slowly he pushed in, and she stretched and resisted and then stretched again, and he gave her a moment of stillness to get used to him inside.

Well, not really a moment because he knew he only

had a few left in him but Jed left it for her to initiate movement, felt the squeeze and the pull on him as she tested herself as she moved herself up and down his long length.

Just when she thought she had adjusted, just when she pulled him in, he beat her to it and drove into her, and she met him and then he did it again and she tried to trip into his rhythm, except he was so hard and fast now it was bliss to not try, to simply let him, only it wasn't a passive response, it was more trusting.

Jed could hear Jasmine's moans and her urging, and he wished for a second she'd be quiet, because it made it impossible for Jed not to come, except she was starting to. He felt the lift of her hips and the arch of her into him, the feel of a slow uncurling from the inside, reluctant almost to give in to him, and then as he moaned his release she shattered.

She did, she just gave in in a way she never had, felt and delivered deeper than she ever had, and found out in that moment how much of herself she had always held back, the intensity fusing them for a moment in absolute bliss.

She lay there trying to get her breath back as he rested on top of her, and still they were one as reality slowly started to intrude.

She wasn't ready for a relationship.

He'd sworn to not get involved with someone from work.

Penny.

Promotion.

Simon.

Single mum.

Simultaneously the real world flooded its lights onto them and they both turned looked at each other for a long moment.

'Well,' Jasmine said. 'We must have both needed that.'

He laughed, actually laughed on the inside too as he had when she had mouthed 'sorry', and the doubts that had started hushed.

And they hushed some more as they lay in bed and drank Vanessa's sparkling wine that hadn't even had time to cool, and they congratulated each other on how fantastic that had been, rather than trying to work out where they were, and then she told him not what was on her mind but the truth.

'I have to go to sleep.'

'And me.'

'I hardly slept yesterday.'

'Me neither.'

'Jed, I don't know what happened. I don't really know what to say.' She was as honest as she could be. 'I'm nowhere near ready to get involved with someone, so I don't really know how we ended up here.'

'I do,' Jed admitted. 'Why the hell do you think I've been avoiding you since I found out you weren't married?'

'What?'

He just shrugged.

'Tell me.'

'You just...' He gave an embarrassed grin. 'Well, you know when you're attracted to someone? I suppose when I saw you talking to Penny and then she said you were here for an interview and then someone called you Mrs Phillips, well, I was relieved you were spoken for.'

Jasmine frowned.

'I don't like mixing work with things and thought I might have trouble keeping to that with you—it wasn't a logical thing, just…'

She did know what he meant.

Maybe it hadn't been quite an instant attraction, but that evening on the beach, when he'd lifted his T-shirt… Jasmine pulled back the sheet, looked at his lovely abdomen and bent over and ran her fingers lightly over the line there. He caught her hand as it moved down.

'I thought you wanted to sleep.'

'I do.'

'Then later.'

She set the alarm for that afternoon, before she remembered another potential problem. Penny.

'And no one at work is to know.'

'Suits me.'

'I mean it,' Jasmine said. 'What happened yesterday at work was wrong.'

'I'll carry on being horrible.'

'Good.'

'So much for clearing the air,' Jed said. 'Now it's all the more complicated.'

'Not really,' Jasmine yawned. 'Just sleep with me often and buy me lots of chocolate. My needs are simple.'

For that morning at least it really did seem as straightforward as that.

CHAPTER NINE

JED WAS NICE and grumpy at work and he deliberately didn't look up when she walked past, and Jasmine made sure there were no private jokes or smiles.

Gossip was rife in this place and the last thing she wanted was to be at the centre of it again.

No one could have guessed that their days were spent in bed. She just hoped he understood that it couldn't always be like this—that night shifts and her mother's help had made things far easier than they would be from now on. In fact, Jed got his first proper taste of dating a single mum that weekend.

Ruby was lovely.

'I'm hoping to work overseas as a nanny,' she explained to Jasmine, 'so I'm trying to get as much experience as I can and hopefully by the time I've got my qualification I'll have a couple of good references.'

She was very good with Simon, happy to sit with him as he tried to bang square pegs into round holes, and Jasmine could tell Ruby was very used to dealing with young children.

'My main problem is late shifts,' Jasmine explained.

'The crèche knows me,' Ruby said. 'I pick Liam up

and I take him back to Vanessa's. I give him his dinner and bath and I try to get him asleep for Vanessa but Liam likes to wait up for her.'

Jasmine laughed. She and Vanessa had got the boys together a couple of times and Liam certainly had plenty of energy.

'Well, Vanessa and I aren't working the same shifts so much now,' Jasmine explained, 'so if we can try and work opposite late shifts...'

'It will all work out,' Ruby said. 'I can always look after them both some evenings.'

Jasmine was starting to think this could work.

So much so that for a try-out Ruby suggested she look after Simon that night, and for the first time in a very long time Jasmine found herself with a Saturday night free. To her delight, when Jed rang a little bit later she found that she had someone to share it with.

'It went well with Ruby, then?'

He asked about the babysitter as they were seated for dinner.

'She seems lovely,' Jasmine said. 'Simon didn't even get upset when I left.'

They were eating a couple of suburbs away from the Peninsula Hospital in a smart restaurant that overlooked the bay. Jasmine had taken a taxi because she hadn't been out in yonks and she wanted a glass or three of wine.

'I would have picked you up.'

'I know.' Jasmine smiled. 'But I've a feeling Ruby might gossip to Vanessa. I feel like I'm having an affair.

It's too confusing to work out...' She looked up from the menu and went cross-eyed and Jed started to laugh.

'I can't do that.'

'It's easy,' Jasmine said. 'You just look at the tip of your nose and then hold it as you look up.'

'You've practised.'

'Of course.' She grinned.

And, cross-eyed or not, she looked stunning, Jed noted.

Her hair was loose as it had been on the day he had met her on her walk on the beach, but it fell in thick glossy curls. Unlike at work, she was wearing make-up, not a lot but just enough to accentuate her very blue eyes and full mouth. 'What do you want to eat?'

'Anything,' Jasmine said. 'Well, anything apart from chicken nuggets.'

So instead of leftover nuggets there was wine and seafood, and conversation was easy, as long as it was just about food, about movies and the beach, but the second it strayed deeper there was a mutual pulling back.

'Will you go back to your maiden name?' Jed asked after a while.

'I don't know,' she admitted. 'I don't know if I should change Simon's...'

'So what is it?'

'Sorry?'

'Your maiden name?'

She didn't answer him, just peeled a prawn. She didn't even get a reprieve when he asked what had happened in her marriage, because for a marriage to break up when someone was pregnant it sounded as if something pretty serious had.

'I've got three hours, Jed.' She smiled, dipping a prawn in lime mayonnaise. 'In fact, two hours and fifteen minutes now. I want to enjoy them, not spend time talking about my ex.'

And later, when they were finishing up their heavenly dessert and he mentioned something about a restaurant in Sydney, she asked why he'd moved. His answer was equally vague and Jasmine frowned when he used her line.

'We've got thirty minutes till you need to be back for Ruby. Do we really want to waste them hearing my woes?'

'No.' She laughed.

But, yes, her heart said, except that wasn't what they were about—they had both decided.

They were going to keep things simple and take things slowly.

But it was difficult to find someone so easy to talk to and not open up, especially when the conversation strayed at one point a little too close to Penny. She'd mentioned something about how good it was to have Ruby, given her mum and sister were so busy with their jobs. As soon as she said it she could have cut out her tongue.

'Your mum's in real estate?' Jed checked, and she nodded. 'What does your sister do?'

It was a natural question but one she'd dreaded.

'She does extremely well at whatever she puts

her mind to,' Jasmine evaded, reaching for her glass of wine.

'Ouch.' Jed grinned. 'Sore point?'

'Very.'

So he avoided it.

It was nice and going nowhere, they both knew that. It was an out-of-hours fling, except with each turn it became more complicated because outside work there were Simon and Penny and unbeknown fully to the other the two hearts that were meeting had both been incredibly hurt.

Two hearts that had firmly decided to go it alone for now.

They just hadn't factored in desire.

'It's like being a teenager again.' Jasmine grinned as he pulled the car over before they turned into her street and kissed her. 'My mum lives in this street.'

'We're not outside...?'

'No.'

'Good,' he said, and got back to kissing her.

They were under a huge gum tree that dropped gum nuts everywhere, but Jed risked the paintwork, grateful for the leafy shield, and they were ten minutes into a kiss that was way better than teenage ones she'd partaken in, right on this very spot, especially when Jed moved a lever and her seat went back a delicious fraction.

She could hardly breathe. He was over her and looking down at her, his hand was creeping up between her legs, and she could feel how hard he was. However, they could not take it even a fraction further here and she was desperate to pay Ruby and have her out of there, wanted so badly to have him in her bed.

And it would seem that Jed was thinking the same thing. 'I could wait till Ruby's gone.'

'No.' She hauled the word out, for if she regretted using it now, she knew she would regret it more in the morning if she didn't. 'I don't want that for Simon.' She looked up at those gorgeous eyes and that mouth still wet from her kisses and it killed her to be twenty-six and for it to feel wrong to ask him in. 'We're keeping things light,' Jasmine said. 'Agreed?' she prompted, and he nodded. 'Which is fine for me, but I won't treat his little heart lightly.'

'I know.'

'Next time we'll go to yours,' Jasmine suggested.

He looked down at her and the rules he'd embedded into his brain were starting to fade, because he had enjoyed being out, but now he wanted in.

'We'll see,' he said, because this was starting to be about a whole lot more than sex. He'd more than enjoyed tonight, had loved being in her company. The only bit that was proving difficult was leaving things here. 'Maybe we'll go out but eat more quickly?'

'Confusing, isn't it?' she said, and again she crossed her eyes and he laughed and then one more kiss and it ached to a halt.

Killed to turn on the engine and drive down the street and then turn into her own street and to park two doors down from her home.

To smile and walk out and to rearrange her dress as she let herself in.

To chat and pay Ruby and carry on a normal conversation, saying that, yes, she'd had a great night catching up with an old friend, and maybe she'd ask Ruby to babysit so that they could catch up again, perhaps as soon as next week.

But a week didn't seem so soon once Ruby was gone.

A night felt too long.

It killed her not to text him to come back.

CHAPTER TEN

'HI, JASMINE!'

She looked up at the familiar face of a paramedic who was wheeling a stretcher in.

'I haven't seen you in ages.'

'Hi, Mark.' Jasmine smiled, but there was a dull blush on her cheeks, and as Jed looked over to see how the new patient was, he couldn't help but notice it, couldn't help but see that Jasmine was more than a little flustered as she took the handover. 'What are you doing out here?'

'We're all over the place today,' Mark said. 'I had a transfer from Rosebud that got cancelled and then we were called out to Annie here.' Jasmine smiled at her new patient. 'Annie Clayfield, eighty-two years old, fell at home last night. We were alerted by her security when she didn't respond to their daily phone call. We found her on the floor,' Mark explained. 'Conscious, in pain with shortening and rotation to the left leg.'

He pulled back the blanket and Jasmine looked at the patient's feet and saw the familiar deformity that was an obvious sign of a hip fracture.

Annie was a lovely lady and tough too—she tried

to hold back her yelp of pain as they moved her over as gently as they could onto the trolley.

Jed came over when he heard her cry and ordered some analgesic.

'We'll get on top of your pain,' Jed said, 'before we move you too much.' He had a listen to her chest and checked her pulse and was writing up an X-ray order when he saw one of the paramedics leave the stretcher he was sorting out and head over to Jasmine.

'So you're here now?'

'That's right.' Jed noted that her voice was falsely cheerful and he had no reason to listen, no reason not to carry on and see the next patient, except he found himself writing a lot more slowly, found himself wanting to know perhaps more than he should if they were planning to keep things light.

'I heard you and Lloyd split up?'

'We did.'

'What's he doing with himself these days?'

'I've no idea,' Jasmine said. 'We're divorced now. I think he's working in his family's business.'

As Jed went to clip the X-ray slip to Annie's door he saw the paramedic give Jasmine a brief cuddle.

'You had nothing to do with it, Jasmine, we all know that. You don't have to hide.'

'I'm not hiding.'

And there was no such thing as uncomplicated, Jed decided, looking at Annie's X-rays a good hour later and ringing down for the orthopaedic surgeons. They'd both agreed to keep it light, to take things slowly. Neither of them talked much, about families or friends or the past, and it should suit him, and yet the more he knew, or rather the less he got to know...

The more he wanted.

Despite all efforts to take things slowly, things were gathering pace between them. They'd been seeing each other for a few weeks now—at least, whenever they got a chance.

They rang each other a lot, and went out whenever shifts and babysitters permitted, or more often than not they ended up back at his for a few stolen hours.

It just wasn't enough, though.

Concentrate on work, he told himself as he ran along the beach that night.

Except she was home, he knew it.

And Simon would be in bed.

And she wanted to keep that part of her life very separate.

So too did he, Jed reminded himself.

He caught sight of the city shimmering gold in the distance. Melbourne offered a gorgeous skyline but a different skyline from the one he knew so well.

He'd come here to get away, Jed reminded himself.

To finally focus on his career and get ahead.

Yet he looked at the tall gleaming buildings of Melbourne and as much as he loved Peninsula, there was something about the city, or rather a busy city emergency department.

And still Melbourne Central beckoned.

CHAPTER ELEVEN

JASMINE STARED AT the roster and gritted her teeth.

Jed was filling out blood forms and suitably ignoring her, and Penny was at her annoying best, suggesting that the nurses join her in Resus so that she could run through a new piece of equipment with them.

A new piece of equipment that had been there as long as Jasmine had and had been used often.

Honestly, the second the place was finally quiet Penny found a job or an activity for everyone.

No wonder she was so unpopular.

The roster had finally been revealed for the next eight-week period and as she tapped the shifts into her phone Jasmine could feel her blood pressure rising.

Yes, she was the new girl.

Yes, that meant that she got the rubbish shifts—but she had more late duties coming up than she could count, and lots of weekends too, which she would usually be glad of for the money, but of course the crèche wasn't open on weekends and, even though she'd been told it was only about once every three months, there was *another* stint of nights coming up in two weeks.

Her mum would be on her cruise by then.

'Problem?' Lisa checked.

'Just the nights,' Jasmine said. 'I thought it was every three months.'

'Well, we try and share it, but especially when someone's new I like to get them to do some early, so that was an extra for you.'

Was she supposed to say thanks?

She liked Lisa, Jasmine really did, and she was running a department after all, not Jasmine's childcare arrangements, but the pressure of shift work and single parenting, let alone trying to date, was starting to prove impossible.

Idly flicking through the patient bulletin, her eye fell on the perfect job for a single mum who actually wanted to have a little bit of a life too.

It was in the fracture clinic and was almost nine to five.

It was a level above what she was on now, but with her emergency experience she would stand a pretty good chance at getting it.

'Fracture Clinic!' Vanessa peered over her shoulder. 'You'd go out of your mind.'

'I'm going out of my mind looking at the roster,' Jasmine admitted.

'Don't think about it,' Vanessa said breezily. 'Something always turns up.'

Jasmine rolled her eyes as Vanessa walked out. 'I wish I had her optimism.'

'Jasmine.' She turned and smiled at the sound of Mark's voice. 'How are things?'

'Good.' Jed saw she was uncomfortable, saw she

glanced over her shoulder to check whether or not he was there, and it was none of his business, he wanted it that way, yet he wanted to know what the problem was, why Mark thought she was hiding.

'Just giving you the heads up, no doubt you'll be alerted soon, but there's a nasty car versus bike on the beach road. Sounds grim.'

'Do we know how many?' Jed asked.

'That's all I've got but they're calling for backup.'

'Thanks.'

Jasmine let Lisa know and the orthopods were down anyway, looking at a fractured femur, and Lisa said to just wait till they heard more before they started paging anyone but that she'd let Penny and Mr Dean know.

Then Mark's radio started crackling and he listened, translating the coded talk of the operator. 'They're just about to let you know,' Mark said. 'One fatality, one trapped, one on the way—adult male.'

The alert phone went then and Lisa took it just as Penny appeared, looking brusquely efficient as usual.

'Car versus motorbike,' Lisa said. 'We've got the biker coming in, he's conscious, abdominal injuries, hypotensive.' She looked up at the clock. 'He's five minutes away and they've just freed the trapped driver, so he's on his way too.'

'I'll take the first,' Penny said. 'If that's okay with you, Jed?'

'Be my guest,' Jed answered, but Jasmine saw the clenching of his jaw and knew that Penny was seriously rattling him—she was always jumping in, always trying to take over anything that was remotely interesting.

'Have we paged the surgeons?' Penny asked.

'Done,' Jasmine said.

'Blood bank?'

'I've let them know.'

Penny gave no response, but with reason as the blast of a siren told them the ambulance was here. As the paramedics raced the patient in, Jasmine didn't blame Penny a bit for the curse she let out when she asked where the hell the surgeons were.

The patient, though conscious, was beyond pale. His pulse was thin and thready and Jasmine set to work, with Greg cutting his leathers off.

'Can you tell me your name?' Penny asked as she examined him.

'Reece.'

'And do you know where you are?'

He answered the questions when prompted but kept closing his eyes and drifting off. Jasmine could only just palpate his blood pressure manually and Penny wasted no time in drawing blood for an urgent cross-match and telling the porters to run it up.

'And I mean run!' he warned. 'Let's put the O-neg up.'

Penny was possibly up there with the most horrible doctors Jasmine had worked with. She was abrupt to the point of rudeness, gave no thanks, only barked demands, except...

She was brilliant.

'If they can't be bothered to get down here,' Penny shouted as Jasmine tried to locate the surgeons again, 'tell them that I'll meet them up in Theatre.'

The patient had had a spinal and chest X-ray, and despite the O-negative blood being squeezed in, his blood pressure was still barely discernible. It was clear he needed Theatre and Penny wanted him taken straight up.

Jed was dealing with the latest admission, and Jasmine quickly prepared Reece for theatre, loading his clothes into a bag and itemising his valuables—rings, wallet... But as she opened up the wallet Jasmine hesitated. There were loads of hundred-dollar notes—at best guess the wallet contained a few thousand dollars.

'Can someone check this with me?' Jasmine asked.

'I'll check it with you later,' Greg called. 'Just put it in the safe.'

'Can we just check it now?' Jasmine pushed, except Greg wasn't listening, so she popped her head around the curtain to where Vanessa and Lisa were assisting Jed. 'Can someone check this, please? He's got a large amount of cash.'

'Just pop it in the safe,' Lisa called. 'I'll count it when things have calmed down.'

'We're supposed to check it before we put it in the safe.' Jasmine's voice was shrill. 'We're not supposed to sign—'

'Here.' It was Penny who stepped in. 'Give it to me, Nurse. I'll put it in the safe.' She walked over and took the wallet, signed the piece of paper and threw the contents into the safe. Jasmine realised that she was sweating and she could feel Jed's eyes on her.

'Right,' Penny said. 'We need to get him up or he's going to bleed out.' She picked up the phone and told

Theatre the same as Jasmine prepared the trolley for
an emergency transfer, but her hands were shaking and
her heart was thumping as she knew she'd made a bit
of a scene.

'All okay, Jasmine?' Lisa checked as Jasmine walked
past to get a space blanket to put over Reece on the way
up to Theatre.

'We're just about to move him,' Jasmine said, and as
Jed briefly looked up she felt the question in his brief
gaze, knew she wasn't fooling anyone that everything
was okay, least of all Jed.

'Reece.' Jasmine tried to explain things as best she
could as she covered him with the space blanket. He
was irritable now and struggling to remain conscious,
and he wanted to wait till his wife got there before he
went up. 'We're going to have to move you to Theatre
now. Miss Masters will explain things.'

Which Penny did.

She was efficient, brusque but also terribly kind.
'I know you want to wait for your wife—I completely
understand, but you're too sick,' she explained gently
but firmly. 'I will talk to your wife myself as soon as
she gets here. Is there anything you want me to say to
her?' She glanced at Jasmine and Greg and at the anaesthetist who had just arrived. 'Could you all excuse
us a moment?'

As Jasmine stepped outside to give Penny and Reece
some privacy, there was a strange sting of tears in her
eyes. It wasn't that she had seen a different side to her
sister, rather she had seen a side to Penny that she had
long forgotten.

Sitting on the stairs, hearing her parents argue, had terrified four-year-old Jasmine. It had been Penny who would take her back to bed, Penny who would sit beside her and tell her not to worry, that she would take care of things, that even if things did get bad, that even if Dad did what he was threatening and left, they would be fine.

'But what if we're not?' Jasmine would argue. 'What if we never see him?'

'Then we'll deal with it.'

And in their own ways and albeit not perfectly they had.

And as she ran up to Theatre with her sister, and Penny told her to head back down, that she wanted to speak with surgeons, Jasmine knew that she hadn't just come back for the support of her family, neither had she taken the job here for the reasons she had so determinedly given.

She wanted to be close to Penny again.

CHAPTER TWELVE

'I'LL COME OVER after work.'

Jed was coming out of X-Ray as Jasmine walked back from Theatre and they found themselves walking together towards Emergency.

'It's fine.' Jasmine shook her head. 'I'll see you at the weekend. Ruby said that she could—'

'But you're upset tonight.'

'Don't worry, I'll be fine by Saturday.' She couldn't keep the brittle edge from her voice. Yes, she was happy keeping things light, but sometimes, on days like today, it was hard.

'I'm not expecting to be entertained,' Jed said. 'What happened back there?'

'Nothing.'

'Jasmine? Why did you get all upset over the safe? You know we can't just drop everything—the guy was bleeding out.'

'Just leave it.'

But Jed wouldn't.

It was a very long shift. Vanessa was on a half-day and Jasmine really wished that she herself was—she could feel Jed watching her, especially much later when Lisa came over and asked her to check the cash.

'Four thousand six hundred dollars. Agreed?' Lisa checked.

'Agreed,' Jasmine said, and because Penny had first signed for it, she had to be there too.

'I just rang ICU,' Penny said. 'He's doing much better. His wife told me that he was on his way to put down a deposit on a car—that's why he had so much cash on him.' She added her signature to the valuables book.

'Oh, the irony of it,' Lisa sighed, because in a car his injuries would have been so much less. 'Now, I know this is a lot of money and that it has to be checked,' Lisa continued, 'but it's not always possible to just drop everything. It's better to put it in the safe.'

'That's not what the protocol says,' Jasmine pointed out, and Lisa pursed her lips. 'It's been six hours now.'

'I didn't know you were such a stickler for protocol and guidelines, Nurse,' Penny smirked. 'The irony of it!'

'What was that about?' Lisa grinned when Penny waltzed off.

'I think that might have been Penny's attempt at humour,' Jed said, but she could feel his eyes on her, knew he was trying to talk to her, but as she had all day she did her best to avoid him.

Jasmine actually thought she had when she finally finished for the day and went to pick Simon up. But heading over to the crèche she found Jed at the vending machine outside.

'I'll come over later.'

'You know I don't want that. I don't want to confuse Simon.'

'We're not going to make out on the sofa,' Jed said. 'And I'm not going to stay the night till you think he's ready for that, but I do want to talk to you. You're nearly in tears and I don't get why. What happened at your old job?' He could see the blush on her cheeks but she said nothing, instead walked past him to pick up Simon.

Simon was happy and scruffy after a day in the sandpit and Jasmine knew that it was time to face things, that she and Jed could not keep skirting around the edges.

Here in her hands was the living proof of an exceptionally difficult relationship, here was the baggage she carried, and yet it felt right in her arms.

She had to be able to talk about it with someone she trusted.

And she had to start trusting Jed.

He was still waiting for her when she headed outside.

'About six?'

'He'll still be up.'

'I don't mind, or I can come over around nine if that's what you'd prefer?' She longed to let Jed closer but she just couldn't take any chances with Simon.

'About nine.'

Simon wasn't at his sunniest and her mum dropped over too. It was just one of those disorganised evenings, not helped by a disorganised brain thanks to the day's events. Jasmine had just got Simon down and was sorting out his bag for the next day when she heard a knock at the door and looked up to see that it was already a quarter past nine.

'I wouldn't have got here at six anyway,' Jed said, following her through to the kitchen. 'I only just got away. It's still busy there.'

'Who's on?'

'Rex!' Jed rolled his eyes. 'And Penny's still hovering. I swear she never sleeps.'

'Do you want something to eat?'

'Are you going to cook for me?' Jed grinned.

'No,' Jasmine said, 'but if you're nice I might defrost something.'

Actually, she did cook. Well, she made some pasta and defrosted some sauce and it was possibly their most normal night together. He ate a large bowl while Jasmine got things ready for the next day. Perhaps realising she wasn't ready to talk yet, he chatted a bit more about himself, telling her a bit about his siblings and their families.

'Don't you miss them?'

'A lot.'

'So how come you moved down here?'

'Just…' Jed shrugged. He knew he had to tell her, but there would be time for all that later—he wasn't here for himself tonight. He could see that she was still upset, see her hands shake a little as she folded some washing and then finally joined him.

'You got upset in Resus today.'

'I didn't.'

'Jasmine?'

'I just get annoyed when people don't check valuables properly,' she attempted. 'Everyone bangs on about how important it is and then if something goes missing...'

'People are busy.'

'I know that.'

'I heard you speaking to that paramedic,' Jed admitted, and he watched as she closed her eyes. 'Jasmine, did something happen at your old job?'

'No,' she broke in. 'Jed, please...' And then she started to cry. 'I found out that my husband was stealing from patients.' It was so awful to say it, to admit to it. She'd made it so huge in her mind that she half expected him to stand up and walk out, but of course he didn't. Instead, he took both her hands.

'Come on.' He was very kind and very firm but he wasn't going to leave it. 'Tell me what happened.'

'I don't know where to start,' she said. 'There was an unconscious patient apparently and there was a lot of money missing.' She knew she wasn't making much sense, so she just told him everything.

'Lloyd,' Jasmine said. 'Simon's father, he was a paramedic. We really got on, but then everyone did with Lloyd. He was very popular. We went out for about three months and—' she couldn't really look at that time properly '—I thought everything was fantastic at first,' she admitted. 'But I know now that it wasn't because I was being lied to even then. I didn't know but there had been a report put in about him.'

'You can't know if someone doesn't tell you,' Jed pointed out.

'I know that, but it wasn't just that he didn't tell me.'

She took a deep breath, because if she was going to tell him some of it, then she had better tell him all. 'Remember I told you that I can't take the Pill?' She blushed as she had the first time she'd told him. 'Well, we were careless.' She went really red then, not with embarrassment, more with anger. 'Actually, no, we weren't. I know it takes two, but I think he was the one who was careless.'

'Jasmine.' Jed was completely honest. 'I nearly forgot our first time.'

'I know,' she admitted. 'But even if you had, I've got a coil now, so it wouldn't matter. It was more that I didn't forget.' She looked at Jed, she knew how they had lost it in bed together, but she never had till him. 'I reminded him, I tried to stop him. I don't know, I can't prove that, but there was an accident, and I found I was pregnant and not sure I wanted to be. I was just so confused and yet he was delighted. He insisted we get married and and then we took three months off to see Australia. As he said, to have loads of fun before the baby. I had lots of annual leave saved up.'

She couldn't even look at Jed as she went on. 'What Lloyd hadn't told me was that he was under investigation for stealing from a patient. It was all kept confidential so not even his colleagues knew, but another patient had come forward with a complaint and they'd placed Lloyd on three months' paid suspension. We were swanning around Australia and I had no idea.'

'When did he tell you?'

'He didn't,' Jasmine admitted. 'I went back to work. I was coming up for six months pregnant by then and he told me that he had another month off and then he started to talk about how, given I love my work, why didn't we think about him staying home to look after the baby? Every word that man said to me was a lie.' She could feel her anger rising as it did whenever she thought about him and wondered, as she often did, if he'd got her pregnant deliberately.

'So how did you find out?'

'The other paramedics were a bit cool with me,' Jasmine admitted. 'They're a pretty honourable lot, they don't take kindly to what Lloyd did and there was I, chatting with them like I used to, about our holiday, about things, and then one of my friends pulled me aside and said it might be better if I didn't rub things in.' She started to cry. 'She said it was fine if I could accept what he'd done, but it was a bit much for them to hear about us having fun with his suspension pay. He'd been fired by then and I didn't even know.'

'Oh, Jasmine.'

'He said that as his wife I should have supported him, but the fact is I wouldn't have married him had I known.' She looked at Jed. 'I wouldn't have. I'm not saying someone has to be perfect, I'm not saying you don't stick together through bad times, but I didn't even know that he was in the middle of bad times when we got married, when he made sure I was pregnant.' She was really crying now. 'I moved out and kept working right till the end of my pregnancy, but it was awful. I think my friends believed I had nothing to do with it, that I hadn't had a clue…'

'Of course they did.'

'No.' Jasmine shook her head. 'Not all of them—
there was loads of gossip. It was just awful at the time.

'I see some of the paramedics now and we're starting to be friendly again,' she continued. 'I think they
really do understand now that I simply didn't know. I'm
just trying to get on with my life.'

'Do you speak to him at all?'

'Nothing,' Jasmine said. 'He came and saw Simon a
couple of times when we were in the hospital, but there's
been nothing since then. He's got a new girlfriend and
so much for being a stay-home dad—he doesn't even
have a thing to do with his son. He's working in the
family business, they're all supporting him, as families do, and making sure it looks like he earns a dollar
a week, so I don't get anything.'

'You can fight that.'

'I could, but I don't want to,' Jasmine said. 'I don't
want any of his grubby money. I stayed close by for a
year because, at the end of the day, I figured that he is
Simon's dad and I should make it as easy for him as
possible to have access to his son. But when he wanted
nothing to do with him...' She was a little more honest than she'd expected to be. 'I was embarrassed to go
back to work too. He just completely upended my life.'

And Jed got that, he got that so much, how one person could just walk into your life and shatter it, could
make a normal world suddenly crazy, and he could have
told her then, but Jed knew that now wasn't the time.

'And I'm the one left holding the baby.' She was the
most honest she had been with another person. 'And I
know if it hadn't happened then I wouldn't have Simon

and I love him more than anything so I can't wish it had never happened, except sometimes I do.'

Of course she heard Simon crying then, just to ram home the guilt of her words.

'I need to go and settle him.'

'Sure.'

Simon didn't want settling, Simon wanted a drink and a play and a conversation.

'He's not going to settle.' She came back into the living room a good twenty minutes later.

'Do you want me to leave?'

'No,' Jasmine said. 'But I'm going to have to bring him in here.'

'Are you sure?' Jed checked.

'It's no big deal,' Jasmine said.

Except they both knew that it was. Jed hadn't seen Simon since that day on the beach when he'd helped get him into the water.

And Jed really didn't want to leave her.

Simon was delighted with the late night visitor, chatting away to him for as long as he could till his eyes were heavy and Jasmine put him back to bed.

'Cute,' Jed said. 'He looks like you—apart from the blond hair. Is his dad blond?'

'No,' Jasmine replied. Simon was a mini, male Penny.

'Have you told Lisa what happened?'

Jasmine shook her head.

'I think you might feel better if you did.' He was very practical. 'You did nothing wrong, but you know what rumours are like and it might be better to just tell

Lisa up front what happened,' Jed said. 'And then you can stop worrying about it. If anyone does bring it up, Lisa will just blow them off.

'And…' he gave her a smile '…she might be a bit more understanding when patients land in the department with their life savings stuffed in a carrier bag.'

'I think I might,' Jasmine said. 'Thanks.' It was actually nice to have told someone and telling Lisa was a good idea.

'I'd better go,' Jed said. 'It's one thing having a friend over, but different me still being here in the morning. What are you on tomorrow?'

'I'm on a late,' Jasmine said. 'Ruby's picking Simon up from crèche.'

'How's that working out?'

'Good,' Jasmine admitted. 'She's really sensible and he seems to adore her. Simon's usually in bed by about seven so she gets her homework done.

'Stay if you like,' Jasmine said, 'I mean…'

'I know what you mean.' And he looked over at Jasmine and for the first time things were starting to get serious, and he didn't feel hemmed in. In fact, he wanted more of this and was sure that Jasmine was someone he could open up to about his past. She just didn't need it tonight. 'Are you sure?' Jed checked. 'He might wake up again.'

'He might.' Jasmine looked up at him. 'Look…' She didn't really know how to say it without sounding needy, but she had Simon to think of so she had to be brave. 'I want to see more of you, Jed.' His eyes never left her face. 'I'm the same as you. I don't want this to carry over to work, which means that if we are going to see more of each other... I'm not asking for for ever, but if you're thinking this isn't working out then say so now.'

'I think it is working out.'

'And I'd like to see you a bit more than a couple of hours once a week.'

'Me, too.'

'Stay, then,' she said.

It was all a bit different having Simon in the house with them.

Like at midnight when they were kissing on the sofa, instead of things leading to wherever they might lead, she had to check on Simon, who was whimpering with his teeth. By the time she'd given him some medicine and rubbed some gel on his gums, Jed was sitting up in her bed, reading his horoscope in one of her trashy magazines.

Except he put it down as she started undressing.

'Don't,' Jasmine said, because he had an unfair advantage, well, two actually. He was already in bed and also with a body like his there was no need to be embarrassed about stripping off in front of another person.

'Why are you shy now?'

'I don't know.' She actually wasn't shy, she felt guilty for what she had said. 'Thanks,' she said as she slipped into bed. 'For hearing me out and what I said about wishing it had never happened.'

'I'd be the same,' Jed said, shuddering at the thought of how much worse things might have been for him—and he closed his eyes for a moment, imagining the last couple of years with a baby added to the mix. And he turned and he almost told her, but he could see her eyes were still swollen from crying and it simply wouldn't be fair to her.

'Imagine if he hadn't stolen the money,' Jed said. 'You could have spent your life married to a guy who was crap in bed.'

He saw the start of a smile.

'Go on,' he said. 'Say it.'

'No.' Jasmine kicked him. 'Anyway, you don't know that he was.'

'Please.' Jed rolled his eyes.

'So much for not getting involved with anyone from work.' He looked down at her before he kissed her. 'I think we should keep it separate, though,' Jed said. 'I really mean that.'

She was incredibly glad to hear it. 'I'm the same.'

'Things are a bit sensitive at the moment,' he said.

'With the promotion?' It was an entirely innocent question, or at least she'd thought it was, but Jed stopped kissing her and frowned.

'You've heard about that?'

'Sorry.' She tried to play for time.

'How did you hear about that?'

She was glad for the lights being off for another reason now. Her face was on fire in the dark from her slip-up.

'I don't know,' she attempted. 'You know what that place is like, there's always talk.'

'I guess.' He let out a long sigh. 'Oh, well, if it's out

there's nothing I can do about it. At least I know no one heard it from me.'

He forgot about it then but it took a while for Jasmine to.

He kissed her till she almost had, she kissed him back till she nearly did, but it was there at the back of her mind, just how complicated things were and he didn't even know.

'Are you all right?' He lifted his head.

'Just tense.'

She almost told him, she nearly did.

Except she'd promised her sister that she wouldn't.

'I can fix that.'

And he slid beneath the sheets and she lay there biting her lip, thrashing with her thoughts as his tongue urged her to give in.

He was incredibly patient.

Didn't seem to mind a jot how long it took.

And she tried to relax to the probe of his tongue. To forget her problems, forget Penny and Lloyd and everything really except...

'Jed?'

He didn't answer.

'Jed?' She had to tell him, had to tell him now. 'Things are complicated.'

'Not from where I am,' Jed said, lifting his head just a little. 'You worry too much.'

Maybe she did, Jasmine realised, closing her eyes to the mastery of his mouth.

He gave her no room to think about it anyway. His hands lifted her buttocks so he could concentrate his efforts and he homed in, she pushed on his shoulders, because she should surely tell him, except he pushed back on the pressure she exerted and obliterated her thoughts with his tongue.

He was determined now, felt the shift in her, and it turned him on further. He loved feeling her unbend beneath him, loved the constant fight with her busy mind, and he would win this one and he felt her quiver as he worked on her most tender spot.

He felt her thighs start to tighten and the moans in her throat and he loved the wrestle within in her, loved how her hands moved from his shoulders and to his head, how her body begged him to continue while her mouth urged him to stop.

And then she gave in to him, shocked that he didn't stop there, that when he should surely abate he worked harder, and she throbbed into him and still his mouth cursed her restraint. Still his tongue told her there was more, and there was.

He rose over her in the dark, his hand moved to the bedside and it was hers that stopped him, stopped a man who, very kindly, never forgot.

'I told you,' she said. 'I've got the coil.'

And he smiled down at her as just once she said it. 'And, yes, as I've since found out—he was crap in bed.'

There was nothing to complicate or confuse right now, just the bliss of him sliding inside her, and for Jed he had never been closer to another, just lost himself in her. It was more than sex and they both knew it—it was the most intimate either had ever been. He thrust into her as he wanted to and she tightened her legs around him. He could hear the purr in her throat and feel the scratch of her nails on his back and she knew that, however they denied it, this was fast becoming serious.

And yet there were secrets between them.

For Jed there were no secrets, or there soon wouldn't be. He'd already made the decision to tell her, he just had to find the right time and tonight wasn't it. He felt her tighten around him, loved the intimacy and feeling her without the barrier of a sheath, loved the sob into his shoulder and the sudden demand within her that gave Jed permission to let go, which he did, but not fully. He lifted up on his arms and felt every beat of pleasure that shot out of him, he felt every flicker of hers, except he held back on the words that seemed most fitting right now.

He lay there afterwards and he should have been glad he hadn't said them. Neither of them were ready for love, but for Jed it was starting to feel like it.

And for Jasmine too, she felt as if they were on the edge of something, something that neither had seen, a place they had never intended to go. Except he was in bed beside her and it felt as if he should be, and she knew what to do now.

She wasn't waiting for the interviews, and Penny would just have to deal with it if it confused things.

Tomorrow, or at the very next opportunity, she would tell Penny.

Then she could be completely honest with Jed.

Then, Jasmine decided, there would be no holding back.

CHAPTER THIRTEEN

JED WAS GONE before Simon woke up, but her resolve was the same and once she'd given Simon his breakfast and got him dressed, Jasmine picked up the phone and rang Penny.

'What are you doing, ringing me at work?' Penny sounded irritated at the intrusion.

'It's the only chance I get to speak to you,' Jasmine said. 'Of course I can talk to you there if you prefer.'

'No, this is fine,' Penny sighed. 'What did you want?'

'I was hoping we could catch up away from work. There's something I'd like to talk about, something I need to check with you.'

'Fine,' Penny said.

'Tonight?' Jasmine asked.

'I'm going out tonight.' And she was working the next one. 'I'm going to Mum's on Sunday for dinner—how about then?'

Jasmine really didn't want to discuss this in front of their mother, but maybe they could go for a walk afterwards, or she could suggest that Penny go back to her place for a coffee?

'Sounds good.'

'So, when are you working again?' Penny asked.

'In a couple of hours' time.' Jasmine smiled. 'I promise to keep on ignoring you.'

As she dropped Simon off at crèche, Jasmine realised that things were starting to work out—she was starting to think that this was maybe doable and that nine-to-five job in the fracture clinic might not be necessary after all. Vanessa's mum was looking after Liam this evening, which meant that Ruby would pick Simon up from crèche and take him back to Jasmine's. Her baby-sitting arrangements were all under control, if a touch too expensive, but it was worth it to be doing a job she loved and for the first time since way before Simon's birth things were starting to look stable.

Well, not stable. Her heart leapt in her throat still at the sight of Jed and she was shaky with all the rush of a new romance, but the rest of her life seemed to be slotting together when just a few weeks ago it had seemed an impossible dream.

There was actually no chance to speak to Lisa about anything personal, or Jed, come to that. The department was incredibly busy and the late shift flew by, so much so that Jasmine blinked in surprise when Lisa caught her on the way up to the ward with a geriatric patient and lightly scolded her for not taking her breaks.

'I had no idea of the time,' Jasmine admitted, surprised to see it was already seven o'clock. 'I'll just take this one up to the ward.'

'Well, make sure that when you get back you take a break,' Lisa said. 'I don't care how busy the place is, I don't want my staff burning out.'

Lisa was always insistent that her staff take their

allotted breaks, and often she would ring Admin and have a nurse sent down from the wards during particularly busy periods.

After handing her patient over, Jasmine realised she was actually hungry and stopped at the vending machine for chocolate to take to her break. 'It's crazy out there,' Vanessa greeted her when she got back to the staffroom. 'Did Lisa tell you off for not taking a break?'

'She did,' Jasmine said, slipping off her shoes. 'Maybe it's going to be a full moon tonight. I don't envy the night staff.'

'It will be your turn again soon.'

'I know,' Jasmine groaned.

'Did you speak to Ruby about staying over while you're on nights?'

'I did,' Jasmine said. 'She can do the first week. The problem is with the weekend on the second.'

'I can help you with that,' Vanessa said. 'If you can help out next month when it's my turn?' She gave Jasmine a nice smile. 'It all works out in the end.'

'I know,' Jasmine admitted. 'I think I've got to stop looking too far ahead and take things more day by day.'

'That's all you can do when you've got little ones.'

Right now, Jasmine was looking forward to it being nine o'clock so that she could go home. Jed got off duty at ten and had promised to bring food, which meant she had just enough time to chat with Ruby and then hopefully have a quick shower before Jed arrived.

Yes, she was starting to think that things might work out.

'Are you going to that?' Vanessa broke into her thoughts.

'Sorry?'

'It's the accident and emergency ball in a couple of weeks.' Vanessa pointed to the rather impressive poster up on the staff noticeboard. 'It's the big fundraiser for the department. Apparently there are still some spare tickets.'

Jasmine's eyes widened when she saw the price of the tickets and she wasn't surprised that there were still a few left.

'I doubt I'll be going.' Jasmine shook her head as she broke off some chocolate. Especially when she factored in the price of the new dress, hair, shoes and paying a babysitter. 'Are we expected to go?'

'Not really,' Vanessa said. 'It's really more for the bigwigs. Mind you, it will be a fun night—there's always loads of gossip whizzing around after an emergency do—we can have our fun with that afterwards, even if we can't be there.' Vanessa gave a mischievous smile. 'Still, it's a shame that we won't get to watch Jed and Penny studiously avoiding each other and trying to pretend that they're not together.'

Jasmine felt her blood run cold. She couldn't quite believe what she was hearing. 'Jed and Penny?'

'Didn't you know?' Vanessa was idly watching the television as she spoke and didn't see Jasmine's appalled expression and carried on chatting, blissfully unaware of the impact of her words. 'They've been on and off since Jed started here, not that they would ever admit to it, of course. Heaven forbid that Penny brings her personal life into work and be so reckless as to display human tendencies.' Vanessa's words dripped sarcasm. 'God knows what he sees in her.'

'Maybe he doesn't.' Jasmine was having great trouble speaking, let alone sounding normal. 'Maybe he doesn't see anything in her. It's probably just gossip— you know what this place can be like.'

'I wish,' Vanessa sighed. 'Jed is just gorgeous. He's wasted on that cold fish. But I'm afraid that this time the hospital grapevine is right—Greg walked in on them once and you can hardly miss the tension between them.' She turned and looked at Jasmine. 'I can't believe you haven't noticed. It's an open secret, everyone knows.' Vanessa stood up. 'Come on, we'd better get back out there.'

Except Jasmine couldn't move.

'I'll be along in a moment,' Jasmine said. 'I shan't be long.'

Her hand was clenched around the chocolate so tightly it had all melted, not that she noticed till Vanessa had gone and Jasmine stood up. She headed for the bathrooms—she didn't just feel sick, she actually thought she might vomit as she washed the mess off her hands. She held onto the sink and tried to drag in air and calm her racing thoughts before heading back out there.

Not once had it entered her head that Penny and Jed might be together.

Not one single time.

And Penny had never so much as hinted that she was seeing someone.

But, then, why would she?

Penny never told Jasmine what was going on in her life. Her engagement had ended and Penny had said nothing about it other than it was over. She certainly never invited discussion. Jasmine, in turn, had never confided in Penny. Even when her marriage had been on the rocks, Jasmine had dealt with it herself—telling her mum and Penny that it was over only when her decision had already been made.

She should have listened to Penny, Jasmine realised. She should never have worked in the same department as her sister.

Jasmine scooped water from the sink into her hand and drank it, tried to calm herself down. Somehow she had to get through the rest of her shift.

Jed was coming round tonight.

Jasmine spun in panic at the thought.

She would talk to him... And say what?

If there was anything between him and Penny she would just end it and move to the fracture clinic.

Or back to Melbourne Central, because that sounded quite a good option right now. And if that sounded a lot like running away from her problems, well, at that moment Jasmine truly didn't care. As much as she and Penny didn't get on very well, never in a million years would she do that her sister.

Except it would seem that she already had.

'You seem in a hurry to escape the place,' Penny commented.

'For once, yes,' Jed said. 'It's all yours.'

He had more on his mind tonight than a busy department.

Tonight he was going to tell Jasmine the truth about what had happened with Samantha.

It was an unfamiliar route Jed was considering taking and one he was not entirely comfortable with. He was way too used to keeping things in. He'd avoided anything serious since his last break-up. Sure, he'd had the occasional date, but as soon as it had started to be anything more than that, Jed had found himself backing away. And as if to prove him right, the texts and tears that had invariably followed had only strengthened his resolve not to get attached and to step away. Except for the first time he felt as if he could trust another person. After all, Jasmine had opened up to him.

Jed wasn't stepping away now.

Instead, he was stepping forward.

He rang ahead to his favourite restaurant and ordered a meal for two, but despite confidence in his decision there was more than a touch of nerves as he paid for his takeaway and headed back to the car, as he built himself up to do what he said had sworn he would never do—share what had happened, not just with someone he was starting to get close to...but with someone he was starting to get close to from work.

'Hi.'

Jasmine opened the door and let him in, still unsure what she should say, how best to broach it. Did she really want to know that he was with her sister? Did she really want Jed to find out the truth?

Surely it would better to end it neatly?

To get out before they got in too deep?

Except she was in too deep already.

'I bought Italian,' Jed said, moving in for a kiss, 'but to tell the truth I'm not actually that hungry.'

She'd meant to carry on normally, to sit down and discuss things like adults while they were eating, but as he moved in to kiss her, just the thought that he might have been with Penny had Jasmine move her head away.

'Jasmine?' She saw him frown, heard the question in his voice about her less-than-effusive greeting, but she didn't know how to answer him. Despite three hours trying to work out what she might say to him, how best to approach this, she still didn't know how and in the end settled for the first thing that came into her head.

'I'm not sure that you ought to be here.'

'Sorry?'

'I don't think this is working, Jed.'

'It would seem not.'

Of all the things he had been expecting tonight, this wasn't one of them. Sideswiped, Jed walked through to the lounge and put the takeaway down on her coffee table, completely taken aback by the change in Jasmine. They'd made love that morning, he'd left her smiling and happy, with no hint of what was to come. 'Can I ask what has changed between this morning and tonight?'

'I just think things have moved too fast.'

'And could you not have decided this before you introduced me to Simon?' He didn't get it and he knew she was lying when he saw her blush. 'What's going on, Jasmine?'

'I heard something at work today,' Jasmine admitted. 'Something about you.'

'So it's gospel, then?' was Jed's sarcastic response. 'And while you were listening to this gossip, did you not consider running it by me first, before deciding we that weren't working?'

'Of course I did,' Jasmine attempted. 'That's what I'm doing now.'

'Is it even worth asking?' Jed said. 'Because it sounds to me as if the jury is already in. So, what is it that I'm supposed to have done?'

'I heard…' Jasmine swallowed because it sounded so pathetic, especially with how good he had been with her secret last night, but still she had to find out for sure. 'I heard that you and Penny…'

'Penny?'

'Someone told me that you and Penny…' She couldn't even bring herself to say it, but the implication was clear and Jed stood there and shook his head.

'Jasmine, we agreed from the start that as erratic as things may be for us you and I wouldn't see anybody else so, no, I'm not seeing Penny.'

'But have you?' Jasmine asked. 'Have you dated Penny in the past?'

'What on earth…?' He just looked at her, looked at her as if he'd suddenly put glasses on and was seeing her for the first time and not particularly liking the view. 'I'm being dumped because the hospital grapevine states that I might be or in the past might have slept with a colleague?' He shook his head. 'I never took you for the jealous kind, Jasmine.'

'I just need to know.'

But Jed wasn't about to explain himself. 'Look, I don't need this.' He didn't confirm it and he didn't deny it and she honestly didn't know what to do. She could feel tears pouring down her cheek.

'Jed, please,' she said. 'Just tell me. I need to know if there's ever been anything between you and Penny.' She was starting to cry and she knew she had to tell him, no matter how awkward it made things for them, no matter the hurt to Penny, she just had to come right out and say it, and she was about to, except Jed didn't give her a chance.

'You want a complete itinerary of my past?' Jed said. 'What do you want, a full list of anyone I've ever dated so you can check them out online?'

'Jed, please,' Jasmine attempted, but he wasn't listening to her now.

'You're the one with the past, Jasmine. You're the one who's just had her divorce certificate stamped and has a baby sleeping in the bedroom and an ex who stole from patients. Did I ask for a written statement, did I ask for facts and details?' He turned to go and then changed his mind, but he didn't walk back to her. He picked up his takeaway and took it. 'I'm hungry all of a sudden.'

He headed out to his car and drove off, but only as far as the next street, and it was there that Jed pulled over and buried his head in his hands.

He couldn't believe it.

Could not believe the change in her—the second they'd started to get serious, the moment he'd actually thought this might work, he'd been greeted with a list of questions and accusations and for Jed it all felt terribly familiar.

After all, he'd been through it before.

CHAPTER FOURTEEN

THE WEEK HAD been awful.

Jed was back to being aloof, not just with her but with everyone, and on the occasions they had to work together he said as little as he could to her.

And now, when she'd rather be anywhere else, she sat at her mother's, eating Sunday lunch with Penny and wondering how on earth she could ever tell her and if it would simply be better if Penny never found out.

Which sounded to Jasmine an awful lot like lying.

'You wanted to talk to me.'

'I just wanted a chat,' Jasmine said. 'We haven't caught up lately.'

'Well, there's not really much to catch up on,' Penny said. 'It's just work, work, work.'

'It's your interview soon,' Louise reminded her.

'You haven't mentioned it to anyone?' Penny frowned at Jasmine. 'I told you about that in confidence. I shouldn't have said anything.'

'I haven't,' Jasmine said, but her face burnt as she lied.

'Well, I've heard that there are rumours going around, and if I find out that it's you...' Penny gave a tight shrug. 'Sorry, that was uncalled for. I just hate how gossip spreads in that place.'

'Are you going to the A and E ball?' Jasmine tried to change the subject, attempting to find out what she simply had to know.

Not that it would change anything between her and Jed.

Not just because of the possibility that he and Penny had once been an item, more the way he had been when they'd had a row. He hadn't given her a chance to explain, had just thrown everything she had confided to him back in her face and then walked out.

She didn't need someone like that in her life and certainly not in Simon's—still, she did want to know if the rumours were true, which was why she pushed on with Penny, dancing around the subject of the A and E ball in the hope it might lead to something more revealing.

'I've been asked to put in an appearance,' Penny said, helping herself to another piece of lamb. 'Why?' she asked. 'Are you thinking of going?'

'Not at that price,' Jasmine said. 'I just wondered if you were, that's all.'

'I have to, really. Jed and I will probably take it in turns—someone has to hold the fort and all the consultants will want to be there.'

'Jed?' Louise asked.

'The other senior reg,' Penny explained.

'The one who's going for the same position?' Louise checked, and Penny gave a curt nod.

'You and Jed...' The lovely moist lamb was like burnt toast in Jasmine's mouth and she swallowed it down with a long drink of water. 'Are you two…?' Her voice trailed off as Penny frowned.

'What?'

She should just ask her really, Jasmine reasoned. It was her sister after all—any normal sisters would have this conversation.

Except they weren't like normal sisters.

Still, Jasmine pushed on.

She simply had to know.

'Is there anything between you and Jed?'

'If you're hoping for some gossip, you won't get it from me. I don't feed the grapevine,' Penny said, mopping the last of her gravy from her plate. 'So, what did you want to talk about?'

And really the answer didn't matter.

She and Jed were over. If he had slept with Penny she just wanted to be as far away from them both as possible when the truth came out. 'I'm thinking of taking the job in the fracture clinic.'

Penny looked up.

'Why?'

'Because…' Jasmine shrugged '…it's not working, is it?'

'Actually, I thought it was,' Penny said. 'I was worried at first, thought you'd be rushing to my defence every five minutes or calling me out, but apart from that morning with the baby…' She thought for a moment before she spoke. 'Well, seeing you work, you'd have said the same to any doctor.' She gave her sister a brief smile. 'You don't have to leave on my account. So long as you can keep your mouth shut.'

Her mum had made trifle—a vast mango one with piles of cream—and normally Jasmine would have dived into it, but she'd lost her appetite of late and Penny ate like a bird at the best of times. Louise took one spoonful and then changed her mind.

'I must have eaten too fast,' Louise said. 'I've got terrible indigestion.'

'I'll put it back in the fridge,' Jasmine said, clearing the table.

'Take some home,' her mum suggested. 'I don't fancy it.' She smiled to Simon, who was the only one tucking in. 'He can have some for breakfast.'

'Jasmine.' Penny caught her as she was heading out of the front door. 'Look, I know I kicked up when I found out you were going to be working in Emergency.' Penny actually went a bit pink. 'I think that I went a bit far. I just didn't think we could keep things separate, but things seem to be working out fine.'

'What if you get the consultant's position?' Jasmine checked. 'Wouldn't that just make things more difficult?'

'Maybe,' Penny said. 'But I don't think it's fair that you have to change your career just because of me. You're good at what you do.'

It was the closest she had ever come to a compliment from her sister.

'Look,' Penny said, 'I do want to talk to you if that's okay—not here…not yet.' She closed her eyes. 'It's…' She blew out a breath. 'Look, you know how I bang on about work and keeping things separate? Well, maybe I've being a bit of a hypocrite.'

'Are you seeing someone?'

'It's a bit more complicated than that.' Penny shook her head. 'Let me just get the interview over with. I mustn't lose focus now.' She let out a wry laugh. 'Who knows, I might not even get the job and then there won't be a problem.'

'Sorry?' Jasmine didn't get it. 'I thought you were desperate to be a consultant.'

'Yes, well, maybe someone else might want the role more than I do,' Penny said. 'Forget I said anything. We'll catch up soon.'

And as Jasmine lay in bed that night, she was quite sure she knew what the problem was.

Penny was worried that if she got the position it might hurt Jed.

For the first time in a long time Penny was actually putting another person before herself. She actually cared about another person.

The same person her younger sister had been sleeping with.

Monday morning was busy—it always was, with patients left over from a busy weekend still waiting for beds to clear on the ward, and all the patients who had left things till the weekend had passed seemed to arrive on Emergency's doorstep all the worse for the wait. Jed didn't arrive in the department till eleven and was wearing a suit that was, for once, not crumpled. He was very clean-shaven and she knew he wasn't making any

effort on her behalf, especially when Penny came back
from a meeting in Admin and her always immaculately
turned-out sister was looking just that touch more so.

Clearly it was interview day.

She had to leave.

It really was a no-brainer—she could hardly even
bear to look at Penny. She made the mistake of telling
Vanessa on their coffee break that she was going to
apply for the fracture clinic job.

'You'd be bored senseless in the fracture clinic.' Vanessa laughed as they shifted trolleys to try to make
space for a new patient that was being brought over.
Unfortunately, though, Vanessa said it at a time when
Lisa and Jed were moving a two-year-old who had had
a febrile convulsion from a cubicle into Resus.

'I'd be glad of the peace,' Jasmine said, and she
would be, she told herself, because she couldn't go on
like this. It wasn't about the workload, more about having to face Jed and Penny every day and waiting for the
bomb to drop when he found out that she and Penny
were sisters.

She could not face her sister if she ever found out
that she and Jed had been together, even if it had been
over for ages.

But then she looked over and saw that Lisa and Jed
were there and, more, that they must have heard her
talking about the fracture clinic job.

She wasn't so much worried about Jed's reaction—
no doubt he was privately relieved—but Lisa gave her a
less-than-impressed look and inwardly Jasmine kicked
herself.

'Sorry,' Vanessa winced. 'Me and my mouth.'

'It's my fault for saying anything,' Jasmine said, but there wasn't time to worry about it now. Instead, she took over from Lisa.

'Aiden Wilkins. His temp is forty point two,' Lisa said. 'He had a seizure while Jed was examining him. He's never had one before. He's already had rectal paracetamol.'

'Thanks.'

'He's seizing again.' Just as Lisa got to the Resus door, Aidan started to have another convulsion. Jed gave him some diazepam and told Jasmine to ring the paediatrician, which she did, but as she came off the phone Jed gave another order. 'Fast-page him now, also the anaesthetist.'

'Everything okay?' Penny stopped at the foot of the bed as Vanessa took the mum away because she was growing increasingly upset, understandably so.

'Prolonged seizure,' Jed said. 'He's just stopped, but I've just noticed a petechial rash on his abdomen.' Penny looked closely as Jed bought her up to speed. 'That wasn't there fifteen minutes ago when I first examined him.'

'Okay, let's get some penicillin into him,' Penny said, but Jed shook his head.

'I want to do a spinal. Jasmine, can you hold him?'

Speed really was of the essence. Aiden needed the antibiotics, but Jed needed to get some cultures so that the lab would be able to work out the best drugs to give the toddler in the coming days. Thankfully he was used to doing the delicate procedure and in no time had three vials of spinal fluid. Worryingly, Jed noted it was cloudy.

Jasmine wheeled over the crash trolley and started to pull up the drugs when, as so often happened in Resus, Penny was called away as the paramedics sped another patient in.

'Penny!' came Lisa's calm but urgent voice. 'Can I have a hand now, please?'

'Go,' Jed said. 'I've got this.'

The place just exploded then. The paediatrician and anaesthetist arrived just as an emergency page for a cardiac arrest for the new patient was put out.

'Jed!' Penny's voice was shrill from behind the curtain. 'Can I have a hand here?'

'I'm kind of busy now, Penny.' Jed stated the obvious and Lisa dashed out, seeing that Jed was working on the small toddler and picked up the phone. 'I'm fast-paging Mr Dean...' She called out to the anaesthetist, whose pager was trilling. 'We need you over here.'

'Call the second on.' Jed was very calm. 'He's stopped seizing, but I want him here just in case.'

'You call the second on,' Lisa uncharacteristically snapped and looked over at the anaesthetist. 'We need you in here now.'

It was incredibly busy. Jed took bloods and every cubicle in Resus seemed to be calling for a porter to rush bloods and gasses up to the lab. Jed was speaking with the paediatrician about transferring Aiden to the children's hospital and calling for the helicopter when Lisa came in to check things were okay.

'We're going to transfer him,' Jasmine explained.

'I'll sort that,' Lisa said. 'Jasmine, can you go on your break?'

'I'm fine,' Jasmine said. After all, the place was steaming.

'I don't want the breaks left till midday this time. Let's get the breaks started. I'm sending in Greg to take over from you.'

Jasmine loathed being stuck in the staffroom when she knew how busy things were out there, but Lisa was a stickler for breaks and really did look after her staff. That didn't stop her feeling guilty about sitting down and having a coffee when she knew the bedlam that was going on.

'There you are.' Lisa popped her head in at the same time her pager went off. 'I just need to answer this and then, Jasmine, I need a word with you—can you go into my office?'

Oh, God.

Jasmine felt sick. Lisa must have heard her say she was thinking of handing her notice in. She should never have said anything to Vanessa; she should have at least spoken to Lisa first.

Pouring her coffee down the sink, Jasmine was torn.

She didn't want to leave, except she felt she had to, and, she told herself, it would be easier all round, but she loved working in Emergency.

Would Lisa want a decision this morning? Surely this could wait.

She turned into the offices, ready for a brusque lecture or even a telling-off, ready for anything, except what she saw.

The registrar's office door was open and there was Penny.

Or rather there was Penny, with Jed's arms around her, oblivious that they had been seen.

He was holding her so tenderly, his arms wrapped tightly around her, both unaware that Jasmine was standing there. Blinded with tears, she headed for Lisa's office.

Her mind made up.

She had to leave.

CHAPTER FIFTEEN

'I'M SORRY!' LISA walked in just as Jasmine was blowing her nose and doing her best to stave off tears. 'I really tried to speak to you first before you found out.'

So Lisa knew too?

'How are you feeling?' Lisa asked gently. 'I know it's a huge shock, but things are a lot more stable now...' She paused as Jasmine frowned.

'Stable?'

'Critical, but stable,' Lisa said, and Jasmine felt her stomach turn, started to realise that she and Lisa were having two entirely separate conversations.

'I've no idea what you're talking about,' Jasmine admitted. 'Lisa, what am I here for?

'You don't know?' Lisa checked. 'You seemed upset... just then, when I came in.'

'Because...' Because I just saw my sister in Jed's arms, Jasmine thought, and then she wasn't thinking anymore, she was panicking, this horrible internal panic that was building as she realised that something was terribly wrong, that maybe what she had seen with Penny and Jed hadn't been a passionate clinch after all. 'What's going on, Lisa?' Jasmine stood up, more in panic, ready to rush to the door.

'Sit down, Jasmine.' Lisa was firm.

'Is it Simon?' Her mind raced to the childcare centre. Had something happened and she hadn't been informed? Was he out there now, being worked on?

'Simon's fine,' Lisa said, and without stopping for breath, realising the panic that not knowing the situation was causing, she told Jasmine, 'Your mum's been brought into the department.'

Jasmine shook her head.

'She's very sick, Jasmine, but at the moment she's stable. She was brought in in full cardiac arrest.'

'When?' She stood to rush out there.

'Just hold on a minute, Jasmine. You need to be calm before you speak to your mum. We're stabilising her, but she needs to go up to the cath lab urgently and will most likely need a stent or bypass.'

'When?' Jasmine couldn't take it in. She'd only been gone twenty minutes, and then she remembered the patient being whizzed in, Lisa taking over and calling Mr Dean, Penny calling for Jed's assistance.

'Penny?' Her mind flew to her sister. 'Did Penny see her when she came in?'

'She had to work on your mum.' Lisa explained what had happened as gently as she could. 'Jed was caught up with the meningococcal child and I didn't want you finding out that way either—unfortunately, I needed you to be working.'

Jasmine nodded. That much she understood. The last thing she would have needed at that critical time in

Resus was a doctor and a nurse breaking down before help had been summoned.

'And Penny told me to get you out of the way.' Jasmine looked up. 'She told me you were her younger sister and that you were not to find out the same way she had… She was amazing,' Lisa said. 'Once she got over the initial shock, she just…' Lisa gave a wide-eyed look of admiration. 'She worked on your mother the same way she would any patient—she gave her the very best of care. Your mum was in VF and she was defibrillated twice. By the time Mr Dean took over, your mum was back with us.'

'Oh, God,' Jasmine moaned and this time when she stood, nothing would have stopped her. It wasn't to her mother she raced but to next door, where Penny sat slumped in a chair. Jed was holding a drink of water for her. And to think she'd begrudged her sister that embrace. No wonder Jed had been holding her, and Jasmine rushed to do the same.

'I'm so sorry, Penny.'

She cuddled her sister, who just sat there, clearly still in shock. 'It must have been a nightmare.'

Penny nodded. 'I didn't want you to see her like that.'

She had always been in awe of Penny, always felt slightly less, but she looked at her sister through different eyes, saw the brave, strong woman she was, who had shielded the more sensitive one from their parents' rows, had always told her things would be okay.

That she'd deal with it.

And she had. Again.

'It's my fault,' Penny grimaced. 'Yesterday she was

ever so quiet and she said she had indigestion. It must have been chest pain.'

'Penny.' Jasmine had been thinking the same, but hearing her sister say it made her realise there and then what a pointless route that was. 'I had indigestion yesterday. We all did. You know what Mum's Sunday dinners are like.'

'I know.'

Jasmine looked up at Jed. His face was pale and he gave her a very thin smile. 'I'm sorry to hear about your mum,' he said, and then he looked from Jasmine to Penny and then back again. 'I had no idea.'

'Well, how could you have?' Penny said, and then turned to Jasmine. 'Can you go and see Mum? I can't face it just yet, but one of us should be there.'

'Of course.'

'She'll be scared,' Penny warned. 'Not that she'll show it.'

'Come on,' Jed said. 'I'll take you round to her.'

Once they walked out of the door he asked what he had to. 'Jasmine, why didn't you say?'

'She'd made me promise not to.'

'But even so…'

'I can't think about that now, Jed.'

'Come on.' He put his arm round her and led her into her mum's room, and even if it was what he would do with any colleague, even if she no longer wanted him, she was glad to have him there strong and firm beside her as she saw her mum, the strongest, most independent person she knew, with possibly the exception of her elder sister, strapped to machines and looking very small and fragile under a white sheet.

'Hey, Mum.'

Jasmine took her hand.

'I'm sorry,' Louise said, but for once her voice was very weak and thin.

'It's hardly your fault. Don't be daft.'

'No.' She was impatient, despite the morphine, desperate to get everything in order before she went to surgery. 'I haven't been much support.'

'Mum!' Jasmine shook her head. 'You've been wonderful.'

'No.' She could see tears in her mum's eyes. 'Most grandmothers drop everything to help with their grandchildren.'

'Mum,' Jasmine interrupted. 'You can stop right there. I'm glad you're not like most mums, I'm glad Penny is the way that she is, because otherwise I'd be living at home even now. I'd be dumping everything onto you and not sorting my own stuff out, which I have,' Jasmine said firmly, and then wavered. 'Well, almost.' She smiled at her mum. 'And that's thanks to you. I don't want a mum who fixes everything. I want a mum who helps me fix myself.'

'Can I see Simon?' She felt her mum squeeze her hand. 'Or will I scare him?'

'I'll go now and get him.' Before she left, Jasmine looked at Jed.

'I'll stay.'

And it meant a lot that he was with her.

Oh, she knew Mr Dean was around and Vanessa was

watching her mother like a hawk, but it wasn't just for medical reasons it helped to have Jed there.

She couldn't think of that now.

The childcare staff were wonderful when Jasmine told them what was going on. 'Bring him back when you're ready.'

'Thanks.'

Jasmine really didn't know if it would terrify Simon or how he'd react when he saw his nanny, but she knew that the calmer she was the better it would be for Simon. 'Nanny's tired,' Jasmine said as they walked back to the department. 'She's having a rest, so we'll go and give her a kiss.'

He seemed delighted at the prospect.

Especially when he saw Penny standing at the bed. Then he turned and saw Jed there and a smile lit up his face.

'Jed!'

He said it so clearly, there was absolutely no mistake, and Penny's eyes were wide for a second as she looked at Jed, who stood, and then back at Penny.

'I'll have to put in a complaint,' Penny said. 'The hospital grapevine is getting terribly slack.'

'Tell me about it,' Jed said, but whatever was going on, whatever questions needed answers, it was all put aside as Simon gave his nanny a kiss and a cuddle. He was amazing, not bothered at all by the tubes and machines, more fascinated by them, if anything, pointing to the cardiac monitor and turning as every drip bleeped. But of course after a few moments he grew restless.

'We're going to take your mum up to the catheter lab soon,' Vanessa said. The cardiac surgeon had spoken to them in more detail and her mum had signed the consent form, and it was all too quick and too soon. Jasmine had just got used to the idea that she was terribly ill and now there was surgery to face.

'Can I just take Simon back?'

'Of course.' And in the few weeks she'd been here, Jasmine found out just how many friends she had made, just how well she was actually doing, thanks to her mum. 'Tell the crèche that I'll pick up Simon tonight. He can stay at my place.'

'You're sure?' Jasmine checked. 'I can ring Ruby.'

'It's fine tonight. You'll probably be needing Ruby a lot over the next few days. Let me help when I can.'

The crèche was marvellous too and told Jasmine that she could put Simon in full time for the next couple of weeks, and somehow, *somehow* Jasmine knew she was coping with a family emergency and single motherhood and work combined.

And she didn't want to lose her job, no matter how hard it would be, working alongside Jed.

Except she couldn't think about it now.

Right now, her heart was with her mum, who was being wheeled out of Emergency, a brusque and efficient Penny beside her, telling the porter to go ahead and hold the lifts, snapping at Vanessa for not securing the IV pole properly, barking at everyone and giving out orders as she did each and every day, while still managing to hold her mum's hand as she did so.

And her heart wasn't just with her mum.

It was with her big sister too.

The time sitting in the Theatre waiting room brought them possibly the closest they had ever been.

'Is that why you were asking about Jed and I?'

They were two hours into waiting for the surgery to finish, an hour of panic, ringing around friends and family, and then an hour of angst-filled silence, and then, because you could only sit on a knife edge for so long, because sometimes you needed distracting, Penny asked the question that was starting to filter into both their minds.

'For all the good it did me.' Jasmine smiled. 'How come we don't gossip?'

'I never gossip,' Penny said. 'I don't do the girly thing and…' Her voice trailed off and she thought for a moment, realising perhaps how impossible for her sister this had been. 'You could have asked me, Jasmine.'

'What if I didn't like the answer?' Jasmine's eyes filled with tears and she couldn't start crying again. She'd shed more tears since her mother had gone to Theatre than she had in a long time.

'You're still not asking me.'

Jasmine shook her head, because if the truth were known she was scared to. Not just for what it would do to her but what the truth might mean for her sister.

'Nothing has ever happened between Jed and I.'

Jasmine felt as if a chest drain had been inserted, or what she imagined it must feel like, because it felt as if for the first time in days, for the first time since Vanessa had inadvertently dropped the bomb, her lungs expanded fully, the shallow breaths of guilt and fear replaced by a deep breath in.

'Nothing,' Penny said. 'Not a single kiss, I promise you.' And Jasmine could now breathe out. 'Who said that there was something going on between us?'

'It's common knowledge apparently, though I only heard this week. My friend couldn't believe that I hadn't notice the tension between you two.'

'The only tension between us,' Penny continued, 'is who might get the promotion.'

'I thought you were worried about getting it and upsetting Jed.'

Penny just laughed. 'Worrying about upsetting or upstaging Jed Devlin is the furthest thing from my mind—believe me. Do I look like someone who would step aside from a promotion for a man?' She actually laughed at the very thought.

'No,' Jasmine admitted. 'But you did say you weren't sure if you wanted the job...'

'Right now I'm not even thinking about work, I just want Mum to get well, that's as far as I can think today. You have nothing to worry about with Jed and I.'

'It doesn't matter.'

'It clearly did.'

But Jasmine shook her head. 'I'm just glad I haven't hurt you—Jed and I are finished.'

'Jasmine!'

But Jasmine was through worrying about Jed. She didn't have the head space to even think about him right now. 'Let's just worry about Mum for now, huh?'

* * *

'How is she?' Lisa asked when an extremely weary Jasmine made her way down to Emergency the next morning.

'She's had a really good night,' Jasmine said. 'They're going to get her out of bed for a little while this morning, can you believe?'

'They don't waste any time these days.' Lisa smiled. 'How are you?'

'Tired,' Jasmine admitted. 'I'm sorry to mess you around with the roster.'

'Well, you can hardly help what happened. Have you got time to go through it now—did you want the rest of the week off?'

Jasmine shook her head. 'I was actually hoping to come in to work tomorrow—Penny's going to stay with her today and I'll come back this evening, but I'd rather start back at work as soon as possible. I might need some time off when she comes out, though.'

'We'll sort something out,' Lisa said. 'We're very accommodating here, not like the fracture clinic.' Lisa winked.

'Sorry about that.'

'Don't worry about it for now. We'll have a chat when you're up to it.'

'Actually,' Jasmine said, 'do you have time for a chat now?'

She sat in Lisa's office and, because she'd got a lot of her crying out when she'd told Jed, Jasmine managed to tell Lisa what had happened with her ex-husband without too many tears, and was actually incredibly relieved when she had.

'You didn't need to tell me this,' Lisa said. 'But I'm very glad that you did. I'd rather hear it from you first and it's a good lesson to us all about being less careless with patients' property. I can see why you panicked now. Anyway...' she smiled, '...you can stop worrying about it now.'

Finally she could, and only then did Jasmine fully realise how much it had been eating at her, how much energy she had put towards worrying about it, running from it.

'Go home to bed,' Lisa said.

'I will. But I just need to have a quick word with Vanessa, if that's okay?'

Vanessa was one burning blush when they met. 'Simon's been fantastic. He's tucked up in the crèche now and I can have him again tonight if you like.'

'I'll be fine tonight.'

'Well, why don't I pick him when my shift's finished and bring him home to you?' Vanessa offered, and as Jasmine thanked her she suddenly cringed. 'Jasmine, I am so embarrassed.'

'Why?'

'All the terrible things I said about Penny. I could just die. I keep going over and over them and then I remember another awful thing I said.'

Jasmine laughed. 'Believe me, you weren't the only one, and you told me nothing about Penny that I didn't already know—Penny too, for that matter. It's fine, I promise.'

'Me and my mouth!' Vanessa grimaced.

'Forget it.' Jasmine smiled. 'Anyway, I'm going to go home to bed, and thank you so much for your help with Simon. I'm just going to pop in and give him a kiss.'

'Jasmine.' Just as he had on the first day they had met, Jed called her as she went to head out of the department. 'Can I have a word?'

'I'm really tired, Jed.'

'Five minutes.'

'Sure.'

'Somewhere private.'

They settled for one of the interview rooms.

'How is your mum?'

'Getting there.'

'How are you?'

'A lot better than yesterday,' Jasmine said. 'I'm really tired, though.'

'Of course.' He took a breath. 'You should have told me that you and Penny were sisters,' Jed said.

'You didn't exactly give me much chance.'

'Before that.'

'I was working up to it. But if we weren't serious there didn't seem any point.' She gave a tight shrug. 'I told you from the start I was trying to keep work and things separate—you were the same.' She turned to go. 'Anyway, it doesn't matter now.'

'We need to talk.'

'No,' Jasmine said. 'I don't think we do.'

'Nothing happened between Penny and I,' Jed said. 'Absolutely nothing. I can see now why you were upset, why you felt you couldn't ask.'

And now it was, Jasmine realised, time to face things properly, not make an excuse about being tired and scuttle off. 'It's actually not about whether or not you slept with Penny.' Jasmine swallowed. 'I mean, had you, of course it would have mattered.' He saw the hurt that burnt in her eyes as she looked up at him.

'You gave me no chance to explain,' Jasmine said. 'I was struggling—really struggling to tell you something, and you just talked over me, just decided I was too much hard work. You didn't even answer my question. You just threw everything back in my face.'

She would not cry, she would not. 'It took guts to leave my marriage,' Jasmine said. 'But it just took common sense to end things with you. In any relationship there are arguments, Jed.' She looked right at him as she said it. 'And from the little I've witnessed, you don't fight fair!'

She saw him open his mouth to argue, but got in first.

'That's a no in my book.'

CHAPTER SIXTEEN

HE RANG AND Jasmine didn't answer.

And she stayed at her mum's, ringing and answering the phone to various aunts and uncles so even if he went over to her place, she wouldn't know and more to the point she wasn't there.

'Cold tea bags help,' Penny said when she dropped around that evening and saw her puffy eyes. 'You don't want him to see that you've been crying.'

'I could be crying because Mum's in ICU.'

'She's been moved to Coronary Care,' Penny said, 'so you don't have that excuse.'

'They've moved her already?'

'Yes. Great, isn't it? And you've got the night off from visiting. She was sound asleep when I left her. Still, if you want to go in I can watch Simon.' She must have seen Jasmine's blink of surprise. 'I *am* capable.'

'I'm sure you are.' Jasmine grinned. 'I might just pop in, if you're sure.'

'Of course.'

'He's asleep,' Jasmine said. 'You won't have to do anything.'

'I'm sure I'll cope if he wakes,' Penny said. 'And

if you are going to see Mum then you need to put on some make-up.'

It didn't help much, not that her mum would have noticed. She was, as Penny had said, asleep. Still, Jasmine felt better for seeing her, but that feeling faded about five minutes after visiting when she saw Jed coming out of X-Ray.

'Hi,' he said.

'Hi.'

'I tried to call,' Jed said, but Jasmine wasn't interested in talking.

'I need to get home.'

'Run off, then,' Jed said, and Jasmine halted for a second.

'Sorry?'

'You said you had to go.'

She opened her mouth to argue. Had he just accused her of running off? But instead of challenging him, she threw him a very disparaging look, and as she marched off, Jasmine knew she didn't need cold tea bags on her eyes—she was through crying.

Her mum was right—it was completely hereditary.

The Masters women had terrible taste in men!

Still, even if she would have liked to avoid him it was impossible at work. Everywhere she went she seemed to be landed with him, but she refused to let him get to her, refused to give him the satisfaction that she was running off.

But worse than the department being busy was the times it was quiet and though she had no idea who knew what, she nearly bit on her gums when Lisa gave her a very sweet smile.

'Could you give Jed a hand, please?' Lisa said, even though there were five other nurses sitting around. 'He's stitching a hand and she won't stay still on the trolley.'

'Her name's Ethel,' Lisa added. 'You'll get to know her soon, she's one of our regulars.'

'Sure.'

She painted on a smile and walked into Theatre.

'Hi, there, Ethel, I'm Jasmine.'

'Who?'

She was an angry old thing, fuelled on sherry and conspiracy theories, and she made Jasmine laugh.

'Why would they knock the hospital down?' Jasmine asked patiently, when Ethel told her the plans were already in and had been approved by the council.

'Prime real estate,' Ethel said. 'Imagine how many townhouses they could put up here.'

'Have you been talking to my mum?' Jasmine grinned.

'All money, isn't it?' Ethel grumbled for a while and then spoke about her children, who, from the age of Ethel, must be in their sixties at least. 'They're just waiting for me to go,' Ethel said bitterly. 'Worried I'm spending their inheritance.' She peered at Jasmine. 'Have you got children?' she asked.

'None,' Jasmine happily lied.

'Husband?'

'Nope.'

'Good for you,' Ethel said. 'Dating?'

'Nope.'

'Quite right, too.' Ethel said. 'They're no good, the lot of them.' And she ranted for a few minutes about her late husband. 'They're all liars and cheats and if they're not now then they're just waiting to be. Nasty, the lot of them—except for the lovely doctor here.'

She caught Jed's eye and they actually managed a slightly wry smile.

'No, we're all horrible, Ethel,' Jed said. 'You're quite right not to listen to their sorry excuses.'

And if he'd looked up then he'd have seen Jasmine poke her tongue out.

'How's your mum?' Jed asked, when Ethel gave in and started snoring.

'Doing well,' Jasmine said. 'She should be home on Monday.'

'How are you?'

'Good,' Jasmine said, and hopped off the stool. 'It looks like she's sleeping. Just call out if you need a hand.'

'Sure,' Jed said, and carried on stitching as Jasmine went to wash her hands.

She knew he was just trying to irritate her as he started humming, knew he was just trying to prove he was completely unbothered working alongside her.

And then she realised what he was humming.

A little song that was familiar, a little song about a little runaway, and when he looked up at her furious face he had the audacity to laugh.

'You'd better go,' Jed said. 'It sounds busy out there.'

There were maybe five patients it the department.

'Or do you need to pop up to visit your mum?'

He teased her with every excuse she had ever made over the last couple of days whenever he had tried to talk to her.

'Or is it time to pick up Simon?'

And then he got back to humming his song.

'I'm not avoiding you or running away.'

'Good,' Jed said. 'Then I'll be over about eight.'

'I don't want to argue.'

As soon as she opened the door to him, Jasmine said it. 'I don't want raised voices…'

'I didn't come here for that,' Jed said. 'And I wouldn't do that to Simon and I certainly wouldn't do that to you.' He saw her frown of confusion as she let him in. 'You are right, though—I didn't fight fair.' He said it the moment he was inside. 'And I'm not proud of that. I didn't give you a chance to explain. I didn't give us a chance.'

He took a seat. 'And I get it that there were things that you couldn't talk about easily. I've thought about it a lot and I can see how impossible it was for you—after all, if you and Penny had agreed not to tell anyone…' He looked up at her. 'You could have told me—I would never have let on.'

'Perhaps not,' Jasmine said, 'but when I thought you two might have been seeing each other…' She looked at him. 'Penny insists nothing ever happened.'

'It didn't.'

'Apparently Greg walked in on you two once?' She wanted to believe her sister, but deep down she was still worried that it was Penny protecting her all over again.

'Greg walked in on us?' Jed gave a confused shake of

his head, raked his fingers through his hair and pulled on it for a moment, then he gave a small smile as realisation hit. 'We had words once.'

'Words.'

'A lot of words. It was a couple of months ago,' Jed said, 'before you were around. In fact...' he frowned in recall, '...it was the same day as your interview. We had a busy afternoon and there was a multi-trauma that I was dealing with and Penny just marched in and tried to take over.'

'I can imagine.' Jasmine gave a tight smile.

'And then she questioned an investigation I was running—Mr Dean was there and I think she was trying to...' he shrugged, '...score points, I guess. I don't do that.' Jasmine knew already that he didn't. 'And I don't mind being questioned if it's merited, but, as I told Penny, she's never to question me like that in front of a patient again or try and take over unless she thinks I'm putting a patient at risk.' Jed looked up at her. 'Which I certainly wasn't and I told her that.'

'Oh!'

'And I asked her to explain her thought process, her rationale behind questioning me,' Jed said. 'Which Penny didn't take to too well.'

'She wouldn't.'

'Your sister's lousy at confrontation, too.' Jed smiled.

'I don't think so.'

'Oh, she is,' Jed assured her. 'She only likes confrontation when it's on her terms. You should remember that next time she starts.'

And Jasmine found she was smiling.

'Greg walked in on us, actually, we were in the IV room, and, yes, I guess he picked up something was going on, but it certainly wasn't that.'

'So why wouldn't you answer me that day?' Jasmine asked. 'Why couldn't you just say that there was nothing going on between the two of you?'

'Because I've spent the last two years convincing myself I'd be mad to get involved with anyone at work.'

'Especially a single mum?'

'You could come with ten kids,' Jed said. 'It was never about that.'

'Then why?'

'Jasmine, please.' He put up his hand. 'This is difficult.' And she knew then he had something to tell her, that she was as guilty as he'd been that night, because she was the one now not letting him speak.

'I left my last job, not because...' He really was struggling with it. 'I got involved with a colleague,' Jed said. 'And there's no big deal about that, or there wasn't then. She worked in the labs in research and, honestly, for a couple of months it was great.' He blew out a breath. 'Then she started talking about children...'

Jasmine opened her mouth and then closed it.

'I wasn't sure. I mean, it was early days, but it wasn't even on the agenda. I told her that. She got upset and that weekend I went out with some friends. I was supposed to go over to hers on the Sunday and I didn't, no excuse, I just was out and got called into work and I forgot.' Jasmine nodded. She completely got it—she forgot things all the time.

'She went *crazy*,' Jed said. And it wasn't so much

what he said but the way that he said it, his eyes imploring her to understand that this was no idle statement he was making. 'I got home that night and she was sitting outside my flat and she went berserk—she said that I was lying to her, that I'd met someone else.' He took a long breath.

'She hit me,' Jed said. 'But we're not talking a slap. She scratched my face, bit my hand.' He looked at Jasmine. 'I'm six-foot-two, she's shorter than you and there was nothing I could do. I could have hit her back, but I wouldn't do that, though, looking back, I think that was exactly what she wanted me to do.'

'Did you report it?'

He shook his head. 'What? Walk into a police station and say I'd been beaten up? It was a few scratches.'

'Jed?'

'I thought that was it. Obviously, I told her that we were done. She rang and said sorry, said that she'd just lost her head, but I told her it was over and for a little while it seemed that it was, but then she started following me.'

'Stalking?'

Jed nodded. 'One evening I was talking to a friend in the car park, nothing in it, just talking. The next day I caught up with her in the canteen and she'd had her car keyed—there were scratches all down the side. I can't say for sure that it was Samantha...'

'What did you do?'

'Nothing for a bit,' Jed said. 'Then my flat got broken into and then the phone calls started. It was hell.'

He had never been more honest, had been so matter-of-fact about it when he'd discussed it with others, but he wasn't feeling matter-of-fact now, because for the first time he was properly reliving that time. The flat tyres he'd come out to, the phone ringing in the night, that he didn't even want to think of dating, not because he didn't want to but because of what she might do to any woman he went out with.

'It all went from bad to worse. In the end she just unravelled—she ended up being admitted to Psych and nearly lost her job.'

'It's not your fault.' She saw the doubt in his expression. 'Jed, the same way I wasn't responsible for what my ex did.'

'That doesn't stop you looking back,' Jed said. 'I go over and over the time we were together and maybe I did let her think I was more serious than I felt.'

'Oh, come on, Jed. She clearly had issues. If it hadn't been you it would have been the next guy.'

'But it *was* me,' Jed said. 'I had more than a year of it. She's getting help now, apparently, but I just couldn't stay around,' Jed admitted. 'I don't think it was helping either of us to work in the same hospital and in the end I didn't want to even be in the same city. That's why I moved.'

'That's awful.'

'It was,' Jed said. 'I wasn't scared for myself, I could stop her physically, but when she started messing with people I knew, that was enough. And,' Jed added, 'I was scared for her too. It was awful to see someone who was basically nice just going to pieces.' He managed his first smile since he'd arrived that evening. 'Do you believe me now when I say I had no intention of getting involved with anyone at work?'

'Yes.'

'And do you understand why, when you got so upset that I might have once dated Penny, I thought it was all just happening again? I mean, the second we got serious, and we did get serious, you know that we did...' He waited till she nodded. 'Well, the next night I come round and you're standing there, crying and begging to know if I've ever hooked up with Penny, if anything, *anything* had ever happened between us.'

'I get it.' Jasmine even managed to laugh. 'I'd have freaked too, if I were you.' She went over to him and he pulled her onto his knee. 'I promise not to stalk you when we break up.'

'Maybe we won't.'

'We'll see,' Jasmine said.

'I know that you wouldn't now, anyway. You handled the break-up brilliantly,' Jed added. 'I mean, a couple of late night phone calls wouldn't have gone amiss—a few tears...'

Jasmine held her finger and thumb together. 'Just a smidge of obsession?'

'Careful what you wish for, huh?' Jed smiled back. 'I think I dreaded a break-up more than a relationship—and you...' He smiled at her. 'You just carried right on.'

'Not on the inside.'

She'd never admitted it to anyone, not just about Jed but about her fears and her thoughts and how more than anyone in the world she hated confrontation, hated rows, and that, yes, she had been running away. 'I've got to stop avoiding rows...'

'I think it's nice that you do.'

But Jasmine shook her head.

'You're a lot stronger than you think.'

She didn't feel very strong sometimes and she told him a little of how it felt to be related to two very strong women who were so accomplished in everything they did.

'Jasmine,' Jed asked. 'What do you want?'

'Meaning?'

'What do you want?'

She thought for a moment, about Simon safe and warm and sleeping in his cot and her job that she loved and her little home right on the beach and a relationship that looked like it might be working.

'What I've got,' Jasmine said.

'And you've worked for it,' Jed pointed out. 'You could have listened to your mum and sister and been some high-powered lawyer or doctor and hating every minute of it, or you could be working in the fracture clinic because the hours are better, but instead you've stood your ground and you do a job you love... And,' Jed added, 'despite a lousy relationship you've got an amazing son and your heart's back out there. I'd say you're pretty strong.'

And he was right. She had everything she wanted, even if wasn't what her mother or sister might choose. She did, even if it was misguided at times, follow her heart.

'I do want a little bit more,' Jasmine said.

'What?' He moved in for a kiss.

'White walls,' Jasmine whispered. 'I'm on my fourth coat.'

And he looked at walls that were still green tinged and he started to laugh. 'Did you put on an undercoat?'

He saw her frown.

'Jasmine,' he groaned. 'I'll do it at the weekend. But for now...'

It was bliss to be kissed by him again, bliss to be back in his arms and to know there were no secrets between them now, nothing more to know.

Except...

'How did your interview go?' She wriggled out of his kiss—there was so much she had missed out on.

'Don't worry about that now.'

'But how did it go?'

'Very well,' Jed said. 'I should know tomorrow.'

'How did Penny go?'

'Just leave it, huh? Suffice it to say I'm quietly confident but I'll be fine if it doesn't come off.'

'Sure?'

'Sure.'

And then he got back to kissing her and this time she didn't halt him with questions. This time it was just about them, at least until Simon woke up. This time she didn't hesitate, and brought him straight through.

'Jed!' Simon smiled when he saw him.

'You outed us to Penny!' Jed grinned and then he looked at Jasmine. 'We need to go out.'

'I know,' she said. 'I'll speak to Ruby. I can't just...'

'I didn't mean it like that,' Jed said. 'I mean that

we need to announce ourselves to the world before Simon does.'

'I think he already has,' Jasmine said. 'Can't you feel them all watching us?'

He just grinned and then he said what he was thinking and it was far nicer than having to censor every word and thought, so much better than having to hold back. 'Do you want to come to the A and E ball?'

'It's too soon.'

'Not for me,' Jed said. 'Though I will probably only be able to stay till ten, so you might be deposited home early, but I want people to know about us. It isn't too soon for me.'

'I meant…' Jasmine laughed '…that it's too soon for me to organise anything. The ball's tomorrow—and I'm working till four and I haven't got anything to wear.'

'You'll look lovely whatever you wear.'

'That's the most stupid thing I've ever heard…' Did he have not a clue as to how much went into getting ready for this sort of thing? Everyone who was going had the afternoon off and had been talking about dresses and shoes for weeks.

'I'm not going to argue with you.' Jed smiled. 'After all, I know how much you hate it. So I'm just going to tell you instead that we're going to the ball tomorrow and I expect you to be ready when I get here.'

CHAPTER SEVENTEEN

A BIT MORE notice would have been nice.

Lisa and Penny were bright orange, thanks to their spray tans, which they would shower off before their hairdresser appointments, Jasmine thought darkly, or after they'd picked up their thousand-dollar dresses from the dry cleaner's.

They were working on a head injury—their newly extended and painted nails hidden under plastic gloves. Penny wanted him admitted to ICU, except there weren't any beds at Peninsula, though they had been told there *might* be one available later on in the afternoon.

'Nope.' Penny shook her head. 'He'll have to be transferred.'

'Okay,' Lisa said. 'Do you want me to do a ring around?' She looked at Jasmine. 'You go and have your break.' As Jasmine opened her mouth to argue, Lisa overrode her. 'You might have to transfer him,' she pointed out, 'so go and have a break now.'

Jasmine didn't have time for a break.

Instead, she raced up to CCU. She was incredibly nervous about tonight and terribly aware of the lack of anything suitable in her wardrobe and she was determined to dash to the shops at lunchtime. She knew it might be her only chance to visit her mum but as she swept in to see her, Jasmine halted when she saw Jed standing there beside her bed.

'Hi, there.' Jasmine smiled, but it was a wary one, because Jed wasn't her mother's doctor. He hadn't even been involved in her admission. 'Is everything okay?'

'Everything's fine.' Louise smiled, but Jasmine was still cautious.

'Your mum's temperature was up a bit up this morning,' Jed explained. 'And Penny's stuck in with that head injury and insisted that I check things out...' He rolled his eyes. 'She's got a slight chest infection but they're onto it with antibiotics and your mum's physio has been increased.' He gave Louise a smile. 'Now that I've seen for myself that you'll live and have spoken to your doctor, I'd better get back down there and reassure your elder daughter.'

She hardly waited till he was out of the door and had she looked over her shoulder she would have seen Jed shake his head as Jasmine anxiously picked up her mother's charts and saw that her temperature had indeed been rather high but was on its way down.

'Jasmine.' Her mum was stern. 'I've got a chest infection.'

'I know.'

'It's not a big deal,' her mum said, and saw Jasmine's anxious eyes. 'Okay, it could be, but they're straight onto it. They've taken loads of bloods and they've got me up and walking and coughing on the hour. It's my own stupid fault,' Louise admitted. 'It hurt to take a deep breath and to cough and I didn't really listen when they said to increase my painkillers. I thought I was doing better by having less.'

'Mum.' Jasmine let out a frustrated sigh. 'You're so…'

'Stubborn.'

'I could think of a few other words,' Jasmine said. 'Why wouldn't you take the medication?'

'I just wanted to go home and I thought the sooner I got off the strong stuff the sooner they'd release me.'

'And because of that you'll probably be stuck here for another couple of days.'

'Well, we don't always do what's right for us, do we?' Louise admitted. 'But I am learning.' And to prove it she pushed her pain medication button and the little pump whirred into life. 'See?'

'I spoke with the insurance and the travel agent,' Jasmine said, 'and you shall have your cruise, but not for a few months.' She saw her mum rest back on the pillow. 'I brought in some brochures—you get to choose all over again.'

'That's such a relief,' Louise said. 'That means that I can help you out a bit more.'

'Mum, the only person you need to be concentrating on right now is you. I'm getting in the swing of things now. Vanessa and I are going to work out our nights and our late shifts, and we've got Ruby. I just needed you for the first few weeks.'

'And I made it hard to ask,' Louise said. 'I'm sorry.'

'Don't be sorry.'

'I am.'

'You gave me a push,' Jasmine said. 'I knew what I was going to get when I decided to come home—and you have helped. I couldn't have started back on shifts without you. But...' Jasmine took a deep breath, '...I'm not going to apply to work in the fracture clinic, I'm going to stay in Emergency. It's what I'm good at. And it might be a juggle, but...'

'You'll sort it.'

'I will,' Jasmine said, feeling far more positive.

'I don't remember much of my time in there, but...' she took her daughter's hand, '...I do know what was done for me and I've seen the nurses hard at it on ICU and in here. I'm proud of what you do, Jasmine, and I'm sorry I haven't been more supportive. I get it now.'

'Good.'

'And it breaks my heart what Penny had to go through, and I am so glad you were spared from that, but apart from that, I can't think of anyone I'd rather have looking after me than you. Don't let your career go.'

'I'm not going to.'

'No matter how easy it is to drop down to part time or—'

'Mum! I've got a one-year-old to support so dropping my hours down isn't even on the agenda. Not for the next seventeen years at least.'

'He seems nice.' Louise's head jerked to the door. 'Jed.'

'He is.'

'Penny said that you two have been seeing each other.'

'Mum!' Jasmine was firm. 'It's early days. Neither of us wants to rush into anything and there's Simon to think of. Still—' she couldn't help but share the news, '—I'm going to the A and E ball with him tonight.'

'What are you wearing?'

'I don't know yet.' Jasmine ignored her mother's horrified expression. 'I'm going to look at lunchtime.'

'In the village?'

Jasmine closed her eyes. There were about two clothes shops near enough to get to in her lunch break and, no, she didn't think they would have a massive selection of ballgowns to choose from.

'I'd lend you something, but…'

'I'm not borrowing something from my mum!'

'I've got very good taste,' Louise said, 'and a black dress is a black dress, but…' she ran an eye over Jasmine '…it wouldn't fit.'

'Just keep pushing that pain medication button, Mum.' Jasmine smiled. 'You might need it soon.'

'What about your wedding dress?'

'Please.'

'Well, it's not really a wedding dress, is it?' Louise pointed out. 'It would look lovely.'

'No.' Jasmine gave her mum a kiss. 'I have to get back.'

'Are you getting your hair done?'

'Yes!' Jasmine lied. 'Don't worry, I'm not going to let the side down.'

'I know. Can you drop by on your way?'

'Mum!' That was too cringy for words.

'Penny is.'

'Oh, Mum,' Jasmine said. 'I think I preferred the old you.'

'Tough.' Louise smiled. 'You've got a new mum now. Right, you have a lovely day and I'll look forward to seeing you this evening.'

Jasmine headed back down to Emergency and gave a brief nod to Penny, who was sitting at the nursing station writing up notes, and beside her was Jed.

'Have you seen Mum?'

Jasmine blinked in surprise. 'I've just been,' Jasmine said. 'She looks well.'

'What's her temp?'

'Down to thirty-seven point five.'

'Good.'

'Well, she's certainly changed her tune,' Jasmine said to Jed as Penny was called back into Resus. 'I'm actually being acknowledged.' She made sure no one was listening. 'Have you heard?'

'What?'

'Jed!' He was so annoying sometimes. 'About the job,' she mouthed.

'Not yet!' he mouthed back. And then she remembered something. 'This is too embarrassing for words, but on the way to the ball Mum wants me to pop in.'

'No problem.'

'For two minutes.'

'It's no big deal,' Jed assured her.

'For you maybe,' Jasmine grumbled. 'I think they bypassed the old mum when they did surgery.'

'Jasmine.' She heard a rather familiar call from Greg and, jumping off her seat, she dashed into Resus to see the head injury Penny had been working on looking significantly worse. His arms were extending to painful stimuli and Penny was sedating him and getting ready to intubate.

Penny was marvellous, barking out her orders as always, but she actually called for Jed's help when the anaesthetist didn't arrive. Whatever way you looked at it, she was fantastic at her job, just a cow around the staff. That was to say, all the staff, so she didn't deliberately take it personally when Penny told her none too politely to hurry up as Jasmine loaded a syringe with propofol, an oily drug that was a bit slow to draw up. And she really was confident in her work. Penny's hands weren't even shaking as she intubated the patient, Jasmine noticed.

And then Lisa spoke and as Jasmine pulled up some more medication she noticed that her own hands were shaking.

'There's an ICU bed at Melbourne Central. The chopper is already out so I've called for MICA and a police escort.' She told the anaesthetist the same when he arrived and then she told Jasmine to prepare the patient and get herself ready.

'It will be fine,' Jed said just a little while later when Mark and his colleague arrived and transferred the patient to the stretcher. 'Jasmine, it will be.'

'I know.'

'No one's going to say anything.'

'And if they do?'

'They won't,' Jed said. 'But if they do, just tell them to mind their own business.'

He gave her shoulder a squeeze. 'If I don't see you before, I'll pick you up about six-thirty.'

Oh, God… Jasmine would have closed her eyes, except she had to move now, had to follow the stretcher into the ambulance. No, she wasn't going to be buying a dress this lunchtime, neither would she be sorting out her hair.

Instead she was going back to Melbourne Central.

With a police escort they practically flew down the freeway. The patient was stable throughout and Craig, the anaesthetist, was very calm, as were the paramedics. It was Jasmine whose heart was hammering as they approached the hospital she had loved and the place it had hurt so much to leave.

'Are you okay, Jasmine?' Mark asked, before they climbed out.

'Sure.'

'No one's going to eat you.'

'I know.'

Of course, it was a bit of an anticlimax. The hospital didn't suddenly stop just because she was back. In fact, she didn't recognise any of the staff on ICU as she handed the patient over.

The paramedics were going to be taking Jasmine and Craig back to Peninsula, but Mark wanted to take a break before the return journey.

'We'll just grab some lunch at the canteen,' Mark told her.

'I'll meet you back at the ambulance,' Jasmine told him. Tempting as it was to hide out in the canteen, Jas-

mine decided that she was tired of running away from
things, tired of feeling guilty over mistakes that weren't
even hers, so feeling nervous but brave she walked into
Emergency.

'Hi.' She smiled at a face she didn't recognise. 'I
was wondering—'

'Jasmine!' She never got to finish her sentence as
Hannah, the charge nurse, came rushing over. 'Where
have you been?'

'I moved back home.'

'You never even let us know you'd had your baby.
Martha said that she heard it was a boy.'

And she was back and her friends were crowding
around her, looking at pictures of Simon on her phone.
Hearing their enthusiasm, she realised just how badly
she had misjudged her friendships and she started crying.

'He was a bastard,' Hannah said when Jasmine told
her why. 'Of course nobody thought you were involved.'

'Everybody was so weird around me.'

'We were embarrassed,' Martha said. 'Upset for you.'
She gave Jasmine a hug. 'You're better off without him,
you know.'

'Oh, God, do I know.'

'Does that mean you're coming back?' Hannah
asked.

She thought for a moment, because she could come
back and part of her wanted to come back except, Jasmine realised then, just as she had told Jed, she was
very happy with what she had now.

'Maybe one day.' Jasmine smiled and then of course

they asked if she was seeing anyone and she was through with covering things up and so she said yes.

'His name's Jed,' Jasmine said. 'Jed Devlin.'

'I know that name.' Hannah frowned. 'Where do I know that name from?'

'He came for an interview here,' Jasmine said.

'That's right.' Hannah nodded and then waved in direction of the door. 'I think your transport's ready.' Jasmine turned and there were the paramedics. 'Don't be a stranger,' Hannah warned. Then she laughed. 'Well, I guess you won't be now.'

Jasmine had no idea what Hannah meant, but she was on too much of a high to think about it, and then when she realised she still had nothing to wear tonight and she wasn't going to get to the shops, she was far too panicked to dwell on Hannah's words, especially when they hit traffic on the way home.

'Can't you put on the sirens?' Jasmine grumbled, but the paramedics just laughed. 'Some of us are going out tonight.'

CHAPTER EIGHTEEN

THANK GOD FOR heated rollers and quick-dry nail varnish, Jasmine thought as somehow she cobbled herself together, cringing as she pulled her old wedding dress on.

It didn't look remotely like a wedding dress.

It was a dark blue silk that her mother had said matched her eyes, and the strange thing was, as she looked in the mirror, she looked better in it than she had on the big day.

Then she had been sixteen weeks pregnant and bloated and miserable and not particularly sure that she wasn't making the biggest mistake of her life, and, no, she hadn't been particularly excited at the prospect of her wedding night.

Now she had curves and a smile and couldn't wait for the formalities to be over just to get Jed into bed!

'Wow,' Ruby said when she opened the door. 'You look gorgeous. I love the dress.'

'Thanks.' Jasmine smiled.

'Where did you get it?'

'I've had it for ages.' Jasmine blushed and mumbled something about a boutique in the city as she stuffed her bag with lipstick and keys. 'I don't think I'll be late back,' she told Ruby. 'Jed has to go into work and cover for Penny.'

'All you have to worry about is enjoying yourself,' Ruby said. 'He'll be fine.'

She knew that Simon would be fine.

It was two other people she was more worried about tonight.

Surely they wouldn't tell them about the job today, Jasmine reasoned. It was the A and E ball tonight so they would no doubt wait till next week to give the verdict.

Oh, God, Jasmine thought, putting in her earrings, she was torn.

Family first, she told herself, except she knew about the delays that had been caused in Jed's career. He was older than Penny and he wasn't where he thought he should be in his career.

And here he was at her door.

Her heart was hammering for different reasons when she first saw him in a tux.

'Wow.' Jed gave a whistle of appreciation. 'I told you you'd look lovely.'

'Wow to you too,' Jasmine said.

'I thought you said you had nothing to wear. Jasmine, you didn't go spending a fortune, did you?'

'No, no,' Jasmine said. 'I've had this for ages. I didn't know if it would fit!' Quickly she tried to change the subject. 'Have you heard about the job?'

'We'll talk about it later.' He sort of nodded his head

in the direction of Ruby. 'We ought to go, especially if you want to drop in to see your mum.'

'I feel stupid walking through the hospital dressed like this.'

'It will be nice for her,' Jed said. 'And knowing that place, Penny will get called just as she gets into her dress and have to do something urgent and be swanning around Resus in pink satin.'

'I guess,' Jasmine said. 'Though I can't see her in pink satin.' Jed smiled, but she could tell he was a little on edge. Maybe he was having second thoughts about them being seen out together so soon and she told him so.

'You're being daft.'

It was worth going in just to see the smile on her mum's face.

'You look great.' Louise smiled. 'You both do.'

'I'm just going to go and ring the unit and check it's okay,' Jed said, and she knew it was because staff were a bit thin on the ground, but it also gave her a chance for a little bit longer with her mum.

'You look so much better.'

'I feel it,' Louise said. 'I told you your wedding dress would be perfect!'

'Shhh!' Jasmine warned. 'I don't want him knowing.'

'Now.' Louise was back to practical. 'Your sister's got something to tell you, some big news.' And her heart should have surged for Penny, except first it sank for Jed and then it surged back up because she was truly torn. 'It's big news and even if it's a bit hard to hear it, I think it's really important that you be pleased for her.'

'Of course I'll be pleased.'

'I know,' Louise said. 'I can't say anything, I don't want to spoil things for her, and I guess that it's her news to share, but just keep that smile fixed on.'

'I will.'

She gave her mum a kiss and then walked out to where Jed was just hanging up the phone.

'Let's get going.'

He was quiet on the car ride there and if he was just a touch tense, at least Jasmine knew why, but he took her hand and they walked in together and she knew that if he was being a bit quiet it had nothing to do with her.

'Hi, there!' Penny came over all smiles, and kissed Jed's cheek and then Jasmine's too.

'You look amazing,' Jasmine said, because Penny did. There was a glow in her cheeks and a smile that was just a little bit smug, and she didn't blame Jed when he excused himself to have a word with Mr Dean.

'Why are you wearing your wedding dress?' Penny asked the second he was out of earshot.

'Because I had about ten minutes' warning about to-night,' Jasmine said. 'And don't tell anyone.'

'Isn't that a bit twisted?' Penny wrinkled her nose. 'Doesn't that make you a bit of a saddo?'

'Stop it!' Jasmine said, but she started to laugh. Penny was such a cow at times, but she was also very funny.

'Any news?' Jasmine asked.

'Not here, Jasmine,' Penny warned.

'Oh, stop it,' Jasmine said. 'No one can read my lips. You got the job, didn't you? I know you did.' She looked at her sister. 'I thought we were going to be more honest from now on.'

'Jasmine,' Penny warned.

'Well, I'm thrilled for you.' She really was. 'Honestly.'

'Jasmine, will you please shut up?' Penny gave a sigh of irritation then beckoned her towards the ladies. Of course it was crowded, so they went outside and Penny waited till they were about twenty metres from anyone before she spoke,

'I did get offered the job,' Penny said, 'and before you jump up and down on the spot and get all emotional and then start worrying about Jed...'

Jasmine took a deep breath.

'I withdrew my application.'

Jasmine literally felt her jaw drop. 'Why would you do that?'

'Because,' Jasmine said, 'and I never thought I'd hear myself say this, but some things are more important in life.'

'Your career is...' Jasmine buttoned her lip but Penny just laughed.

'Exactly,' she said. 'There needs to be more. I've been a terrible aunt,' Penny said, 'and an appalling sister, because I've been so incredibly jealous of you. I always have been. And I guess I still am. I want what you have.' And she smiled as Jasmine frowned. 'Not Jed, you idiot. The other guy in your life.'

'A baby?'

'It seems Mr Dean was right. They train you up and what do you go and do...?'

'You're pregnant?'

'Not yet,' Penny said. 'But I'm hoping to be in the not-too-distant future, and from everything I've heard about IVF, well, I'm not going to be the sunniest person.'

'Penny!' Jasmine was stunned.

'I'm in my mid-thirties and I just...' Penny gave a tight shrug. 'At the moment I have about sixty-three minutes a week to devote to a relationship. There are not many men who would put up with that.'

'There might be.'

'Well, I want my baby,' Penny said. 'And I've thought long and hard and I'll work right up to the last minute and then—'

'But IVF?' Jasmine queried. 'Don't you just need a donor?'

'I tried for a baby with Vince.' Jasmine watched her sister's eyes, which were always so sharp, actually fill with tears. 'We had a few problems.' She looked at her sister. 'Or rather I had a few problems in that department. It meant IVF and Vince and I...' She swallowed her tears down. 'Well, I think we weren't really up to the challenge.'

'Is that why you broke up?'

'In part.'

'Why couldn't you talk to me?'

'I am now,' Penny said, and Jasmine realised what her mum had meant about some big news. But, no, she didn't need to be told to keep her smile on, she was genuinely thrilled for her sister. 'You have to give me my injections, though.'

'I can't wait to stick another needle in you.' Jasmine grinned and gave Penny a hug.

'And I'm not giving up my career,' Penny said. 'I'm just not complicating things for now. I have no idea how I'm going to work things out.'

'You will,' Jasmine said.

'I think I'll have to get a nanny.'

'We can share one.' Jasmine grinned.

'I want this,' Penny said. 'And I'm not waiting around for Mr Right. Anyway, I've seen both you and mum stuff up—we have terrible taste in men.'

'I guess.'

'Not this time, though.' Penny smiled. 'Mind you, don't you go telling him I got offered the job.'

'Penny! I'm sick of lying.'

'I mean it. If he has got the job and that's what he's all worked up about, the last thing he needs is to be told I turned it down. Just be all happy and celebrate when he gets the news.'

'Do you think he's got it?' Jasmine wasn't so sure—Jed seemed really tense.

'I'm pretty sure. There was an external applicant who was pretty impressive but I think Mr Dean wants to keep it in-house. He should hear any time soon.'

She had a terrible feeling that he already had.

Jed was lovely as they drove back from the ball a couple of hours later, but she could tell that he had something on his mind—it had stung when she had thought he had lost the job to Penny. She knew how his career had been sidetracked dealing with what he had, but losing it to an outsider would really hurt.

'Where are we going?'

Only then had she noticed they were driving to the city.

'Somewhere nice.'

'But you have to work.'

'Nope.' He grinned. 'Mr Dean arranged a locum, well, not really a locum—he's going to be working there in a few weeks so it's good if he gets a feel for the place.'

She looked over and tried to read his expression.

'Working there?'

'The new consultant.' He gave a small grimace.

'Oh, Jed.' She really didn't know what to say. 'I know it's hard for you…'

'Hard on me?' He turned and looked at Jasmine. 'It's hard on you, though Penny didn't look as upset as I thought she'd be,' Jed admitted. 'I thought she'd be savage.' He shook his head. 'She seemed fine.'

Jasmine looked out of the window to the bay. Penny had been right. Working in the same department was way too complicated. She could hardly tell Jed the real reason Penny was so delighted and she definitely didn't want to tell him that Penny had actually turned down the job.

They chatted about this and that but she could feel his tension and she was so irritated that they had told the applicants today of all days. Couldn't they just have enjoyed tonight?

'We can't stay out too long.' Jasmine glanced at her watch—half an hour really, if she was going to be back by midnight, though maybe she could stretch it till half past. It was hardly his fault. He just wanted to go out somewhere nice and wasn't used to factoring in a one-year-old and his babysitter.

'What are we doing here?' she asked as they pulled up at a very nice hotel.

'I told you I wanted to take you somewhere nice.'

'Just a drink at the bar, then.' She hoped he hadn't booked for dinner. He popped the boot and as Jasmine stepped out of the car, she frowned as he gave his name to park it and frowned even more at the sight of her rather tatty case being hauled out.

'Jed?'

'Ruby packed it,' Jed said. 'It's all sorted.'

'Oh.'

They went to check in. It was the nicest thing he could have done for her, but she felt terrible because surely he had been planning a celebration, or maybe he hadn't factored in that he'd know.

It was like holiday where it was raining and everyone was pretending it didn't matter, all grimly determined to enjoy themselves, and she would...she was. Jasmine was thrilled to have a night away with him, she just knew how hard this must be for him.

'Wow!' She stepped into the hotel room and tried not to notice the champagne and two glasses. Instead, she stared out at the view but Jed poured two glasses and it tasted fantastic and, yes, it was fantastic to be together.

'I am sorry about the job,' Jasmine said.

'Shhh,' he said. 'Let's just celebrate.'

'Cheers!'

'You don't know what we're celebrating,' Jed said.

'That we're here's good enough for me.'

'And me,' Jed said, and then he smiled. '"Oh, ye of little faith".'

She didn't understand. 'Sorry?'

He pulled back one of the curtains. 'Have a look over there. What do you see?' It was just a busy city. 'Over there.' He pointed to a tall building. 'That's where I'm going to be working. I got offered a consultant's position on Thursday, so I withdrew my application.'

'Oh!' She could have thumped him. 'You let me drive all that way thinking you were disappointed!'

'No,' Jed said. 'I knew that you *were* disappointed—it's awful for Penny. I really thought when I took the position at Melbourne Central that Penny was a certainty for the job. I think Mr Dean's really got it wrong. The new guy seems great by all accounts, but it's going to be tough on your sister.'

'No, you don't understand.' She opened her mouth, but again she couldn't say anything.

'What?'

Jasmine shook her head. 'Leave it.'

'I can't.'

'You can.'

'I can't.'

Jasmine was firm. 'She's my sister.'

She looked over to where he'd be working. 'I thought you were happy at Peninsula.'

'I've been incredibly happy,' Jed said. 'I applied to a few hospitals when I first thought of moving here and it was a close-run thing. I love big city hospitals but when Mr Dean hinted at a consultancy... Anyway, Central rang me last week and asked if I'd be interested in a more senior position than the one I interviewed for last year, and given the tension at work, given a lot of things, the choice was actually easy.'

'That's good,' Jasmine said, trying to mask the little edge of disappointment in her voice, that just when they were finding each other he was upping sticks, but, still, it was just an hour or so away.

'I like to keep work and home separate,' Jed said.

'I know that.'

'And I haven't been doing a very good job of it of late.'

He started to kiss her and then pulled his head back. 'You're sulking.'

'No.' She looked up at him and she was too scared to admit it, because he meant so much more than she dared reveal. They'd agreed they were going to take things slowly and, yes, they were back on track, but maybe once he got to a big hospital, maybe when things were more difficult, when Simon was sick and he was on call and it all became too hard to have a single mum as a girlfriend who lived a good hour away, maybe then things would go wrong for them.

'It's been a hell of a week.'

'And now it's over,' Jed said. 'Now you can enjoy being spoiled.' He gave her a smile. 'Come on, tell me, how come Penny's looking so pleased if she didn't get the job.'

Jasmine closed her eyes. 'Actually, come to think of it, it's a good job that you're going to Melbourne Central. I'm not breaking my sister's confidence.' She looked at him.

'Fair enough.'

'She's family.'

'I'm not arguing.' Jed grinned. 'I think you want to, though.'

'I don't.'

Jasmine didn't. She didn't want anything to spoil this night. 'So…' She forced her voice to be upbeat. 'When do you start?'

'Four weeks,' Jed said. 'It's going to be fantastic—it's a great hospital.'

'Good.'

'It's everything I want.'

He pulled her into his arms and he was smiling. She would not ruin this night, would not nit-pick, but how come he was so happy to be leaving? How come he had been so tense all night? Though he wasn't tense now, he was *delighted* with his good news, thrilled to be moving an hour away, and she swallowed down her tears.

'I can't wait to start,' Jed said. 'And tomorrow I thought I might go and look for somewhere to live.'

Some bachelor city apartment, Jasmine thought bitterly, but she kept her smile there.

'The staff there seem really friendly,' he added.

She thought of Hannah, who was gorgeous and flirted like crazy, and Martha, and the wild parties they often had, and he would be there and she would be home with Simon.

'And I can't wait…'

'Okay.' Her lips were taut with smiling. 'I'm thrilled for you.'

She reached for her glass as she did not want to

argue; she took a sip of champagne and swallowed down a row, but it was fizzing. Yes, she was happy for him, yes, she was thrilled, but... 'Do you have to keep rubbing it in?'

She didn't get why he was smiling.

'Sorry?'

'Do you have to keep telling me how *thrilled* you are to be leaving, how fantastic it is to be moving away?'

'Come on, Jasmine.' He grinned. 'Don't spoil tonight with a row.'

'I want one!' She did. For the first time in her life she wanted her row and stuff it if it was an expensive one. So what if she was spoiling a wonderful night? Did he have to be quite so insensitive?

'Go for it.'

'I will,' Jasmine said. 'I'm thrilled for you. I really am, but do you have to keep going on about it?' She just said it. 'Do you have to keep telling me how delighted you are to be going away and all the parties...'

'I never said anything about parties.'

'Oh, but there will be.'

And he just grinned.

'And I'll be home with Simon and you'll be an hour away and, yes, I am happy for you and, no, I didn't expect you to take Simon and me into consideration, but I can't keep grinning like an idiot when the fact is you're moving away.' She started to cry. 'And I don't understand why you're laughing.'

'Because I love how you row.'

And he pulled her into him. 'I've been goading you.'

'Why?'

'Because.'

'Because what?'

'I want just a smidge of obsession.'

'Well, you've got it.' And he kissed her and it was lovely. She'd said what she thought, had had a good row and no one was any the worse for it. Then he stopped kissing her and looked at her for a very long time.

'I am pleased for you. I honestly am. I know you'll love it there.' And she realised then what Hannah had meant when she'd said that she'd see her around. If she was going out with Jed she'd be with him at times. 'I'm just sad you're leaving, that's all.'

'I have to,' Jed said. 'Because I'm not working alongside a woman who turned down my proposal.' And he took out a box containing a ring but she didn't even look at it properly, just looked straight back at him. 'And if she doesn't turn it down then I'm working in the same department as my wife and sister-in-law. That would be way too complicated and I already have trouble enough concentrating on work when you're around. So which one is it?'

'The complicated one,' Jasmine said, and watched as he put a ring on her finger.

'It won't be complicated for long,' he assured her. 'I'm taking time off before I start my new job and for the next few weeks I'm going to take some time to get to know that son of yours and you're going to get to know me properly. We'll go to Sydney and meet my family. We'll just take some time. I don't want you to feel you're being rushed into anything again. We'll wait as long as it takes for you to feel okay with it.'

'I already am.' She had never been more sure of anything in her life. 'And I don't feel as if I'm rushing into things this time. I know.'

'I know too,' Jed said. 'And you're coming to look for somewhere to live with me. Midway, maybe? Or we can just carry on as we are and I'll sort out the travel, but I promise you that you and Simon will always be my first consideration.'

She believed him, she really did, and her heart filled not just for her own happiness but because her son was going to have such an amazing man to help raise him, for all the happy times to come.

'Mum's going to have another heart attack when she finds out.'

'She already knows,' Jed said. 'What, do you think I'd ask you to marry me without asking for her permission?'

'You asked her?' So that was what her mum had been banging on about not dropping her hours or losing her career—she already knew.

'Of course I asked her.'

'You're an old-fashioned thing, aren't you?'

'Yep,' Jed said. 'But I'm filthy-minded too. I want to do you in your wedding dress.'

She blinked.

'I'm sure you will.'

'I mean this one.'

She just about died of embarrassment, right there on the spot. 'You knew?'

'Your mum told me.' He smiled, and then pulled her back into his arms. 'And now, seeing as I'm almost family, you can tell me what's going on with Penny.' She started to, but he stopped her.

'Not yet.' He was kissing her face, kissing her mouth, and making her feel wanted and beautiful in her wedding dress for the very first time, as he told her just how much the future was theirs. 'We've got ages.'

* * * * *

SECRETS OF A CAREER GIRL

BY
CAROL MARINELLI

First published in Great Britain 2013
by Mills & Boon, an imprint of Harlequin (UK) Limited.
Harlequin (UK) Limited, Eton House, 18-24 Paradise Road,
Richmond, Surrey TW9 1SR

© Carol Marinelli 2013

ISBN: 978 0 263 89901 6

Harlequin (UK) policy is to use papers that are natural, renewable
and recyclable products and made from wood grown in sustainable
forests. The logging and manufacturing process conform to the
legal environmental regulations of the country of origin.

Printed and bound in Spain
by Blackprint CPI, Barcelona

PROLOGUE

THE PATIENTS LIKED her, though.

Emergency Consultant Ethan Lewis glanced up as an elderly lady in a wheelchair, with a younger woman pushing her, approached the nurses' station and asked if Penny Masters was working today. The lady in the wheelchair still had her wristband on and was holding a bag of discharge medications and a tin of chocolates.

'I think she's on her lunch break,' answered Lisa, the nurse unit manager. 'I'll just buzz around and find out.'

'No, don't disturb her. Mum just wanted to give her these to say thank you—she really was marvellous that day when Mum was brought in.'

'It's no problem,' Lisa said, picking up a phone. 'I think she's in her office.'

Yes, Ethan thought to himself. Unlike everybody else, who took their lunch in the staffroom, Penny would be holed away in her office, catching up with work. He'd been trying to have a word with her all day—a casual word, to ask a favour—but, as Ethan was starting to discover, there was no such thing as a casual word with Penny.

Ethan had been working in the emergency department of the Peninsula Hospital for more than three months now. It was a busy bayside hospital that serviced some of Melbourne's outer suburbs. The emergency department was, for the most part, a friendly one, which suited Ethan's laid-back ways.

For the most part.

He watched as Penny walked over. Immaculate as ever, petite and slender, her very straight blonde hair was tied back neatly and she was wearing a three-quarter-sleeve navy wraparound dress and smart low-heeled shoes. The female equivalent of a business suit perhaps, which was rather unusual in this place—most of the other staff, Ethan included, preferred the comfort and ease of wearing scrubs. Penny, though, dressed smartly at all times and gloved and gowned up for everything.

'Mrs Adams, how lovely to see you looking so well.' Ethan watched as she approached her ex-patient. Without being told, Penny knew her name. Though the greeting was friendly, it was a very professional smile that Penny gave and there was no tactile embrace. Penny stood there and enquired how Mrs Adams was doing with more than mere polite interest, because even though they had clearly just left the ward, the daughter had a few questions about her mother's medication and Penny went through the medication bag and easily answered all of them.

'Thank you so much for explaining,' Mrs Adams's daughter said. 'I didn't like to keep asking the nurse when I didn't understand.'

'You *must* keep asking.'

Yes, the patients loved Penny.

They didn't mind in the least that she was meticulous, thorough and incredibly inflexible in her treatment plans.

It was the staff that struggled—if Penny wanted observations every fifteen minutes, she accepted no excuses if they weren't done. If Penny ordered analgesia, it didn't matter to her that there might be a line-up at the drug trolley, or that there was no one available to check the dose, because her patient needed it now.

Penny walked Mrs Adams and her daughter to the exit, and stood talking for another couple of moments there. As she walked back through the department, Jasmine, a nurse who also happened to be Penny's sister, called her over to the nurses' station.

'What did you get?' Jasmine asked.

Penny glanced down at the tin she was holding. 'Chocolate macadamias,' she said, peeling off the Cellophane. 'I'll leave them here for everyone to help themselves.'

She wasn't even that friendly towards her sister, Ethan thought as Penny put down the chocolates on the bench and went to go. He would never have picked Penny and Jasmine as sisters—it had had to be pointed out to him.

Jasmine was dark and curvy, Penny blonde and very slim.

Jasmine smiled and was friendly, whereas Penny was much more guarded and standoffish. Ethan refused to play by her silent, stay-back rules and he called her as she went to head off. 'Can I have a quick word, Penny?'

'I'm actually at lunch,' Penny said.

The very slow burning Taurus within Ethan stirred a little then—his hazel eyes flashed and, had there been horns hidden under his thick black hair, Penny would now be seeing her first glimpse of them. It took a lot to rile Ethan, but Penny was starting to. Ethan had always known that there might be a problem when he had taken this job—two of the department's senior registrars had also applied for the consultant position.

Jasmine's new husband Jed was one of them.

Penny the other.

Knowing the stiff competition, Ethan had been somewhat taken aback when he had been offered the role. He had since learnt that Jed had taken a job in a city hospital, but Penny was still here and, yes, it was awkward. Ethan often reminded himself that her ego might be a touch fragile and that it might take a little while for her to accept him in the role that she had applied for.

Well, it was time that Penny did accept who was boss and, for the first time, Ethan pulled rank as she went to head back to her lunch.

'That's fine.' He looked into her cool blue eyes. 'But when you're finished, can you make sure that you come and find me? I need to speak with you.'

She hesitated for just a second before answering. 'Regarding what?'

No, there was no such thing as a casual word with Penny. 'I'm on call next weekend,' Ethan said. 'Is there any chance that you could cover me for a few hours on Sunday afternoon? I'm hoping to go to a football match with my cousin—' He was about to explain further, but before he could, Penny interrupted him.

'I've already got plans.'

She didn't add 'sorry'.

Penny never did.

As she turned to go Ethan's jaw clamped down and, rarely for him, his temper was rising. He was tempted to tap her on the shoulder and tell her that this was more than some idle request because his team was playing that weekend. His cousin was actually on the waiting list for a heart transplant.

No, he wouldn't waste the sympathy card on her and with good reason—Ethan actually smiled a twisted smile as Penny walked off.

'Did you use it?' Phil would ask when Ethan rang him tonight.

'*Nope.*'

'Good,' Phil would say. 'Save it for women you fancy.'

Yes, it was a black game, but one that got Phil through and gave them both a few laughs.

He certainly wouldn't be using the sympathy card on Penny.

'We're going to the airport to see Mum off on Sunday.' Jasmine had jumped down from her stool to help herself to the chocolate nuts and offered an explanation where her sister had offered none. She was trying to smooth things over, Ethan guessed, for her socially awkward sister. Except Penny wasn't awkward, Ethan decided—she simply wasn't the least bit sociable. 'It's been planned for ages.'

'It's not a problem.' Ethan got back to his notes as Jasmine, taking another handful of the chocolate nuts, headed off, but as he reached to take a handful himself Ethan realised that Penny hadn't even taken one.

She could use the sugar, Ethan thought darkly.

'You could try asking Gordon,' Lisa suggested when it was just the two of them, because Ethan had told her while chatting a few days ago about his cousin, and, no, he hadn't been using the sympathy card with Lisa!

'I'll see,' Ethan said. Gordon had three sons and another baby on the way. 'Though he probably needs his weekend with his family, as does Penny.' He couldn't keep the tart edge from his voice as he mentioned her name.

'You don't know, do you?' Lisa was trying to sort out the nursing roster but she too had seen the frosty exchange between Penny and Ethan, and though she could see both sides, Lisa understood both sides too. 'Jasmine and Penny's mum was brought in a few months ago in full cardiac arrest. They were both on duty at the time.'

Ethan grimaced. To anyone who worked in Emergency, dealing with someone you knew, especially a family member, was the worst-case scenario. 'Did you manage to keep it from them?'

'Hardly! Well, we kept it from Jasmine while the resuscitation was happening so at least she found out rather more kindly than Penny did.' Lisa put down her pen and told Ethan what had happened that day.

'Penny was just pulling on her gown when the paramedics wheeled her mother in,' Lisa said. 'You know how she gowns up all the time.' Lisa rolled her eyes.

'Penny takes up half of the laundry budget on gowns alone. Anyway, you know how she usually starts snapping out orders and things? Well, I knew that there was something wrong because she just stood there frozen. She asked for Jed—he was the other registrar on that day—but he was stuck with another patient. Penny told me that the patient was her mum and then just snapped out of it and got on with the resuscitation, just as if it were any other patient. And she kept going until we got Mr Dean here to take over. She did tell me not to let Jasmine in, though.'

Lisa gave a wry smile. 'I didn't even know, till that point, that Penny and Jasmine were sisters. Penny likes to keep her personal life well away from work.'

'I had noticed.'

'The cruise is a huge thing for their mother. Do you see now why Penny couldn't swap?'

'I do,' Ethan said, and got back to his notes. But that was the problem exactly—he'd never have heard it from Penny herself.

And then he stopped writing, took another handful of chocolate nuts as it dawned on him...

Like him, Penny had refused to play the sympathy card.

CHAPTER ONE

'HAVE YOU THOUGHT about letting a few people at work know what's going on?'

Penny closed her eyes at her sister's suggestion and didn't respond. The very last thing Penny wanted was the people at work to know that she was going through IVF.

Again.

It was bad enough for the intensely private Penny that her mum and sister knew but, given that Penny was seriously petrified of needles, she'd had no choice but to confide in Jasmine, who would be giving Penny her evening injections soon.

While she couldn't get through it without Jasmine's practical help, there were times when Penny wished that she had never let on that she was trying for a baby.

Yes, her family had been wonderfully supportive but sometimes Penny didn't want to talk about it. She didn't want to hear that they were keeping their fingers crossed for her, didn't always want to give the required permanent updates and, more than anything, she had hated the sympathy when it hadn't worked out the first

time. Naturally they had tried to comfort her and understand what they could not—they had both had babies.

The two sisters were walking along the beach close
to where they both lived. Penny lived in one of the smart
townhouses that had gone up a couple of years ago and
took in the glittering bay views. Jasmine lived a little
further along the beach with her new husband Jed and
her toddler son Simon, who was from Jasmine's first
marriage. The newlyweds were busily house hunting
and trying to find somewhere suitable between the city,
where Jed now worked, and the Peninsula Hospital.

Now, though, the sisters lived close by and, having
waved their mother off from Melbourne airport for her
long-awaited overseas trip, they walked along the beach
with Simon, enjoying the last hour of sunlight.

'It might be a good idea to let a couple of people in
on what you're going through,' Jasmine pushed, because
she wanted Penny to have the support Jasmine felt that
she needed, especially as Penny was going through this
all alone.

'Even my own friends don't really understand,'
Penny said. 'Coral thinks I'm being selfish, and Bi-
anca, though she says I should go for it if that's what
I want...' Her voice trailed off. 'If I can't talk about it
with my own friends, what's it going to be like at work?'

'Lisa especially would be really good.'

'Lisa is a nurse unit manager,' Penny broke in. 'I'm
not a nurse.'

'She runs the place, though,' Jasmine said. 'She'd be
able to look out for you a little bit.'

'I don't need looking out for.'

Jasmine wasn't so sure. She could see that the treatment was taking its toll on her sister, not that Penny would appreciate her observations.

Jasmine wanted so badly to help her sister. They had never really been close but Penny had always looked out for her—several years older, Penny had shielded her from the worst of their parents' rows and their mother's upset when their father had finally left. It had been the same when their mother had been brought into Emergency—Penny had made sure Jasmine hadn't found out about their mother in the same way that she had.

'I know this is all a bit new to you, Jasmine,' Penny said. 'But I've been living with this for years. I've known for ages that I had fertility problems.'

'How long did you and Vince try for?'

Penny heard the tentativeness in Jasmine's question. They were both working on their relationship, but there were still areas between them that were rarely, if ever, discussed.

'Two years,' Penny finally answered.

One year of serious trying and then a year of endless tests and consultations and a relationship that hadn't been able to take the strain. 'We didn't just break up over that, though,' Penny admitted. 'But it certainly didn't help. I can tell you this much.' She gave a tight smile. 'We'd never have survived IVF. It doesn't exactly bring out the best in you.'

'How are you feeling this time?' Jasmine asked.

'Terrible,' Penny admitted. 'I'm getting hot flashes.'

'Are you serious?'

'I'm completely serious. I'd forgotten that part—you

know, at the time you think that you will never forget, but you actually do.'

Jasmine opened her mouth to agree with her sister and then closed it again as Penny turned around.

Penny knew that Jasmine had been about to admit to the same thing, but for very different reasons—Jasmine's breasts were noticeably larger and she'd had nothing to eat at the airport and had then screwed up her nose when Penny had suggested they get some takeaway for dinner, choosing instead a slow walk on the beach.

Jasmine was pregnant.

Penny just knew.

'I don't need the whole department watching me for signs of a baby bump,' Penny said, though it was the opposite for Penny with her sister. She had been trying so hard to ignore the signs in Jasmine, but more and more it was becoming evident and Penny wished she would just come out and tell her now. 'Or gossiping,' Penny added.

'It wouldn't be like that.'

'Of course it would,' Penny snapped. 'And, of course, they'll all have an opinion on whether I should be doing this, given that I haven't got a partner.' She gave an exasperated sigh. It wasn't a decision she was taking lightly, not in the least. At thirty-four there was no sign of Mr Right on the horizon and with her fertility issues, even if he did come along, it was going to be a struggle to get pregnant.

After many long conversations with the fertility consultant, more and more Penny felt as if time was running out. 'If there's good news at the end of this, I'll tell people, but they don't need to know that I'm trying.'

'But the treatment is so intense. If people only knew...'.

Penny didn't let her finish. 'You don't walk into the staffroom and tell them that you've come off the pill and had sex with Jed last night.' When Jasmine laughed, Penny carried on. 'No, you feed the sharks when you're good and ready.' Penny paused, waiting for her sister to open up to her, because even if Penny snapped and snarled a bit she wasn't a shark, but Jasmine changed the subject.

'I can't believe that Mum has finally made it to her cruise.' Jasmine smiled. 'Well, she's made it to her flight.'

'And she'll make it to her cruise.' Penny was firm.

'What if something happens while she's stuck in the middle of the ocean?'

'There's a medical team,' Penny said, but of course that didn't reassure her sister. 'Jasmine, are you going to spend the next month worrying about things that might happen and every imagined scenario while Mum is no doubt having the absolute time of her life?'

'I guess,' Jasmine conceded. 'Though I really did think we were going to lose her.'

'We didn't, though,' Penny broke in.

While Louise Masters's heart attack and emergency admission had been a most difficult time, from there good things had sprung—an urgent reminder for all concerned that you should live your life to the full.

Which was why their mother would soon be sailing

around the Mediterranean, why Jasmine had followed her heart and opened up to Penny's then fellow senior registrar Jed, and why Penny was, at this moment, walking along the beach with a face that was bright red and breaking out into a sweat as she experienced yet another wretched hot flash. Not that Jasmine noticed; her mind had moved on to other things.

'What do you think of Ethan?' Jasmine asked for Penny's thoughts on the new consultant, but Penny didn't answer; instead, she suggested a walk in the shallows, much to little Simon's delight. Both holding his hands, they lifted him up between them, swung him over the water, and finally Penny felt herself calm, the heat fading from her face, her racing heart slowing, and then Jasmine asked her again what she thought of Ethan.

'He thinks that he's God's gift.'

'So do a few other people,' Jasmine pointed out, because since Ethan had arrived, a couple of hearts had already been broken. 'He is funny, though.' Jasmine grinned.

'I don't think he's funny at all,' Penny said, but then again she didn't sit in the little huddles at the nurses' station, neither did she wait for the latest breaking news to be announced in the staffroom. Penny loathed gossip and refused to partake in it, though, given it was Jasmine, there was one thing she did divulge. 'He seems to think that he got the job over me.' Penny gave a little smirk. 'He has no idea that I declined to take it.'

'He doesn't know?'

'God, no!' Penny said. 'I would assume he knows that Jed turned it down to take the position at Melbourne

Central, but it would be a bit much for him to know that he was actually the third choice.'

'Wouldn't Mr Dean have told him?'

'Mr Dean wouldn't discuss the other applicants with him—you know what he's like.' Penny rolled her eyes. Mr Dean had put her through the wringer over the years—he was incredibly chauvinistic and had been reluctant to promote Penny to senior registrar. Penny was quite sure it was because she was a woman—she'd heard Mr Dean comment a few times how you trained women up only for them to get pregnant. Still, Penny had long since proven herself and, though Ethan might think otherwise, the consultant's position had been Penny's. She had chosen not to take it, deciding it would be too much on top of going through IVF, and more and more she was glad she had made that decision.

'Ethan's gorgeous.' Jasmine nudged her. 'He's so sexy.'

'Jasmine!'

'What? Just because I'm married I'm not supposed to notice just how stunning he is?'

Penny conceded with a shrug. Yes, Ethan Lewis was stunning. He had thick silky black hair that seemed always to be just a day away from needing a good cut and had unusual hazel eyes. He was very tall and broad shouldered and so naturally he stood out. He was also a bit chauvinistic, not that the women seemed to mind.

'The trouble with Ethan,' Penny said, 'is that he knows how gorgeous he is and he uses it unwisely. Someone should stamp "not the settling-down type" on his forehead. It might have helped warn the nurse in CCU who keeps coming down to the department to try and speak to him, and also that physiotherapist.'

Penny frowned as she tried to think of the young woman's name, but gave up. 'And that's just two that I've seen and heard about, and given that I'm the last person to know anything, I'm quite sure there must be a few more.'

'Well, at least he doesn't pretend he's interested in anything more serious,' Jasmine said. 'I was talking to him the other day and I apologised for going on too much about Simon and he just laughed and said he enjoyed hearing it, as it's the closest he'll ever get to having one of his own. He's lovely,' Jasmine sighed. 'You should have a fling with him.'

Jasmine would so love to see her very uptight sister unbend just a little. 'She should, shouldn't she, Simon?' Jasmine said as she picked up her little boy, who was finally starting to tire.

'Don't bring Simon into this.' Penny smiled fondly at her nephew. 'And don't you listen to your mother.'

Simon smiled back. He adored his aunt and he held out his hands for Penny to hold him, which she did. 'You're the cause of all this,' Penny teased, because seeing her sister pregnant and later as a mum had stirred already jumbled feelings in Penny and she desperately wanted a baby of her own.

'You tell Aunty Penny that she *should* listen to me and have some fun before she's ankle deep in nappies and exhausted from lack of sleep.' Jasmine smiled at her son and then turned to her sister. 'Just one last wild fling before you get pregnant!'

'I've never had a wild fling in my life and I'm certainly not about to start now. You've never had IVF, have you?' Penny's voice was wry. 'Believe me, Ethan Lewis and sex and wild flings are the very last thing on my mind right now.' Penny did suddenly laugh, though. 'Could you imagine if I did and then twelve weeks later announced that I'm pregnant?'

'Oh, I would just love to see that.' Jasmine was laughing too at the thought of the confirmed bachelor Ethan Lewis thinking for a moment that he was about to become a father. 'It would kill him!'

CHAPTER TWO

'WHERE THE HELL is X-ray?' Penny snapped at Jasmine the next afternoon, just as she would to anyone—they weren't sisters here and no feelings were spared.

They were struggling to stabilise a patient in congestive heart failure who wasn't responding to the usual treatment regimes. John Douglas had presented to the department struggling to breathe, his heart beating dangerously fast and his lungs overloaded with fluid. It was a common emergency that Penny was more than used to dealing with, but what was compounding the problem was that John was also a renal patient and undergoing regular dialysis at a major city hospital so Penny was trying to sort out the far higher drug doses that were needed in his case.

'I'm just going to lean you forward, John,' Penny said, and listened again to her patient's chest. The oxygen saturation machine was bleeping its alarm. Vanessa, another nurse, returned with John's blood-gas results and it was confirmed to Penny that things were really grim. She had already paged the medics to come down urgently and was now considering putting out a crash call, because even though he hadn't gone into cardiac arrest he was very close.

'Give him another forty milligrams,' Penny called out to Jasmine, though she wasn't cross when Jasmine hesitated. 'He's a renal patient,' Penny explained, 'so he'll need massive doses of diuretics.'

Still, Penny was concerned about the amount of medication she was having to give and was carefully checking the drug guide, wishing the medics would hurry up and get there. She had just decided to put out a crash call when Ethan approached.

'Problem?' Ethan asked, and Penny quickly brought him up to speed.

'He's not responding,' Penny said. 'And neither are the medics to their fast page. I'm going to call the crash team.'

'Hold off for just a moment.' Ethan scanned the drug sheet to see what had been given. He had just come from working a rotation in the major renal unit in a city hospital, so he was familiar with the drug doses required in a case like this and he quickly examined the patient. 'He needs a large bolus.'

Ethan saw Penny's face go bright red as he took over the patient's care. 'Penny, where I worked before...' He didn't really have time to explain things and he wasn't about to compromise patient care by pandering to Penny's fragile ego—she was spitting with rage, Ethan could see it. In fact, he was tempted to lick his finger and put it onto her flaming cheek just so that he could hear the hiss.

'Go ahead,' came Penny's curt response, and she

thrust the patient notes into his hands and walked off quickly.

'Have we ordered a portable chest X-ray?' he asked Jasmine.

'It's supposed to be on its way,' Jasmine answered.

'You're going to be okay, sir.' Ethan listened to his chest and considered calling the crash team himself.

He could see Jasmine was blushing too at her sister's little outburst and was sorely tempted to ask Jasmine just what the hell her sister's problem was, though of course Ethan knew. Well, he wasn't just going to stand back, and if Penny didn't like it, she'd better start getting used to it. Penny Masters was an absolute... Ethan kept the word in his head as he saw the fluid start to gush into the catheter bag. The patient's oxygen saturations started to rise slowly. He was just ordering some more morphine when the radiographer arrived for the chest X-ray, along with a much calmer-looking Penny.

'Thanks for that,' she said, completely unable to look him in the eye. She had fled to her office, which had a small sink in it, and splashed her face with cold water and run her wrists under the tap. Penny would never have left the patient had Ethan not been there, but she had never had a hot flash so severe. She knew that Ethan was less than impressed, especially when, without a further word, he stalked off.

'Are you okay?' Jasmine checked as they waited outside while the patient was being X-rayed, Vanessa staying in with him.

'Of course I'm not.' Rarely for Penny, she was close

to tears. 'He thought I was cross at him for making suggestions and that I just walked off in a temper.'

He'd thought exactly that, Jasmine knew. She had seen the roll of his tongue in his cheek and the less than impressed rise of Ethan's brows. 'Penny, if people just knew—'

'What?' Penny interrupted. 'Do you really think that I'm going to explain to him that I just had a hot flash?'

Penny was mortified—absolutely and completely mortified. The down-regulation medication to stop her own cycle was in full effect, and she had a splitting headache as well, another of the side effects. The headache she could deal with, but for a woman who was usually so able to keep things in check, the rip of heat that had seared through her face and the rapid flutter of her heart in her chest had felt appalling. She had hardly been able to breathe in there but she had absolutely no intention of telling Ethan Lewis why. 'Do you really think that Neanderthal would be understanding?'

'Neanderthal?' Jasmine grinned in delight at her sister's choice of word.

'Just leave it,' Penny snapped.

Ethan didn't leave it, though.

Before heading for home, he passed her office, where Penny sat busily writing up her notes. She was sitting very straight, like some schoolmarm, Ethan thought as he knocked a couple of times on her open door.

In fact, it was rather like walking into the headmistress's office as those cold blue eyes lifted to his and gave him a very stern stare.

'What time are you on till?' Ethan asked.

'Midnight,' Penny answered—she knew that he hadn't just popped in for a chat.

'How is Mr Douglas doing now?'

'He's a lot better, but the medics are still stabilising him and then he'll be transferred so he can have his dialysis.' She wished he would just leave; she really didn't want to discuss what had taken place. 'Thank you for your help with him.'

'It didn't feel very welcome.' Ethan waited a moment, but Penny said nothing, just turned her attention back to her notes and, no, he would not just leave it. 'What the hell happened back there, Penny?'

'I don't know what you're talking about.'

'I think that you do,' came Ethan's swift retort. 'If there is an issue then it's time that we discussed it.'

'There is no issue.'

Ethan begged to differ. She was the most difficult woman that he had ever met and he'd met a lot of women! Yes, she was a fantastic doctor. Ethan had no qualms there, and in fact he was quietly surprised, having seen her work, that she hadn't been given the consultant's position. He could well understand how angry she must be, but somehow they had to work together and if she was going to storm off every time he stepped in on a consultation, something had to be said. 'We have to work together, Penny.'

'I'm aware of that.'

'Which means that at times we'll disagree.'

'I'm aware of that too.' Her face was starting to burn again, but from embarrassment this time. 'Look, thank you for stepping in with Mr Douglas, it was much appreciated. I'm not as familiar as I would like to be with renal patients so I'm very pleased that you were there. We do seem to have our wires crossed, though.' She gave tight smile. 'I wasn't cross or upset.' She saw his incredulous look.

'You walked off.'

Penny said nothing, just stared at this huge, very masculine man. She didn't know how to tell him and she didn't really want to try, except her silence invited him to continue speaking.

'I wasn't trying to take over. You seem to have formed an opinion that I'm—'

'Formed an opinion?' Penny stopped him right there. 'I'm actually a bit busy in my life right now. I haven't had time to think, let alone form an opinion of you.'

His lips twitched almost into a smile at her not-too-subtle putdown. 'Oh, but I think that you have,' Ethan said, and there and then he took the gloves off. He'd tried niceness, he'd tried politeness, he'd accepted that the situation might be a little difficult for her, but at the end of the day Penny needed to get over it and accept that he had been given the job. 'Do you know what, Penny? I'm starting to form an opinion of you, and your behaviour this afternoon is leading me to think it might be the right one.'

'Whatever!' Penny hadn't got this far in her career on charm. To do her job you needed to be tough and she certainly wasn't there to make friends. 'You carry right on forming your opinion of me and, while you do, I'll get back to my patients.' Penny stood. 'Or is there anything else you want to discuss?'

'Nothing that won't keep.'

She brushed past him and he was terribly tempted to catch her as she walked past, to turn her round and just have the row that was so clearly needed. Perhaps it was wiser to just let it go, Ethan thought, letting out a rare angry breath as he heard her heels clip down the corridor, but he turned at the sound of Lisa's voice. 'There he is.'

'Kate?' Ethan smiled when he saw that Lisa was with his sister, wondered, albeit briefly, what on earth she was doing at his workplace, and then properly read her face. 'One of the kids...'

'The kids are fine, Ethan.' She took a breath and he knew what was coming. 'It's Phil—we need to get to the hospital.' And still his brain tried to process things kindly. He waited for her to smile, to hold up crossed fingers and to say 'this is it,' that a heart had been found for their cousin, but she just looked at him. 'Carl's watching the kids. We need to hurry and get there.'

No, it would seem that Phil wasn't going to get that heart.

Ethan was glad that Kate hadn't told him by phone, realised that had he not stopped to talk to Penny he could have been sitting in his car, stuck on the packed Beach Road and finding out that Phil was about to die.

'I'll meet you there.' He was already heading to his office to grab his car keys but Kate shook her head. She knew how close Ethan and Phil were.

'I'll drive.'

It was just as well that she did, because the rush-hour traffic didn't care that there was somewhere they

needed to be. Ethan could feel his temper building
as they inched towards the hospital, could sense the
mounting urgency, especially when his mother called
to see how far away they were.

'A couple of minutes,' Ethan said.

'Get here,' came his mother's response.

They were pulling into Melbourne Central and again
Ethan was very glad that Kate had been driving. He was
grateful that there was no competition in the grief stakes
between him and his twin—she knew that he and Phil
were like brothers. Kate dropped him off at the main
entrance and then went to find a place to park the car
as Ethan ran through the hospital building, desperate
to get to his cousin in time, still holding a small flame
of hope that something could yet be done.

It was extinguished even before he got to Phil's room.

Because standing outside was Phil's ex-wife, Gina,
and unless he was dying she'd never be there otherwise.
She'd be sitting outside in the canteen as she usually
did when she brought Justin in to visit. It had been a
wretched divorce and Phil's parents hadn't exactly been
kind in their summing up of Gina—and not just behind
her back. There had been some terrible arguments too.

'Gina,' he said, but she just flashed him a look that
said he was a part of the Lewis family and could he
please just stay back.

'I'm here for Justin,' Gina said, and Ethan nodded
and went in the room. His eyes didn't first go to Phil
but to Justin. Ethan could see the bewilderment and fear
on the little boy's face as Vera and Jack, Phil's parents,
told him to be brave. Ethan felt his head tighten, wanted

to tell them to stop, but then his eyes moved to the bed and to his cousin and there wasn't even time to say to Phil all he wanted to.

It was all over by the time Kate arrived.

CHAPTER THREE

PENNY PARKED HER car and took a couple of moments to
sort out her make-up and hair. She wondered, not for
the first time, how she was going to get through this.
It was eight a.m. and she had just come from having a
blood test and vaginal ultrasound. If the results were
as expected, she would be starting her injections this
evening.

She collected her handbag and the little cool bag
holding the medication and told herself that lots of
women worked while they went through this.

And she told herself something else, something she
had decided last night—at the very first opportunity she
would apologise properly to Ethan. Penny had come up
with a plan. She wouldn't tell him everything, just explain to him that she was on some medication and that
yesterday she hadn't felt very well. If he probed, she
might hint that it was a feminine issue.

Her lips twitched into a smile as she pictured Ethan's
reaction—that would soon silence him.

Walking towards Emergency, Penny saw a dark blue
car pull up in the entrance bay, where the ambulances
did, and she watched as a security guard walked to-

wards it to warn the occupants that they couldn't park there.

Except the woman wasn't parking her car.

Instead, she was dropping Ethan Lewis off.

Penny tried not to look as they shared a brief embrace and then a thoroughly seedy-looking Ethan climbed out. He was unshaven and unkempt, dressed in yesterday's rumpled scrubs. She tried to turn her attention away from him, but her gaze went straight to the car he had just come from. And it was then that Penny felt it— the red-hot poker that jabbed into her stomach as she glanced at the woman, a red-hot poker that temporarily nudged aside her loudly ticking biological clock. And at six minutes past eight and a few months later than most women at Peninsula Hospital, Penny realised that Ethan Lewis really was an incredibly sexy man and it wasn't a hot flash that was causing her to blush as they walked into the department together.

'Ethan.' She tried to keep to the script she had planned. 'I was wondering if I could speak to you about yesterday. I realise that I—'

'Just leave it.' He completely dismissed her, so much so that he strode ahead of her and into the male changing rooms.

Charming!

Ethan ignored her all day and Penny decided that she wasn't about to try apologising again.

She took her lunch break in her office, waiting for the IVF nurse to ring, which she did right on time. Penny took a deep breath as she found out that, as expected, she was to start her injections that evening, which meant she needed to call Jasmine.

'I'm on till six,' Penny said. 'I don't think I'll be able to get away early.'

'Penny, when do you ever get away early? It's not a problem, I'll come and give it to you at work, but Jed won't be home so I'll have to bring Simon in.'

Penny grimaced. She did not want to make a fool of herself in front of her nephew as it would terrify him. Simon, like his mother, was very sensitive. Still, there was no choice.

There really wasn't time to worry about her upcoming jab. The department was busy enough to keep her mind off it and she smiled when she saw her next patient, an eight-week-old named Daniel.

'He's had a bit of a cold,' Laura, the mother, explained. 'I took him to my doctor yesterday and he said that he didn't have a temperature and his chest sounded fine. I've been putting drops up his nose to help with feeding,' Laura continued. 'But this afternoon I came in from putting out the washing and went to check on him and he was pale, really pale, and he'd been sick. I know he's fine now...'

He seemed fine and Penny examined Daniel thoroughly, but apart from a cold and a low-grade temperature there was nothing remarkable to find.

'Has he been coughing?'

'A bit,' Laura said, as Penny listened carefully to his chest, but apart from a couple of crackles it was clear.

Still, Penny was concerned and it did sound as if he

might have had an apnoeic episode so she decided to ring the paediatricians, who were very busy on the ward.

'They're going to be a while,' Penny explained to the mum. 'I'm going to take some bloods and do some swabs, so hopefully we'll have some results back by the time they get down here. And I'll order a chest X-ray.'

To show that she wasn't, in fact, too up herself to value Ethan's opinion, late in the afternoon when she was concerned about the baby and the paediatricians weren't anywhere around, instead of speaking with Mr Dean, Penny decided that she would ask Ethan.

He barely looked up from the form he was filling out when Penny asked if she could have a word.

'Sure.'

'I've got an eight-week-old I'm concerned about.' He glanced up. 'Mum found him very pale in his cot after his nap and he'd vomited, but he picked up well. He's had a cold, struggling to feed, he's a bit sniffly, just...' She moved her hand to show she was wavering. 'His chest is clear, and he's got a small cough, which is un-remarkable. I've done some swabs and some bloods.'

'What did paeds say?' Ethan asked.

'They'll come down when they can, but they're busy and they're going to be ages,' Penny said. 'Mum just wants to take him home now that he's had the tests and wait to get the results, but I'm not sure.'

Ethan came and though he had been scowling at Penny, he was lovely with the mum. He carefully checked the infant, who was bright and alert and just hungry. Penny put some saline drops in his nose and they watched as the baby latched on and started to feed

happily, but just as Ethan was about to go, Daniel splut-
tered and broke into a coughing fit. As he came off the
breast Ethan took him and held him and Penny watched,
the diagnosis becoming more and more evident as he
broke into a prolonged paroxysmal cough and then
struggled to inhale and then cough again. Ethan was
holding him up and tapping his back as Penny turned
on the suction, but thankfully it wasn't needed.

'He wasn't doing that.' Laura was beside herself,
watching her son. 'He's just had a little cough.'

'That might have been what happened this afternoon,' Penny said, 'when you found him in his cot.'
She had to explain to the mother that it would seem her
baby had whooping cough.

'He's not making any noises, though.'

'People, especially babies, don't always, but he's
struggling to get air in during the coughing attack,'
Penny explained. 'It's not evident straight away but he's
moved into the coughing stage now.' She looked at the
baby Ethan was holding—he had stopped coughing
and was again desperate to be fed. 'I'm going to call
the paediatricians…'

'Can I feed him?'

'I'll watch him feed while you go and call Paeds,'
Ethan said to Penny, handing the crying baby back to
his mum. 'Wait one moment before you feed him.' He
stepped out with Penny. 'He's to be transferred. I know
he seems fine at the moment but, given his age, he needs
to be somewhere with PICU.'

'I know.' Penny nodded.

'Can you get Lisa to come in and watch him feed? I'll stay in for now.'

Penny nodded. The coughing episodes were scary at best and someone calm and experienced needed to be in with the mum to help deal with them. 'I've never actually seen whooping cough,' Penny said to Lisa.

'I've had it,' Lisa said. 'Hundred-day cough they call it and I know why. Poor baby and poor mum having to watch him. I'll go and relieve Ethan.'

Penny spoke again to the paediatrician and started the baby on antibiotics, but really there was no treatment that could stop the coughing attacks and, as Ethan had said, given his tender age, he really did need to be somewhere with paediatric intensive care facilities in case he suddenly deteriorated.

'They're going to come down and see him just as soon as they can,' Penny said when Ethan came out. 'I'll go and let mum know.'

'She's in for a tough time,' Ethan said. 'Are you immunised?'

'All up to date,' Penny said, because though she was terrified of injections, before embarking on IVF she had *made* herself get all her immunisations up to date and poor Jasmine had been the one who'd had to do them. Still, it was worth it, Penny realised, for days such as this.

'Right.' Ethan glanced at his watch. 'I'm going home.'

'See you tomorrow,' Penny said, but Ethan shook his head.

'I'm on days off now.'

'Enjoy them.'

He didn't answer. In fact, since her attempt to apologise, unless it was about a patient, Ethan had said nothing at all to her and she felt like poking her tongue out at his back as he and his bad mood walked off together.

Maybe it was just as well he was on days off. Hopefully by the time he was back they could put yesterday's incident behind them and start again.

And she'd hopefully be finished with the hot flashes by then.

As predicted, there wasn't a hope of her getting away at six, but when it neared, Penny told Lisa she was taking a short break and, seeing Jasmine walking down the corridor with Simon in his stroller, the moment she had been silently dreading all day was finally here.

'I don't want Simon seeing me upset.' Penny was starting to panic. 'It could make him as terrified of needles as I am.'

'There'll be someone in the staffroom who can watch him for five minutes,' Jasmine said. 'You go on and get everything ready and I'll come in.' They both knew it wasn't a question of Penny being brave because her nephew was there—it was the one thing, apart from her fertility, that Penny couldn't control, and her response to injections was varied and unpredictable.

'Vanessa's watching him,' Jasmine said when she came into the office a few minutes later.

'I don't know if I can do this again,' Penny said. Her hand was shaking as she checked the doses the IVF nurse had given her.

'In a couple of moments you'll be one evening down.'

'With God knows how many more to go,' Penny said. She took a deep breath and undid her skirt. 'Just do it.'

She closed her eyes but could not stop shaking as Jasmine walked over. She had hoped so much that things would be different this time, but she was crying again, just as she had that morning at her blood test, and she was very glad that Simon wasn't there to see his aunt make an absolute fool of herself.

'It's done.' Jasmine massaged in the medication. 'You're done for the day.'

'It's ridiculous,' Penny whimpered. 'I've given so many injections today, I've taken blood from an eight-week-old…'

'Don't worry about it,' Jasmine said. 'You're actually better than you used to be.'

'Really?'

'A bit,' Jasmine lied. 'How are the hot flashes?'

'Only two today.'

'How's Ethan been?' Jasmine asked as Penny tucked herself in.

'Horrible,' Penny said. 'He's still sulking about yesterday. I tried to apologise but he wasn't having any of it. There's not much more that I can do.'

But even if she shrugged it off to her sister, Penny was rattled because, yes, she had wanted to put it behind them, had wanted to start again, and, no, she didn't want to but she felt the tiniest bit attracted to him.

CHAPTER FOUR

ETHAN HAD LONG known that his cousin might die but on the eve of the funeral he couldn't really acknowledge that Phil had.

Kate kept ringing and asking him to come over, except he didn't want to talk about it, not even with those closest to him. Ethan had been dreading the funeral, had found himself starting to tear up when he'd asked Gordon to cover for him for the day, though he had kept the details minimal. Then Gordon rang to tell Ethan that he was up in Maternity as his wife, Hilary, had gone into early labour so he wouldn't be able to cover Ethan's shift after all.

'Someone else should be able to cover you, though.'

'It's fine, Gordon,' Ethan said. 'I'll sort something out, you just do what you have to.' He wished him good luck and then looked at the roster. There were several doctors he could change with, he and Penny were on till six today, but tomorrow…

As she walked past he called over to her. Penny was perhaps not his first choice to ask, but it was a pretty straight swap.

'Can I ask a favour?'

Please, don't, Penny thought as she saw him look-ing at the roster because, in her impossible schedule, for the next couple of weeks there really was no room for manoeuvre, not that Ethan would know that.

'Tomorrow I'm on from nine till six and you're twelve till nine—is there any chance we can swap?' She just blinked. 'Though I might not get in till one.'

'I can't swap tomorrow, Ethan.' She couldn't. Not only did she have an ultrasound and blood test booked for tomorrow, she had a meeting with the specialist at nine.

'I've got to attend a funeral,' Ethan pushed, but didn't go into detail, didn't tell her that this was personal, he simply couldn't. 'Gordon was supposed to be covering for me, but his wife has gone into labour—premature labour,' he added.

Penny hesitated; she knew she couldn't say no.

Except she couldn't say yes either, she simply could not miss her blood test—it was as essential as that.

She'd ring the IVF nurse, Penny decided, see if she could fiddle around her appointment, but for now, till she had, she'd have to stand firm.

'Is there anybody else you can ask?'

'A few.'

'Well, see if they can help and if not, let me know.'

If she occasionally smiled, Ethan thought, she would actually be exceptionally attractive, but even then, with her terse attitude and unfeeling ways, Penny could never be considered beautiful. A black smile spread across his lips. She really was the limit and instead of leaving it there, Ethan found that he couldn't. 'What is your problem, Penny?'

'Problem?' Penny frowned. 'I don't have a problem. I simply can't come in early tomorrow, that's all.'

'It was the same when I asked you to come in for a few hours the other day.'

'So that you could go to a football match.' Penny stared back coolly, looking into his angry eyes and surprisingly tempted to tell him that she had a vaginal ultrasound and a blood test booked for ten past eight tomorrow, just so that she could watch him squirm. 'I'm sorry, Ethan, I have things on. I'm not able to simply change my schedule at a moment's notice. If you can check with the others…'

'Like it or not,' Ethan said, 'there has to be a senior staff member on at all times, and that sometimes means making last-minute changes to the roster.'

'I'm aware of that,' Penny responded.

'Yet you don't…' He watched two spots of colour rising on her cheeks, and then she turned abruptly to go, but Ethan refused to leave it there. 'You're going to have to be more flexible.'

Her back was to him and he watched as Penny stilled, her shoulders stiffened and she slowly turned around. 'Excuse me?'

'In the coming days you're going to have to be more flexible—Gordon will need some time after all.'

'If Gordon's wife having a baby leaves us short-staffed then it might be prudent to look at getting a locum because—and I am warning you now—I am not going to be dropping everything and coming into work and leaving here late and changing shifts at the last moment to accommodate Gordon, his wife and their baby.'

Penny was angry now and with good reason—part of her mandatory counselling before she'd commenced IVF had addressed problems such as this. Timing was important. These weeks were incredibly intense and to keep it from becoming a staffroom topic of conversation Penny had worked out her appointments very carefully around her work schedule. And now Hilary had gone into labour and she was supposed to juggle everything.

Well, Penny was doing this for *her* baby.

'You're such a team player,' Ethan said.

'Oh, but I'm not,' Penny responded. 'Ask anyone.'

'I don't need to ask, I'd say it's already common knowledge.' It was—Penny was the ice queen. He'd heard it from many and had seen it for himself, but she hadn't finished yet, pulling Ethan up on a very pertinent point.

'You're talking as if Hilary is about to deliver a micro-prem when, in fact, she's actually thirty-five weeks' gestation.' Ethan at that point actually had to suppress a smile, because she had well and truly caught him out. When he'd said premature labour he had been appealing or rather searching for the softer side to Penny, but he was fast realising that she simply didn't have one. 'I don't respond to bells and whistles, Ethan. Give me a real drama and I'll deal with it accordingly.' She walked off and Ethan watched.

She was absolutely immaculate. Her straight blonde hair was tied low at the back of her neck. Her sheer cream blouse looked as if it had come straight off a mannequin at an expensive boutique and her charcoal-grey skirt was perfectly cut to show a very trim figure. If she had been just a few inches taller she could be walking down a runway instead of the corridor of the emergency department.

'What do you respond to, Penny?' The words were out of Ethan's mouth before his brain had even processed them, and how he wished, the moment they were uttered, that he could take them back.

He was more than aware of the not-so-slight sexual undertone to them, and Ethan half expected her to turn on her low heels and march back to give him a sharp piece of her mind, or perhaps to head straight to Mr Dean's office, but what happened next came as a complete surprise.

Ethan watched as Penny threw her head back and laughed and then glanced over her shoulder at him. He saw not the glitter of ice in those cold blue eyes but something far more fetching. And her mouth was parted in a slightly mocking yet somehow mischievous smile as she answered him. 'That's for me to know!'

Ethan found himself smiling back, a proper smile this time. He almost called out that he was looking forward to finding out but then he checked himself, the smile fading, and he turned back to the roster he had been viewing before Penny had come along, and wondered what the hell had just happened. She had been completely immutable with the roster, thoroughly unfriendly and yet somehow it had ended in a smile.

A flirtatious one at that.

Ethan had no trouble with flirting—he was an expert

at it, in fact. He had just never expected to find himself going there with Penny, but more to the point, Ethan thought darkly, he still didn't have anyone to cover him for the funeral.

'Not now!' Penny said a few moments later when Jasmine knocked on her office door as she came in to start her late shift. Penny was seriously rattled by the small confrontation she'd had with Ethan and wanted a few moments alone to process things and to ring the IVF nurse to see if she could possibly swap. More unsettling than that, though, was the flutter in her throat and the blush on her cheeks at her response to him. Her face still burnt red even as she tried to put off her sister from coming in, but Jasmine wanted a quick word.

'It won't take a second—I'm just letting you know that Mum rang this morning from a satellite phone.'

'Where is she?' Penny smiled and it was genuine. She was thrilled to hear from her mum.

'Heading for Mykonos,' Jasmine said, and Penny groaned her envy.

'I'm sure that I don't need to ask if she's having a good time.'

'Completely loving it,' Jasmine said. 'She said that she should've done this years ago and...don't fall off your chair, but I think she might have met someone.'

'You mean a man?' Penny blinked in surprise. 'I don't know what to say...I don't know what to think.'

'I know.' Jasmine smiled. 'I can't imagine Mum with anyone.'

Louise Masters had been single since the day her

husband had left. A very volatile marriage had made
Louise swear off men and instead she had focused heav-
ily on her career and had done her best to instil the
same very independent, somewhat bitter values into
her daughters.

'Anyway,' Jasmine continued, 'we didn't talk for
long. I've no idea how much it would have cost her to
call. She just wanted to send her love and to find out
how you were getting on. I told her that you were doing
fine.' Jasmine hesitated. She'd heard a few whispers,
knew that Penny was putting noses out of joint everywhere, which wasn't unusual. Penny was known for
being tough, it was just a lot more concentrated at the
moment. '*Are* you doing fine, though?'

'Not really,' Penny admitted. 'Actually, Jasmine, I
think you're right, I might have to let a few people at
work know. It's proving impossible. I've just had an
argument with Ethan—he needs me to come in early
tomorrow so that he can go to a funeral. God.' Penny
buried her face in her hands. 'Imagine saying no to
that—it's a funeral!'

'Penny, it was a football match a couple of weeks
ago that Ethan asked you to cover him for.' Jasmine
was indignant on her sister's behalf. 'And Mr Dean has
a corporate golf day on Thursday and Rex is getting a
divorce. The fact is that this place needs more doctors,
but they still won't employ another one.'

'A funeral, though.' Penny groaned.

'Penny, you go to more funerals than anyone I know.'
It was true. Of course they couldn't attend the funeral of
every patient who died, but Penny's black outfits were

taken for a trip to the dry cleaner's more than most. 'You *have* to keep the next few weeks clear.' Jasmine was firm. She knew how hard this was for Penny and just how hard her sister worked. 'And I do think you should let your colleagues know. Not everyone, but if you told Lisa…'

'How can Lisa help with the doctors' roster?'

'Well, just tell Ethan or Mr Dean…' Her voice trailed off.

'It's hopeless, isn't it?' Mr Dean wasn't going to be exactly thrilled to find out that his senior registrar was trying to get pregnant—it was the reason he had hesitated to promote her a few years ago—of that Penny was sure.

'Penny, you can't come in early tomorrow. You can't miss a blood test, it determines the whole day's treatment.'

'I know. I just really thought I could handle working and doing this. I thought that it might be easier the second time around, that I'd know more what to expect, that I'd at least be used to the needles.'

'Penny.' Jasmine sat on the edge of her sister's desk. 'I think you are going to have to face the fact that you are never going to get over your fear of needles.'

'I'm an emergency registrar!'

'With one weakness.' Jasmine gave a sympathetic smile. 'It's just a horrible weakness to have when you're going through IVF.'

'I made a right fool of myself this morning at my blood test.' Penny shuddered at the memory. 'It took two of them, one to hold me and one to take the blood. I was crying and carrying on like a two-year-old!'

'Then it's just as well that you're not having your IVF treatment here.'

Penny blanched at the very thought of that happening. Even if Peninsula Hospital offered IVF, which they didn't, Penny wouldn't take it. Oh, for the convenience, it would be wonderful to just pop upstairs for the endless blood tests, injections and scans that were part of the tumultuous ride she was on, but not so convenient would be to have your colleagues see you a shivering, terrified mess. She was bad enough at the best of times, but right now, tired and with her hormones all over the place, it was the worst of times.

'Do you have to work?' Jasmine asked gently.

'I took time off last time,' Penny said. 'And I had all that time off when Mum came out of hospital. I'd actually like to have some annual leave up my sleeve if I ever do get pregnant.'

'You will.' Jasmine slipped off the desk and gave her sister a hug, but it wasn't returned. Penny wasn't particularly touchy-feely. 'You're going to get your baby.'

'Easy for you to say.' Penny tried to keep the bitterness out of her voice. She loved Simon very much, but he had been an accident. Just one mistake had seen Jasmine pregnant. Yes, Jasmine had had a terrible time with a horrible husband and later as a single mum before she'd married Jed. But now, just a few months into her marriage, she was pregnant, although she hadn't told Penny.

Penny felt her sister's arms around her tense shoulders and it was time to face the white elephant in the room before it came between them.

'When are you going to tell me, Jasmine?' There was a long stretch of silence. 'You're pregnant, aren't you?'

'Penny, I...'

Penny heard the discomfort in her sister's voice and forced a smile before turning her face back to Jasmine. 'How many weeks?'

'Fourteen.' Jasmine flushed.

'Have you told Mum?'

'Not yet. We haven't said anything to anyone yet. I wanted to tell you first but I just didn't know how.' Jasmine's eyes were same blue as her sister's and they filled with tears. 'You were so upset when your last IVF attempt failed and then you've been building up for this one. I know how hard it is for you right now, and to find out my news right in the middle of an IVF treatment cycle, well, I know...'

Except Jasmine didn't know, Penny thought, though at least she tried to understand.

Penny took a deep breath. 'Even if it isn't happening easily for me, it doesn't mean that I can't be pleased for you.'

'You're sure?'

'Of course I am. I know I wasn't the best sister and aunt to Simon at first, but I've told you why. I was jealous when you were pregnant with Simon, but it's different now—I'm honestly pleased for you and Jed.' Penny gave a wry smile. 'And, of course, terribly, terribly jealous.'

'I know.' Jasmine smiled back. 'I'm so glad that we can be more honest with each other now.'

'We can be,' Penny said. 'Which means you won't be offended if I tell you I really need five minutes alone right now.'

'Sure.'

Penny waited till the door was closed and then put her head back in her hands.

Fourteen weeks.

She just sat there, a hormonal jumble of conflict.

She was pleased for her sister.

No, she wasn't!

She was jealous, jealous, jealous, and now she felt guilty for feeling so jealous, yet she was pleased for her sister too.

Oh, hell!

Penny really had forgotten just how awful the treatment made her feel. It was far worse than feeling pre-menstrual. The last time had been bad enough but she had gone through it at home, concentrating solely on her appointments.

Trying to work through it was unbearable.

And then she remembered her confrontation with Ethan—the reason she had come to the office in the first place—and reached for her phone and rang the IVF nurse to explain her problem. 'I'm booked in for ten past eight,' Penny said. 'I was wondering if I could come in on the early round. And also if, instead of my appointment, I could have a phone consultation with the specialist.' There was a bit of a tart pause, which Penny took as a warning. You had to be fully on board, she had been told this on many occasions, and she tried so hard to be.

Except she was also expected to be fully on board at work.

'There's a spot at six-twenty a.m.,' the nurse said, and an already exhausted Penny took it. She headed out of the office and back through to the department to catch up with Ethan and to show him what a *team player* she could be, but he was stuck with a baby who had suspicious injuries and later interviewing the parents. Oh, well, Penny thought, it would keep for later. He might already have someone else. Of course, Penny got caught up with work of her own and at the end of a very long shift, with a needle to look forward to, Penny wasn't in the happiest of moods when, just to cap it all off, Gordon came into the department with a huge smile on his face.

'It's a boy!'

'How lovely!' Penny offered her congratulations and Ethan came over and did the same, and they headed over to the nurses' station and stood while Gordon sat showing the many, many photos he had taken on his phone of his gorgeous new son.

'He's doing really well,' Gordon enthused. 'Though they will probably keep him in the nursery for a few days, given that he's a bit small, but we should get him home soon. Hilary's a paediatrician after all.' He gave a tired yawn. 'It's been a long day—do you want to join me in celebrating? Hilary is catching up on some sleep. I thought we could go and have a drink before I head back up there.'

'I'd love to,' Penny said as her phone alarm buzzed in her pocket to remind her that it was injection time. 'But I'm afraid that I can't right now.' She didn't dash straight off, though, and looked at a couple more photos. 'How is Hilary doing?'

'Really well,' Gordon said. 'She's a bit disappointed, of course, but she'll soon come round.'

'Disappointed?' Penny looked at an image of the tiny but, oh, so healthy baby.

'She really wanted a girl this time. Which I guess is understandable after three sons.'

'Didn't you find out what you were having?' Ethan asked Gordon, but Penny wasn't really listening. She could feel the incessant buzz from a phone in her pocket and she needed to go.

'Congratulations again!' Penny said to Gordon. 'But now you'll have to excuse me. Tell Hilary that I shall come up and visit her soon.'

A bit disappointed.

The words buzzed in Penny's ears as she walked around her office. She was being hypersensitive, Penny told herself. It was just that it seemed so easy for everyone else at the moment. Maybe if she had three sons she'd be disappointed too at not getting a girl, except she couldn't imagine it. Worse, she couldn't imagine having three babies—it was hard enough trying to get one.

And then she thought about the baby that Ethan had been looking after that afternoon and all the social workers and police that had been involved, and it just didn't seem fair that some people who had babies didn't even seem to want them.

'Hi, there.' Jasmine was waiting for Penny in her office. She had everything set up for the tiny injection that really should only take a minute, except Penny needed to be talked down from the ceiling each and every time. Penny hated the weakness. She'd had hypnosis and even counselling in a bid to overcome it, not that it changed a single thing. Every needle that went into her had her shaking with fear and this evening was no exception. If anything, this evening she was worse.

'I can't do this today,' Penny said as she closed the office door and let out a shaky breath. 'I'm honestly not just saying it this time, Jasmine. I'm really not up to it.'

'Penny.' Jasmine was very patient; she was more than used to this. 'You know that you can't miss one injection.'

'I don't think I want to do the treatment anymore.' Penny just said it. 'I can't keep going on like this. I'm snapping at everyone, I'm in tears all the time.'

'The same as you were last time,' Jasmine said.

'I was going to ring in sick tomorrow, or ask Mr Dean if I could take annual leave, but now with Gordon's wife having the baby...' Penny closed her eyes at the impossibility of it all. 'I don't want the injection.'

'You're *going* to finish this course.'

'And what if it doesn't work?'

'Then you'll have a proper break before you put yourself through this again,' Jasmine said firmly. 'It's no wonder that you're teary and exhausted. Let's just get this needle over and done with and then we'll talk.'

And she would have, except there was a sharp knock on Penny's door.

'Penny?' There was no mistaking Ethan's low voice, but Penny didn't answer. She'd forgotten to lock it and when he knocked again, it was so impatient that Penny wouldn't put it past him to simply walk in.

'What?' Penny asked angrily when she opened the door just a fraction.

'I was wondering if you could change your mind and come out for a drink with Gordon and I. There is no one else around to ask and Rex needs to stay here.'

'I can't,' Penny said. 'I've got the case review to prepare for.'

'One drink,' Ethan said. Surely she could manage one quick drink. 'Come on, Penny, I'm asking for some help here. I'm really not in the mood to go out celebrating tonight and I don't know how to do the baby talk thing.'

'Oh, and because I'm a woman, I do?'

'God, you just don't let up, do you?' Ethan snapped. 'I was just asking for some backup. It would be nice to do the right thing by the guy, the sociable thing. His wife's just had a baby, it's right to take him out.'

'It's right that the consultant takes him out!' Penny retorted sharply. 'I'm not a consultant, which means I get to go home and sign off from this place occasionally, and I'm signing off now. Good night, Ethan!'

Penny closed the door on him and promptly burst into tears. And because Jasmine knew her well, or rather better than anyone else knew Penny, she didn't try to comfort her at first. Instead, she undid her sister's skirt as Penny stood there and sobbed. Jasmine looked at her bruised stomach and, finding a suitable spot, swabbed her skin and then stuck in the needle. Penny continued to sob and then, having disposed of the needle, Jasmine went over and gave her sister a hug.

'It's done.'

'It's not just that,' Penny said.

'I know.'

'I made a right fool of myself just then. Ethan thinks that I'm jealous because I didn't get the job. I know that's what he's been thinking and I've just gone and proved it to him.'

'You're not jealous, though, Penny.' Jasmine tried to get her sister to see reason. 'He doesn't know what's going on. You turned down the job so that you could concentrate on your IVF.'

'No! I turned down the consultant's position so that I could have a baby.' Penny gulped. 'But the way things are going, I don't think that I'm going to get one.'

CHAPTER FIVE

ETHAN PAID THE taxi and let himself into his apartment.

A celebratory drink on an empty stomach, the way he was feeling right now, possibly hadn't been the best idea and it hadn't been just the one.

Given it had only been him with Gordon, he hadn't exactly been able to get up and leave after one, so instead he'd had to sit there and listen as Gordon had gone into spectacular detail about his day, or rather his wife's day.

Ethan had been hoping that now that the baby had been born, Gordon would come back to work.

He'd had no idea how it all worked.

As it turned out, Gordon was now on paternity leave and would be juggling toddler twins and a six-year-old's school run.

'Not a problem,' he had said to Gordon.

It was, though, a huge one.

Ethan had gone through everyone to cover for him in the morning and the only person who might possibly have been able to help had an *appointment*.

Well, Ethan had his cousin's funeral to attend.

He'd been dreading it, but he would far rather be there than not.

He would love to just ring in sick tomorrow, to let someone else sort it out, to just sign off on the place, as Penny had tonight.

Still, he had expected more from her.

She was senior too.

Ethan loaded some toast into the toaster and some tinned spaghetti into the microwave and tried not to think about Justin and how he'd be feeling tonight. Though, he consoled himself, Gina would surely be handling things better than his own mother had, given they had broken up a couple of years ago.

He couldn't not be there tomorrow and not just for appearances' sake—Ethan wanted to see for himself that Justin was okay.

Ethan thought about Phil and the black game they'd played and, sorry, mate, he said to his cousin, because even if he didn't fancy Penny, he was going to have to play the sympathy card.

He was scrolling through his phone to find her number when it rang.

'Ethan?' He didn't answer her straight away; instead, he frowned at the sound of her voice. 'It's Penny. Penny Masters from work.'

'Hi, Penny.'

'I'm sorry to call you so late. I meant to tell you before I left for home—it just slipped my mind. I changed my appointment. I can get into work by nine tomorrow, if you still need me to.'

'I do.' The words just jumped out of him. 'Thank

you.' Ethan closed his eyes in relief and it took a second to realise that she was still talking.

'I'd also like to apologise for my words before.' She sounded very prim and formal. 'I really wasn't in a position to go out tonight, but I didn't explain myself very well.'

Penny had explained things perfectly, Ethan thought privately, but he was so relieved that he would be able to get the funeral tomorrow that he let go the chance for a little barb, and instead he was nice. 'I don't blame you in the least for not wanting to come out tonight.' Relief, mixed with just a little bit too much champagne, had him speaking honestly. 'I really don't think that I'm going to be able to look Hilary in the eye when I go and visit her.'

'Too much detail?' He *heard* her smile.

'Far, far too much.'

'That's Gordon for you. He's very...' Penny really didn't know how to describe him.

'In tune?' Ethan suggested.

'Something like that.'

'I felt as if I was listening to him describe *his* labour,' Ethan said, and was rewarded by the sound of her laugh. 'Hold on a second.' The microwave was pinging and he pressed Stop on the microwave rather than ending the call, not that he thought about it. 'Look, thanks a lot for tomorrow. I hope it wasn't too much trouble.'

'It was!' Penny said, which had him frowning but sort of smiling too. 'Don't rush back.'

'I'll be back by one.' Ethan really didn't want to stand around chatting and drinking and talking about Phil in the past tense. He would be glad of the chance to slip away and just bury himself in work.

'Whose funeral is it?' Penny asked, and not gently, assuming, because he was fine to dash off from the funeral by one, that it was a patient from work and her mind was sort of scanning the admissions from the previous week as to who it might be, when his voice broke in.

'My cousin's.'

Penny closed her eyes, guilty and horrified too, because she'd been so upset tonight she had almost forgotten to ring him. 'You should have told me that! Ethan, I assumed it was a patient. You should have told me that it was personal.'

'I was just about to call you and do that,' Ethan admitted.

'Is that why you've been so...?' Penny's voice trailed off.

'That's fine, coming from you,' Ethan said, but it actually came out rather nicely and Penny found herself smiling into the phone as he continued. 'Yes, it's been a tough few days.'

'How old?'

'My age,' Ethan said. 'Thirty-six.'

'Was it expected?'

'Sort of,' Ethan said, and felt that sting at the back of his nose. 'Sort of not. He was on the waiting list for a heart transplant.'

There was silence for a moment. 'Was he the one you were going to go to the football with?' For the first time he heard her sound tentative.

'Penny...'

'Oh, God!' She was a mass of manufactured hormones, not that he knew, and this news came at the end
of a very upsetting day. 'He missed the football match
because of me.'

'It wasn't something at the top of his bucket list.'
Ethan actually found himself smiling as he recalled
the conversation he'd had with Phil when he'd told him
that he couldn't get the time off, the one about the sympathy vote.

And, no, he didn't fancy Penny, he'd just had a bit
too much to drink, he must have, because he was telling
her that they'd often gone to watch football. 'He went
anyway—with Justin, his son.' And he told Penny about
the illness that had ravaged his cousin. 'He got a virus
a couple of years ago.' And he could understand a bit
better why the patients liked her, because she was very
matter-of-fact and didn't gush out her sympathies, just
asked pertinent questions and then asked how his son
and wife were doing.

'Ex-wife,' Ethan said, and he found himself mus-
ing—only he was doing it out loud and to Penny. 'They
broke up before he got ill, she had an affair and it was
all just a mess. It must be hell for her too and she's coming tomorrow. She's bringing Justin.'

'How old is he?'

'Six,' Ethan said.

She asked how his aunt and uncle were.

'Not great,' he admitted. 'They're worried that they
won't get to see Justin so much anymore. It's just a
mess all round.'

And he told Penny the hell of watching someone so vital and full of life gradually getting weaker. How he hated that he had only just made it to the hospital in time. He let out more than he had to Kate, to anyone, and during that conversation Penny found out that it had been his sister who had dropped him off at work, but there was no room for relief or dousing of red-hot pokers, or anything really, as she could hear the heartbreak in his voice.

'Thirty-six,' Ethan repeated, and was met by silence. He would never have known that her silence was because of tears. 'So, while I suppose we were expecting it, it still came as a shock.' He didn't really know how better to explain it. 'And it will be a shock for Justin too.'

'Poor kid,' Penny said.

'Anyway, thanks for swapping.'

He hung up the phone, poured his spaghetti on the toast and then frowned because it was cold. He'd surely only been on the phone for a moment and so back into the microwave it went.

They'd actually been talking for a full twenty minutes.

At five a.m. Penny stood, bleary-eyed, under the shower, trying to wake up. She got out and then dried her hair. At least she didn't have to worry about make-up yet, given that she would be crying it all off very soon.

And normally the terribly efficient Penny didn't have to worry about what to wear because her work wardrobe was on a fourteen-day rotation, except it wasn't so simple at the moment because her arms were bruised from all the blood tests and so her sleeveless grey top wasn't an option.

Even the simplest thing seemed complicated this morning.

A sheer neutral jumper worked well with her black skirt, except it meant that she had to change her underwear because it showed her black bra, and with all her appointments and tests the usually meticulous Penny's laundry wasn't up to date. Racing the clock, she grabbed coral silk underwear that she'd never usually consider wearing for work and then raced downstairs, so rushed and tired that by mistake she added orange juice instead of milk to her coffee and had to make her drink all over again.

Still, Penny thought, she was glad to have been able to help out Ethan, and there was just a flutter of something unfamiliar stirring. Penny hadn't fancied anyone for ages. Not since she and Vince had spilt up. Well, that wasn't strictly true—she'd had a slight crush on someone a while ago, but she certainly wasn't about to go there, even in her thoughts. She drove for what felt like ages until at last, at a quarter to seven, she lay with her knees up, loathing it despite being used to it, as she underwent the internal scan to find out how her ovaries were behaving. And if that wasn't bad enough, afterwards she headed for her blood test.

'Morning, Penny!'

They all knew her well.

Penny was determined not to make the scene she had yesterday. She was there willingly after all. But her resolve wavered as she sat on the seat and one of the nurses held her head as she cried while the other strapped down her arm—it was just an exercise in humiliation really.

'I'm not doing this again,' Penny said as she felt the needle go into her already-bruised vein.

But she'd said that the last time, yet here she was again, locked in the exhausting world of IVF.

Penny sorted out her make-up in the hospital car park and was, in fact, in the department well before nine.

'Morning, Penny.' Mr Dean was especially pleased to see her, because it meant that he could soon go home. 'I hope that you had a good night's sleep—the place is wild.'

Of course it was.

'Where's Penny?' was a frequent cry that she heard throughout the day and Penny didn't really stop for a break, just made do with coffee on the run, but by one o'clock she knew that she had to get something to eat, which she would, just as soon as Mrs Hunt's chest pain was sorted out.

'Cardiology knows that you're here,' Penny explained to her patient. 'They haven't forgotten you. They're just a bit busy up on CCU.' The medication patch wasn't working and Penny was just writing Mrs Hunt up for some morphine when the department was alerted that a severe head injury was on its way in.

'Can you sort out that medication, Vanessa?' Penny asked as she pulled on a fresh gown and gloves and her eye shield. 'Maybe you could give Cardiology another page, just remind them that she's here?' Penny said, because one look at her new patient and Penny knew she wouldn't be back in to see Mrs Hunt for a while.

'Fight at school,' a paramedic said as they lifted the young man over. 'Fell backwards...'

The teen was still in his school uniform and was, she was told, eighteen. Penny shut out the horror and focussed on her patient, feeling the mush of his skull beneath her gloved hands.

'CPR was started immediately and continued at the scene...' Penny listened to the paramedics' handover as she worked. He'd been intubated and they'd got his heart started again, but it wasn't looking good at all. She flashed a torch into his eyes but they were fixed and dilated. Still, he'd been given atropine, a medication that, amongst other things, dilated the pupils, which could account for that.

Hopefully.

'Has anyone seen Penny?' She heard Jasmine's voice.

'Curtain one, Resus,' Penny shouted. 'What?' she asked a moment later when Jasmine popped her head around.

'Nothing.' Jasmine saw the seriousness of the situation and came and helped Lisa with the young man. The trauma team arrived then as well, but despite their best efforts and equipment things were looking seriously grim.

'We'll get him round for a head CT.' The trauma consultant was speaking with Penny and she glanced up as Ethan came in. He was wearing a black suit and had taken off his tie. His face was a touch grey and he looked down at the young man on the resus bed and then at Penny. 'I'm just letting you know that I'm back. I'll get changed.'

'Before you do, could you just check in on curtain three?' Penny said. 'I had to leave her for this.'

Ethan never did get to change. Mrs Hunt's chest pain was increasing.

'Vanessa!' Penny was trying to concentrate on her patient but she could hear a commotion starting across the room. 'Did you give her that morphine?'

'I'm giving it now.'

It was a horrible afternoon.

Once the young patient was being dealt with by Trauma, Penny had an extremely tart word with Vanessa but she was just met with excuses.

'I was trying to get through to Cardiology and then I was waiting for someone to come and check the drug with me, but everyone was in with the trauma or at lunch…'

And Penny said nothing. She didn't have to, her look said it all.

'Two staff members have to check morphine.' Lisa stuck up for her nurse, of course. 'And nurses do have to eat!' Penny bit down on a brittle response, because she'd really love to have made it to lunch too. There was a gnawing of hunger in her stomach but more than that she was annoyed that Mrs Hunt had been in pain for a good fifteen minutes when the medication had been ordered well before that. 'We do our best, Penny,' Lisa said.

It just wasn't good enough for Penny, though she held on to those words.

The police came in and so to did the parents and as the trauma team had taken the young man from CT straight to Theatre, it was Penny who had to speak to them.

'Do you want me to come in with you?' Lisa offered, but Penny shook her head.

'I'll be fine.'

Ethan watched as she walked towards the interview room and thanked God that today it wasn't him about to break terrible news.

'Mr and Mrs Monroe.' Penny introduced herself and sat down. 'I was the doctor on duty when Heath was brought in.'

And she went through everything with them. They didn't need her tears, neither did they need false hope. She told them it was incredibly serious but that their son was in Theatre, and she watched as their lives fell apart. As she walked out of the interview room, Penny wondered if she could really bear to be a mum because the agony on their features, the sobbing that had come from Mrs Monroe was, Penny realised, from a kind of love she didn't yet know.

'How are they?' Ethan asked when she came back to the nurses' station.

'They're just having a nice cup of tea…' Penny bristled and then checked herself. She was aware she was terribly brittle at times. Jasmine had happily told her that on several occasions, but speaking with Heath's parents had been incredibly hard. 'Awful,' she admitted, then looked at his black suit and up into his hazel eyes and she could see they were a little bit bloodshot.

Normally Penny didn't ask questions, she liked to keep everything distanced, but she had seen his eyes shutter when he'd looked at the young patient, remembered the raw pain in his voice last night, and for once she crossed the line.

'How was the funeral?' Penny asked.

'It wasn't a funeral apparently, it was a celebration of life.' He turned back to his notes. 'It was a funeral to me.'

'How was the son?'

'Trying to be brave.' He let out a breath.

He looked beautiful in a suit; in fact, Penny couldn't believe that she'd never noticed until recently that he was a very good-looking man. Still, her mind had been in other places in recent weeks, but it was in an unfamiliar one now, because she wanted to say something more to him, wanted to somehow say the right thing. She just didn't know what.

'I need to get something to eat.' Penny, of course, said the wrong thing, but she was actually feeling sick she was so hungry. 'I'm sorry, Ethan, that sounded...'

'It's fine.' For the first time that day Ethan actually smiled. Penny really was socially awkward, Ethan realised. It just didn't offend him so much today.

'Can I have a word, please, Penny?' She turned at Jasmine's voice, remembered she had been looking for her earlier.

'Away from here.' Penny saw how pale her sister was and even before they had reached her office, Penny couldn't help but ask.

'Is it the baby?'

'No.' Jasmine swallowed before speaking. 'Jed's mum had a stroke this morning.'

'Oh! I'm sorry to hear that. How bad is it?'

'We're not sure yet. Jed's trying to get away from work and then he's going to fly over there.'

'You need to go with him.' Instantly, Penny understood her sister's dilemma—Jed's family were all in Sydney.

'I can't leave you now.' Jasmine's eyes were full of tears.

'Jasmine. Your husband's mum is ill, possibly seriously. How can you not go with him? You know how people had to just drop everything when Mum was sick.'

'You're mid-treatment and I promised you—'

'You made a bigger promise to your husband when you married him.' Penny was incredibly firm. 'I will be fine.' Jasmine gave her a very disbelieving look. After all, she was the one who gave Penny her injections and knew just how bad she was. 'I will be,' Penny insisted.

'You'll stop the treatment,' Jasmine said.

'I won't. I'll ring the clinic now and make an appointment or I'll go to my GP. Jasmine, you know that you have to go with Jed.'

She did.

There really wasn't a choice.

But what Penny didn't tell her was that there was little chance of her getting to the clinic by six and even if she did, tomorrow she was on midday till nine.

'Are you okay?' Ethan frowned as she joined him at the nurses' station.

'I just had some bad news,' Penny said. 'Jed's mother has had a stroke.'

'I'm sorry to hear that.' He saw tears starting to fill her very blue eyes and her nose starting to go red. 'Are you close?'

'No.' Penny shook her head. 'They live in Sydney, Jasmine is on her way there now.'

'I meant close,' Ethan said, as Penny seemed a little dazed, 'as in are you close to her?'

'Not really. I just met her once at the wedding.' Penny blinked. 'She seemed pretty nice, though. Ethan...' Penny took a deep breath '...could I ask...?' No, she couldn't ask him to cover for her now, because even if he said yes to tonight, what about tomorrow and the next day? 'It doesn't matter.'

She went to walk off to her office and Ethan sat there frowning. Really, all he did was frown any time he spoke to Penny. She really was the most confusing woman he had ever met.

Cold one minute and then incredibly empathetic the next.

Ethan looked up and qualified his thought.

Make that empathetic one minute and a soon-to-be blubbering mess the next. Her face had gone bright red and she had stopped in the corridor by a sink and was pulling paper towels out of the dispenser, and her shoulders were heaving.

He didn't know very much about Penny, she'd made sure of that, but from the little that he did know, Ethan was quite sure she would hate any of the staff seeing her like that. She was trying to dash off, but Lisa was calling out to her and he watched as the trauma registrar came into the department and caught a glimpse of her and, patient notes in hand, went to waylay her. Ethan stepped in.

'I need a quick word with you, please, Penny.' He took her by the elbow and sped her through the department into one of the patient interview rooms, and the second they were inside Penny broke down.

CHAPTER SIX

'PLEASE, GO, ETHAN.'

He just stood there.

'Ethan, please, just go.'

'I'm really sorry about your sister's mother-in-law.' He saw her forehead crinkle and then intermingled with sobs she let out a strange gurgle of laughter.

'It's not that.'

'Oh.'

'I'm not that nice.'

Ethan stood there awkwardly, not knowing what to do. He could handle tears from patients and their relatives but this felt more personal than that. She had a handful of paper towels so he couldn't even offer her a tissue.

Then she blurted it out.

'I'm having IVF.'

And any fledgling thoughts that possibly he might rather like Penny in *that* way were instantly doused. Still, at least, in this, he did know what to do. My God, he did, because he wrapped his arms around her and gave her a cuddle. As he did so he was filled with a sense of déjà vu, because his twin sister had been through it so many times and had taught him what to do. Often Kate had wept on him, on anyone who happened to be passing really.

Except there was no feeling of déjà vu when he actually held Penny in his arms. She was incredibly slim and, he was quite sure from her little wriggle to escape, that she wasn't someone who particularly liked to be held. 'It must be horrible,' Ethan said, because Kate had told him that that was a good thing to say when he'd messed up a few times and said the completely wrong thing.

'I'm a mess,' Penny mumbled.

'You're not a mess,' Ethan said. 'It's just that your hormones are crazy at the moment.' He would ring Kate tonight and thank her, Ethan thought as he felt Penny relax in his arms. Then he ventured off the given script. 'So that's what's been going on?'

She nodded into his chest and Ethan realised then that her on IVF was the only Penny he had ever known. 'It's my second go. That's why I was away when you started here. I should have taken time off this time.'

He realised now why she'd been so inflexible with the roster on other occasions, all the appointments she would have been juggling would have made it impossible to change—and yet yesterday, at short notice, she had. 'Why didn't you just say?'

'I didn't want anyone to know. But now I'm just being a bitch to everyone.'

'You're not.'

'Everyone's saying it.'

'No,' Ethan lied, 'you just come across as a bit

tough.' He gave in then. 'I bet you're normally a really nice person.' He held his breath, worried that he had said the wrong thing, but he felt her laugh a little. 'I bet you're a sweet, warm, lovely thing really.'

'No,' Penny said. 'I *am* a bitch, but you've just met the exacerbated version.' And then she started to cry again. 'You missed going to the football with your cousin because of me. I'm a horribly selfish person.'

'Penny, stop it.'

Except she couldn't stop crying, just wished she could take back that day and he could have had that time with his cousin.

'Phil and I often went to football, it really wasn't a big deal, and remember Phil got to spend precious time with Justin that day.'

Finally she felt herself calming, embarrassed now at being held, and she pulled away.

'You need to go home,' Ethan said. 'Were you at the clinic this morning?'

Penny nodded.

'I can cover more for you now that I know. You come in to work a bit later some mornings, just text me.'

'It's not just because I'm tired that I'm crying.' She took a big breath and told him the embarrassing truth. 'I'm terrified of needles and Jasmine has been the one giving the injections to me. I'm due for one at six. I'm going to ring the clinic and see if they can give it to me, but I'm not sure what time they close, and then there's tomorrow...'

Ethan sat her down. 'Surely one of the nurses can give it to you?' Ethan suggested, but realised that, of course, she didn't want anyone to know she was on IVF. 'I can give you your injections.'

'God, no.' Penny shook her head. 'I'm not just a little bit scared of needles. I get in a right state sometimes—even worse than I am now.'

'Can't your partner come in?' Ethan asked, because Carl had given Kate hers. 'Surely he'd—'

'I don't have a partner. I'm doing this by myself.'

'You're doing this on your own?'

'Yes.'

'You mean you'd choose…' As Penny looked at him sharply, luckily Ethan had the good sense to stop talking. He just couldn't really believe someone would choose to be a parent, let alone a single one—babies really weren't his forte. But, whatever his thoughts on the subject were, they really weren't relevant here. Penny wasn't asking for his opinion, just some help with logistics. Instead, he asked where the clinic was and then looked at his watch.

'You really do need to get going if you're going to have a hope of making it there, but if the travelling gets too much, any time you need me to give you an injection, I'm more than happy to.'

'I don't think you realise how bad I am with needles.'

'There's a straitjacket in the lock-up room,' Ethan said. And he wasn't joking, there *was* a straitjacket in the lock-up room and he knew exactly how petrified some people were of needles. 'I do know how to give an injection to someone who doesn't want one, Penny. I tend to do it quite a lot.' He gave her a smile but she shook her head.

'I'll sort something out.'

'Go, then,' Ethan said. 'And thank you for today.'

Of course, it wasn't quite so straightforward as simply leaving the department and getting to her car. Three people stopped Penny on her way to her office, which she had to go to, because that's where her bag and keys were, and also her medication.

Penny dashed to her car and pulled out of the car park, ringing the IVF nurse as she did so and being put straight on hold.

Penny hit the beach road and it wasn't five in the morning, it was nearly five p.m., so the traffic was bumper to bumper. Ringing off, she turned the car round—it took fifteen minutes just to get back to work.

'I thought you'd be back.' Ethan smiled.

'Can I talk to you for a second?' She just had to let him know what he was getting into. 'I need these every night at six. I don't know how long Jasmine is going to be gone and we don't always work the same shifts.'

'I know I'm lousy at commitment, Penny,' Ethan said. 'But I think I can manage this. I can come into work if I'm not on, or you can come into me, or we can meet in a bar and go into a quiet corner.' He almost made her smile.

'From the noises I make they'd think you were attacking me!' Penny said. 'I'm not just a little bit scared of needles—I try not to, but sometimes I start crying. I just lose it.'

'It's fine.' He was annoyingly calm.

'I don't think you understand. You will not calm me

down and even if I say no, I don't want it, you have to ignore me. Just undo my skirt and stick it in.'

'I'm not even going to try to respond to that.' Ethan saw the flush spread on her cheeks and he met her eyes with a smile. 'Go and get something to eat and sit down for a while and then remind me closer to six.'

Penny tapped him on the shoulder at five to six.

'Could I have a word in my office, please, Ethan?'

'Of course.'

'I need you for a moment, Penny,' Lisa called as they walked past.

'It will have to keep.' Ethan's voice was gruff. 'Only buzz me if something urgent comes in. I need to speak with Penny.'

'It sounds as if I'm about to be told off.'

'Exactly,' Ethan said. 'So we shan't be disturbed.'

They walked into her office where Penny had things all set up and, she noted, he actually thought to lock the door. 'Is this what you were doing when I knocked for you to come for a drink with Gordon?'

Penny nodded.

'You really never know what goes on behind closed doors.' He gave her a smile and then, ever the doctor, he checked the vials and the use-by dates.

'I've already checked everything.'

'Good for you,' Ethan said, refusing to be rushed and taking the time to make sure, but it was all too much for Penny. It was bad enough that she was having a needle, but with Jasmine gone and everything it was just a whole lot worse. Seeing Ethan pick up the syringe,

Penny started to cry, and not as she had before. This was, Ethan realised, the sound of real fear.

'Okay.' He kept his voice practical, he was just going to go in and get this over and done with.

'No!' Penny shouted. She had worked herself up to try and stay calm. She could think of nothing worse then Ethan seeing her in such a terrible state and having to face him again, but her resolve had completely broken when she'd seen him pick up the injection. The last thing on Penny's mind was the result and the possibility of a baby; she just wanted to get out of there.

'No.' She said it again as he walked over with the kidney dish. 'Ethan, no, I've changed my mind.'

'Tough.'

Even as Penny said no, she was trying to undo her skirt and failing, and then when Ethan stepped in she tried to brush off his hands but failed at that too.

'Ethan, please!' Penny was doing her best not to sob and make a complete fool of herself. He put the kidney dish down on the desk behind her, his hands finding the side zip of her skirt. He pushed her against the desk and held her in place with one hip as he pulled her skirt down a little bit and reached for the alcohol swab on the desk behind him. Then Ethan turned her, resisting and crying, around and she felt the coldness of the alcohol on the top of her buttock. 'What the hell are you doing?' Penny shouted. 'It's sub-cut, you idiot...'

He turned her quickly to face him and before she even knew it, Ethan had swabbed her stomach and the needle was in.

'I know.' Ethan smiled, massaging the injection site

with one hand as he threw the needle into the kidney dish with the other. 'That's called a distraction technique, in case you were wondering.'

Only the distraction had been for him—the image of coral-coloured silk knickers and just a glimpse of the top of her bottom were branded in his mind. Now he was looking down at her lovely pale stomach as he massaged the injection in, and he saw the dots of bruises and his fingers wanted to wander there too. More than that he knew she was watching his fingers, knew he should stop now, or that she could take over, but they both just stood very close, looking down. And he actually wondered if it was wrong just how turned on he was now and, no, he did not want to fancy her.

It had been a hell of a day, a completely wretched day, and he blamed it on the funeral as he lingered a little too long. And Penny looked at his mouth and blamed it all on the hormones she was taking, because she was holding back from kissing him.

'Okay!' It was Ethan who took control, whose mind sort of jolted and alerted him to the fact that the woman he was very close to kissing, the woman he was hard for now, was very actively trying to get pregnant.

'You're done,' Ethan said. He picked up the kidney dish, turned his back and made a big deal about tipping the contents into the sharps dispenser.

She was a close colleague too, Ethan told himself. And an absolute cow to work with, he reminded himself a few times—except he knew why now.

No, he did not want to fancy Penny.

As Penny did up her zipper and smoothed down her

blouse she was not sure what, if anything, had happened just then. She was embarrassed at her tears, of course, but there was something else swirling in the room with them, an energy that must not be acknowledged.

'Thank you.'

'No problem,' Ethan clipped. 'Same time tomorrow, then?'

'Please,' Penny said. 'I mean, yes.'

CHAPTER SEVEN

ETHAN WAS ACTUALLY on a day off the next day.

He woke late, saw the black suit over the chair and tried not to think about yesterday.

Tried not to, because it had been a day of hellish emotion and it seemed impossible to think that Justin would be back at school today and the world was moving on, but not for some.

The transplant co-ordinator had been called up for the head injury patient, Heath, later in the evening, he had heard. Ethan had seen the boy's parents sobbing outside the ambulance bay on his way home.

Waking up to grief was a lot like waking up with a hangover, Ethan decided as he pieced together the previous day and braced himself to face the upcoming one. He lay there, eyes closed, trying to summon up the energy to move, to get on with his day. He should maybe ring his aunt and uncle, Ethan thought, see how they were, but he couldn't stomach it. Or ring his sister and find out how the rest of the wake had been.

Except he just wanted to be alone, just as he had wanted to be alone last night. He hadn't been able to face a bar. Even Kelly, a friend, who was more than a friend sometimes, had called, and knowing how tough the day would have been had suggested coming over.

He hadn't wanted that either.

He could go and do something, maybe a long drive down to the Ocean Road, just stay a night in Torquay or Lorne perhaps, watch the waves, get away, except, just as he thought he had a plan Ethan remembered he had to be at the hospital at six to give Penny her injection.

Penny.

Ethan blew out a breath as he recalled the near miss last night.

What the hell had he been thinking? Or rather, he hadn't been thinking in the least.

Still, he kept getting glimpses of coral underwear flashing before his eyes throughout the day.

He'd expected flesh coloured.

Not that he'd thought about it.

But *had* he thought about it, then flesh coloured it would be.

Sensible, seamless, Ethan decided as he drove to the hospital. Not that she'd need a bra.

Not that he'd noticed.

Ethan pulled into his parking spot and tried to go back, tried to rewind the clock to a few days ago, when he hadn't remotely thought of her in that way. When she had just been a sour-faced colleague who was difficult to work with, one who hadn't turned round and bewitched him with a smile.

'What are you doing here?' Rex asked as Ethan walked through the department, for once out of scrubs and dressed in black jeans and a black top.

'I need to take some work home. Is it just you on?' Ethan asked casually.

'Nope,' Rex said. 'Penny's on.' He pulled a poker face. 'She's just taking a break.'

Ethan knew that because he'd texted her to say that he was here, but he didn't want anyone getting even a hint so he stood and chatted with Rex a moment before heading to Penny's office.

'Sorry to mess up your day off.'

He checked the dose again, and she undid her zipper and just stared at the door as she lowered her skirt. Penny closed her eyes and hyperventilated but managed to stay much calmer, even if her knuckles were white as she clutched the desk behind her. In turn, Ethan was very gruff and businesslike and what they had both been silently nervous about happening was nowhere near repeated. In fact, it was all over and done with very quickly.

'Thanks for this.'

'No problem,' Ethan said.

'Will you carry on working?' Ethan asked, and Penny frowned as she tucked her shirt in. 'When you have the baby I mean.'

'If I have one,' Penny said. 'Did you ask Gordon the same question?'

'No.' He was so not into political correctness. 'But then again, Gordon isn't a single dad. And,' he added, 'despite his account of it, Gordon wasn't actually the one who got pregnant and gave birth.'

Penny laughed.

'Shall we go and see them?' Ethan said. 'It's quiet

out there at the moment and Rex is in. We could head up and just get it over with.'

'Get it over with?' Penny smiled. She had been thinking exactly the same thing. Gordon really could be the most crushing bore and she'd never really had a conversation with Hilary, a paediatrician, that hadn't revolved around baby poo.

'Sorry.' Ethan didn't know he was being teased. 'That was a bit…'

'Don't you like babies?' Penny asked as they headed towards the lifts that would take them to the maternity unit.

'Actually, no.' Ethan was honest. 'I don't actively dislike them or anything. My sister has had three now. I like the five-year-old, he makes me laugh sometimes.'

'How old is your sister?'

'Thirty-six,' Ethan said, and she remembered their phone conversation.

'You're a twin.' Penny smiled. 'On anyone else that would be cute.'

They stopped at the gift shop and bought flowers and balloons and Penny wrote a card but Ethan had forgotten to get one and asked if he could just add his name.

'You're giving me injections,' Penny said. 'Not sperm. Buy your own card.'

She was the most horrible person he had ever met, but she did make him grin, and Ethan was still smiling when they both walked into Hilary's room together.

'Penny!' Gordon seemed delighted to see them. 'Ethan!' He shook Ethan's hand. 'He's just woken up, we're just feeding.'

'Well, don't let us interrupt you. We just came in to give you these and say a quick hello.'

'Don't be daft,' Gordon said. 'Completely natural. What do you think? He's a good-looking little man, isn't he?'

Ethan peered down at the baby and to Penny's delight he was blushing. 'Congratulations,' he said to Hilary. 'He's very handsome.'

'He's gorgeous,' Penny said. 'He looks like you.'

'He looks like Gordon,' Hilary corrected her.

She could feel Ethan's exquisite discomfort beside her and to his credit he did attempt conversation, but she almost felt him fold in relief as his phone bleeped and he excused himself for a moment.

'I heard about Jed's mum,' Hilary said. 'Have you heard any news?'

'She's actually improving,' Penny said as Ethan came back in. 'They should be home in a couple of days.'

'I'm hoping to get him home soon.' Hilary looked down at her baby. 'He's a bit small, though, and the labour—'

Thankfully Penny's pager crackled into life, urgently summoning her down to Emergency.

'I'll come and see if they need me too,' Ethan offered.

'That was you.' Penny grinned as they fled out of Maternity.

'I'm sorry!' Ethan said. 'I just couldn't sit there while she fed the baby. I'm fine with patients, with women in cafés, but when I know someone...' He was honest. 'I was the same with my sister. I just break out in a sweat.

Please,' he said. 'I beg of you, when you have your baby, please don't feed it when I come to visit.'

'I promise I won't,' Penny assured him.

'I know that sounds terrible.'

'Absolutely not.' Penny could think of nothing worse than feeding a baby in front of Ethan. 'I don't even know if I want to feed it myself.'

'Stop!' Ethan said. He just didn't want to think about Penny and breasts and babies and the black panties she was wearing today.

Yes, he'd seen, even if he'd tried very hard not to.

'Sorry.' Even Penny couldn't believe she was discussing breastfeeding with him. 'You don't approve, do you?'

'Of bottle-feeding?'

She didn't smile at his joke. 'I meant you don't approve of me doing this on my own.'

'I can't really say the right thing here.'

'You can,' she offered, because she didn't mind people's *invited* opinions.

'No.' He was honest. 'I just can't imagine that someone would choose to be a single mum. My mum raised my sister and I on her own and it wasn't easy.'

'My mum got divorced,' Penny said, 'and, believe me, things got a whole lot better when Dad wasn't around.' Then she checked herself. 'Actually, things got a whole lot worse for a couple of years, but then they got better. And my sister was a single mum for a while.'

'By choice?'

'No,' Penny said. 'Well, yes, by choice, because she

had no choice but to leave Simon's dad. I really have thought things through.'

'Tell me?'

'I've got to work.'

'Dinner?' Ethan said, because he really was starting to like Penny, well, not fancy like, he told himself, but then he remembered the flash of her knickers and what had almost happened yesterday. Maybe he should recant that invitation to take her out for dinner, except he'd already asked.

'Why?'

Ethan shrugged. 'Well, I've been out with a new father and listened to his labour and if I add a woman going through IVF, I figure by the end of the week I could qualify as a sensitive new-age guy.'

Penny smiled and he had been right—she really was attractive when she did.

'Okay, then.' Her acceptance caught him just a little by surprise. He'd sort of been hoping, for safety's sake, that she might decline. 'Tomorrow,' she said. 'After you stab me.'

Penny was on a day off, so it was she who *dropped in* just as Ethan was finishing up.

She was wearing a dress that buttoned up at the front and her heels were a little higher. He caught the musky scent of her perfume as he followed her into the office and locked the door.

'I'll do it,' he said, taking her little cool bag.

She told him her doses and he heard the shake in her voice as she did so.

'I am so sorry about this.' He turned and she was try-ing to undo the little buttons on her dress. It really was a very genuine fear, made worse today because she'd had the whole drive here to think about it. Ethan actually saw her break out into a cold sweat as he approached and she was trying very hard not to cry.

'I need a bit more skin than that, Penny.' She'd only managed two buttons. 'Here.' He undid a couple more and felt the splash of a hot tear on the back of his hand. 'You must really want this baby.'

'I do.'

He could see tiny goose bumps rising on her stom-ach. He was really impressed with himself because he was completely matter-of-fact and, despite a glimpse of purple underwear and the heady scent of her, he was not a bit turned on. Two evenings in a row now!

He just kept reminding himself that there'd be a baby in there any time soon and that those small breasts would soon look like Hilary's.

'Done,' Ethan said.

'Thanks.'

'Where do you want to go and eat?'

Penny didn't care, so they ended up in the same pub near the hospital where he had been with Gordon, and they took a booth and sat opposite each other. He saw the dark smudges under her eyes and the paleness of her skin. The treatment must really be taking its toll by now.

'Jasmine's coming back the day after tomorrow,' Penny said. 'Well, as long as Jed's mother keeps im-proving, so tomorrow should be the last time you have to do it.'

'It's not an issue.'

'I am very grateful to you, though. Jasmine was worried that I'd just stop the treatment and I think she was right.'

'Have you told her I'm giving them?'

'Yes.' Penny nodded. 'She sends you her sympathies.'

He'd prefer self-restraint.

'When's your next blood test?'

'Seven a.m. tomorrow.'

'Do you want to change the next one?' Ethan asked. 'Go in a little bit later?'

Penny shook her head. 'Thanks, but it has to be done early.'

She ordered nachos smothered in sour cream and guacamole and cheese, and it surprised him because he'd thought she'd order a salad or something.

And usually she would but this was like PMS times a thousand so she just scooped up the cheesiest bit she could find and sank her teeth into it with such pleasure that Ethan wished he hadn't ordered the steak.

'Have some.' She saw his eyes linger on them.

'Who'd have thought?' Ethan said.

'I'm good at sharing.'

'I meant the two of us being out together. What a difference a week can make.'

Penny smiled and he rather wished she hadn't.

'How come you're so petrified of needles?'

'I'm not as bad as I used to be,' Penny said. 'I did hypnosis, counselling and everything, just to get to where I could let someone give me one.'

'So you think hypnosis works?'

She saw his sceptical frown. 'I don't know,' Penny admitted. 'I mean, I'm still scared of needles but the hypnotherapist did get me to remember the first time that I freaked out—I was at school and we were all lined up to get an injection and the girl in front of me passed out.'

'Mass hysteria?'

'Possibly.' Penny had thought about it practically. 'But my father had just left my mother a couple of weeks before, so apparently, according to the counsellor, it was my excuse to scream and cry.' She gave a very wicked smile. 'Load of rubbish really.' She took a sip of her drink. 'All I know is that the fear is there and I'm having to face it over and over and over. Sometimes it's terrible, sometimes it's not so bad. I was good at my blood test this morning.'

'You were good tonight.'

'Yep,' Penny said. 'And had Jasmine's mother-in-law not had a stroke, you'd never have known and we'd have been able to look each other in the eye.'

'I'm looking you in the eye now, Penny.'

She looked up and so he was. She saw that his eyes were more amber than hazel and there was a quickening to her pulse. How could she possibly be thinking such thoughts? She couldn't be attracted to Ethan. She had to stay focussed on her treatment—her plan to become a mother. Except thinking about babies had her thinking about making babies the old-fashioned way! With Ethan?

It was very warm in the bar; it must have been that causing this sear of heat between them, and Ethan wished he'd asked for his steak rare because it was taking for ever to come.

'Do you have any phobias?' she asked when thankfully his order had been delivered and normality was starting to return.

'I don't think so.'

'Flying?'

'Love it.' Ethan smiled.

'Heights?'

'They don't bother me in the least.'

She did, though, Ethan thought as he ate his steak and tried to tell himself he was out with a colleague, but Penny was starting to bother him a lot, only not in the way she once had. He was just in no position to say. To his absolute surprise where Penny was concerned, since that morning when she'd turned round and smiled, there had been a charge in the air.

One that to Ethan really didn't make sense, because he liked his women soft, curvy and cute, which was a terrible word and one he'd never admit to out loud, but that was what he liked.

And there was nothing soft about Penny and there wasn't a curve to be seen, and as for cute…

'What are you smiling at?' Penny frowned.

'Nothing.' He reminded himself of the reason they were actually out. 'So,' he asked, 'assuming this round of treatment is a success, how many embryos are you having put back?' He saw her blink at the rather personal question.

'Two.'

'I think I've just found my phobia.'

Penny grinned. He made no secret of the fact he had no desire to ever be a parent, so she asked him why.

'I'm not sure really,' Ethan admitted. 'It's the responsibility, I guess. I save it all for work. I've just never wanted to settle down, let alone have a baby.' He gave her a wide-eyed look. 'And certainly not two at the same time.'

'Twins would be lovely,' she said, 'then I'd never have to go through this again.'

'You should speak to my mum first,' Ethan said. 'I guarantee if you did you'd only put one back.'

'You said she was a single mum?'

'No,' he corrected her. 'I said that she raised us on her own. My father died when we were six.'

'I'm sorry.' She looked at him. 'Same age as Justin.'

He gave a small mirthless smile, her hit just a little too direct.

'How did you deal with it?'

Ethan gave a shrug. 'You just grow up overnight.' He never really talked about it with anyone. 'It's tough, though. I heard Vera, my aunt, telling Justin to be brave, and it was all the same stuff she told me. Then there was Jack, my uncle, he's my dad's brother, giving me lectures over the years about how I was the man of the house and I needed to be more responsible. I hope they don't say the same to Justin, it scared the life out of me.'

Maybe that was why he held on to his freedom so much, Penny mused, and she couldn't help asking more.

'And were you the man of the house?' Penny asked, and she gave a thin smile when he shrugged.

'I tried to be,' Ethan said. 'And resented every minute of it. Then being a teenager sort of got in the way of being sensible.'

'Did you miss having a dad?'

They were both being honest, and after all she had asked, and he wasn't going to sugar coat his response just because it was what she wanted to hear.

'Yes,' Ethan said. 'But I do accept that things are very different now. Back then there weren't so many women raising children alone. I used to feel the odd one out. I'm sure that yours won't feel like that.' He reminded himself to smile. 'Anyway, what would I know?'

They ordered coffee and then chatted about work, about her case review tomorrow, where once a week the senior staff got together and reviewed a case. It was Penny's turn and, no, she told him, she wasn't nervous. 'Just ill prepared,' Penny admitted. 'So I'd better get home and rectify that.'

They walked out to their cars and there was a strange moment because had she not been doing her level best to get pregnant, had they just been out, Ethan would have done his usual thing and kissed her. Right now that would prove no problem at all, because as they stood by her car, he actually forgot about needles and ultrasounds and little people that made an awful lot of noise and demanded to be fed a lot.

"Night, then,' she said, going into her bag for her keys and then looking up at him.

"Night, Penny.'

He went to give her a kiss on the cheek, but changed his mind midway. Except it was too late for that so he went ahead, but there was an awkward moment because he missed his mark and his lips landed a little close to her mouth.

He felt the warmth of her blush on his lips and knew he should say good night and walk away. Except he wasn't holding a needle and she wasn't crying or asking him to stop and he could smell her hair and that musky perfume. He thought of the purple underwear he had glimpsed earlier.

It was all just a second, a very long second, and Penny was a guilty party in this too. Had been complicit as she'd carefully selected her underwear that morning, was as attracted as he was and, yes, she wanted his mouth. Now here it was, just the graze of his lips, and she felt as if a feather was stroking her from the inside. There was just a flare that lit between them and mouths that were a beat away from applying pressure, but neither did. Just two mouths mingling and deciding to linger, two minds racing and about to quiet and give in, but then they were literally saved by the bell, or rather by his pager.

'Did you arrange that one too?' Penny asked.

Ethan just grinned, because had he been thinking straight he might have arranged one for a few moments ago because he did not want to start anything with Penny.

Well, not Penny.

He didn't want to start anything with a soon-to-be-pregnant Penny, Ethan reminded himself as he telephoned work to find out what was happening.

'The place is steaming,' Ethan said when he came off the phone.

'Should I come in?'

'It's packed and they're not getting through them. I'll just go in for a couple of hours and help them clear the backlog. You go home.'

'You're sure?'

Ethan nodded, gave her a light kiss on the cheek that was definitely just a friendly one, a token effort to erase the one that had happened before, saw her into her car and then headed to his.

One more needle to get through, Ethan told himself.

He was almost as nervous about it as she was.

CHAPTER EIGHT

PENNY KNEW THE drill only too well.

After a very sleepless night, trying to prepare for her case presentation then later going over and over their near kiss, Penny was up at the crack of dawn and about to have her ultrasound. She went to hitch up her skirt, but she was wearing her wraparound dress and it was a bit too tight.

'Just open it up, Penny,' the sonographer said, and offered her a sheet, which she pulled over not just her stomach but her chest, because everything was exposed.

Damn.

She had been dressing for her presentation.

Or had she?

Penny honestly wasn't sure.

It *was* her presentation outfit, which had been sitting in its dry-cleaner bag for two weeks now, waiting for today. It was her grey wraparound and even though she didn't have a cleavage, it was a bit too low so underneath she wore a silver-grey cami with a bit of lace at the top, and because it was Penny she wore matching panties, which were rather more lace than silk.

And tonight she'd be getting her needle from Ethan.

It was too much, Penny decided. She'd just change into scrubs, except there was a part of her that wanted his eyes on her, a part of her that refused to be silenced, that wanted more than last night, and Penny was most unused to such strong feelings. Even now, walking to get her blood done, she was thinking of the near miss last night and what might have unfolded if they hadn't been interrupted by the pager. She blinked in astonishment at the depravity of her own thoughts.

'Morning, Penny.'

It took two attempts to get the blood this morning. She was stressed about her case presentation, worried about her choice of clothes, exhausted after a night of thinking and trying not to think about Ethan and a kiss that never happened and must never happen! This meant Penny sobbed like she never had as they took her blood.

'Finished.' The nurse smiled as she pressed down on the cotton swab. 'I think I left a bruise.'

'It's my own fault,' Penny said, because despite being held down her arm had jerked when the needle had gone in. As Penny blew her nose, instead of standing up and getting out of there as quickly as possible as she usually would, she asked a question. She was a typical doctor and had read up on things herself, but there was one bit now that was honestly confusing her. 'Can I ask a question?'

'Of course.'

'About…' She was going bright red but tried to sound matter-of-fact as she spoke. 'Increased libido?' Her voice came out as a croak and Penny cleared her throat, but the nurse was completely unfazed by her question.

'You're a walking cocktail of hormones at the moment, Penny,' the nurse said. 'Often women could think of nothing worse at this stage, but for some...'

'So it's normal?'

'Sure. Just make sure that you use protection,' the nurse said. 'It's only once we've done the embryo transfer that you need to refrain, and not just from sex, no orgasms either—which is unfortunate...' she smiled '...because an increase in libido is commonplace then.'

Penny blinked. She'd sort of skipped over all those parts, thinking that it would never really be a problem for her.

'You'll get a phone call later and we'll sort out your doses,' the nurse said. 'You'll be ready for your trigger injection any day soon. So just enjoy it for now.'

She certainly wouldn't be enjoying it! Penny just wanted these feelings to pass, wanted a neat explanation as to why she was nearly climbing the walls at the thought of Ethan. Did she fancy him or was it the medication?

And did it really matter?

Would it be so terrible to have sex with someone you really fancied even if it was going absolutely nowhere?

Stop it, she told herself as she drove to work.

Just stop it right there!

Of course the second she walked into work she saw Ethan. She tried to douse the fire in her cheeks, only it wasn't working—he was dressed in scrubs and very unshaven. He was scowling at the bed board and had clearly been up all night.

'Good sleep?' His voice was wry.

'Fantastic.' Hers was equally wry as she walked past, because she'd be lucky to have slept for more than a couple of hours, though she was glad now that she hadn't accepted the consultant's position. There was no way she could have juggled it all, she would not have coped if she'd been called in last night and had still been expected to work through the next day.

Penny got through the busy morning, doing her best to avoid him, and she had a feeling Ethan was trying to avoid her too. Both were trying to pretend that the near miss last night hadn't happened.

She headed to the lecture theatre and set up her computer, nodding a greeting as her colleagues filed in. She wasn't nervous as she was a very good public speaker, but her heart was fluttering as Ethan walked in. He'd been firing on coffee all morning but from his yawn as he took a seat in the lecture theatre for her presentation, she wouldn't be in the least surprised if he fell asleep midway through.

Penny had decided not to present about Heath, the young man with the head injury, and instead spoke about the renal patient who had come in with cardiac failure. She went through it all—the medication, the dosages, admitted to her own hesitation—suggesting a protocol sheet be implemented, and Ethan didn't fall asleep as she spoke. Instead, he watched her.

Watched her mouth move and speak, but hardly heard a word, his mind more on her pert bottom as she turned and pointed to the whiteboard. All he wanted to do was go home—why did he have to fancy Penny?

He knew that the extra jewellery and make-up and

heels were not for his benefit. It was the way Penny was and she was always going to make an extra effort for this type of thing. Except he could see the flash of lace on her cami and he wanted the effort to have been for him.

Then his eyes lingered on the tie of her dress and his mind wandered as to how he was going to get it off, or up, and it was then that she caught him looking. Her voice trailed off and they both just stared.

Really stared.

Ethan clamped his teeth together because he was incredibly tempted to silently mouth something *really* inappropriate to her, just to see those burning cheeks flame further.

'Penny?' Mr Dean asked when the silence dragged on. 'You said he was then given a bolus?'

'That's right.' She snapped back to her presentation and apart from that, apart from nearly jumping off the stage and straddling Ethan, Penny got through the rest of her speech really well. Attempting to be normal, Ethan congratulated her a little while later.

'Well done,' he said. 'I'm sorry if I offended you that day. I didn't mean to just walk in and take over.'

'But you didn't offend me.' Penny frowned and then remembered. 'I was having a hot flash, Ethan.' She watched his face break into a smile. 'It was the drugs— that was a glimpse of menopausal Penny.'

'Well, remind me, if we're both still working here then, that it's time for me to look for another job,' Ethan said laughingly.

'Are you heading off, Ethan?' Mr Dean walked past. 'You were here all night.'

'Soon,' Ethan said, then he looked at Penny. 'If I go home now I'm going to crash and I won't get back.'

'I'm so sorry.' He really did look exhausted.

'I'm going to go into the on-call room and sleep,' Ethan said. 'Get everything ready and then come and get me at five to six.'

'Thanks.'

She tried to ignore the on-call room, but every time she walked past, the thought of Ethan lying in there asleep flashed like a strobe light in her mind. If she was like this now, what the hell was she going to be like after the embryo transfer? She might be needing that straitjacket after all.

Penny set up her needle and swab and had it all laid out in her office and then, because she could at times be nice, she made Ethan a coffee before she knocked on the door of the on-call room. He was so zonked she could actually hear the low sounds of snoring.

'Ethan.' She knocked again and put her head around the door. 'Ethan, it's nearly six.' He sat up and sort of shook himself awake.

'Can you bring it in here?' He just wanted to get the injection over and done with and then go back to sleep but then he changed his mind and with good reason. 'I'll be out in a minute.'

'I brought you a coffee.'

She walked over in the darkness and he got a waft of her scent. He heard the slight rattle as she put his coffee down on the bedside table and it was right that her hand was shaking, Ethan thought, because she was seconds away from being pulled into his bed.

'Thanks,' Ethan said. 'I'll be there soon.'

He had to get himself under control—physically and mentally—before touching her.

Hurry home, Jasmine.

He'd never met Jed, let alone his mother, but he wished her the speediest, most uneventful of recoveries from her stroke. Ethan gulped his coffee and splashed his face in the sink and then walked to Penny's office.

'Ready?'

'Yes.' She was fiddling with the tie of her dress and he could hear her starting to cry, just sort of breathy sobs that she was trying to keep in.

'Okay, then.' He walked towards her, and she was a mess, a hot mess at that, Ethan thought as he looked at her eyes. They showed a mixture of fear and lust and if she said no to the injection this time, he would drop the needle.

He didn't want her to do this.

He wanted her to stop so that they could do what people who fancied each other did.

A lot.

He wanted to go out and have more dinners and have nachos himself next time and go far too far in a car park and then go even further back home.

'No.' She pushed at his hand as it reached for her dress tie, and he was breathing very hard now—tired, turned on, pissed off. He didn't want to do this either.

'What do you want, Penny?' He forgot he wasn't supposed to ask, he was supposed to go ahead and give her the needle. Her hands were on his arm and he tried to ignore the feel of her fingers on his skin. He tried to undo the tie for her as if he hadn't been thinking about doing just that all day.

She had on silver-grey knickers and a matching cami, and through the silk he could tell her chest was almost completely flat. He liked curves, Ethan told himself, except he wanted his mouth to lower to the thick nipples he could see rising out of the fabric, and as he swabbed her stomach he caught a glimpse of blonde hair above her panty line and he could see a bit through the lace too.

And he did *not* want to give her this needle. He could hear her gulping and soft whimpers and feel her breath on his cheek, and he did not want to do it.

But he'd signed up for the gig so he swabbed her skin and though he hesitated over her stomach, he finally stuck the needle in.

'There,' he said. 'You're done.'

Ethan rubbed her stomach and then she took over. His hand did not linger, he just wanted this over and done, wanted out and home. Maybe tonight he'd call Kelly, get this Penny fantasy out of his head once and for all.

Then he saw the lust in her eyes and her lips were moving towards his and he jerked his head backwards. 'Penny!' he warned.

She screwed her eyes closed at his rejection. She'd have to resign, it was all just so unlike her. 'I'm so sorry, Ethan. I think it's the drugs, it's like I'm on heat.'

He'd embarrassed her, Ethan knew that, which he'd

never wanted to do. She had no need to be embarrassed. He wanted her too, so he tried to soften things, except he was rock hard. 'I just don't want to start something with someone who's trying for a baby.'

'I know. I get that completely. I'm never like this...' She attempted her excuses again as he dropped the needle into the dish behind her. 'It's the drugs.'

'It's not the drugs, Penny,' Ethan said, because he wasn't taking any, but hormones were certainly raging and he stopped fighting it then, his mouth coming down on hers the way it had wanted to last night.

She almost came just at the pressure of his mouth as her stomach hollowed with lust. It wasn't a brief kiss, it wasn't unsure and whatever the opposite of tentative was should be called Ethan, because his tongue was deliciously crude, his unshaven jaw surely shredding her skin. Penny was no saint either. Her hands were in his hair, her scantily clad body pressing into him, feeling his fierce erection, and he pulled away just a little.

'Penny...'

'I know,' she said. 'I know this is going nowhere.'

'You understand?'

'Of course.' She was in her office, with her dress undone, and it was all so inappropriate, especially for someone like Penny, so much so that she fought an incredible urge to laugh. Then she stopped fighting and laughed a little bit. 'If you knew me, you'd know that it *is* the drugs. I'm going to be so embarrassed later.'

'Why?' He smiled down. 'It's just a kiss,' Ethan said, 'a one-off.'

'An anomaly,' Penny said. 'Never to be repeated or

mentioned again. As soon as you walk out the door we're done.'

'I'm not out the door yet.'

She was more than happy with the ground rules, just for the bliss of the return of his mouth.

It was just a kiss but it was a kiss with a secret. His fingers were working her nipples through the silk of her cami till she moaned in his mouth and then he slipped his hand up the cami so that skin could meet skin. He worked them a little more firmly. Normally she loathed that, hated the beat of disappointment when they found out that she really was quite flat-chested, but it just didn't matter right now. If anything he was even more turned on because he pressed his erection hard into her, and she almost came undone—a ball of hot tension in his arms.

And it was still just a kiss, but the secret was deepening, his hand now sliding into her panties, and they would both never repeat or mention it again, but in this too he knew what to do. He cupped her for a moment before he began to stroke her with precision, and he couldn't for a moment kiss and concentrate, so he let her mouth work his neck, and then he warned her to be careful because there must be no evidence, and as she removed her mouth, Penny lost her head.

She just gave in to the bliss and the scent of him, her hands around his neck to steady herself, her legs shaking as she fought the urge for him to lift her, to wrap her legs around his waist, yet she stood as she forgot how to breathe.

Ethan felt the rip of tension and her quiver and her

thighs clasp around his hand and he stroked through her pulses as frantic need left her and leached into him, and he got back to kissing her, but with urgency. Pressing himself hard into her, Ethan's hands moved to lift her, a fierce need to be inside her, but then sense reared its head and moved into his and he released her hips, because if he didn't, he would have her over that desk.

And, no, Ethan told himself, that he did not want.

Except he did.

No wonder he didn't like being responsible, Ethan thought, peeling them apart. 'And now I'm handing you back to Jasmine.' He looked down and smiled and she looked up and nodded, and there was that awkward bit, because she had come and he hadn't, and she wanted more too, yet he was releasing her, about to head out there to where this had never happened.

'Ethan...' She wanted more of him, wanted more than a corner of chocolate before it was wrapped and returned to the fridge, and she didn't care if they were in her office; right now, she simply didn't care.

'Penny.' He gave her a small kiss to interrupt her invitation, and then he made it very clear where they were. 'You go and concentrate on getting that baby.'

CHAPTER NINE

IT WAS ALL happening.

It was like a train she had boarded and she so badly wanted the baby at the end, but she'd lost something along the way. Ethan was a bit aloof and she was back to being frosty but she missed the Ethan she had glimpsed and, in turn, he wanted more of Penny, just not *that* much more.

Because Ethan knew what was happening now. He didn't turn a hair when she asked if they could swap their days off at short notice.

'Sure,' was all he said.

He asked no questions, though he did look things up on the internet, knew that when she came back after her couple of days off, there was a high chance she would be as horny as hell.

But no orgasms allowed, Ethan thought with a black smile as he knocked on her office door to update her on one of her patients.

'I feel like a delivery boy,' he said, holding a card and chocolates.

She wished she had a delivery boy who looked like Ethan—she'd be ringing for pizza every night, Penny thought as he handed his wares over. 'Heath's parents asked me to give these to you.'

'You should have buzzed me.' Immediately Penny stood, but Ethan shook his head.

'I went to, but they were getting upset so they asked if I could just hand these to you. I think they were a bit overwhelmed being back in Emergency.'

Penny nodded and sat back down.

'I spoke to them for a bit,' Ethan told her.

'How were they?' Penny asked as she read the letter.

'Just struggling through. They said they knew that one day they'd be pleased with the decision they had made for Heath to be a donor, but not yet.' And Penny nodded because the letter said much the same—thanking her for her care that day and for gently preparing them for what was to come a few hours later. She showed the letter to Ethan and as he read it he forgot to be aloof, forgot he didn't really want to be talking with Penny at the moment.

'I couldn't have dealt with it that day,' he admitted.

'I'm not surprised.'

'Phil used to feel guilty about that. He said he was lying there basically hoping someone would die.'

'You can't think like that.'

'But you *do* think like that,' Ethan admitted. 'Because even I was thinking that if Phil had lasted for just a few more days…'

'There are a lot of people waiting for hearts.' Penny said, practical with the facts. 'And a lot of hearts are wasted. How's Justin dealing with it all?'

'I don't know,' Ethan admitted, and saw the rise of

her eyebrows. 'It's all a bit of a mess. Gina wants nothing to do with Phil's side of the family and I can't say I
blame her. She wasn't exactly treated well by my uncle
and aunt.' He gave a tired shrug. 'Anyway, there's nothing I can do.' He went to ask how she was doing, but
changed his mind—he really didn't want a conversation
about egg retrieval and a five-day wait before embryo
transfer. 'I'd better get back out there.'

'Sure,' Penny said, but there was an impossible tension between them.

And so they muddled through and it was a bit easier
to be aloof than he'd thought it might be, because he was
a bit fed up too, not just with Penny but with himself.
He didn't particularly like the superficial Ethan who, a
couple of weeks later, had this guilty image of Penny's
test results being negative and asking her for a night
out in the city to cheer her up and then taking her back
to his apartment to make love, not babies.

And, yes, he was glad it was a long weekend coming
up and that in one hour from now he'd be out of there.

Hopefully without seeing Penny, because she was
about to start a stint of nights and was off today.

Then, just when he thought he'd got through it, in
Penny walked. She had Jasmine's toddler son with her—
must be picking him up from crèche to help Jasmine
out. He saw Jasmine give her a brief, excited hug, saw
Penny warn her to hush, and even without that, Ethan
knew that she was pregnant, he just knew from the
timing, because he'd been back on the IVF site again.

And, no, there was no avoiding her and no avoiding

the fact he was crazy about a woman who was pregnant, and not with his child.

'Hi, there.' Jasmine had taken Simon to the vending machine and he came over when she caught his eye. 'Ready for nights?' he asked.

'As I'll ever be.'

'So?' he asked, because even if he didn't want to know, he knew. 'How are you?'

'Good,' Penny said, and her back teeth clamped down because she wanted to tell him her news but it was far too early. But more than that she wanted to flirt, she wanted him and he was just out of bounds. She wanted dates and dinners and laughter and fun, yet she badly wanted the baby inside her too. 'What are you doing for the long weekend? Anything nice?'

'Yep.' Ethan nodded. It had been a long day and now, with the unspoken news hanging between them, more than ever he just wanted to get away. 'I've got the long weekend and then two days off, I'm not back here till Thursday. I'm going out on a boat and hopefully we'll all be eating too much, drinking too much and talking too much.'

'With friends?' She thought her face would crack from smiling.

'Family,' Ethan said. 'We do it every year.'

'Sounds great,' Penny said. 'Kate will have her hands full.' Penny could imagine nothing worse than being at sea with toddlers—she'd have a nervous breakdown.

'God, no.' Ethan pulled a face. 'Once a year my mum has them all for her so she can get away. Kate says it keeps her sane. It would never happen otherwise.'

'I don't blame her,' Penny said. 'She'd be worried sick trying to keep tabs on them on a boat.'

'I meant I wouldn't be going if she brought them.' He hesitated, tried to turn it into a joke and then stopped, but he'd said it all, really—he was Mr R&R, heading off, kicking back and just so removed from the world she was about to join.

'It sounds lovely,' Penny said, because a few nights out at sea with Ethan, well, there was not a lot she could think of that sounded nicer than that.

He looked at her for a very long time, wished she could come along, could almost see her in a sarong with sunburnt shoulders, and he couldn't help but regret all the things they could have done, all the dates they could have been on and he was, for a ridiculous moment, tempted to ask her to see if she could swap her nights with someone and come with him, but he stopped himself, because even if the impossible could be achieved, he soon saw the real picture.

No wine, because she wasn't drinking.

No seafood either.

And throwing up on the hour every hour as Kate had done one year.

'Have a good break,' Penny said.

Oh, he fully intended to!

Only it wasn't that great.

Given what had had happened in recent weeks, it was a far more sombre affair, of course.

'You're quiet,' Kate commented on the Saturday

morning. It was a glorious day, the sky blue, the wind crisp and the sun hot.

'I think we're all quiet,' Ethan said.

'I rang Gina.' Ethan looked over, hoping there had been some progress, but Kate shook her head. 'I said maybe we could get the kids together, but she said no. Surely she can't keep Justin from his grandparents?'

'I guess she can,' Ethan said. 'Or she can make it as difficult as possible for them to see him, which she is.' He shook his head. 'I'm staying out of it.'

'Ethan, you can't do nothing.'

'I can,' he interrupted, 'because if I say what I really think about the situation, it's going to be a few very long days at sea.'

'Say it to me,' Kate pushed.

'Are you sure?' He looked at his sister, who nodded. 'Phil should have sorted this.' He watched her jaw tighten and Kate struggled for a moment before she could respond.

'He didn't know this was going to happen.'

'Yes, he did,' Ethan interrupted. 'I told him to sort this. I told him he had to work things out between his parents and Gina. Phil knew full well the mess he'd be leaving behind if he didn't sort something out. I know he did, because I told him. Frankly, I don't blame Gina for wanting to have nothing to do with us. Maybe Jack and Vera should have thought about the future before they opened their mouths when Gina had the audacity to break up with their son.'

'No one knew then how sick Phil was going to get.'

'No one ever knows what the future holds.' Ethan

refused to turn Phil into a saint and even if his aunt and uncle were grieving, it didn't suddenly make them infallible. 'I love Jack and Vera and I loved Phil, but the fact is that some of this mess is of their own making,' Ethan said. 'See now why I'm staying out of it?'

Kate nodded and looked at her rarely angry brother and was positive something else was eating him. 'Is there anything else going on?'

They were close, they were twins and they spoke a lot, but Ethan had only once before said what he was about to. 'I like someone.'

Kate saw his grim face. 'Married?' she groaned.

'No.'

'How long have you known her?'

'Since I started my new job, well, just after. She was having a couple of weeks off.'

'What's she like?'

'Moody, angry, funny, single…'

'Kids?' Kate checked, because there had to be a 'but'.

'Pregnant.' He looked at his sister. 'Only just.'

'Ethan!' Kate couldn't keep the excitement from her voice, but she didn't get carried away when she saw his face. 'I know you said it's not for you, but—'

'The baby's not mine!' Ethan quickly interrupted. 'Penny's on IVF. She's determined to be a single mum, she'd already started her treatment when we met.'

'Oh, Ethan.'

'I was giving her the shots.'

'Why?'

'Because she's petrified of needles and I didn't fancy her then, or maybe I did.' He shook his head. 'Kate, I don't even think I want kids, you know it broke Caitlin and I up. But even if I could somehow wrap my head around that, I mean even if I'd met Penny and she already had a child...' He pulled a face. 'I don't know, Kate. I can't walk around watching her get bigger with someone else's child.'

'Ethan,' Kate said. 'You know Carl and I were both having problems.' She was very careful not to say too much, but he knew that they had both been having problems, that all three of their children were Carl's in everything but genes.

'I get that,' Ethan said. 'But I bet Carl took a bit of time to get his head around it, and I bet he said a few things while he did that he wished he could take back now.'

And Kate stayed silent, because her brother was right—it had taken a lot of talking and a lot of soul searching before Carl had come round. 'And that was with two people who both desperately wanted kids and I don't even know that I do. I just walked in on the end of Penny's decision and I'm supposed to be fine with it? Well, I'm not and I'll tell you this much. I can't even...' He shut his mouth. He wasn't going to discuss *everything* with his sister and he couldn't explain properly, even to himself, the strange possessiveness that had gripped him when he'd almost slept with Penny.

'What do *you* want, Ethan?'

'Penny,' Ethan said. 'But I want time with Penny. I want to get to know her some more, it's still early days. I don't want to start something with someone who has a baby on board and be the one holding the sick back when I didn't cause it.' He looked at his sister. 'Selfish?'

'Honest.'

'And I'm angry too.'

'Why?'

'It doesn't matter.'

'Ethan?'

'It really doesn't matter,' Ethan said, even though he hated it when others did that. 'Because it's not relevant now.'

They couldn't carry on talking as they were being called for. The engines were still and he stood there as Phil's ashes were scattered. He looked at his aunt and uncle, who had been so strong at the funeral, celebrating his life, weep as the wind carried away the last thing they could do for him.

Only it wasn't just Phil that Ethan was thinking about as they stood in silence on deck. He wanted Penny to be happy, he was pleased for her, just terribly disappointed for them. Maybe he could do it, maybe he would wrap his head around it in a few months' time, but he felt as if there were a gun to it now and he looked at the ashes sinking into the waves and he was crying.

Not a lot and he didn't stand out, there wasn't a dry eye on board. He had every reason to be choked up, but he was, Kate knew, shedding a tear for other reasons too.

Penny didn't mind working nights, and she was actually glad that Ethan was on leave because she just wanted a pause to sort out how she felt about him. She wanted the hormones to calm down so she could look at things a bit more objectively. Not that she'd had even a moment to think about Ethan tonight; the place had been busy from the start of her shift and she was trying to put an NG tube down a very restless patient.

'Come on, Mia, swallow,' Penny said. 'You need this.'

'I don't want the tube.'

'Then you have to drink the charcoal.'

Mia had taken an overdose and to stop the tablets from being absorbed further, she had to be given a large drink of activated charcoal. It looked terrible, it was black and chalky, but as Penny and Vanessa had told the patient over and over, it actually didn't taste too bad. It was all to no avail, though—despite a lot of coaxing they'd only managed to get half the liquid into Mia.

'If you can let me put this tube down your nose and into your stomach, we can put the rest of it down and you won't have to taste it,' Penny said, 'and then you can have a rest, but it's imperative that you have the charcoal.'

'I can't.' The poor girl was upset already—after a huge row at her boyfriend Rory's house she'd stupidly swallowed some pills and when she'd got home her parents had thought she'd been drinking. When Mia had finally admitted what she had done, before calling the ambulance, there had been another row for Mia with her parents shouting at her, even as the paramedics arrived.

They'd started shouting again when Rory had arrived at the hospital, when most of all Mia needed calm, and

Penny was doing her best to ensure that Mia got it, but first she *had* to get the charcoal in.

'Do you want Rory to come in?' Penny suggested. 'He offered before.'

Mia nodded and Penny called the young man in. At eighteen Rory was very mature and he held both Mia's hands as Penny got ready to have another go at putting the tube down.

'Big breath,' Penny said, 'and then start to swallow when the tube hits the back of your throat.'

Except she didn't swallow. Instead, Mia vomited all over Penny's gown, so much so that it soaked through to her clothing.

'It doesn't matter,' Penny said soothingly as Mia started sobbing her apology. 'Let's give it another go.'

The cubicle looked as if someone had been playing with a black paintball and the staff and patients didn't look much better either, but finally the tube was in. Penny checked its position, relieved that the tube was in the right spot.

'Right, let's get the charcoal in and then you can have a rest.' The medication was poured down and Penny had a word with the intern, Raj, before she headed to the changing rooms. She was incredibly tired and couldn't wait for the couple of hours till the end of her shift.

Penny kept a spare set of clothes at work, but it was five a.m. and she was past caring so, rarely for her, she pulled some scrubs off the trolley, filled the sink with water to try and soak her shirt, and it was as she did so that Penny felt it—a cold feeling down below. She wanted to be imagining things, wanted to be wrong, so she dashed to the loo, but as she pulled down her panties it was confirmed that, no, she wasn't imagining things.

'Please, no,' Penny begged as she sat with her head in her hands, trying to tell herself it was normal, just some spotting, that it wasn't her period she was getting.

Penny couldn't stand to call it a baby; it was the only way she had been able to get through it last time. So she told herself that it was just a period, said over and over to herself that most women wouldn't have even have known that they were pregnant at this stage.

Except Penny knew that she fleetingly had been.

'Penny!' She heard Vanessa come into the changing room.

'Can I have two minutes?'

'Mia's not well.'

'I'm on my way,' Penny said through gritted teeth.

'She's seizing,' Vanessa went on.

'Then what are you doing in here, talking to me?' Penny shouted. 'Put out an urgent page for the medics.'

As Vanessa fled, with shaking hands Penny had to find change to buy a pad and then pulled on scrubs and dashed back to Mia. Raj was there and had given Mia diazepam; she had stopped seizing but was clearly very unwell.

'She's taken something else,' Penny said, because the medications Mia had admitted to taking would not have caused this.

'I've just spoken to the family.' Vanessa's voice was shaky. 'The boyfriend's ringing his mum to go through all the bins and things as they were at his house when she took them.'

'Good.'

Penny was tough, she *had* to be tough, she just didn't let herself think about personal things; instead she focussed on saving a sixteen-year-old girl who had made a stupid mistake that might now cost her her life. As soon as Rory came off the phone she spoke to the distressed boyfriend to try and get more clues as to what Mia might have taken.

'Mum's on anti-depressants.' Rory looked bewildered. 'I didn't even know that she was, but she's had a look and one of the packets is missing. She thinks—'

'Okay, what are they called?'

He told her and Penny kept her expression from reacting—she didn't want to scare the young man any more than he already was, but tricyclic antidepressants were very serious in overdose and could cause not just seizures but cardiac arrhythmias.

Leaving Rory, Penny told the medics what the young girl had taken and then dealt with the parents, who were still blaming the boyfriend.

'He has been very helpful,' Penny said. 'If it wasn't for Rory, we wouldn't have known what Mia had taken, and he also helped us to get the tube down. Mia's actually had the right treatment—the charcoal will stop any further absorption, but she'll need to go to Intensive Care for observation.'

'When can we see her?' the father asked.

'I can take you in there now,' Penny offered, because Mia was awake now, though very drowsy, but first she just wanted to clarify something with the parents. 'I know you're very upset at the moment, but it has to be put aside for now. Mia needs calm, she is not to be distressed.' Penny looked up as Rory walked in.

'What the hell did you say to upset her enough to take all those pills?' the father flared. 'You caused this.'

'I'm sorry!' Penny stood. She'd heard enough. 'Until you calm down, you're not coming in to see Mia.'

'You can't stop me from seeing her.'

'Absolutely I can.' Penny stood firm. 'Mia is to be kept as calm as possible. We're trying to prevent further arrhythmias or seizures, not actively bring them on.'

She walked off and started writing up her notes, and finally a rather more contrite father asked if he could go in and see his daughter now, assuring Penny he would not cause her any further distress.

'Of course.'

She stepped behind the curtain to have a quick word with Vanessa before letting them in.

'Mia's parents want to come in,' Penny said. 'Don't take any nonsense from the dad if he starts getting angry. Just ask him to leave.'

'I don't take nonsense from the patients and their relatives,' Vanessa said, and as Penny turned to go she heard the nurse mutter, 'I've got no choice with the staff, though...'

Penny didn't have the time, let alone the emotional capacity, to respond to Vanessa, or even to dwell on it. She had no alternative other than to drag herself through the last part of her shift, then she got into her car and finally she was home.

Penny took off her scrubs. Her stomach was black

from the charcoal and she showered quickly then put on a nightdress and picked up the phone.

'I'm bleeding.'

The IVF nurse was very practical and calm and, yes, a bit of spotting was normal, but this was more than a bit of spotting and they went through the medications, but Penny could feel herself cramping.

'Should I rest?' She wanted to ring in sick but she knew deep down that it wouldn't make any real difference.

But she rang in sick anyway.

Work was less than impressed, because it was the long weekend and one consultant was out on a boat and Mr Dean was on a golf weekend, but whether or not it would make a difference to the outcome, Penny couldn't have gone into work anyway—she just lay in bed, trying to hold on to something she was sure she'd already lost.

'I'm sorry, Penny.' It was Tuesday night. She'd actually stopped bleeding but didn't dare hope, yet there was a tiny flicker there when she took the call, only to hear that her HCG levels were tumbling down.

All that for twenty-four hours of being pregnant.

Jasmine's periods were later than that sometimes.

'Oh, Penny, I'm so sorry!' Jasmine, who the second she'd heard that Penny had called in sick, had been in and out of her home all over the weekend. She was there too when the nurse called with her blood results and Jasmine wrapped her in a hug when Penny put down the phone after the news. But Penny could feel Jasmine's belly soft and round and pressing into her stupid empty flat one and Penny said some horrible things.

Horrible things.

Like, no, actually, Jasmine didn't understand.

And that it was all right for Jasmine to stand there and be so compassionate and understanding when she didn't actually have a clue how it felt to not even be able to get pregnant. Except it was a bit worse than that because Penny used the F word and then asked her sister to get out.

'Penny, please!'

'No!'

She was back to being a bitch.

CHAPTER TEN

THERE WERE DISADVANTAGES to being a consultant, as Ethan was finding out, because when he came back from his long-awaited days off, which had actually turned into more of an extended wake, half his colleagues were sulking because he'd been out of range and they'd been called in to work.

'Penny's sick?' Ethan frowned when Lisa told him.

That Penny might be ill wasn't the problem apparently, though it was the problem for Ethan. 'We had a locum for two nights and Mr Dean came in, but he wasn't too pleased.' Lisa brought him up to speed.

'But if she's sick, she can't help it,' Ethan pointed out as a knot tightened in his stomach. 'When did she ring in?'

'Saturday morning.' Lisa sighed. 'At the beginning of a long weekend. It's been a bit grim here, to say the least.'

But it wasn't just Penny they were annoyed at.

'Did you have a good break?' Mr Dean gave a tight, mirthless smile as he walked past, but Ethan just rolled his eyes. He didn't give a damn about things like that—he worked hard when he was here and was entitled to his days off. The only person Ethan was worried about now was Penny.

Except when he tried to call her, she didn't pick up her phone.

'How's Penny?' Ethan asked a worried-looking Jasmine when she arrived for her late shift.

Jasmine's cheeks flushed and she just gave a brief shake of her head.

'Did she lose it?'

Ethan grimaced when Jasmine gave a reluctant nod.

Ethan headed to his office and rang Kate and told her the little he knew.

'Don't call it *it*,' Kate suggested.

'I didn't mean it like that.'

'I know,' Kate said. 'Poor thing.'

'I don't know what to do.' Ethan didn't even know how he felt. He was gutted for Penny as he thought of all she had been through.

But there was guilt there as well.

'I don't know what you can do either,' Kate admitted, because Carl had been as invested in the procedures as she had and had been right there beside her when on many occasions the news hadn't been good. But though she utterly understood where her brother was coming from, he wasn't going to react as Carl had.

'Do I just not mention it? I mean…'

'No,' Kate said, but then halted. 'I don't know. You said she hadn't told you she was pregnant?'

'I can't just ignore it,' Ethan said. 'She won't pick up the phone.'

'You really like her?'

'Yes.'

'Then I think you ought to go over there and just be ready.'

'For what?'

'For anything.'

Even as he rang the bell, Ethan had absolutely no idea if he was doing the right thing.

It just couldn't go past without being noted.

That was all he knew.

She opened the door in her dressing gown, except it was undone and underneath she had on a short night-dress. Ethan hadn't known many woman who wore silky nightdresses and matching dressing gowns, but this was Penny, he reminded himself, and even if she was a bit washed out, she still looked stunning.

'I'm so sorry, Penny.'

She looked at him, all brown and healthy and brim-ming with energy from nearly a week off, and she felt drab and pale in comparison. 'How do you know?' Penny asked. 'Did Jasmine say something?'

Ethan hadn't even made it through the door and he'd already put his foot in it. 'No,' Ethan said. 'I asked her when I heard you'd called in sick.'

'She shouldn't have said anything.'

'She didn't say a word,' Ethan said. 'I asked if you'd...' He breathed out. 'Penny, I knew before you went away that you were pregnant.'

'How?'

How? Because she was buried so deep in his skull, he'd been on IVF sites and working out dates and watching her unseen, constantly tuned in to her, though she didn't need to hear that. 'I just knew,' Ethan said. 'Jasmine didn't say a word.'

Penny opened the door further and let him in.

'I didn't know what to bring.' He was very honest with his discomfort and it helped that he didn't try to hide it. It helped that he had come too.

'Wine would have been nice.'

'I can go out and get some.'

'I've got some open.' Penny looked at him warily. 'I'm not very good company.'

'I'm not here for a party.'

'Well, you won't get one. I'm boring even me now in my quest for a baby, so I'd run for the beach now if I were you. I know it's not your thing. I'll be back to normal soon.'

'Come here,' he said, and he gave her a cuddle. She wriggled a bit as she had the first day he'd held her and then she gave in; it felt really nice to be held by him.

'Do you want me to go out and get a bottle?'

'No. I'm drinking alone. Well, not alone, I've got my cat.'

And an ugly cat it was too, Ethan thought as feline eyes narrowed in suspicion at a big male stomping through the room. He followed Penny to where she was retrieving her glass and bottle from her bedside table and hovered at the door.

'I'm a cliché,' Penny said. 'I'll be the mad aunt, if Jasmine ever lets me see them again.' She closed her eyes. 'I had a terrible argument with her when I found out. I'm a horrible sister.'

'I'm sure you're not.'

'I am.' Penny sniffed. 'We've never been that close, but for the last few months we've both really tried, and now I've gone and ruined it. I told her that she had no idea how I felt.'

'She doesn't,' Ethan said.

'But she tries so hard to. It's not her fault, I just...' She was embarrassed to admit just how bad she'd been, but was too guilt ridden to gloss over it. 'She gave me a cuddle and I could feel her stomach and I told her that, no, she didn't know, but I said it more nastily than that.' Worried blue eyes lifted to him and a dark blush spread on her cheeks. 'It wasn't just that she's pregnant, though.' She stopped. She certainly wasn't about to share her shameful truth. 'It doesn't matter.'

'Tell me.'

'I can't.'

'You can.'

'I really can't.'

'I hate that,' Ethan said. 'I hate it when people go, oh, it doesn't matter, when clearly it does, and then they say they can't tell you, and you know that it's something relevant, except you're not allowed to know.'

She actually smiled a little when she responded to him. 'You're *not* allowed.'

'Fine.' Ethan sulked.

'If I told you and you ever said anything, I'd have to kill you.'

Ethan couldn't help but smile but more than that they were sitting down on the sofa together and Penny was, Ethan realised, actually going to reveal. 'When my mum was bought in in cardiac arrest, it was awful. I mean, just awful. Jasmine was on duty but I managed to keep it from her…'

'While you worked on your mum?'

'And I was upset. I mean, really upset.'

'I would imagine so.'

'And Jed gave me a cuddle, nothing more. What I didn't know then was that Jasmine was seeing Jed. Confused?'

'Not yet.'

'But Jasmine saw us together, before she knew about Mum, I mean…'

'And thought you two were together?' Ethan checked, and Penny nodded. 'And were you?'

'Never.'

'Not a little bit?' Ethan checked.

'Not a smudge,' Penny confirmed. 'But…' She just couldn't bring herself to say it.

'You liked him?'

'A bit.' She was just this ball of guilt. 'I wasn't having dirty dreams or anything.' She went red as she looked at Ethan, because she was having the rudest ones about him. 'But, yes, I sort of liked him. I don't remotely in that way now, I mean that, but at the time…'

'It hurt to find out they were together.'

'Yes,' Penny admitted.

'And now she's got the baby.'

'Two.'

'Penny.' Ethan was honest too. 'Can I tell you something?' He took her hands. 'I think it's completely normal to like someone, to fancy them. I like and fancy people all the time, it's not an issue, even if the two of you…'

'Nothing happened.'

'Which makes things a whole lot easier. But…' he didn't really see the issue '…suppose,' Ethan said, 'just suppose Jasmine was single, and given all we've done is had one kiss, well, a bit more than that…'

And Penny felt the heat of breath in her nostrils, and it burnt a whole lot more than it had with Jed, except she couldn't really tell him that when he was trying to prove a point about how inconsequential it was.

'Okay, bad example.' Ethan scrambled for other scenarios. 'Suppose—'

'I get your point.' She did. In one fell swoop he'd made her realise just how teeny her feelings for her— unknown at the time—future brother-in-law had been. She thought of Jasmine walking alongside her on the beach, admitting how gorgeous Ethan was, and what a tiny deal it had been then.

'You've done nothing wrong,' Ethan said. 'Are you not supposed to like anyone, just in case your sister might?'

'I guess.' Penny couldn't believe how easily a simple conversation had dispersed the complicated into nothing. 'I don't want Jed, and I am pleased she's pregnant.' She looked at Ethan. 'It was just all too much that day. Do you ever feel jealous that Kate has a family?'

'No.' He was honest. 'I just can't imagine ever being settled like that, just one person for the rest of your life. And…' he gave a shrug '…I think we've found another phobia of mine.' He took a deep breath; there was one thing he needed to know. 'Will you try again?'

'I don't know,' Penny said. 'Probably. But they like you to wait a couple of months.'

'You're thirty-four, Penny,' Ethan said.

'Thirty-five,' Penny said. 'It's my birthday.'

He didn't know what to say.

And clearly neither did Jasmine, because the phone rang then and Penny took it into her bedroom. It was a very short, terse phone call and when it was over Penny looked up at him in the doorway, only this time he came in.

'Do you ever fight with your sister?' she asked as he sat with her on the bed and put his arm around her.

'Not really,' Ethan said.

'With anyone?'

'No.' He gave her a smile. 'You.'

But it wasn't enough for Penny. She wanted him to have done something as terrible as she had, and so he thought for a moment, searched his brain for someone he'd had a huge stand-up row with, just to make her feel better.

'With Phil.'

'When?' Penny frowned.

'Last year. There was stuff that needed dealing with and Phil wasn't dealing with it. And I told him so and pretty loudly too.' Ethan gave her a nudge. 'So if you feel bad, imagine having a shouting match with someone who has a heart like a balloon about to burst.'

'But it didn't.'

'No, it didn't. Well, not for another year.' Ethan shook his head; he wasn't going to go there.

'You really loved him, didn't you?'

'Yep.' Ethan nodded. 'But I'm here about you.'

They were lying on the bed now, more two friends chatting than this being about anything sexual, even as the conversation turned to sex. 'Have you ever thought about going about it the old-fashioned way?' Ethan asked. 'Meet someone, fall in love, live the fairy-tale.'

'Been there, done that. Well, I thought it was love and we were frantically trying for a baby for a very long time.'

He'd been doing really well, Kate would have been proud of him, but he grimaced a bit then and she noticed.

'What?'

'Nothing.' Ethan shrugged. He just didn't like the image of her *frantically* trying with someone else.

'I'm not very fertile—I'm sub-fertile. Isn't that the most horrible word? It put a terrible strain on our relationship. It wasn't just that, though, he was...' She was about to say it didn't matter, but Ethan hated it when she did that. 'Vince was all for the modern working woman, or so he said, yet I was the one who was going to be the stay-home mum.' Ethan looked at her. 'I earned more than him, yet it was just assumed that I'd be the one to stop work.' She saw him frown. 'What?' Penny asked again.

'Why, if you're doing all you can to have a baby, would you want to work?'

'I love my work, I'd go crazy without it, but I would

certainly slow things down. It wasn't just that, though, there were other things.'

'Like what?'

'Like I was starting to resent that it was always me stopping at the supermarket on the way home from work and getting dinner. Aside from the fact that I can't have babies, I don't think I'd make a very good wife.'

'What's for dinner, Penny?'

He made her smile.

'What about you?'

'I have no idea,' he said, and turned and smiled at her now-frowning face on the pillow beside him. 'I've never had my fertility checked.'

'You think you're funny, don't you?'

'I know I am,' Ethan said, 'because you're trying really hard not to smile.'

'I meant, have you been in a serious relationship?'

'Apparently,' Ethan said. 'Though I didn't know it at the time.' He sighed at the memory. 'I thought it was great, she wanted to move in...'

'Oh.'

'Or look for somewhere to live, or get engaged and then married and make lots of babies one day.'

'What was her name?'

'Caitlin. I led her on apparently, but I didn't know that I was, I just thought we were having a good time. I didn't realise it had to be leading somewhere—so now I make things a little more clear from the start.' He waited, his eyes checking that he had.

'I get it, Ethan.' She gave him a smile and then she

told him. 'Jasmine said I should have a wild fling with you before I got pregnant.'

'I'm that much of a sure thing, am I?'

'Apparently,' Penny said. 'She thought I should forget about making babies and just enjoy myself for once.'

'Have you ever had sex for the sake of it?' He screwed up his face. 'I mean, how long since you've had sex without trying for a baby?'

'A very long time.' She looked at him. 'There was one time that I would have, but he declined.'

'Well, maybe he was just being all male and territorial and couldn't quite get his head around...' He screwed up his face again, tried to spare the details. 'You know in a few days' time you...'

'Might have been pregnant?'

'No, not just that.'

Penny frowned and then got it. 'With someone else's baby!' She actually laughed. 'You *are* a caveman!'

'Nope, just a normal man.' Ethan grinned, glad to see her smile. 'And the only one I want you *frantically* describing is me.'

And he was getting his words wrong, because he meant that he didn't want to sit here and listen about her ex and her in bed, or did he mean that he wanted to give her something to frantically describe?

That wasn't what he'd come here for.

'I'm going to go.'

He pulled up on his elbow and gave her a kiss, though it was a bit pointless to pretend it was a friendly one, given what they'd been like, and that they were lying on the bed, but Ethan did kiss her with no intention other than to say goodbye.

Except he'd forgotten just how much he liked kissing her till he was back there, and Penny was remembering all over again too. It was so nice to be lying down being kissed by him, nicer too when a little while later his hands crept to her breasts that clearly didn't disappoint because she could feel him harden against her thigh as he stroked.

Only this time he did what he had wanted to that time, his mouth moving down, slipping down the fabric and licking around the areola and then taking her in his mouth.

She was on her back, his expert mouth suckling her hard, and Penny was gasping, wanting to turn to get to him, to explore him too, but loath to end the bliss of his mouth.

He turned her to him, gave her other breast the same attention. Ethan, who loved breasts, actually loved that she hardly had any. Penny was grappling to pull out his top, desperate to feel his skin as his mouth sucking her breast drove her to higher pleasures.

But Ethan moved her hands away, his intention to take his time, but as his hand slid down the jut of her hips, her nightdress had ridden up and he found his hand cupping her bare bottom. 'Hell, Penny,' he moaned, 'have you been walking around all this time with no knickers on?' He blew out a breath, remembered then the reason he was there, and when Kate had said to be ready for anything, he was quite sure she hadn't meant that. 'Sorry.'

'For what?'

'Taking things too far.'

'You've never taken things too far,' Penny said. 'You haven't taken things far enough.'

They were at each other again, a knot of arms and legs and deep kisses, her hands going to his buckle, but he halted her.

'Penny.' He took her face in his hands and he wrestled with indecision, not sure if it was Hot Mess Penny he was talking to, whom he completely adored and could deal with, or Baby Making Mode Penny, who terrified him, and she got that much.

'I'm not asking you to get me pregnant.'

'Isn't it too soon?' Ethan checked.

'Nope.' And she thought of sex for the sake of it, and how lovely he had been and how badly she wanted the rest of that chocolate bar out of the fridge now. And so too did Ethan. They were back to kissing, only pausing to strip the other off and pray for condoms in his wallet, which, hurrah, there were.

She buried her head in his chest and smelt and felt close-up and naked Ethan. He was stunning, muscled but not too much with a smooth tanned chest and flat brown nipples that shifted from view as his mouth slid down again, only this time not to her breasts. He licked down to her stomach and he did what he had wanted to do that first day he had given her her injection, and he kissed her till she was writhing.

Penny had felt like a pincushion these past weeks, a failed baby-making machine at times, but his mouth was slowly turning her back into a woman as he lingered at each step. Penny closed her eyes in bliss as his mouth moved lower still and with each measured stroke she lost a little more control but gained mounting pleasure. Her hands pulled tight on his hair as Ethan revelled in the taste of her. The scent that had been alluring him for weeks was now his to savour and he carried on kissing her deeply there as she throbbed to his mouth and he returned her to herself.

A new self.

'Ethan.' Penny lay catching her breath, went to say something, she didn't know what. She wanted to sit up and face him, wanted to go down on him. It took a moment to realise it wasn't her decision to make. He was over her, sheathed and poised at her entrance.

'Love-thirty,' he said, sexy and smiling and not a moment too soon for Penny, through with being patient.

She moaned as he filled her. Ethan folded his arms behind her head so that her face was right up to him, and she had forgotten how lovely sex could be. Or rather, Penny amended as he moved deep inside her, she'd never really known just how lovely sex could be. Then, as Ethan shifted tempo she made one final amendment before she lost rational thought. She'd never known sex could be so hot.

She didn't get poor-Penny sex; she got the full bull in Ethan. A surprise birthday present that had her as wild as him. One of his arms moved down to her hips and he practically lifted her off the bed each time he thrust into her. Had Penny ever had any doubt as to all those times she'd thought him aroused, they were gone, because every missed opportunity, every subdued thought

Ethan had had seemed to be being banished now over and over deep in her centre.

His want, his desire, the absence of tentativeness had Penny flooded in warmth, her legs wrapping around him, her skin scalding, grinding into him as she tipped into climax.

'Penny…' Ethan was trying to hold on, but feeling her shatter, feeling her jolt as if she'd been stunned, by the time he felt her strong, rapid clenches Ethan was on the way to meeting them.

Almost dizzy, he collapsed on top of her and then moved to the side, pulling her with him, more than a bit bewildered about what had happened, because Ethan loved sex but had never had sex like that, and while going down on her his intention had been to be gentle.

'Did we land on the beach?' Ethan asked.

'I'm not sure,' Penny admitted. 'I can't actually see.' She felt a gurgle of laughter swirl inside her, only it wasn't laughter, she realised, just this glimpse of being free. 'And it's actually thirty-fifteen now,' Penny said. 'You forfeited the last game if I remember rightly.'

He'd had no idea what to expect when he'd arrived tonight at her door, but felt as if, in that small conversation, he'd met the real Penny, the one that he'd sometimes glimpsed. Or was it more that it was a different him? Usually Ethan was snoring his head off right about now, but instead it was Penny dozing as he went and dimmed the lights before climbing into bed beside her.

'Happy birthday, Penny.'

And as she lay there, feeling his big body beside her, she thought that it really shouldn't have been a happy birthday; it had had every ingredient for it not to be, except it had just turned into her most memorable, possibly favourite one.

'Thank you,' Penny said, and then turned over to him. 'You were right—it wasn't the drugs.'

CHAPTER ELEVEN

'IT'S MY MUM.'

Unfortunately Penny hadn't come into the bathroom to join him in the shower later the next morning. They were up to deuce after a much more tender lovemaking session and Penny was fixing some breakfast while Ethan showered when the intercom buzzed. 'I know this sounds like I'm eighteen…'

'You want me to hide?' Ethan grinned as she pulled on her nightdress and then her dressing gown.

'Not hide, just don't come out of the bedroom,' Penny said. 'She'll tell Jasmine and, honestly, by the time we get back to work they'll all have us engaged or something.'

'Mum!' Penny opened the door and stood as her mum gave her a cuddle.

'I'm so sorry, Penny, I wish I'd been here. I told you not to try till after my trip.'

And there were so many things she could have said to that, but Penny buttoned her lip and forced a smile.

'How was the cruise?'

'It was amazing!' It must have been because Louise *looked* amazing! She was suntanned and relaxed-looking and wearing new clothes and jewellery, and her hair was a fabulous caramel colour and very well cut. 'I had the best time, Penny. You'd love it!'

'I think I might,' Penny said, because till her mother had set off, she'd never even considered one, but she was seeing the benefits now.

'All you do is eat and be pampered—I've got so much to tell you!'

And Ethan lay on the bed, reading magazines, listening as Penny did her best to limit his exposure to her mother's love life, because Penny kept asking her to describe islands, but her mum just kept talking about a man she had met. 'I go all the way to Greece and Bradley's from Melbourne and he's so romantic. One night—'

'Hold on a minute, Mum,' Penny interrupted. 'I'm just going to get changed.'

She brought Ethan in a coffee, which she would pretend she'd left in her room, not that her mother would notice. She was way too busy discussing Bradley and comparing the differences with Penny's father.

'I'm so sorry.'

'It's interesting.'

It was, and it became more so because Penny could not stop her mother from talking, and Ethan heard how useless her father had been and that maybe Louise had been a bit harsh in her summing up of *all* men to her daughters, because Bradley was nothing like that at all.

They were serious, in fact, he heard her tell Penny.

'It's a month, Mum.'

'And I'm old enough to know what I like and that this is right.'

'Well, why not just see how it goes now you're back?' He could hear Penny's wariness and then her mother's exasperation.

'Can't you just be happy for me, Penny?'

'Of course I am.'

But they all knew it was qualified and then the strain was back in Penny's voice, especially when her mother asked how she felt about losing the baby.

'It wasn't a baby, Mum! I got my period.' Ethan closed his eyes. Kate had been right—it was different for everyone, because Kate had had photos and named every embryo. 'It just didn't work.'

'Okay, Penny.'

They chatted some more and then with Penny promising to go round tomorrow she finally got her mother out of the door. Ethan looked up at Penny's strained features as she came through the bedroom door.

'Sorry about that.'

'No need to say sorry.'

'She just goes too far.' Penny let out an angry breath. 'I can't think of it as a baby.' Ethan was terribly aware suddenly that he was lying not in a bed but a minefield. 'I'd go mad otherwise, if I thought like that.'

'I know.'

'I bet she didn't ask Jasmine to hold off trying to conceive till she got back.' Ethan swallowed, thought it best not to say a thing, though was tempted to fire a quick SOS to his sister just in case he said the wrong thing. 'Well, she can go over there now and hear Jasmine's latest happy news.' Penny joined him on the bed. 'She's met the love of her life, apparently.'

'Bradley,' Ethan said, and she gave a little laugh.

She turned to him. 'I'm supposed to be happy for her.'

'Aren't you?'

Penny looked back at him. 'From past experience I really don't trust my mother's taste in men so no, I'm not going to clap hands and get all excited. He's the first person she's seriously dated since my father left.'

'Do you ever see him?'

'Never,' Penny said. 'And I've never wanted to. I see enough of his sort at work and I've stitched up enough of his sort's handiwork too.' She didn't want to talk about her father. 'What did you do while we were talking?' Penny asked.

'Read,' Ethan said. 'Had a little walk around the bed, worked out that you rotate your wardrobe...'

'Of course I do,' Penny said. 'I haven't got time to think what to wear each day.' She climbed off the bed. 'I'm going to have a shower.'

'Good,' Ethan said. 'And I'll find you something to wear.'

'I can choose my own clothes, thank you.'

'You don't know where we're going.'

'Ethan, I don't want to go out.'

'Which is exactly why you should.'

Penny chose her own clothes, thank you very much. A pair of shorts and a T-shirt and wedge sandals and Ethan watched in amusement as she applied factor thirty to every exposed piece of skin. When they walked out of her smart townhouse and didn't head straight for his car, Penny actually felt a bit shaky.

'I've been inside too long.'

'I know you have.'

Really, since her walk on the beach with Jasmine it had been work and appointments and stopping at the supermarket on the way home, she told Ethan as they walked down to the beach.

'I'm a terrible wife even to myself,' Penny said, taking off her sandals and holding them as they walked down the path to the beach. 'I try to remember to make lots of meals and then freeze them and I always mean to make healthy lunches and take them in.'

'Same,' Ethan said.

'And I do it for one day, sometimes two.'

'That's why there's a canteen, Penny.' Ethan smiled. 'For all the people who have rotting vegetables in the drawer at the bottom of their fridge and didn't have time to make a sandwich, and if they did they don't have any super-healthy grain bread.'

Penny smiled. It was actually really nice to be out. It was a very clear day, the bay as blue and still as the sky, and the beach pretty empty. It was just nice to feel the sand beneath her feet and she thought of the last time she had been here with Jasmine and Simon, having hot flashes and carrying petrified hope and talking about wild flings with Ethan.

Penny glanced over at him, glad and surprised that the one thing she hadn't wanted that day had transpired.

'How come you ended up at Peninsula?' Penny asked.

'I wanted a change.' Ethan's voice was wry. 'I thought a nice bayside hospital would mean a nice laid-back lifestyle—I mean, given we don't have PICU and things.' He gave a shrug. 'I didn't count on catchments and that we'd get everything for miles around and then end up transferring them out.'

'You don't like it?'

'I love it,' Ethan mused. 'It just wasn't what I was expecting it to be—and I know that I don't do this sort of thing enough.' Ethan thought about it all for a long moment as they walked—thought about the wall of silence he had been met with because he hadn't been able to suddenly come back when Penny was sick. Thought about all that was silently expected of them. Ethan wasn't a rebel, just knew that there had to be more than work, and he told her that.

'You go out,' Penny said, because she'd heard that Ethan liked to party hard.

'I do,' Ethan said, 'but...' Just not lately. Ethan had once thought of days off counted in parties and bars and women and how much he could cram in. But since Phil's death it had all halted. Right now, just pausing on the beach on his one day off, Ethan actually felt like he'd escaped.

'I'm going to join a gym.' Penny broke into his thoughts.

'So you can feel guilty about not going?'

He made her smile because, yes, over the years she'd joined the hospital gym and the one near home many times.

'Why don't you just walk here more often?' Ethan suggested.

'Why don't you?'

They took the path off the beach that led into town and ordered brunch—smoked salmon and poached eggs on a very unhealthy white bread, washed down with coffee and fruit juice, and it was nice to sit outside and watch the world passing. Ethan was right, it was so good to be out, but being out meant exposure and after half an hour sitting at a pavement café she heard a woman call his name.

'Ethan.'

Penny looked up and it was the woman who had dropped him off that time, except she was pushing a stroller with a three-year-old and a very young baby.

'Kate.' Ethan smiled and looked down at his niece and nephew and gave them a wave then remembered to make the introductions. 'This is Penny from work and, Penny, this is my sister, Kate.'

'Of course you should join us,' Penny said when Kate insisted she didn't want to interrupt. She sat but when there wasn't a waiter to be found Ethan headed inside to order coffee and a milkshake for the three-year-old.

It was horribly awkward for Penny, because she and Kate were just so different; both lived close by yet both moved in completely different circles.

Both had a bit of what the other wanted.

'Days off?' Kate asked.

'Yes,' Penny answered. 'Well, I've been off sick, but I'm back tomorrow.'

'I'm sorry to hear that,' Kate said, aching at the defensiveness in Penny's voice, because she knew so much more.

'Ethan said you had three children?'

'Yes, the eldest is at school,' Kate said, nodding towards the school over the street. 'You work in Emergency with Ethan?' she checked, as if she didn't already know. 'I think I saw you when I dropped Ethan off one morning.'

'That's right.' Penny did her best not to blush, because it had been the morning she had actually realised just how gorgeous Ethan was.

Yes, it was awkward because Penny just said as she always did, as little as possible about herself. If she'd only open up, Ethan thought when he returned, then Kate would tell her all about the hell she had gone through to get her three, but instead they talked about work and weather and things that didn't matter, till Kate had to go. 'I'll catch up with you soon, Ethan.' She gave her brother a friendly kiss on the cheek. 'It was lovely to meet you, Penny.'

'And you.'

'She seems nice,' Penny said.

'She is,' Ethan said, but if she'd just spoken properly to her, then Penny would know that Kate didn't just *seem* nice, she actually *was*.

Penny, Penny, Ethan sighed in his head. What to do?

'Shall we go to the movies?'

'The movies?' Penny frowned. 'I haven't been to the movies since...' She thought for a moment. 'I can't remember when.'

At her insistence, Penny bought the tickets and he

went and got the popcorn and drinks and things, but as she walked over she saw him talking to a woman and a young boy and stopped walking.

The woman was being polite, but her face was a frozen mask. The young boy beside her was smiling up at Ethan and she just knew then that it was Justin. He looked like Ethan.

She was shaking a bit inside, her mind racing. She'd got it wrong with his sister; she couldn't keep jumping to the conclusion that every woman he spoke to he'd slept with. Penny made a great deal about putting the tickets into her purse, pretending to jump in surprise as Ethan came over.

'Okay?' Penny checked.

'Sure.'

She could tell he wasn't.

Still, the movie was a good one and it was so nice to sit in the darkness—so nice not to have to think. They sat at the back in a practically empty cinema and ate popcorn and just checked out of the world for a little while, which for Penny was bliss. It was nice too for Ethan to not go over and over the terse conversation with Gina. To just accept that Gina didn't want her ex-husband's cousin involved in her son's life.

He turned in the darkness to Penny about the same time she turned to him. There was the rustle of popcorn falling to the floor as they acted more like teenagers than a responsible couple in their thirties. After the movie Ethan wished he had brought the car as they walked quickly along the beach, almost running, not just to be together but away from problems each needed to face.

It felt so good to fall through the door, to lift her arms as he slid her out of her top, to undo the zipper of her shorts, as she did the same to him.

'Why did we leave it so long?' He was kissing her, not thinking of anything else but her mouth and her body and all the times they had missed, and how much better the boat would have been if he'd had Penny there with him.

'You know why.'

Ethan's head was in two places as he remembered what had kept them apart, but that problem had gone now and he just wasn't thinking, or rather he was thinking out loud, but before he had time to stop himself suddenly the words were out.

'Maybe it's for the best.'

CHAPTER TWELVE

'YOU DIDN'T SAY that?' Kate grimaced. 'God, Ethan.'

'I can't believe I said it.' The once laid-back Ethan had his head in his hands as Kate grilled him further.

'What did she do?'

His look said it all because Penny had said the F word again, quite a few times, as she'd kicked him out.

'I'm not saying you have to tiptoe around her, but honestly, Ethan, it is the most awful time. Carl and I never row, but we have every time I've been on IVF, and if he'd said that...' Kate let out a long, angry sigh that told Ethan her reaction would have perhaps been as volatile as Penny's.

'I can understand you'd be upset if Carl said it, but I didn't mean it like that,' Ethan said. 'I meant...' He stopped talking then.

'What?' his sister pushed.

'That I can barely get my head around a long-term relationship and having kids of my own, let alone going out with someone who was pregnant with someone else's child. When I said it was for the best I just meant that at least now we had a chance.'

'You need to tell her that.'

'You've met her,' Ethan told his twin. 'She's the most difficult, complicated…' And there it was, she was everything he wanted, the one woman who could possibly hold his attention. And she was still holding it fully on her first day back at work.

Penny was wearing a grey skirt with her cream sleeveless blouse but she'd lost weight around her hips and maybe he *was* a bit of a caveman because he wanted to insist she take some proper time off and haul her to his bed, and feed her and have sex with her and then watch late-night shows in his dark bedroom while she slept, while she healed. He wanted to take care of her. Instead, he had to stand and watch as she nitpicked her way through the department, upsetting everyone. Any minute soon he was going to have to step in.

'Why hasn't his blood pressure been done?' Her voice carried over the resuscitation room. Penny was checking the obs chart on her patient. She had ordered observations to be taken every fifteen minutes and when she saw that they hadn't been done for half an hour she called out to Vanessa.

'It has been done,' Vanessa said, taking the chart. 'Sorry, Penny, I just didn't write it down. It was one-eighty over ninety.'

'Which means nothing if it isn't written down.' Penny held her breath and told herself to calm down, but she'd told Vanessa about this a few times. 'You *have* to document.'

'I know.'

'Then why don't you do it?' Penny said, and as she walked off, she was aware that Ethan was behind her. He tapped her smartly on the shoulder but she ignored him.

'Stop taking it out on the nurses.'

'I'm not,' Penny said. 'What's the point of Vanessa knowing the patient is hypertensive and not telling me or even writing it down? If he strokes out—'

'Penny.' He knew all that, knew that she was right, but he could see the dark shadows under her eyes and could feel her tense and too thin under his hand on her shoulder. 'I'm sorry for what I said.'

'I don't want to discuss that.'

'Tough.' She had marched to her office and Ethan had followed and stood with his back to the door. 'I said the wrong thing. I say the wrong thing a lot apparently.'

'You said how you felt.'

'How could I have when I don't even know how I feel?' Ethan couldn't contain it any longer and to hell with lousy timing, it had been lousy timing for him as well. 'I'm sorry that I didn't arrive in your life with a fully packed nappy bag, ready to be a father to another man's child.' Penny closed her eyes. 'Instead, I walked in on the end of a huge life decision you'd made.'

'I didn't make it lightly.'

'But I was supposed to,' Ethan said. 'I was supposed to be fine with it, delighted that you were pregnant, and for you I was, just not for us!'

And she was just so bruised and raw and angry and lost she didn't know how to respond anymore.

'Just leave it.'

'How can I leave it?' Ethan demanded. 'Because I'm

trying to sort the two of us out and you're talking about going for it again.'

'No, I'm not.'

Today, Ethan wanted to add, but just stood there, trying to hold on to his temper, because only a low-life would have a row with a woman going through this. 'Okay, let's just leave it,' Ethan said, 'but I will not have you taking it out on the nurses. You've upset Vanessa.'

'Vanessa knows me.' Guilt prickled down her spine. 'I've worked with Vanessa for years.'

'Hey,' Ethan snapped. 'Do you remember that guy I stitched who'd just had a remote control bounce off his skull?'

She had no idea what he was talking about. 'Well, maybe you weren't working that day, but he said the same. "She's never moaned, we've been married for years."' His eyes flashed at Penny. 'People will put up with so much, Penny, but not for ever.'

'I get that!' Penny screwed her eyes closed on tears. 'I've always been strict with observations, I've always been tough.'

'There's another word to describe you that's doing the rounds right now, Penny.'

'I know that. It's just been so intense.'

'I know that,' Ethan said, 'but the staff don't. I'm not going to stand back and let you take it out on them, Penny. Please.' He was trying to pull her up, trying to talk her down; he just wanted to take her home, but she didn't want him to and as he tried to take her in his arms Penny was backing off.

'I know it's been hell for you,' Ethan said.

'Well, it's over.' Penny swallowed down her pain. 'I just want to get back to my life, back to my career. I can't believe that I turned down a prom...' She stopped herself.

'Say it.'

Penny looked at him.

'It doesn't matter.'

'You know how I really hate that.' And so he waited.

'I turned down a promotion so that I could concentrate on IVF.'

'You mean you turned down my job?' Ethan checked, and she gave a tight shrug. Then he was on side with the masses—Penny could be such a bitch at times. 'Thanks a lot, Penny.'

She wanted to call him back, except he walked out, and if that wasn't enough to be dealing with, a moment later there was a knock at her door.

'Hi, Lisa.' Penny gave a tight smile. 'It's not really a good time.'

'No, it isn't a good time,' Lisa said. 'My nurses work hard, Penny, and they put up with a lot and they do many extra things to help you that you probably don't even notice.' Penny swallowed as Lisa continued. 'But you might start to notice just how much extra they did for you when they stop.'

'It will be okay,' Jasmine said.

Penny had left work early, to Mr Dean's obvious displeasure, and the second she had got home she had rung her sister and said sorry, and Jasmine had come round. They'd had a cuddle when Jasmine had arrived at her door and, this time, when Penny had felt the swell in her sister's stomach, while it had hurt, overriding that Penny was happy for her sister and just so pleased to see her that she told Jasmine about work.

'I've upset all the nurses.'

'Penny!' Jasmine flailed between divided loyalties. 'You haven't been that bad. Lisa can be a cow at times—and Vanessa's always forgetting to write things down, but if you were more friendly, if people knew more what was going on in your life...'

'I don't know how to tell people.'

And Jasmine got that, because since she had been a little girl it had been Penny who had taken care of things, who had let her little sister open up to her about all the scary stuff going on with their parents and had said nothing about her own fears.

'You told Ethan.'

'Because I had to.'

'So how did the Neanderthal do?' Jasmine asked.

'He was great,' Penny said, and she let out a sigh as she remembered that day, how he'd stepped in when she'd broken down, how he'd actually said all the right things. 'Not just with the injections.'

'You like him?'

Penny nodded. 'And I just hurt him,' she said. 'I let it slip about the promotion.'

'You didn't just let it slip,' Jasmine said. 'You did what you always do whenever anyone gets close.'

'Probably,' Penny admitted.

'Try talking to him,' Jasmine said.

'I don't want to talk to him about this, though,' Penny

said. 'It's all we talk about and I'm tired of it. I wish I'd met him without this damn IVF hanging over me. I want us to have a chance at normal.'

'Tell him, then,' Jasmine urged.

'I can't yet,' Penny admitted. 'I need to sort out myself first, work out how I feel about other things.' Penny took a deep breath. 'I've just been going round in circles and I can't anymore and I'm not going to dump on Ethan. I need to think of myself.'

When Jasmine had gone she rang Mr Dean.

Told him she was struggling with some personal issues and that she was taking some time off.

Just let him put a word wrong now, Penny thought.

'That's fine, Penny.' Mr Dean must have heard the unvoiced warning in her tone, because he told her to take the two weeks of annual leave she had left and more if she needed it, and even though he could be very insensitive, for once he was incredibly careful not to say the wrong thing.

Unlike a certain someone, Penny thought as she stripped off her work clothes and headed for the shower.

Unlike Ethan.

Penny's eyes filled with tears then because part of what she liked about Ethan was that he did say the wrong thing and wasn't always careful at times, wasn't tentative and constantly wearing kid gloves around her, which she hated.

He'd never deliberately hurt her, he'd just been trying to say how he felt about her losing... Penny screwed her eyes closed, tried to block the pain, but she couldn't do it anymore. There wasn't a needle in sight but she let it all out then, folded up on the shower floor, crying and sobbing as she mourned. Because it wasn't just a failed IVF, she hadn't just got her period that horrible time. For a little while there she had thought she'd got her baby.

While she might feel better after a really good cry, Penny thought, she certainly didn't look better.

Huddled on the sofa in her nightdress, watching but not watching the news, Penny surveyed the damage. Yes, IVF was expensive, and she wasn't just talking dollars.

Penny rang her mum and had a nice talk with her, a really nice talk, because her mum told Bradley she was taking the call upstairs and they spoke for a good hour. Louise offered to come over but Penny didn't want her to.

Next.

Unable to say it, she fired off Ethan a text saying she was sorry for being such a bitch about his job.

And then he sent her a text with a photo attached—a big bear with a tiny dart in it.

Just a bruised ego—all mended now.

Which made her smile, and when a little while later her doorbell rang she wasn't sure if it was Ethan or her mum, but as she opened it, Penny knew her response would be the same.

'I really want to be on my own.'

'Why?' Ethan said. He'd come straight from work and was in his scrubs and looking far too gorgeous for someone feeling as drained as Penny did.

'Because I'm such good company.' She didn't need

to tell him she was being sarcastic. He looked at her swollen eyes and lips and the little dark red dots on her eyelids and he couldn't let her close the door.

'I need to talk to you, Penny,' Ethan said. 'I lied to you.'

'That's fine.'

'You don't even want to know when I lied?'

'No,' Penny said. 'I want to think about me.' But she did let him in. Ethan pulled her into his arms for a cuddle but he felt her resistance and just wanted to erase it, wanted to take some of her hurt, but she simply wouldn't let him. 'I wish you'd spoken to my sister. Kate's been through it many, many times. I wish you'd let people in.'

'I wish I would too,' Penny said.

'Then why don't you?' He could see the confusion swirling in her eyes, guessed she was trying to answer that by herself. He was going to make her talk, was determined to sort things out, and he led her to the couch and sat down beside her. 'You don't have to keep it all in. It's not good for you. You said you didn't get upset when your dad left and then a few days later—'

'Oh, don't start.'

'I have started,' Ethan said.

'Of course I was upset when he left,' Penny said.

'You just couldn't show it.'

'No!' Penny said. 'Because Jasmine was sobbing herself to sleep, Mum was doing the same on the couch, and someone had to do the dishes and make Jasmine her lunch and...' She swallowed the hot choking fear she had felt then. 'How would falling apart have helped?'

'It might have stopped you falling apart now,' Ethan suggested. 'It might have meant your mother would have stepped up. It might have meant someone stepping in.'

'I'm not falling apart,' Penny said, and she meant it. 'I did that a couple of hours ago.'

He looked at her swollen face. 'I could have been there for you.'

'Oh, no,' Penny said. 'I'm so glad that you weren't.' She gave him a smile, a real one, because there were things she simply didn't want another person to see, and she actually felt better for her mammoth cry and was ready now to face another truth.

'So when did you lie?'

'I *was* serious about Caitlin.' The smile slid from her face when she didn't get the answer she was expecting. 'Not quite walking-up-the-aisle serious, but serious. And then Phil got sick and the thought of being married, having kids, leaving them behind?' He was honest. 'It just freaked me out.'

'I do understand. It is scary to think of being responsible for another person,' she admitted.

'But you want it,' Ethan said. 'You're brave enough to do it your own.'

'Not on my own,' Penny said, 'because even if we fight I do have my sister and mum, and if something happened to me, they'd be there.' She looked at him. 'I thought you were about to tell me you had a son.'

He gave her a barking-mad look.

'I saw you at the cinema.'

'That was Justin.'

'He looks like you,' Penny said, smiling now at her own paranoia.

'Phil looked like me,' Ethan said, then changed the subject because she was getting too close to a place that hurt. 'You do too much on your own.'

'Better than not doing it at all.' She smiled and nudged him, except Ethan didn't smile, and to her horror she watched him swallow, watched him struggle to get a grip, saw him pinch his nose and it was her arm around him now.

'Ethan?'

'Sorry.' He let out a slightly incredulous laugh, shocked how much was there just beneath the surface, how much he had just refused to let out.

'Is it Phil?'

He shook his head and again he got how the patients liked her because she sort of went straight to the really painful bit rather than tiptoeing around it. 'Justin?'

'If you get famous and they name a perfume after you, it won't be called Subtle, Penny.'

'No, it will be called Pertinent,' Penny said. 'You *need* to be there for him, Ethan.' And he nodded, rested his head in his hands, and Penny felt the tension in his shoulders, heard him struggle to keep his voice even as he gave a ragged apology. 'This was supposed to be about you.'

'How selfish of you.' Penny smiled.

'I don't know what to do—I've been trying to stay out of it but I can't. And it's not just the family stuff and that Gina's keeping him from his grandparents. The thing is, I know how he feels. It's like I'm looking at a mini-me. I saw him at the hospital, heard my aunt saying the same things she did to me when my father died—to be brave, be strong. It's not what he needs to hear right now.'

'You can be there for him.'

'I don't want to go rushing in and make promises I might not keep,' Ethan admitted. 'I've never been able to commit myself to anything except work. Penny, I don't want to let him down.'

'You won't.' She saw him blink at the certainty in her voice. 'I know you won't let him down, precisely because you haven't rushed in. Just take your time and you'll work something out.'

'I don't know what, though.' He looked to where she was sitting and pulled her onto his lap, and this time she didn't resist when he pulled her in for a cuddle. 'So much for cheering you up.'

'You have, though.' Penny smiled and he smiled too. 'Thank you for everything,' Penny said. 'Not just the injections but…' she looked at the man who was still there despite all that had gone on these past weeks '…thank you for being my friend through this.'

'A bit more than a friend.' And to confirm it gave her a kiss. A kiss that seemed at odds with the way she was feeling, because there was this well of happiness filling her at what should have been the saddest of times.

'Are you wearing no knickers again?' Ethan smiled again and he had possibly the nicest mouth a man could have, and she was looking into his hazel eyes and it hadn't just been manufactured hormones that had been raging that time. Penny could fully see it now. It had been lust, all the flush of a new romance, the big one, because right now for Penny it was looking like something a lot bigger than lust.

Something she'd never really felt before—an L word that would probably be as shocking to Ethan as the F word had been to Jasmine, and if that mouth returned to hers now, she might be tempted later to say so, and again it was just too much and too soon.

'You need to go,' Penny said.

'Do I?'

'Yes,' Penny said, 'because I want to go to bed and have sex with you and I want to get up tomorrow and do it again, and then I want you to take me out tomorrow night, but I think I need to think about things properly. I need to work some stuff out.'

'And you can't do that with me?'

Penny looked at him and, no, she didn't want to try to do this with Ethan—her fertility issues were conversations that should be had far later along in a relationship, dark places a couple might visit later that had instead been thrust on them at the beginning.

'It's a girl thing,' Penny said, because with or without Ethan in her future she needed to properly know how she felt. And as to the other issue, the L one—well, she didn't need him by her side to work that out.

Penny already knew.

So much for a wild fling—of all the times to go and fall in love with someone.

'I could make love to you on the sofa and then leave,' Ethan said, cupping her naked bottom and making her laugh.

'I suppose that might be a compromise.'

He kissed her again, pulled her around on his lap so she was facing him, and his hands were everywhere and so too were hers. 'I'm crazy about you, Penny.'

'I know,' she said, kissing him back and trying to hold on to a word he might not be ready to hear. 'I'm crazy about you too.'

Her hand went to his back pocket, which gave him lovely access to her neck. She could feel his tongue, his mouth most definitely leaving evidence that hers hadn't been about to, but it was bliss and she had a whole two weeks off, so she let him carry on, working her neck and his hands stroked her breasts as she slid the condom on him.

'You'll call me if you need me,' Ethan said as she sank herself down onto him.

'You'll call me too,' Penny said, locked in an erotic embrace, hardly able to breathe. 'But not for this.'

'Penny.' He was lifting his hips and thrusting into her, protesting her impossible rules.

'I mean it,' Penny panted, because she could bury herself in Ethan and stay there forever, just as he was burying himself deep in her now.

Yes, a good cry and a good orgasm and Penny felt a whole lot better as she kissed him goodbye at her door. Still stuck on deuce but with play suspended.

Penny *was* going to sort herself out.

And so too would Ethan.

CHAPTER THIRTEEN

'PENNY!' KATE SMILED as she walked past the café and ignored Penny's burning cheeks.

'Oh, hi,' Penny said, as if she just happened to be sitting there at a quarter to nine in the morning, as if she hadn't been looking up school times on the internet, as if she hadn't spent forty minutes trying to cover the marks on her neck and her puffy eyes. 'How are you?'

'Good.' Kate smiled. 'Though I could do with one of them.' She nodded to Penny's coffee and, yes, she'd love to join her and, yes, Penny thought, it was another woman she needed for this and this link was thanks to Ethan.

'How's work?' Kate asked, taking a seat.

'I'm taking some time off.' She told her why and Penny realised that Kate probably already knew.

'Did Ethan tell you?'

'Do I have to answer that?'

'No.' Penny shook her head.

'Then I won't.'

Kate had been there and knew, though she couldn't have a second coffee, not at the café anyway because the baby needed feeding. In truth, she shouldn't really have stopped for the first, but she'd been where Penny was.

'We could take a coffee back to mine,' Kate suggested, 'and talk there.'

It *was* another woman Penny needed, one who'd been there and knew—who knew it so well that she took phone calls for a support group.

'Everyone was pregnant when I started trying,' Kate said, making up bottles for Dillon a little while later as Penny sat at the kitchen table.

It *was* so nice to talk and to hold someone else's baby and not feel guilty for shedding tears. She'd always tried to smile with Jasmine and friends, and say, no, no, she was fine. It was nice to hold one and have a little weep.

'I think I've gone a bit mad,' Penny admitted.

'It's par for the course.'

Penny looked at Dillon and though she'd never be disappointed with a boy, Penny admitted to herself that deep down she would have loved a girl too. Oh, a boy would be fantastic, but she'd have loved a mini-Penny. A little girl who she could do everything right by and fix the world for, who she could unashamedly show all the love that bubbled and fizzed inside.

But she could do it for herself too, Penny realised.

'I've just had a text,' Kate said a little while later. 'My brother's coming around.'

'I'll go, then.'

She thanked Kate for the morning and they had a hug and she handed back little Dillon. It wasn't that she didn't want to see Ethan, it was more there was something she was ready to face and she wanted to face it alone. Penny headed to the beach and walked for a while, adding up all the months, all the years, all the time she'd lost trying. She was ready to stop and so she said it out loud—but to herself first.

'I'm not going to be a mum.' She actually didn't cry as she said it, just felt relief almost as she let go of something she had never had, anger shifting towards acceptance; sadness a constant ache but one she could now more readily wear.

Yes, times alone were needed for both of them, yet Kate was the strange conduit that linked them.

'She's been here.' He could just tell, when about ten minutes after Penny left he was at his sister's door and Kate was blushing and flustered when she answered.

'Why do you say that?'

'Because I can smell her perfume,' Ethan said.

'You really have got it bad,' Kate said. 'What did you do to her neck?'

Ethan wasn't going to answer that one, so he asked a question instead. 'What was she talking about?'

'Not about you,' Kate said, then added, 'She's really nice.'

Not *seems*, Ethan noted—finally, it would appear, Penny was letting people in.

'She is.'

'Well, I hate to chuck you out so soon, but I've got nothing done today and I'm on fruit duty at playgroup.' Kate was putting sandals onto her daughter's feet. The baby was asleep and instead of letting her wake him, as usually Ethan would, he offered to watch him instead.

'Are you sure?' Kate checked. 'There's a bottle in the fridge if he wakes up.'

'Go.'

And later he sat with Dillon on his lap and stared at a very little man who would, God willing, grow up.

And, Ethan realised, taking out his phone, it was time for him to as well.

Just not yet.

He made every decision alone—it was simply the way he was, but instead of ringing who he meant to, he dialled Penny.

She probably wouldn't pick up.

'Hi.'

'Hi, Penny,' he said. 'What are you doing?'

'Sitting on the beach. What about you?'

'Watching my nephew. Kate's at playgroup.' He took a deep breath. 'I'm going to ring Gina.'

'That's good.'

'I think I need to say sorry first, for how the family has been.' He was really just thinking out loud.

'Maybe,' Penny said, 'but are you ringing on behalf of the family?'

'No.'

'You could just keep it more about you,' Penny said, and they chatted for a while about what he might say till the baby on his lap decided that a bottle might be a good idea, and Penny could hear his little whimpers in the background.

'You'd better go,' Penny said. 'It sounds like the baby needs feeding.'

As he hung up the phone he sat for a moment, wondering if he'd upset her with the baby crying and everything, but she'd seemed fine. It had been their first full conversation without a mention of babies.

'Apart from you,' he said to Dillon as he headed to the fridge.

Ethan offered the baby his bottle but he spat out the cold milk so Ethan warmed it up. 'It was worth a try.' He grinned at his new friend and they settled back down on the sofa. There was no putting it off any longer and Ethan again picked up his phone.

'Gina...' He took a deep breath. 'It's Ethan.' He was met with a very long silence. 'I'm really sorry for all that the family has put you through.'

'You didn't.'

'No,' he said. 'But I do know what happened and I know too what Jack and Vera can be like.' He took a long breath. 'But I'm not ringing about them, I'm ringing about Justin. I lost my dad around the same age.'

'I know.'

They chatted for a bit and it was awkward at first and there was a long stretch of silence when he made his suggestion. 'I was thinking, if it's okay with you, I could get Justin his football membership. I can't take him every week, it depends on the roster, but...' He thought of Penny, because he so often did and, yes, she'd swap now and then and so too would the others.

This he could do.

Would do.

'I would be able to take Justin to most games.'

'He'd love that,' Gina said. 'But...' She hesitated for a moment.

'I'm not starting something I won't see through,' Ethan said. 'I'm not saying I'm never going to move, but I will be there for him. I wouldn't be offering otherwise.'

Only that wasn't what Gina was hesitating about. 'Maybe you could take him to his grandparents' after the match, but not every week. Maybe he could stay over?' Gina let out a sigh. 'But I can't face picking him up.'

'I can do that,' Ethan said. 'We can work out times.'

'Would you talk to Vera and Jack first?' Gina said. 'I don't want Justin going there and being told what a terrible person I am.'

'I'll talk to them,' Ethan said. 'And if it's not working out, I'll talk to them again, but whatever happens there, I'll be around for Justin.'

They chatted some more and it was agreed he would ring Justin and tell him the good news that night. When Ethan hung up the phone he looked into the solemn eyes of his nephew.

'How did I do?'

He got no answer.

'When you're a bit bigger I might take you to the football too.' He got a smile for that and again his mind tripped back to Penny. 'I'll be the mad uncle.'

And so the weekend came around and he picked up a six-year-old with a pinched, angry face. He knew that look only too well and sat where they always had, only this time without Phil.

And they shouted at the opposition and the umpire and let off a bit of a steam, but instead of talking about the game on the way to Justin's grandparents' they spoke about what mattered.

'Well, if he wanted to live so much then he should have tried harder,' Justin said, because he was tired of hearing that his dad had tried so hard to be there for him. And he got to be six and very angry instead of being told to be brave and strong. And maybe Penny has sprayed Ethan with some Pertinence before he left because instead of being subtle, instead of dropping him off at his Vera and Jack's and hoping for the best, Ethan warned him how things might be.

'They're upset,' Ethan said, 'and you remind them of your dad, and it's just so hard on everyone.' He blew out a breath because there was just so much hurt all around, but so much love too.

'They hate my mum.'

'They don't,' Ethan said, and then corrected himself, because it was Justin who was dealing with this. 'Well, if they do, you shouldn't have to hear it. You tell me if they say anything that hurts. And if they are less than nice about her, it's because they don't know your mum,' Ethan said. 'She's great.'

He saw the smile lift the edge of Justin's lips as finally someone in the Lewis family said something nice about his mum.

Yes, Ethan decided, having dropped Justin off—this he could do.

CHAPTER FOURTEEN

'MORNING, ETHAN.' VANESSA was just coming on duty and smiled when she saw him, but then pulled a face. 'I'm guessing, from the state of you, that you're going off duty?'

Finishing up a week of nights, Ethan was aware that he probably wasn't looking his best. He had meant to shave before he'd come on last night, and had also meant to shave the night before that too. 'So, if you're going off duty...' Vanessa said, looking at the board that Lisa was filling in—it showed all the on-take doctors and who was on duty today. 'Oh, no!' Vanessa said as she watched Lisa write 'Penny Masters' in red. 'She's back.'

'She will be soon,' Lisa teased the nurses. 'Party's over for you lot.'

'Tell me about it. Who knows what her problem is,' Vanessa groaned, and Ethan wanted to tell them to give her a break, that the two of them had no idea what Penny was going through.

But Penny would hate that.

She was just this tough little thing choosing to go it alone, and for the last couple of weeks he'd had to force himself to respect that while trying to sort out how he felt about IVF and babies and things. Ethan still didn't know. He couldn't work out how he felt about dating someone who wanted a baby, oh, say, about nine months from now.

He'd bought flowers for the first time in his unromantic life and they were waiting in her office, along with an invitation for dinner. Maybe they could just take it slowly, start at the beginning without those blasted needles hanging over them.

Though he'd rather liked giving them!

Play was resuming, Ethan thought with a smile.

He heard the bell from Triage and Lisa stopped writing on the board and sped off with Ethan following. They got outside to find nurses trying to get an unconscious woman from the back seat of a car onto a trolley as her panicked husband shouted for them to hurry up. Security was nowhere to be seen.

'What happened?' Ethan asked the man.

'I just came home from work and I couldn't wake her...' The man was barefoot and jumping up and down on the spot. As his wife was placed on the trolley Ethan tried to get some more information, but apart from a urine infection there was nothing wrong with her, the agitated husband said.

'You're going to have to move your car,' Lisa told him as they started to move the patient inside, but he ignored her, instead running alongside his wife.

'You need to move your car,' Ethan said, because even if it sounded a minor detail, it wasn't if there was an ambulance on its way in with another sick patient.

'Just sort my wife out!' the man roared at Ethan.

'Stop worrying about the car.' There was a minor scuffle; the man fronted up to Ethan, fear and adrenaline and panic igniting. Ethan blocked the man's fist, but Ethan was angry too.

'Man up!' Ethan said. 'You want me to stand here fighting, or do you want me to sort out your wife? Go and move your car.'

He did so, but as they sped the woman through, the usually laid-back Ethan, who let things like that go, glared over at Lisa.

'Where the hell was Security?'

Lisa didn't answer.

'I want that reported.'

'He's just scared.'

'Yeah, well, we're all scared at times.'

They were now at the doors to Resus and Ethan was dealing with the patient, who was responding to pain and her pupils were reacting. He could smell what was wrong—there was the familiar smell of ketones on her breath. Lisa was attaching her to monitors as Ethan quickly found a vein and took bloods. 'Add a pregnancy test,' Ethan said, because she was of childbearing age and a diabetic crisis could be dangerous for any foetus. By the time the husband returned from parking his car there was saline up and Lisa was giving the patient her first dose of insulin. His anger was fading, but still it churned.

'Are you all right, Ethan?' Lisa checked.

'Sure.'

'I'll do an incident form after...'

'Forget it.' He gave a small smile that said he had overreacted.

'Touched a nerve, did it?' Lisa smiled back.

'Must have,' Ethan said.

He thought of his own fear as he'd raced to get to his cousin, yet it wouldn't have entered his head to front up to anyone, and he thought of Kate, who had done the right thing and not just left the car, even though she must so badly have wanted to. 'I want to know where Security was, though,' Ethan said, and then got back to the patient. The medics were on their way down but for now Ethan went in to speak with the husband.

'I'll come in with you,' Lisa said.

'No need,' Ethan said.

'I wasn't offering.' Lisa had worked there a very long time and gave him a smile that told him there was no way she was leaving the two of them in the same room.

'Come on, then.'

They walked in and the man was sitting in there, his head in his hands.

'Mr Edmunds.' Ethan looked at the patient sheet that had been handed to him.

'Mark.' He looked up. 'Sorry about before.'

Ethan would deal with that later. He was actually glad Lisa had insisted on coming in as there was still this strange surliness writhing inside Ethan and he looked down at the patient card again for a moment before talking.

'Your wife, Anna, did you know she was diabetic?'

Mark shook his head. 'No…she's been fine, well,

tired, but like I said, she thought she had a urine infection.'

Ethan nodded. 'One of the signs is passing urine a lot but we're checking for any infection.' He explained things as simply as he could to the very confused and very scared man—that his wife had type one diabetes and she was in ketoacidosis—her glucose was far too high and would be slowly brought down. But it affected everything and she would be very closely watched, and while she was very sick, he expected her to soon be well.

'She'll still be diabetic?'

'Yes.' Ethan nodded. 'But she'll be taught to manage it and this will hopefully be the worst it ever is.' Ethan took a breath. 'Is there any chance that your wife might be pregnant?'

'We're trying.'

'Okay,' Ethan said.

'Would it damage the baby?'

'Let's just wait for results and then we'll see what we're dealing with. Do you want to come in and see your wife?'

Mark nodded and then said it again. 'I am sorry about earlier.'

'And I accept your apology,' Ethan said. 'But there is no place for that sort of carry-on here.'

'I was just—'

'Not an excuse,' Ethan broke in. 'There were two women there and your fist wasn't looking where it was going. We've got doctors here who are barely five foot...'

Yes, there was his problem—everything went back to Penny.

But, hell, Ethan thought, it could have been Penny on duty and she could have been pregnant, and he stood up and walked out and took a deep breath.

'Where was Security?' Ethan asked Lisa.

'Over in the car park,' Lisa said. 'Someone was trying to break into a car. They can't be everywhere, Ethan.'

He knew that, but he wanted them everywhere, wanted two burly guards and an Alsatian walking alongside Penny at all times.

Maybe he was a caveman after all.

CHAPTER FIFTEEN

YES, SHE HAD always rotated her clothes, mixing and matching her outfits with precision, changing them with the seasons. Not anymore. Today she had *chosen* a floral dress that buttoned at the front. Instead of low, flat heels, she wore sandals, and because she hadn't been meticulous with her factor thirty, Penny's legs were sun-kissed and she wore her hair loose.

She smiled as she walked into work and Ethan, tired after his night shift, chatting to the medics, noticed the glow in her and had a feeling her decision had been made and that there were embryos about to be taken out of storage in the very near future.

'Morning, Vanessa,' Penny said as she walked past.

'Er, morning, Penny.'

'Hi, Lisa.'

'Penny.'

Penny swallowed. 'Lisa, can I have a word with you, please?'

It was the hardest word and Lisa gave her a smile as they moved into an empty cubicle, and Penny said it. 'I've been going through some things and I should never have brought it to work. It was just...' And she did what Jasmine had advised all along and what Penny had thought she would never do—let Lisa know what had been going on.

'Well, you can't really leave your hormones at home.' Lisa smiled. 'You could have said.'

'I know.'

'I am discreet.'

'I know that too,' Penny said. 'I'll have a word with Vanessa and apologise. Anyone else?' And then Penny gave a guilty smile. 'Should I just call a staff meeting?'

Yes, it really was the hardest, hardest word because sometimes when you had to say it, it meant that you'd really hurt someone.

'I'm so sorry, Vanessa.' Penny saw the red cheeks and the flash of tears in her colleague's eyes and it wasn't actually the blood pressure she hadn't written down or the delays in medication that were the problem. There was another morning Penny hadn't properly apologised for, and though she didn't want to play the sympathy card, Penny did want Vanessa to know that her outburst hadn't been aimed at her.

Penny took her into an interview room.

'You were right to come and get me that morning and let me know what was happening. I know you'd never leave a patient and that Raj was there. I wasn't angry at you—I was just upset. When you came to find me I'd just got my period,' Penny said. 'I'd been trying for a baby and I thought I was finally pregnant.' And, no, she didn't tell her that for twenty-four hours she had been pregnant, neither did she say anything about the IVF, but it was enough for Vanessa to put her arms around her. Penny gave a little self-conscious wriggle, but then found out that it was nice sometimes to have a friend and be held.

Ethan watched them walking out of the interview room, smiling and chatting, and he excused himself and walked over.

'Morning, Penny.'

'Morning.'

'Nice break?'

'Very.'

'What did you get up to?'

'Not much.' How lovely it was to say that.

'Glad to be back?'

'Not yet.' Penny took a deep breath. 'I'm sorry I've been such a cow to work with.' Even though he knew why, she still felt she ought to say it here in the workplace and not just to Ethan. 'I should have recorded my apology before I came back to work. You're the third and I haven't even got halfway down the corridor.'

'Maybe you could ask the receptionist to play it over the loudspeaker?' Ethan grinned.

She walked off to her office and turned and flashed that smile but he didn't follow at first.

He just stood there thinking, because he knew how he felt now, and he checked with himself for a moment and the answer was still the same so he headed to her office to tell her.

'I would have loved your baby.' Ethan stood at the door and whether it was the wrong or right thing to say, he told her what he now knew.

'Ethan...'

'I'm not just saying that.' He wasn't and he told her why. 'I know you're going to go for it again,' Ethan said, 'I could see it when you walked in. I'll tell you this, if you were pregnant now, if it had worked out for you, well, I might have taken a while to come around but I would have, because it wouldn't change the way I feel. It's just taken a bit of a time for me to understand that.'

'I'm not going for it again.' She saw him frown. 'This is Tranquil Penny.'

'Oh.' He came over and took her in his arms and introduced himself. 'Pleased to meet you.' Then he frowned. 'What do you mean, you're not going to try again?'

'I can't have children.' She'd practised saying it, not just to Ethan but at other times in her future. 'I know I might want to try again someday, but now I just want a break from it—I want lots of sex for sex's sake, preferably with you.' She reached into her bag and took out a packet of pills and waved them. 'It's probably over-kill—left to their own devices my ovaries squeeze out two, maybe three eggs a year—but I'm taking the pressure off.'

She gave him a smile. 'Yes, please, to dinner.' He kissed her and he had never been so pleased to kiss a woman, just relieved to find her mouth and what had been missing in every other mouth he had kissed.

Here it was, the love he hadn't been looking for.

'I'm going home to sleep,' Ethan said.

'Not yet,' Penny grumbled.

'I am, and then I'm going to set my alarm so I've time

to tidy up in case I end up bringing my date back.' He gave her a smile. 'You've never seen my home.'

Penny blushed. Yes, there was a lot to get to know and lots of fun to be had before a guy like Ethan might settle down. And it might never happen, but she wanted him in a way she never had. There was a love inside Penny so much bigger than this kiss. A love that crowded out so many other things, and she just had to hold on to her feelings a bit, not terrify him with them by jumping in too soon.

'Or maybe…' Ethan said, and he undid a couple of buttons and had a peek and she was in coral, his favourite '…we could skip the restaurant and eat at my place?'

'What's for dinner, Ethan?'

They had the tiniest of histories, but it was enough to make the other smile.

'That all depends on what you pick up at the supermarket on your way home from work,' Ethan said.

And he glimpsed then a future and there would be no remote-control flinging because they would look out for each other, argue and tease each other, and then kiss and make up and not let things fester.

'Do you want to go to the football on Sunday?'

'No!' Penny pulled a face; she could think of nothing worse, but then it clicked. 'Are you going with Justin?'

'It will be our second week,' Ethan said.

'Gina agreed?'

'More than that. Afterwards I'm taking him to my aunt and uncle's and he's staying the night, and then in the morning I'll go and collect him and take him back to his mum's. We'll be doing that a couple of times a month and it's working out well.'

'That's some commitment.' Penny smiled at her commitment-phobe.

'I'm getting good at them.'

Yes, there was still a lot she didn't know about Ethan, because as he stood there looking at her he was doing the maths. She was thirty-five and at a rate of two to three eggs a year there weren't a whole lot of chances, but he was prepared to take them now. Ethan picked up the pill pack she was still holding and, just as Penny had with the needles to get what she wanted, he faced his fears over and over, twenty-eight times, in fact.

He punched each pill into the sink, even the sugar-coated ones, and then turned on the tap and watched them swirl in the water. Then he broke out in a sweat because it was *him* now talking about making babies when he'd never thought he might.

'I've got more at home.'

'I want whatever happens,' Ethan said. 'And I don't want to take away even one of your chances.'

'And I don't want to ruin this,' Penny said. They were chasing the same dream from different directions, both terrified to miss or even to clash and blow them apart. Penny was standing at the silver lining of acceptance that there might never be babies, and Ethan was just starting to accept that there might be. 'I don't want you to find out you do want babies after all and then be disappointed.'

And he was the most honest, sexiest, funniest man

she had ever met, even as he voiced her unspoken fears. 'And then go off with someone years younger...'

'Ha, ha,' Penny said, because they could talk about things, tell each other things and, yes, they could tease each other too. 'Someone soft and curvy and cute.'

'Did I really used to go for cute?' Ethan smiled. And he looked at her and he knew where his heart was. 'Actually,' Ethan said as he faced another of his fears, 'for one hot mess you'd make a very cute bride.'

She blinked at him.

'I want to see Menopausal Penny and I want you to see Midlife Crisis Ethan.'

'So do I.' She was kissing him again. 'Going out in your sports car and joining a gym and things.'

'And if there are no babies, we'll be the mad aunt and uncle who spoil all their nieces and nephews but make their parents jealous as we go off on cruises and travel around the world. But,' Ethan said, 'if we're really clucky, we'll move to America and adopt little twin monkeys.'

'And dress them in tutus.'

'No,' Ethan said, because it was his future they were planning too. 'Not the boy one.'

EPILOGUE

'IT'S CALLED A spontaneous pregnancy,' her GP explained as Penny sat there, stunned. 'Some women do get pregnant naturally after IVF.'

It would seem so.

Penny honestly didn't know how she felt.

She'd imagined hearing she was pregnant so many times, but now that it was here, she actually didn't know how to deal with the news.

They had just returned from their honeymoon—Louise had given them the cruise bug and they had sailed around the Mediterranean, getting brown and being spoiled. Penny closed her eyes at the thought of the champagne and the things she had eaten, though now, when she thought about it, she hadn't really indulged that much.

'We nearly didn't go,' Penny admitted as she chatted to the doctor. She'd thought they'd have to call it off because Mr Dean had told them that they couldn't both take annual leave at the same time.

'We're hardly going to go on separate honeymoons,' Ethan had said—that was how they had announced their news—and given Ethan didn't actually have any annual leave and would be taking it unpaid, they could afford a locum to cover him.

'Be glad that you had your cruise.' Her GP smiled. 'Because you won't be doing that sort of thing for a while.'

And Penny was glad that they had, so glad, because they'd had nearly a year of just them and it had been amazing—dating for all of a week before Penny had put her house on the market and she and the cat had moved in with him, then just getting to know each other and learning how to laugh and to love.

Penny drove home. She was supposed to be getting her hair done as it was her mother's wedding in a few hours' time, but instead she'd have to make do with heated rollers.

She just had to see Ethan, had to find out how he would take the news.

'Your hair's nice,' Ethan said when she got back. He was in the bathroom, shaving, the cat sitting by the sink watching him.

'I didn't get my hair done.' Penny had to laugh.

'Oh,' Ethan said. 'Well, it still looks nice. Where did you go?' He saw her hesitate and he pretty much guessed she'd been to her GP.

Penny had been fantastic and absolutely adored Jasmine's little baby girl, Amelia, and they'd just found out that Kate was going to try for a fourth. There were so many friends and relations getting pregnant that Ethan was noticing and he was starting to feel little pinpricks of disappointment when Penny's period rarely came.

And not just for Penny.

He liked the time spent with Justin, and Penny was good with him too. He wanted now what Penny had wanted—a baby—though he couldn't really tell her that. No doubt soon they'd be off to America to look at little monkeys, but first...

'You'll be all right at the wedding?' He rinsed his face and then turned round. 'You're all right with your mum and Bradley?'

'Apart from his name,' Penny said. 'And do they have to be so affectionate in public?'

She was the oddest person he had ever met and he loved her all the more for it. And maybe the timing wasn't right, maybe he should bring it up after the wedding because he didn't want to upset her beforehand, but right or wrong he said what was on his mind.

'If you want to go again...'

'Go again?'

'On IVF,' Ethan said. 'I'd be fine with that.'

'You're sure?' Penny's eyes narrowed. 'That doesn't sound very enthusiastic.'

'Okay.' He tried again. 'Why don't *we* go on IVF?' He thought for a moment. 'That makes me sound like Gordon.' And then he was serious. 'If you want to then so do I.'

'What do you want, Ethan?'

'I can't believe I'm saying this,' Ethan admitted. 'But I'd like to try for a baby...' He rushed into his 'but if it doesn't work then I won't be disappointed' speech, but she halted him. There was no need for that. She loved it that he wanted this too, that it wasn't something she was foisting on them too soon.

'We don't need to try,' Penny said. 'I've just come from the doctor's.'

He was scared to get too excited, just in case it was like last time, only it was nothing like last time.

'I'm thirteen weeks,' Penny said, and she watched his reaction as it sank in that while they'd been busy with weddings and football matches and honeymoons and juggling work and falling deeper and deeper in love, she'd been pregnant.

'Can we tell people?' Ethan asked.

'I guess,' Penny said, because they were out of the first trimester. 'But not just yet. It's Mum's day today.'

And it was just as well she didn't get her hair done because it would have been messed up anyway as they were soon off to bed to celebrate. Ethan had the good sense to set the alarm just in case they got a bit carried away.

'Can't be late for your mum's wedding,' he said as a very tanned Penny stripped off.

They were on two sets to one, with Ethan winning, and each game spent an awful lot of time at deuce.

Record times!

'Hey, I bet when you were fantasising about having your wild fling with me,' Ethan said as he dropped his towel, 'you never imagined it ending up like this.'

'No,' Penny said, because the best she had been able to imagine then had been a shocked reaction and a baby that wasn't his.

The truth was so much better.

* * * * *

MILLS & BOON®
Book Club

oin the Mills & Boon Book Club

Subscribe to **Medical** today for 3, 6 or 12 months and you could **save over £40!**

e'll also treat you to these fabulous extras:

- **FREE L'Occitane gift set worth £10**
- **FREE home delivery**
- **Rewards scheme, exclusive offers…and much more!**

Subscribe now and save over £40
ww.millsandboon.co.uk/subscribeme